The Next Parish Over

The NEXT PARISH Over

A Collection of Irish-American Writing

Edited by
Patricia Monaghan

Many Minnesotas Project Number 7

NEW RIVERS PRESS 1993

The publication of *The Next Parish Over: A Collection of Irish-American Writing* has been made possible by a generous grant from the Star Tribune/Cowles Media Company.

Additional support has been provided by Liberty State Bank, the National Endowment for the Arts (with funds appropriated by the Congress of the United States), the Tennant Company Foundation, and the contributing members of New Rivers Press. New Rivers Press is a member agency of the United Arts Fund.

New Rivers Press books are distributed by:

The Talman Company
131 Spring Street, Suite 201 E-N
New York NY 10012

The Next Parish Over: A Collection of Irish-American Writing has been manufactured in the United States of America for New Rivers Press, 420 N. 5th Street/Suite 910, Minneapolis, MN 55401.

Contents

Introduction

I NEVER SAW IRELAND UNTIL I WAS THIRTY. NOT WITH THE FLESH EYE, that is. But it seemed, as I touched down in Dublin and saw the forty shades of green of that little bit of heaven, that I had always seen my dear native land with inner eyes.

Or, more accurately, heard it with inner ears. It was the songs that did it. From earliest memory, Irish songs were, in my grandparents' and parents' homes, part of every gathering fit to be called a party or a holiday. There was Uncle Jack, prancing with a blackthorn stick and singing "The Hat Me Father Wore." There was my father's resonant tenor as he sang "Danny Boy." And all us kids, packed in the back of the green-topped station wagon, singing song after rebel song.

This being America, there was recorded music too. The Little Gaelic Singers on our first hi-fi, and the grackle-voiced Tinker Lady. The music changed with the decades: Mickey and Mary Carton at first, then the Clancy Brothers, most lately Clannad and Enya.

Being Irish, it seemed to me as a child, meant mostly that you knew a lot of songs. It was a way we had of absorbing the details of our history: I knew all about Roddy McCorley going to die on the Bridge of Tuam that day, and about Father Murphy of old Kilkormick, raising up the rocks with a warning cry. I knew about Kelly the Boy from Killane and O'Donnell Abu. I knew about rebels and quislings and the patriot game.

It was the songs that taught me what I knew about the woes of immigration, more than I ever heard direct from my grandparents, for whom talk of home was allusive, as though to a pain they feared to enliven. But "Boys from the Country Mayo" taught me to sing out the tongue-twisting names of my countryside of origin: "Ballihaunis, Bellmullet, Tourmakedy (God love it)" – and yes! my grandfather's own town, "Bohola, whose great men are famed near and far."

It was the songs that taught me about the rural life my forebears had abandoned, where sweet buttermilk watered the lanes and where you might, or might not, give Mr. Maguire a chair. I always knew that I would find in the Irish country side sweet-voiced linnets and dew-covered heather. And, of course, those forty shades of green.

Other things bonded us as Irish-Americans: the church, often; politics, sometimes; other institutions, like the military or the police force. Drink, and the corrosive denial that accompanied its abuse. A repressive puritanism offset by a heedless wildness. And the strange necessary suffocation of family.

If we Irish-Americans are hypenates rather than assimilates, it is because of the family that both holds us up and holds us in. We do not learn our Irishness in church or in school. We absorb it in the living room, in song and sometimes story, in verbal play and frequent cruelty. We learn it in the dining room, in fierce arguments and rousing debates. We learn it in the quiet night, when an American-born mother hums an ancient Gaelic lullabye whose words she never understood.

Here on this side of the water, we tend to think of ourselves as simply Irish rather than Irish-American. Where I live now, in Chicago, people wear T-shirts proclaiming that they're "South Side Irish" and talk about going to an "Irish bar" after work. But we are, in fact, really Yanks. We learn that the first time we go home to Ireland – it's always called "going home," even if you've never been there before. We have each absorbed too much of the multiplicity and individualism of America to be Irish. We're noisy and brash. We barge in with questions where significant quizzical looks would suffice. We rashly assume we're unique, even in our clannishness. We're not really Irish, and the real Irish know that.

But we're not simply American either. We often resent being mistaken for generic "white ethnics" (as Chicago polls so baldly put it). We think we're more than that. We're not so much immigrants here as displaced persons. Our grandparents instilled in us a sense of displacement from a magical green island, our real home. Perhaps this, in turn, derives from the ancient Gaelic idea of Tir na nOg, the isle of the blessed that we humans forever seek. Somewhere, we grow up believing, we are at home. It just isn't here, it isn't now.

It is this conflicted sense of belonging and not-belonging that marks Irish-American life. Within the family, the conflict can be extreme. If to be Irish-American is to be in exile, what can you do but despise and cling to your fellow exiles? If home is by definition not-here, what else can you feel but traitorous should you ever feel truly at home?

I don't remember if I thought I'd be at home in Ireland, that first time I went back. I certainly know it wasn't so. If I'd never felt completely American over here, over there I suddenly felt nothing *but* American. But in Mayo, where the rocky fields look out to the gray stormy Atlantic, I learned how close connections can be, even when they're hugely distant.

In the west of Ireland, they say that "the next parish over is America." It's said jocularly, but of course there's truth in the joke. The Irish and the Irish-American are an ocean apart, but it's an ocean that unites as well as separates. We sing much the same songs: of exile and cunning, of rebellion and betrayal. But we sing them in different accents, with different cadences. It makes a new music over here.

Part One

The Stories, Like Hidden Tongues

Traces

My grandmother used to tell me stories
of her mother's people, the Nortons
from Mayo — who moved to Scotland,
Wisconsin, anywhere. You know the Irish,
she said — too poor to stay at home.

No, I didn't know the Irish,
not even when I went to Dublin,
Galway, Cork — years later, searching
for that trace of recognition
I was so sure would come to me.

You know the Irish, my grandmother said —
we had royalty back there, Lady Jane
Dempsey I think it was, who eloped with
her footman — which doesn't surprise me.
There was a lord, too, though that name's lost.

Everyone from Ireland has royalty somewhere,
she said. And each time I heard them,
those old stories changed again.
I asked my father at her funeral.
She talked to you, not me, he said.

Now *he's* gone, and when my children
ask sometimes, I trace those old tales again,
a little more unsure each journey through.
You know the Irish. It's what we have.
It's all we have. I've come to say it too.

Spilled Milk

MY GRANDMOTHER HAS TOLD ME THE STORY SO OFTEN, I VIVIDLY recall the milk house although I have never been there. It is built of gray stone gathered from the fields and held together with chalky mortar. A patch of moss by the door looks like a velvet pincushion. Inside: a cream separator, the churn, gleaming tin pails, and butter paddles, their wood frayed from years of use. I see them through her eyes as she recites them like the rosary, like a charm.

Even though she died three years ago, she comes to me in dreams to add more detail—an inch-long tear in the screen patched with black darning thread, the speck of the man coming toward her on the road, framed by the door. So tiny is he that at first she mistakes him for a fly, as she lifts the pails of raw milk and pours them into the separator's mouth. Not a cloud mars the sky.

She whistles "The Prisoner's Lament" off-key to take her mind from the milky smell, faintly sour in the August heat. Uncle Mike and Aunt Rose have gone into town to buy a part for the mowing machine. My grandmother's gingham dress is plastered to her back and a damp, red curl sticks to her flushed cheek. At thirteen she is gangly, still frail from her years in the orphanage.

"It wasn't so bad, living on Uncle Mike's farm," she tells me long afterward when her pale hair is blue from a rinse bought at the five-and-dime. "Certainly not as bad as with the nuns." The beatings and long days spent mending buckets of stockings, the cruelties handed out by the children who had parents, but nonetheless were boarded at the home, weren't the worst. Those were nothing compared to the man who rented the orphans to beg for him.

He wore a bowler hat and a scratchy black wool coat, and he always arrived right before Christmas. "You make more of a profit begging around the holidays," my grandmother lets me know. Her housedress pulls tight against her hips, as solidly plump as the flowered cushions on her brand-new Sears loveseat.

"He'd ask for about a dozen of us, and I'd hide because I didn't want to go," she says as she dusts. "But since I looked so pitiful, I was always picked. He'd take us on the ferry to Milwaukee, take our coats away from us, and dump us out in the street." She stops her work now to hug me, and my nose fills with the scent of Tabu bath powder. "He'd paid the nuns a certain amount, and we had to make that back from him plus a profit or else he wouldn't let us eat our supper. Stale bread."

Her face closes with remembering. "The snow was never white in Milwaukee, always dirty gray like pigeons." A shudder passes through her. "Dirty and cold, so cold. Sometimes he'd rip our clothes to make us more appealing to the fine folks with money, and when he'd return us, he'd tell the nuns we tore them playing. They'd slap us and send us to bed without eating." My grandmother and I spend the remainder of the afternoon playing bingo, and she teaches me to play cards.

The Christmases she produces are spectacular and always include a reading of "The Little Match Girl." Her lace-covered table is crammed with ham and turkey, mince and pumpkin and apple pies. A mountain of presents spills from beneath the tree to fill the living room. Each year I receive more dolls to make up for the ones she never had.

"You're spoiling her," my mother grouses annually.

"I have a right," is my grandmother's ritual reply, jaw set, eyes flashing blue fire as if gas jets burn behind them.

I am not afraid of her temper. She turns it against me only once, on Saint Patrick's Day, when she pinches me hard enough to bruise my arm for wearing the orange ribbon that my mother insisted on tying in my hair. Crying harder than I do, she then bakes me a custard with nutmeg and cinnamon. "All's fair in love and war," she warns me sadly as I eat the peace offering from her best china. "It's part of being Irish."

There are other parts of being Irish. We don't cry over spilled milk, not for long anyway. As proof, she instructs me to consider our wakes: whiskey- and tear-soaked celebrations of passage for a stiffening corpse laid out in a coffin on the dining-room table. We keen, wailing heart-wrenching sobs, and later tell jokes and stories, laughing ourselves silly with just as much enthusiasm. Some of us drink. "We know how

to live," she teaches me, "and we know how to die. And we know how
to tell about it, too."

On rainy afternoons I stay with her to keep her company while
Grandpa works, and she fills me in on what she's learned of the Easter
Rising, secondhand of course, because she, after all, was living with
her Uncle Mike here in Michigan. While my grandfather reads meters
for the water department, we take turns standing on the ottoman,
waving our arms and raising our voices in impassioned speeches for
home rule. Since neither of us will pretend to be the hated English,
we Irish volunteers wedge ourselves behind the sofa, aiming our
fingers at invisible troops.

A voracious reader, she glibly paints word pictures of Dublin
Castle and Connolly Street, of De Valera and Pearse, but she lets me
direct the scenes she sets. "I don't know how to play," she tells me. "All
I learned to do was mend stockings and scrub floors, so you will have
to teach me." I take delight in showing her how to barricade Connolly
Street with a card table tipped on its side, how to make a Sinn Fein
flag from a dish towel tied to a broomstick.

My mother is not pleased when she comes to pick me up. "Your
grandmother's time in the orphanage affected her," Mother warns in
the car later. "She's never even been to Ireland, and we aren't *that*
Irish." She grinds the gears. "Well, *she* may be, but I'm certainly not,
and you're even less so." Her hands grip the De Soto's steering wheel.
"She's always stretched the truth. Next thing she'll be telling you
about the stone angel falling on her father. It was a load of stone
blocks." Two bright spots of color appear on her cheeks. "With her,
everything is high drama."

Afterward I am forbidden to be alone in my grandmother's
presence for two months because she is a bad influence on me. So for
two months I shell peas and snap beans for canning. Standing on a
tall chair, I iron my father's shirts, wondering all the time how
Grandma will ever manage to play without me.

One afternoon when my work is done, my mother curls my hair,
using sugar water for setting lotion. As she winds the curls in tight
spirals, she holds the metal bobby pins between her teeth. I have never
been quite so afraid of her. Then she sends me out with a quart jar
of water to pick dandelions in the yard between our house and the
barn. Standing in the kitchen window, she watches as bees swarm
around my head like a buzzing brown cloud. I try to defend myself
with the water, but even so, two of them sting me. When I run to the

house, shrieking and crying, she orders me to my room to wait for my father to come home. "She deliberately poured water on herself," she says to him, and he spanks me to calm her. I believe that my grandmother was lucky to live in an orphanage.

When my grandmother and I are finally reunited, I ask her to tell me the story about her father and the stone angel. She pulls a tin of butter cookies from the cupboard and brews tea in the pot with the shamrocks on it. "Patrick was a dancer and a drinker," she tells me as we get cozy on the loveseat. The faint scent of Grandpa's cigars lingers in the room. "A boxer, too," Grandma continues. "A devilishly handsome man with blue eyes and black hair, a black Irishman with a black heart to match, Patrick was. He was a master stonemason." She pours more milk into my tea and stirs it. "Before I was born, before Ma died, he helped to build the Catholic orphanage where I stayed."

"How did she die?" I would rather listen to my grandmother than listen to the radio or even go to the movies.

"I was two and she was thirty-six when she died," Grandma says. "She was big with a baby inside of her when she went out to the back yard to boil the wash and hang it. She took a chill and she died of pneumonia two days later, on Christmas day, coughing blood. They called the priest, who came in his black coat, smelling of whiskey, and gave her last rites. I don't remember much else — just my da crying and then lying on the floor later in his own vomit from drink. I was so young I couldn't figure out why we didn't open the presents." When she recounts this suffering, it is as though it had been inflicted on someone else.

My grandmother's mother was beautiful, the daughter of a lumberjack who farmed when the virgin timber in Michigan had all been cut. After marrying her off to the Irish stonemason, he moved to northern California to fell redwoods. There are no pictures of him or of his daughter, so I must take her at her word. "He ached to feel his saw blade bite into the soft wood of the biggest trees in the world, just like a knife going through butter," my grandmother recounts. "And he died when one of those very trees fell on him." She thinks for a moment and hints that this family history of having heavy objects fall upon us with crushing force may be a curse.

Then she goes on. "After Ma went to heaven, Da would be gone for days at a time, drinking and womanizing. Min, who was eleven, did her best to raise us. Frank had a paper route. Every night when he was finished, he'd bring me a cream puff wrapped in paper from the bakery since I was the baby and he liked me best. Sometimes when Da came back, he brought us money, so we got by."

By then the orphanage was long finished and Patrick was working on Saint Alphonsus Church. A statue he was carving toppled and smashed the bones in one of his legs, crippling him. She describes the angel to me, how it had her mother's face, how its gray wings arced toward heaven like a prayer, defying the weight of the stone they were carved from. "It was as if his heart was already flawed," she tells me. "When the angel fell on him, it broke wide open." We both nod wisely at the poetic justice in this.

She tells me that nobody cares to take the time to make such angels today. If I want to see good work like that I will need to visit a cemetery or the church. She herself will no longer set foot in a Catholic church, not after the nuns. When she must pass either church or nun, she hurries to the other side of the street. Even so, she teaches me to say the beads, to cross myself, and to recite at least one Hail Mary before I go to sleep each night, silently so my mother won't know.

If her father couldn't work, he still could drink, and that became his full-time occupation. He returned home only to move his children from tenement to boardinghouse – rough places as my grandmother remembers them. "Finally we were out in the street where it was even rougher," she says. "My grandparents couldn't afford to take us in and the other relatives only wanted Anna and Mabe, who were old enough to keep house. Min found a live-in job caring for an *Episcopal* priest's children." She frowns at this disgrace.

"Then, of course, neighbors told the nuns on Frank and me, who were the youngest, and they locked us in the home like prisoners." Abruptly she switches the subject. "Let's play Easter Rising." We do, making believe that the British have taken us captive in Dublin Castle and we must break out. While we plan our escape, my grandmother sings "The Prisoner's Lament." "If I had the wings of an angel," her voice strains and crackles. I join in, "Over these prison walls I would fly, I'd fly to the arms of my darling, and there I'd be willing to die." By the time Grandpa comes home from work, we have managed to break free and put supper on the table.

When I see her the next week, she has decided I will write her story and the story of the Irish race after I am grown. Someone must stand witness to what has occurred, even a distant witness. We have the gift of gab, she allows. It is in our blood from the famine time and well before. It comes from the pain of being misunderstood for centuries, and if we do not write about the pain or tell it in a story, it often gets us into trouble. Since she has only an eighth-grade education, she judges I might be the better grammarian, and therefore the task falls to me. "When you do it," she insists, "you must change our name to Kelley, so no one will recognize us."

For months, her storytelling escalates. I learn of bright spots in the orphanage, about how she wore out her shoes sliding down the hill in winter because there were no sleds. And when the nuns whipped her, she would look at them defiantly and say, "Thank you very much, Sister. Have you finished?"—which would set off another round of beatings. Once, on a bet, she pulled off a nun's wimple to see if sisters shaved their heads as was rumored. They did, and that prank earned her yet another whipping. She teaches me to read tea leaves, and invariably tells me I am coming into money. She shows me how to twist the stems carefully from apples to discover the last initial of the man I will marry. She instructs me on the art of avoiding black cats and ladders.

In the home, her big brother Frank watched after her, holding her hand whenever he could, and when he couldn't, smiling a rakish smile at her from across the room like Patrick's ghost. Mostly the boys and girls were separated, though. Her eyes fill with tears when she talks about the morning she came down to breakfast, took her place on the bench, and looked across the room for Frank, who wasn't there. For days the nuns wouldn't tell her what happened to him; finally, one informed her that he'd died, to forget about him. Months later, she learned that some second cousins had taken him since he'd grown old enough and strong enough to help on their farm.

She teaches me to wear spotless white gloves when we go to town. She shows me where the fairies sleep in her garden and promises me I will one day see one because she knows in her heart I have the sight. Every year we celebrate our birthdays together, since they fall only a few days apart.

The worst part about the Irish is that they drink, my mother informs me repeatedly. They drink because their imaginations work overtime. There are other bad things that she won't detail because I am too young to hear them. My grandmother has never touched a drop of spirits and she forbids my grandfather to drink, because she has seen the power of whiskey. Lips that touch liquor, will never touch hers. Her sisters are all slaves to drink, though, and even her beloved

Frank has succumbed. "Sins of the fathers," my mother grumbles on our way to a meeting of the Women's Christian Temperance Union at the Methodist church, and she adds something about whores and barflies. I wonder if they are as black and ominous as the fly on the milk-house screen in my grandmother's best story.

In late summer, as my grandmother and I inspect the snapdragons and the phlox in her garden, she gets to the part about the fire in the orphanage. She had no place to go except with Uncle Mike and Aunt Rose, the latter a dreaded Protestant. "When they saw how bad off I was," she tells me, "Uncle Mike, a good Irishman, told the nuns they could go to hell before he'd send me back to that place. I couldn't even sit in a chair; I didn't know how to anymore from sitting on the benches. 'You'll take this poor girl back over my dead body,' Mike told them." Her voice is as brave and clear as when she gives her home-rule speeches. I feel like clapping and cheering.

"When the trustees from the orphanage came to get me, Uncle Mike held me on his lap and put his arms around me. He threatened to punch the man's lights out." She smiles. "And he would have, too, if the terrible fellow hadn't left right then. So they served us with papers and took us to court. I can still remember how the nuns said that because Uncle Mike hadn't married in the Church, he and Aunt Rose were living in sin and that I'd lose my mortal soul if I stayed there. I was born and baptized a Catholic so I belonged to the nuns lock, stock, and barrel. But the judge at the hearing just looked at those old nuns and said, 'I married this couple right in this very courtroom. If you keep saying they aren't legally married, I'll hold you in contempt. Case dismissed.'" My grandmother's fist pounds the side of the tool-shed like a judge's gavel. She smiles so broadly she shows her teeth, which she is ashamed of because they are crooked.

Her teeth may be less than perfect, but she has good legs, which she shows off to her advantage and my mother's chagrin. Like a racehorse's, they are *very* good legs. In fact, it was those very legs which attracted my grandfather's eye when she was eighteen and on her own, working in a candy store. Both of them ended their engagements to other people, she to a handsome boy named Frank. My grandparents married within the year, but that is another story.

Her best tale remains the one about the day in the milk house that faraway August. The black spot through the screen slowly spread like a stain, and she saw it was a man. Frozen, she was terrified it was the orphanage official who had lain in wait for her to be alone. Many a night she had stayed awake, rigid with fear she'd be kidnapped and returned to the sisters. Now, since there was only one door, she was cornered like an animal.

As the stranger came closer, she could tell he was just a raggedy hobo with matted hair. His shoes were tied together with twine and his pants were so dirty and old they fairly glistened in the sun. Her shoulders relaxed, and she heaved a sigh . . . until she recognized the stranger as her long-lost da, and the pail of milk she'd been lifting flew crashing to the stone floor as if it had wings.

What could she do but hurl herself out the door with the fury of a banshee and start pounding her old man's chest with her fists? His yellowed teeth were rotting, his face was bearded, nose red-veined from years of drink. Oh, but she would have known those eyes anywhere. They haunted her dreams. She hated those eyes burning into her, wanted to put them out.

He was pitiful, she says, and stank to high heaven, but she was relentless. And he wouldn't fight back like an honest Irishman, but whined, begging her to forgive him and take him in, could she do anything but refuse him? Mother of God, once she knew for certain he wouldn't kill her, she knew without doubt that she would kill him, finish the job the stone angel started. Someone seemed meant to die that day. Suddenly afraid of the consequences of that murderous rage on her mortal soul, she took off on her racehorse legs, running toward the farmhouse with him flapping and wheezing behind her. "I slammed the door in his face." Her voice rings with triumph. "I told him I hoped he rotted in hell; he'd have me back as a daughter over his dead body." Giddy with excitement, although I've heard the tale at least six times, I let out the breath I have been holding. "And that was the end of it," she concludes. Before I can fully recover, she directs me to find the cardboard bingo cards and goes off to look for her button box for markers.

Obviously it is *not* the end of it because she tells and retells the story for the rest of her life. During the Alzheimer's years, it blurs like a bad print of an old movie. The images are nearly unrecognizable, but since you know the story line by heart, you make allowances. After the fatal heart attack, she began invading my dreams, and the focus has become so painfully sharp, it hurts me to view it directly.

In the time between my childhood and my grandmother's death, I managed to escape the weight of my mother, but my lips did touch liquor and, nearly crushed by the bottle, I forgot to write Grandma's story. Instead I married a man from the South Bronx who, although he was not Irish, resembled my great-grandfather Patrick in more ways than I care to recount. Let's just say he was a boxer in his own right. Later, too long after I'd turned from drink, I ejected him from my life, cursing his dark heart and telling him I hoped he rotted in hell. In the days before my thirty-sixth Christmas, I let the dirty clothes pile up, afraid that if I did the wash it would seal my fate. I read my tea leaves that always foretold I would be coming into money which never arrived.

Finally, sick and tired of grieving over spilled milk — mine, my mother's, my grandmother's, which lay mingled in a clotted puddle — I decided to wipe up the mess by sending away to the orphanage, the county courthouse, and the department of health for the records that would substantiate or disprove my grandmother's history.

My great-grandmother did die on Christmas Day in 1902, exactly as I'd been told. Her husband deserted his children shortly afterward, and my grandmother was committed to the Grand Rapids Catholic Home for Orphans when she was seven, along with Frank, the brother she idolized. I have the papers to prove it, those and the court records from the custody battle the nuns waged against Mike and Rose five years later. There are newspaper clippings, too, about the orphanage fire. And Frank's boy, now an old man with pacemaker, confirms the begging in Milwaukee.

As it turns out, Patrick lay cold and decomposing long before my grandmother's thirteenth summer. He was buried in a pauper's grave outside the churchyard, and since the drink finally caught up to him in winter when the frozen earth was difficult to spade, he shares his final resting place with two other derelicts, one of them nameless, none of them properly waked. And although that blackhearted drunkard of an Irishman did lay the stones for the orphanage that would imprison his own daughter's mind and heart throughout her life, he was no stone-carver. Saint Alphonsus Church doesn't have any stone angels. It never did.

Why My Grandmother Could Never Escape Ireland

for Evelyn Case Hassard

She slept above the creamery, her dreams
rising into the neck of Dublin's bottle
until she herself slowly separated
out of the thin milk of a dead mother.
She told me her father did not drink
though the chill of iron tankards ruled his hand
as he doled out love, cheating his daughter
by a farthing's weight for every quart,
ladling on the beatings like a man
dumping the spoils into a stone gutter.
Once he shattered her eardrum, then left
for Liverpool. She, unaccountably, followed,
the harsh buzz of his constant fault-finding
planted permanently inside her skull,
badgering her across a greased Atlantic.

For My Irish Grandfather

I am stung now with a different shame than then,
That day in front of Kresge's five-and-ten
When my urchin friends and I ran into you,
Staggering, unshaven, your crushed felt hat askew.
You swooped down with unbounded love to hug me,
Then stopped and rocked in grieved uncertainty.
You must have sensed my recoil, my debate,
Young as I was. (Was it seven or eight?)
Lips tobacco flecked, blue eyes clouded and remote,
You fished in the baggy pockets of your coat
(That coat so oversized
The sleeves fell past your fingertips). Your eyes
Found sunlight. You held up a dime,
(One you had just bummed, maybe) black with grime
And chew tobacco, and tendered it to me.
I ran and left you gesturing helplessly.

They say the whole town knew you, Tommy Dwyer,
That you had a voice like one of heaven's choir,
That silver voice my mother used to call
Your "sad and tragic downfall."
In those depression years, in the saloons,
They plied your weakness. One would importune,
"Have another drink Tommy. This one's on me."
And another, "Sing us your beautiful 'Mother Macree.'"
Whole seasons you would disappear.
When I'd ask mother why, she would look severe.
"He's riding the rails," she'd whisper. "Who knows where?
Let's pray God's mother keeps him in her care."

In laurel time I think of you the more.
That's when you'd show up at the door.
Mother would argue you to a hot tub.
My father, when you were sobered up and scrubbed,
Would cut your hair and shave you, find you shoes,
And one of his old suits. For a month or two
You'd be a different man. Then you'd be gone
As suddenly as summer moving on.

I wish I could have known you in your heyday,
When your eyes were like the May and every payday
You courted pretty Bridget Rooney
With ballads of the times, all Juney-moony;
Before the years of drudging in the coal mines,
Her early death, the booze, the brooding bread lines.

I keep a priceless memory
Of an hour or two you spent with me
When mother left me in your care one day.
You made up games in a grandfather's way.
I'd run and hide behind the chair.
You'd pretend to look for me everywhere
Till you suddenly spied me. Then you sang,
(How tenderly your tenor rang)
"Peek-a-boo,
I see you
Hiding behind the chair.
Peek-a-boo
I love you
Hiding behind the chair."
Did you remember, hopping a freight in the bitter midnight
    air?

The last time I saw you alive we cried.
It was when mother died.
We never knew how you heard the news.
You appeared out of nowhere, like sorrow's muse.
I sat in the living room all alone
With mother. (She lay as if carved in stone.)
The front door opened slowly, slowly.
You stood there, bowed and bald and holy,
Your felt hat crumpled in your hands,
Your too-big overcoat strangely grand.
You ignored me and moved to the coffin and stood
A long time looking, still as the wood
Of the crucifix above her head,
One with the silence of the dead.
Down our cheeks ran the drops of our shared loss.
You made a gigantic sign of the cross,
Shouting, "Jesus, Mary and Joseph have mercy
On my darling, my girl, my little girl . . .
She forgave me all my sins.
She took me in
When I had nowhere to lay my head.
She's with Christ and his angels and saints." You spread
A kerchief over your nose and blew it.
Then (young as I was, I knew you'd do it)
You started to sing.
Your voice had the lilt of an angel's wing.
"My wild Irish rose . . .
Sweetest flower that grows . . . "
From dining room, kitchen, from the street outside,
Family and neighbors gathered, wet-eyed.
"You may go everywhere,
But none can compare . . . "
My memory fails here, and my art,
With you singing her beauty, your hand on your heart.

John McCormack

THE DAY WAS COOL AND GRAY AND SMELLED OF APPROACHING RAIN.
We wore sweaters even though it was August. We would have stayed
inside to watch television that morning, except that our visiting uncle
from Chicago sat in the big chair in the living room, smoking and staring at nothing. We were a little afraid of him, although he was kindly
and gave us quarters when we bought him bags of popcorn or bottles
of Pepsi at the store. He always had a glass of Pepsi beside him on the
floor. He was supposed to be leaving in a few days. He was a plasterer,
and there were some unfinished jobs waiting for him back in Chicago.
He had been up north taking the "cure" he told us. "Cure for what?"
we asked. "Booze," he had answered in a low voice. "But don't tell your
mother I told you so."

We made cocoa in the spaghetti pot and sat around the picnic
table in the back yard with our hot mugs, reading the new mystery
books we had checked out of the library yesterday. Our oldest sister
sat on the step, copying recipes from a thick *International Cookbook.*
She had been reading cookbooks for a month and had a whole notebook full of recipes with ingredients we had never heard of before.

"How does this sound?" she would ask, interrupting us. "Nor-
wegian Baked Herring."

"Awful!"

"It's layers of herring and potatoes. I think it sounds good.
I've never tasted herring. Or how about this? Rice and Spinach
Armenian."

"You don't like spinach," we told her. "You know you don't."

"I might, if it were cooked like this. I'd leave out the garlic,
though."

We returned to our books. It was pleasant to look up occasionally
to watch one of the cats roll in the mint that grew under the garage
window or to listen to the piano next door. But after awhile, when we

began to get chilly, we went inside to refill our mugs and decided to read at the kitchen table.

Our brother Joe, who had been over at the archery range all morning, suddenly appeared at the screen door, panting. A misty rain had begun, but he stayed outside on the steps. There were droplets in his dark blond hair.

"Something's happened at the lake!"

"What?" we all asked at once. "On our side?"

"This side of the bridge," he said. "I don't know what it is. But there's lots of police cars. I'm going back."

He jumped down the steps. We heard his shoes pounding on the walk around the side of the house. Our oldest sister hastily dropped the dipper back into the cocoa, and turned off the burner.

"Let me get my sweater," she said.

"Hurry!" We edged into the dining room to wait for her, setting off a tinkle of glasses in the sideboard. Our uncle, his back to us, was standing over the record player in the living room, humming "tura-lura-lura" to himself. He was about to play our father's old Irish record again. We heard the click as he changed the speed to 78, and noted the shiny red bald spot on the back of his head. His hair always seemed greasy, the way it parted over the bald spot. Yet he took a shower every morning, and when he shaved, he left the bathroom door half open, so that we had all seen him patting his cheeks with blue after-shave lotion.

Two police cars had been driven across the grass to the edge of the lake. We saw that first. Then we saw the boat and the diver in the wet suit who was putting the oars in the oarlocks. A small crowd of people had gathered at a short distance from the black cars, mostly children in shorts, but there were a couple of mothers, too, and the old man who lived in the tiny, unpainted house down at the end of our alley. The surface of the lake was dark and absorbed the drops of light rain without ripples.

Joe waved at us as we hurried across the thick, wet grass.

"They're dragging the lake," he said anxiously when we reached his side. "Somebody drowned."

"Who?"

"A woman." He pointed to one of the police cars. A man was

hunched in the back seat, his head turned away from us to look out at the lake. "That's her husband."

"Was she swimming?"

Joe shook his head. "It's awful," he said. "She jumped from the bridge."

"Jumped?"

We all turned to look at the concrete bridge which arched across the lake at its narrow neck. We were at the smaller, shallower end of the lake, but there were still DANGER and DEEP WATER signs posted on the bridge pilings. We noticed how some of the cars crossing the bridge slowed down as they spotted the police cars on the shore.

"Why would she jump?" our brother Pat asked in a puzzled voice.

"To kill herself."

Pat stared at Joe, frowning. He ran his hand absently through his short, almost white hair. "Why?"

"She was unhappy, I guess." Joe looked out at the cold lake. "But I don't know how anyone could be that unhappy."

We watched the diver and one of the policemen row out toward the bridge. The diver attached his face mask and dropped silently into the water. He had a breathing tube, but it was hard to spot it on the dark surface. Occasionally his head emerged. Twice he climbed back into the rowboat, and the policeman poured something to drink from a thermos. The other policemen paced up and down the shore, rubbing their chilled hands together, sometimes listening to the static and strange bursts of talk on their radio, occasionally speaking in low voices to the man in the back seat, who would roll the window down and lean out.

We squatted down, trying to cover our bare legs with the tails of our sweaters. The light rain turned into a fine mist, and the bridge looked silvery and insubstantial. The trees in the little woods behind the archery range were obscured by fog. More mothers had arrived. Some had come to fetch their children, but had remained standing near other mothers, talking in subdued voices and glancing out at the boat. Our oldest sister had found a stump to sit on, a little away from the crowd. Joe plucked at his bowstring absently and in a while went to sit by himself under the willow tree.

"Let's go home," one of us said after an hour. "I'm hungry."

We stood up. Our legs were stiff from the damp. The grass had printed greenish lines into our knees.

"Pat!" we called.

He ignored us. He was staring intently out at the lake.

We started home without him, glancing back at the police cars once or twice. We planned to come back after lunch. On the other side of the park road, where the grass was smooth and cropped for baseball, we broke into a run. We were out of breath by the time we reached our yard. The inner door was open, and through the screen we could hear two voices singing "The Harp That Once Thro' Tara's Halls." Once voice, sweet and far away, was spoiled by static and crackles. The other voice, loud but weak and interrupted by a hacking cough, was our uncle's. We stood outside by the blue spruce for a minute or two, listening in embarrassment.

Finally we entered the house. Our uncle did not even hear us at first. His head was tilted toward the ceiling, his eyes were closed, and his hand was wrapped around his throat as he sang, as if he were controlling the pitch by the pressure of his fingers.

The song came to an end. Our uncle opened his eyes during the short band of static that followed and saw us as we crossed the living room.

He blinked and cleared his throat. "He was the best," he said to us thickly. "This old record doesn't do him justice."

"John McCormack?" we asked politely.

"John McCormack," he repeated. "I heard him sing once. That was at the ballroom of the Lakeshore Palace Hotel. It was at a banquet. All the men were wearing tuxedos, and all the women had on strapless gowns – I was a waiter. I never told you I was a waiter, did I?"

"No," we said as we backed shyly away from him, trying not to be rude.

"When he started to sing, I forgot I was supposed to be filling the water goblets. I just stood there, my mouth open. I felt it all the way up my spine, up and down every bone, in my skull –"

"Felt what?" one of us asked.

"I felt like I was dying, but it was so sweet . . . he had the voice of an angel, a voice like the harp of an angel. I hope it's like that when I die; I hope the angels will sing 'Ireland, Mother Ireland' as beautifully as John McCormack."

"Somebody died at the lake," we said.

The vague, dreamy look on his face disappeared. "I know. One of the neighbors knocked at the door." He stood up heavily. "I need a walk. I suppose you're all going back there after lunch?"

We nodded.

"I'll go with you," he said as he headed toward the bathroom. "Your mother's at the store with the baby."

He came into the kitchen a few minutes later, and absently placed the John McCormack album on the table where we were making our sandwiches. He poured another Pepsi into his smudged glass. We stared at the album as we chewed. A brown castle had been sketched against the turquoise background, next to a portrait of John McCormack, who looked very handsome and foreign. He reminded us of our father in the old photographs on the mantel where he was wearing his army uniform and had a thick wave in his hair.

We did not like to be seen in public with our uncle, who walked stiffly, as if his legs hurt, and sang or hummed out loud even when he was passing a stranger on the sidewalk. His baggy trousers, splattered with paint around his cuffs, seemed about to fall down around his ankles. His black dress shoes were unpolished and worn at the heels. The back of his shirt was creased. The skin under his eyes was thick and swollen, his nose and cheeks reddened by broken veins. He always had a vacant, faraway look in his light blue eyes.

We were ashamed of our reluctance to be seen with him, however, and had never spoken of it to each other. We stayed close to his side as we crossed the park to the lake, pointing out interesting features of the neighborhood—the bus wye, the sycamore which had been split by lightning, the red ring of paint around a diseased elm, the archery range where Joe practiced with his bow and arrow, even the grove of trees in the distance where a man had exposed himself to some third-grade boys.

The rain had let up completely and the sun was coming out. The crowd had grown; now it was mostly adults, all of them silent, standing shoulder to shoulder as we came toward the shore of the lake. We recognized Mrs. Wagner, who lived across the alley; she was still in her nurse's uniform, standing on tiptoes in her white, rubber-soled shoes, trying to see over the heads in front of her. An ambulance had been parked next to the police cars. As we joined the crowd, we saw two policemen come around the side of the ambulance with a bundle. The doors were opened, then slammed shut. The crowd began moving apart.

Our oldest sister saw us, and jumped off the stump which must have given her an excellent view of what had happened.

"They found her," she said flatly. She tried to smooth her damp hair, which was beginning to dry in frizzy peaks.

"What did she look like?"

"I couldn't look after all. I only looked after they had her in the boat, covered up." She shivered. "But I saw her foot when they carried her out on shore."

"Where's Pat?" our uncle asked.

"Over there." Our oldest sister pointed to some bushes. "I think he's throwing up. I should have sent him home—" She frowned, thrusting her hands into the pockets of her shorts and turning away.

We looked out at the lake. The surface was scaled with silver now that the sun was out and a wind was rising. The ambulance and the police car with the husband in the back pulled silently away. The diver stood by the rowboat, smoking and talking to two policemen.

Pat came up beside us. There were deep circles under his eyes, and he was wheezing slightly.

"You better use your inhaler," our oldest sister said.

"I'm all right."

"What did you see?" we asked.

"Her hair was so long it was caught in the weeds. They had to cut her free." He swallowed. "She was stiff. Her blouse was muddy."

Our uncle crossed himself.

Pat watched him closely. "Can you do that?"

"What?"

"Pray for her?"

Our uncle blinked. "Of course you can pray for her. For her soul."

"Isn't her soul in hell?"

Our uncle glanced down at Pat, then gripped his shoulder. "Now who told you that? Only God knows about the soul."

Pat trembled. His lips were blue and bitten, and for the first time we realized that he had seen something that was going to haunt him—something that he could not describe to us in words. We did not know whether to be envious or relieved that we had not seen it, too. Our oldest sister's guarded face told us nothing.

"We need to light a candle for her soul," our uncle said, bending closer to Pat. "I lit a candle when John McCormack died. That was in 1945 before any of you were born. I'd been sent home from the war with a bullet in my thigh. That candle burned for weeks and when it was almost out, I lit two more from the same flame. I like to think that other candles were lit from my flame, for other souls, and that my flame is still burning somehow . . . or burned until John McCormack got out of purgatory, the good man."

He brushed his hand across Pat's face, as if he had seen a tear which we had missed. "What do you say? Shall we go up to church and light a candle for this poor drowned lady?"

"Our new church doesn't have candles," we said.

"What? It's a Catholic church. Of course it has candles."

"We've never seen any candles," we said emphatically. "We go to mass every Sunday."

"There are candles," our oldest sister said. "In the vestibule on the far side, near the pamphlet table. It's the side we never go in — and they're way back in the corner."

"Let's go," our uncle said. "You can light the candle, Pat."

Pat nodded, and we started off across the grass which smelled fresh and sharp as the sun dried the blades. Other people who had seen the drowned woman brought ashore were moving slowly across the park, too, or standing in small groups, talking quietly. As we passed one group of women, which included Mrs. Wagner in her white uniform, we looked secretly up at their faces, but their moving lips and eyelashes and slightly knitted foreheads did not tell us what we needed to know.

We climbed the hill to the church, pausing a few times to let our uncle catch his breath. His face grew red and congested. The exertion caused his hair to stick to his forehead in wet coils.

Our church was a modern building of yellow brick, with a squat bell tower and a curved facade. It was attached to the older, three-story grade school. A few cars were parked in the lot.

"They must be hearing confession," we told our uncle.

He looked up at the church. "What a pity. You don't have any stained glass windows."

"The windows are colored glass," we said. "When the sun shines it turns all blue inside."

We led him to the nearest door, and held it open for him.

"Did you ever see Sacred Heart in Chicago?" he asked in a low voice. "When you go to mass at dawn, the whole church is as bleak as the inside of a mountain. You can't see the ceiling it's so high. Then the sun comes up — it pours through the center window, the Sacred Heart window, and you've never seen red that red. It's the color of wine or rubies or real, wet blood — " he coughed, glancing suddenly at Pat. "There's a gold canopy over the altar, too, and the candlesticks are massive silver. But the candles you light yourself are at the side altars."

We were inside the vestibule, a low, square room where a few metal folding chairs had been stacked against the wall. Another door, which our oldest sister opened, led into the church itself.

"The candles are on the other side," she said.

We dipped our hands into the aluminum holy water font as we entered. The water was cool and soft as we splashed it on our foreheads. The church was dim, for the sun was not hitting the blue windows this time of day. When we reached the center aisle, we genuflected. A large, abstract sculpture hung above the altar instead of the usual crucifix, and although we had gotten used to seeing it, we always felt a little funny when we crossed ourselves. Only two people were in line at the confession box on the left. The red light on the box at the right had already been turned off.

The vestibule on the other side of the church was shadowy, for the venetian blinds were shut. The pamphlet table was empty except for a few out-of-date copies of *The Catholic Messenger*. We looked curiously at the tiered metal rack in the corner. Each shelf contained little red glasses with white votive candles inside. A black box with a slot in the top was attached to the side of the rack.

"That's strange," our uncle said, fumbling with the change in his pocket. "None of them are lit." He handed a dime to Pat. "Put that in the box."

The dime made a hollow clink as Pat dropped it in the slot.

"Let's see if I've got any matches, now." Our uncle began going through his other pocket. He pulled out nail clippers, ticket stubs, the broken end of a pencil, crushed grains of popcorn, three finely wrinkled one-dollar bills, and finally produced a matchbook with softened edges.

He was lighting a match for Pat when the inner door of the church opened. Father North, one of the three parish priests, appeared before us in his long, black cassock. He had just come from hearing confessions, for the purple stole still hung around his neck. We felt our throats constrict. His face was stern as if he had been listening to terrible sins.

He looked at our little group and his face darkened.

"You're the new children in the parish, aren't you?" he asked briskly.

"Yes, Father," we whispered back.

"Who is this man?" he asked. "Are you children all right?"

We stared at him, not understanding.

His lip twitched impatiently. "Is this man bothering you?"

We looked at our uncle then, stunned and horrified at what Father North was suggesting. He stood there in front of Pat with a match burning down to his finger, his mouth open a little, a slightly dazed look on his face. The white lining of his pockets hung partly out.

"Please, Father," our oldest sister said in a voice that was high and shaky. "This is our uncle." And then, although we had never seen her touch anyone affectionately before, not even our father or mother, she put her arm around our uncle's shoulder.

"He's from Chicago," we said, all of us speaking at once for we saw that our uncle's face was beginning to redden in shame. "He's our favorite uncle. You should hear him sing. We've come up to light a candle."

"Fine," Father North said. "But I'd like to lock the doors. Confession is over."

"Do you lock the doors in this church, Father?" our uncle asked in a soft voice, his eyes on the floor.

"It's not safe to keep the doors open when no one is here — it's a sorry comment on the world, I'm afraid."

Our uncle nodded.

Our oldest sister moved away from him, then, dropping her arm self-consciously.

Our uncle handed the matchbook to Pat. "Be careful," he said hoarsely.

Pat lit a match above the long wick of a candle in the first tier. It caught immediately and made the dark red glass translucent. He made the sign of the cross and bowed his head. We watched him pray for the woman who had drowned herself.

Then we turned to go.

Father North cleared his throat. "I'd appreciate it if you'd blow the candle out before you leave."

"Blow it out?" Pat looked at our uncle in surprise.

Father North pointed to a small sign taped to the side of the candle rack.

"What grade will you be in, son?"

"Fourth," said Pat.

"Can you read the sign?"

Pat swallowed. "'Please do not leave candles burning. Fire –'" he hesitated.

"'Hazard'," Father North finished emphatically.

Pat looked at the candle flame. "I just lit it," he said, his voice quivering. "It's for a dead soul."

"Let it burn for a while, Father," our uncle asked in a voice so humble that we squirmed with embarrassment. "In most churches . . . " his voice trailed off inaudibly.

Father North pointed at Pat. "Please blow out your candle. What if the curtains caught on fire? I know you lit it for a soul. Very nice. But it's not the candle that counts, it's the prayer behind it."

"I always thought it was the candle, Father," our uncle said.

Father North shook his head. "It's only a pretty custom."

"But I've lit a lot of candles over the years," our uncle said, his voice trembling. "You mean my candles did no one any good?"

Father North hesitated. Then his somber face lit up with a smile, the first we had ever seen across his face. We could see the edges of his teeth. "If they did you good, that's fine. That's important, too."

"I thought I was helping the poor souls of purgatory."

A flicker of annoyance crossed Father North's face. "Only God decides about that." He tugged nervously at the stole hanging from his neck, and pulled a set of heavy keys from his pocket. He looked severely at Pat.

Pat bent over the flame. We all drew our breath in and held it down in our lungs a long time until our chests ached, as if we could keep the flame burning by not breathing. We wanted a miracle, and when Pat's weak mouthful of air caused the flame to brighten, instead of go out, we thought we had been granted our prayer.

"Blow harder," Father North said.

"He has asthma," our oldest sister said.

Pat closed his eyes, then spat at the candle. The flame disappeared with a hiss. We knew it was the sound of a soul slipping into darkness, a soul that might have lit her way to heaven by the light of Pat's candle. That was our fancy, at least, when we glanced into Pat's cold and vacant face as he brushed past us and ran out the door.

"Good-bye, Father," we said hastily, to cover Pat's violent departure and the gloom which had fallen over our uncle's face, sealing his lips.

"Tell your brother to come see me sometime when his heart isn't so hard," Father North said. "You seem like a nice family."

"Thank you, Father," we said.

We walked home beside our uncle. He did not hum or talk about John McCormack, and we were afraid to mention the singer now. Our uncle's ankles seemed to hurt, for he walked even more slowly and carefully than usual, and he stumbled in places where the sidewalk was uneven or badly cracked.

Later that night we got out the box of old black and white photographs to show our uncle, who seemed despondent. We showed him pictures of ourselves at every age, in high chairs, in teeter-totters, in strollers, in matching dresses, in funny bonnets. When we held the photographs up to the light to see them better, we saw his ghostly fingers shining through the paper upon which our smiling faces had been, as we thought, permanently fixed.

Memories

it came into our lives unexpectedly
like an unwanted child
rudely shoved into the living room
through the narrow doors
by two white-shirted beer-bellied
brutes heaving and grunting like
pigs in heat

i remember it arriving
on a hot summer afternoon
charged on dad's meager pay

once in the house
our lives would never
be the same

many a night
i would sneak from bed
down the hallway
to peek through the door
where mother and the beast
engaged in battle
like knights of old
jousting for honor

mother slouched over the stool
her eyes dreamlike
half-shut
hair disheveled
each magical musical note
bringing her back to kinder times
before the weight of marriage
crushed her like a bulldozer

her fingers tickling those
ivory keys with tender notes of love
looking like a chinese sewing lady
in a garment shop

as if each note were
a perfect stitch binding
her life to a new scrap
of cloth

An Irish-American Air

For my uncle, Pfc. John Thomas McNeil,
killed in action, 1918 (and for my daughter-in-law, Kathy)

My grandmother loved to be told
there was auburn left in her hair;
as I combed it I'd tell her I'd found some,
though I never had seen any there.

We'd move from the bath to the kitchen
where I'd finish her beauty care.
"You're the only one has any patience,"
she'd say of the waist-length hair.

"He went for the Navy," she'd tell me,
"he went for a sailor to be."
And I'd think how the blue of the jacket
would have looked, with his eyes, like the sea.

"It was safer, you see, in the Navy,
we'd heard there were less of them dead;
but his eyes wouldn't do for the Navy,
he went down for the Army instead.

They promised them all six months' training,
and the war would be over by then;
but they shipped him to France in the morning,
and Wilson was lying again."

She hated the name and it crackled
through my hand in her ivory hair,
and the teeth in her face and my comb
snarled as they bit down where

her memory locked in the rocking,
and she groaned into one of her tunes,
"We'd sit on the swing together
and sing 'The Innisfallen Dragoons,'

Mrs. Gallagher and myself together,
and we'd wait for the boys to come home,"
and her fist beat the side of the rocker
like an Irish metronome.

O she moved back and forth with the music,
though she never stopped marking the time,
when she would be with him somewhere,
who had both been cut down in their prime,

he in the joy of his manhood,
and she in her pride as his mother;
when he fell, the whole of her bearing
told the world that all life was over.

And now there's a different woman,
and now there's another son;
and another name in the White House,
and another "last war" to be "won."

"You know, you're the image of mama,"
says a voice from behind me, where,
this May, in a Michigan garden,
my mother puts a curl in my hair.

Memorial Day, 1971

Grammudder

for Ann McCardy Murphy

I.

1943. You hummed
"Over There" absently,
but another war

throbbed in memory.
You poured Irish tea
into white enamel cups

steaming pale rinds
of smoke into casks
of afternoon silence.

I ate scones and heard
pipers, Robert Emmett's last
speech on the dock.

Finnians, republicans
lined up, your brother
Jack beaten with a horse

crop, bleeding in his own
velvet fields, the brocade
lands of Mullingar.

Your stories held onto
that world, useless
as the blind collie

sleeping at our feet.
You gave the stories
like hidden tongues

that might speak later on,
might wake a partisan heart.
I have always remained Irish,

missing something
I cannot name.
It has given me an edge.

II.

"Your grandmother was
motherless from birth,"
my mother said.

Then keeping the muscles
of her mouth tight,
she told me of your childhood.

Jack to Australia
Katherine to Chicago,
only Pa and you, alone

with the mares and sheep
in those sodden
hills of Athlone.

When you are twelve,
the old man begins
or ends love, simple as loss.

A cap of rain
wheeled the clotted glens
when he hitched the mare.

At the dock he placed
a tag around your neck
that read:

Ann McCardy: Chicago.
He said, "God bless,
wait for Katherine."

Then a whistle,
gulls reeling in the
slate sky's finality.

Ireland lurching
further and further
through the swelling mists.

The mare and himself
waving the old cap.
"Oh Pa," is all you say.

William Keough

Last Word on a Pink Dress

EVEN BEFORE MY GRANDFATHER HAD BECOME ONE OF THE DEARLY departed from eating too much of the Halloween candy he snitched from me and my brother Joey, my grandmother went flying off to Florida every spring with one of her widowed friends to play kitty-whist in the sun, gossip about their heartless children back in Boston and eat oranges. Back she came after a week or so with a mottled tan and a shopping-bag full of Mexican jumping beans, souvenir saucers, rattles, and jars of real Atlantic sand.

"Look at her," my mother sneered as she emerged at Logan one March day, "she thinks she's eighteen again, the old fool."

"Never mind her raving," my grandmother would shout above the roaring of the planes, holding tightly to her wide-brimmed yellow sunbonnet – the sleeves of her immense coat taking the wind like kites at Nantasket Beach. "Imagine a girl jealous of her own mother." She would snuff up her tiny nose, secretly gloating, and turn her moon-face upon us children. "Here," she would say, slipping a Mexican puppet into my hands, "I've only the one so keep your trap shut." Then she'd go around distributing the rest of her largesse from the large and overflowing shopping bags she carried everywhere.

On her return one late March day, a freak storm had swept in and deposited three-foot drifts beside the runway and a bitter east wind blew in off the water. "Mother of God," she exclaimed to no one in particular, "do they expect us to live in igloos? I, for one, am not about to take to rubbing noses."

"Who asked you to," my mother scoffed. "You out gallivanting around the country, how do *you* suffer?"

"Go ahead and start," my grandmother said, squinting up her eyes, "we all have our crosses if you know what I mean. I'm ready for you."

"Ah, come on, Lil," my father interceded, "wait till you get your coat off."

But that night, when my grandmother took one look at the lot of us with our rheumy eyes and runny noses, she decided that something had to be done — and immediately. Scouring the paper, she spotted an ad for cottages in some woods down the Cape. "Riviera Lake Shores, they call it," she said, sticking the ad under my grandfather's chin, "exclusive estates for less than $3500." Despite her appeal, Papa maintained a stony silence, probably dreaming he was back at his tavern up on Chauncy Street.

"Oh, aren't you the great one for how-do-you-do's and a sunny Saturday at the track," she railed at him. "Oh, sure, you can be generous to foreigners, but tight as a clam when it comes to us. When it comes to us, you squeeze a dollar so tight the ink runs in your hand." She shot out a short, stubby finger. "May the Blessed Mother in heaven forgive you, John Joseph Delehanty, because I certainly can't. Ninety-eight dollars down it says in black and white, and thirty-eight a month which I'll pay myself out of the Christmas Club money. *I* can go without!" Papa fidgeted in his easy chair — visibly weakening. "I'll ask no more," my grandmother closed, "just the down payment, John."

Sighing, my grandfather pulled out his wrinkled black leather wallet and fingered the bills like skin before slowly handing them over. "As God is my witness," my grandmother cooed, crossing her heart and stuffing the bills in her bra.

The next morning she set off on foot and returned with the deed in her pocket and a photo of the cottage, which she stuck under our noses for approval. "Our new summer home!" she exulted. Papa slouched in his chair, smoking a cigar and flipping through a green racing tout.

The following months she collected the family in a flotilla of second-hand cars, and we set off to view our new summer home. What greeted us was an unpainted plywood shack set among some scrawny pines. Undaunted, she bustled about, organizing work details so everyone was busy hanging up drapes and hammering shingles, moving bunks into the two tiny bedrooms and painting the walls her choice of a particularly lurid pink.

Soon all was set to rights, and hordes of distant relatives appeared to join us on bright June Sundays to cadge free beers and have a dip in the lake. "You told them yourself," my mother would say, to which my grandmother would just raise her chin to pronounce, "*I* never refuse *my* blood."

My grandmother bought an aluminum chaise longue with emerald-green ribbing (her throne, we called it) which she stationed in the front yard in order to preside over the incredible welter and from which she complained about her blood pressure and gossiped about the odds and ends of summer to all and sundry. My grandfather, a wise man, remained safe in Boston behind the counter of his bar. "So Bill Kelley," she would call out to my dad, starting in on one of her fierce and breathless monologues, "I suppose you don't think we need screens on all the windows even if the mosquitoes are eating me alive, and it's fine with me, even if I did, squeezing pennies out of dust, buy it for your enjoyment, and sure it's fine for you, you don't have to live here all week, so I guess my old knees will have to do the job, they have before, I feel so wicked." Then she would make as if to struggle out of her seat, groaning against her own weight until my father went over to soothe her back down. He would shake his head and bring his beer out to the windows where he hammered away at new screens in order to drink in peace.

But despite its exotic title, Riviera Lake Shores was something of a disappointment. The lake was really a pond — a lily pond at that — and thick with mosquitoes; and some cranberry people had water rights for their bogs which meant that some mornings we would awaken only to find the water level mysteriously dwindled. We didn't much care, Joe and me. As long as we had something to splash in, we were happy — even if lilypads did wrap around our legs like water snakes and even if the water did sometimes taste like cranberry juice.

But it did put a slight crimp in one of my grandmother's fondest dreams. She wanted a nice picture of Riviera Lake Shores to impress her friends back in Boston, and she certainly did not think highly of the lilypads. "Maybe they can poison them," my father shrugged. "I'd like to poison Mister What's-his-name, that developer," snorted my grandmother, "selling lots next to a bloody swamp."

Finally, my dad came up with an ingenious solution, photographing just before sunset when the light shivered on top of the ripples so everything was all black and shimmering and the lilypads were lost on the negative. "It's positively romantic," my grandmother exulted, "you're a real knight among men, Bill Kelley," and she laid off him for two whole days after that.

If it was bad enough that Riviera Lake turned out to be nothing more than a glorified frog-pond, the cottage's concrete blocks sat on sandy waste that tolerated only scrub pines the needles of which soaked the ground with acid. This seemed to scotch her plans for a nice green lawn. But when the men just shook their heads sadly, she ranted at them to just go and get seed, and no degree of masculine logic could put her off. It was all quite simple: she would have her lawn or *they* would be sorry. She knew a man could do anything he put his mind to—and that no man ever did unless he was hounded into it.

So my Uncle Richie the carpenter brought down a truckload of loam from Quincy, and she put Joey and myself to work raking up the brown pine needles and spreading thick black loam about the yard. As my grandmother sat out in her chaise longue, her tiny blue eyes fastened like leeches on our narrow, sweaty backs. "Look, Jimmie," she shouted at me, "you missed a spot, oh Jesus, Mary, and Joseph, there's too many rocks in it, oh Joey, are you blind, do a good job or I'll tell your father, I hope to Christ it'll do." And then, sunset slipping down all green and gold as we slipped away for a merciful swim, we could still hear her voice chasing us, her face lost in the shadows, "It's too thin, Mother of Mercy, too thin for a growing thing."

With the intercession of Saint Fauna or Saint Flora or whoever is the patron saint of botanical miracles, something did manage to fight its way through the acid and pine needles—crabgrass it was. And dandelions flourished. How she hated the dandelions, moving despite her bulk with incredible swiftness about the yard, stooping and grunting, snipping off their heads with house scissors and shoving them into the pockets of her apron. "Mother of Mercy, look at the yellow worms," she shrieked, "I knew the soil was too thin but do you think they'd listen?" No one dared tell her about the crabgrass, she seemed happy enough it was green.

But after a while the lawn ceased to satisfy her—she wanted a real tree. She had once seen groves of willows along the road on an excursion into the country, and that was what she wanted. "Willows always look so pretty hanging down," she announced, "and not so sad as they look, just what a tired soul needs to sit under and think about the hereafter, take me to the tree place, Bill Kelley."

"They'll rob her blind," my mother muttered, "she doesn't know a blessed thing about trees. She wouldn't know an elm from a pussy-willow."

All the same she was not to be denied her willow, and so off she went to the nursery with my dad, and when they returned my father was carrying what looked like a broken branch in a brown paper bag.

"All that talk," she said with a flourish in my mother's direction, "all that talk about prices and ignorance and it was only $5.98."

"And now what are you going to do with it," said my mother, "keep it in a bowl in the house for a year or two?"

"Shut your face," she growled, snatching the willow from my father and cradling it in her arms. "It'll be full-grown in nine years."

"And who do you expect is going to take care of it?"

My grandmother turned her back on her. "I'll do it myself like I do everything else around here, come on, Jimmie."

So I trooped off to the yard after her, and after surveying the crabgrass for the longest time she finally lit on a spot just to the left of her chaise longue. "Dig," she said, and I did. "Deeper," she cried, "do you want the squirrels to be eating its legs?"

"Are we planting it or burying it?"

"Never mind with the wise stuff, smarty-pants, just like her always with the smart answers, just dig." At last she was satisfied and placed the willow in the hole, fanning the roots against the ground until it almost disappeared.

"Here, Lil," my father interrupted, coming from the house, "that's not right."

"Look out with your hands, Bill Kelley," she barked, "you're with her, and we both know she doesn't want me to have anything." My father retreated to his windows.

So afterwards I would water the willow three times a day under her baleful eye until a puddle formed about a yard around. "She's drowning it," my mother informed the walls, "she thinks it's a fish, the fool."

My grandmother stuck a fat finger under my nose. "Remember, Jimmie, you can't drown anything with love."

During the week my dad and uncles would go back to Boston to work, so Joey and myself were left to do their bidding. One morning it poured, and Joey and I were playing dice baseball when my grand-mother came into the bedroom. "Jimmie," she whispered, "Jimmie, the willow hasn't been watered, quick before she sees you and quiet now." Joey giggled — he was always giggling — but she silenced him with a glare. I could hear the rain outside clattering noisily down on the roof and swishing against the pines, but I knew there was no appeal. So I put on my sneakers and my Red Sox windbreaker and slipped out the kitchen door to get the garden hose. I was soaked to the skin almost at once, and a considerable puddle had already spread around

the willow, and I was tempted to turn back until I saw my grandmother's nose pressed against the front window. I just nodded, my
hair matted and my clothes dripping, licked the rainwater from the
corner of my mouth, and watered the willow.

Suddenly my mother appeared at the front door. "Are you out of
your mind? Get in here before I throttle you. You're as bad as she is.
Get in here, Jimmie!"

So I shut off the hose and slipped inside, shaking like a spaniel.
"Here, put these on," my mother said, handing me some dry clothes.
"She told you to do that didn't she?" I shrugged my shoulders. "Crazy
as loons, the both of you." When she batted my head with an open
hand, I could see she was working herself up to a real froth, and I
sincerely wished I was back in the rain. "Wait till I tell your father.
Raining cats and dogs, and you're out watering a dead tree."

"It is not dead," my grandmother said, "it's growing every day,
cruel you are, *cruel* to your own mother and *cruel* to your little boy and
have always been, sure I told him to water the willow and if you want
to do something, girl, then turn on me. " She grabbed me up from my
mother's side and shoved me behind her.

And it was only then that my mother started to throw things,
cups and saucers at first, then pots and pans and plates, while my
grandmother ducked and finally hurled a chair against the wall. They
toppled lamps and tables and even overturned the couch until they
both began to cry, my brother and I watching from the bedroom and
laughing into our fists to keep them from hearing, and the cottage a
shambles of wounded furniture and broken crockery.

After that it was spooky. For days the rain kept up so we had to
stick to the house, but still they refused to talk to each other, even at
meals. "Could you tell *her* to pass the salt," my grandmother would
say. "Tell *her* she can take it herself," my mother would sputter back,
right under my grandmother's nose. And so I passed the salt and
carried messages, proud at last to be man of the house.

Yet in spite of all our attention, that willow refused to grow.
Scrawny and leafless, it crouched forlornly in the front yard beside the
chaise longue, and my grandmother glared at it as if she wanted to bat
its ears from limb to limb. One morning when she decided she had
enough, she dragged me off by the arm to the variety store up at the
highway. "Hello there," she called to attract the owner's attention, "I
want some willow-food here, it's for an emergency."

"How's that lady?" The owner ventured, coming cautiously over from behind the candy counter.

"Willow-food I said. Precious Blood, don't you understand the English language, look here, some vitamins or something to make a tiny tree grow up big and strong."

The owner nodded slowly and disappeared. He returned with a yellow box of something which looked like washing detergent but which he said was good for all growing things. My grandmother snatched it up and handed it to me, "It better be guaranteed, how much does it cost, do you take pennies, of course you have to." And she counted out the change on the glass counter coin by coin — quarters, dimes, nickels, and many pennies — and double-counted just to be sure. As we left the owner whispered, "Good-bye, son," and I smiled back bravely to assure him I hadn't been kidnapped.

We fed the willow a spoonful a day as directed, but still it shriveled. My grandmother rained such curses on it I was reminded of how she had urged my childhood bowels on by prophesying it would come out my ears if I didn't loosen up so that to this day when constipated the first thing I check is my ears in the bathroom mirror. That willow, I knew, was in big trouble. I was amazed it didn't just one night pluck itself up and run away instead of perching there so bare and brown and defiant. Finally, with fall approaching, she couldn't stand to look at its frailty any longer and pulled it up by the roots. She threw the willow in with the rubbish, then thought better of it and took it to the sand pile in the back yard where she burned it together with some newspapers until nothing was left but ashes. "It's sad, Jimmie, my heart's desire gone up in smoke, well, it's the least I can do for the poor thing, a decent end for one and all." She stared back at the cottage. "She killed it, killed it with all of her hard talk as God is my witness. So cruel she didn't even want me to have a willow tree, that one wouldn't give you the time of day."

"It's four o'clock," I said checking my Mickey Mouse watch proudly, glad to oblige.

"My poor Jimmie!" She pulled me to her immense soft bosom and started weeping. "It's a wonder to me how anyone can be so smart and so stupid at the same time, I hope to God you never get lost in the woods."

Of course I did get lost in the woods – as we all do eventually. Time passed and so did my grandfather, which shocked me because like all kids I thought that everyone lived forever. I remember peeking into the coffin only to see this dead stranger with orange color on his face – not at all a convincing model of my grandfather who I knew had gone to heaven somewhere over Hawaii where he was now at last sitting in peace, smoking his great cigars, and playing with his green racing sheets. They couldn't fool me.

My mother turned thinner and shriller with the years. Her blue eyes got as crazy as winter sky, and doctors gave her small bottles of pills in colors various as the rainbow, and she still took fits and my dad took to coming home later and later. I took refuge in books like *Robinson Crusoe* and *Around the World in Eighty Days*, dreaming of flight, constantly dreaming.

My mother refused to loose her hold so easily. "Kiss me," she demanded sometimes as I lay in my pajamas after the strap. "On the cheek." And I would relent, my lips cold and white with rage, all the time assuring myself: *It doesn't count, it's not a real kiss – it's not a real kiss if I don't mean it.*

"The Irish are a miserable people," my Uncle Richie used to say when he was drunk, "we hate ourselves."

"You hate yourself," my father would object furiously, "I don't hate myself." Uncle Richie would laugh at this until tears came and then pour himself another drink.

Uncle Richie had made money in the contracting business, and he had taken to traveling outside the family circle. Every winter he went off to Las Vegas for a week, and he even went hunting in Alaska with Protestants. "He thinks he's too good for his own shit," my father would snort. But Uncle Richie would whisper to me, "You're going to make it out of here, you little bastard, because you have a good head on your shoulders and you can see it for what it is – a goddam loony bin of spit and spite. Go on, I say, and good luck to you." But once sober, he would change his tune. "Listen, Jimmie," he would say, "never forget where you come from. *Never.* It may not seem like much at times but it's all you have. Who really cares but your family? You'll see – you'll see."

As soon as I could I fled to college out in the flat American plains of the Midwest, hibernating for long winters before returning home. My mother railed at my betrayal and considered me not only a heretic but a traitor to the family. And she was right. I lost my religion,

I lost faith. What love I had left I threw in my grandmother's ample lap and we mourned the lost generation in between, and it was always she who pieced together my tatters and sent me off for another fall.

Still they argued, the two of them, still fierce and unrelenting as before but (more ominously) from a distance, each other's bitter obsession. "*She* needs help," my mother would pronounce, "she's losing her mind." "*She's* plotting to put me in an early grave," the other said in her kitchen, "there's the devil in that girl, damned if I know where she gets it, treats me something wicked." "Now Granny," I would say, an uncomfortable co-conspirator, "you know she cares." "It's a wonder I've lasted this long," she would sigh, reaching for the canasta cards.

I felt like a crumb being pecked apart by pigeons. In self defense, I stayed away two years, choosing to do without a telephone and writing crisp adult letters home about how well I was doing in Political Science and how much I missed everyone but neglecting to mention the Iowa co-ed I was living with or any of the details of that jumble of confusion which was my real life. Finally, disgusted with my vacillations and hauntings, the girl took off with another Peace Corps volunteer to save South America instead of me, and I took a bus back to Boston.

Before going home, I went to a bar across from the Park Square Greyhound Station where I sat soaking in the broad *a*'s and the flood of dangling participles that meant Boston and listened to a couple of old men changing their rehearsals of their lives from drink to drink. The old "God-forbids" and "Jesus-help-mes" brought me back, and as I sat there sipping a cheap draft I could only think how much I hated my family and how much I had missed them and how hard it is to be always reasonable.

I found my mother in the kitchen. "You need a haircut," she said tipping up her head to demand a kiss. She looked strange, older of course but sadder somehow. Her eyes had lost their bright madness and gone somewhere. I took my suitcase to my old room, which had been kept intact like a museum, then came back down to my mother. She heated up some fish chowder while filling me in on family things. But when she hadn't even mentioned my grandmother to complain of, I became worried.

"How's Granny?" I asked as casually as I could manage.

"Not well," my mother said, dropping her eyes, "do you want some crackers with the chowder?"

Later that night, after my parents had gone to bed, I cornered Joey. I've always considered Joey the sane one, even if he did once confess to wanting to be president of the United States and even if he did continue to live at home.

"You'll need a drink," Joey said, laughing in that strange high-pitched way of his. "That you'll need." Then he filled me in on how my grandmother had slipped on the ice the previous winter and taken a good crack on the head and the police had taken her to the City Hospital where a young doctor had done the worst thing imaginable and pronounced her fit as a fiddle without even having the good sense to tell her how terrible it really was and giving her a bottle of placebos with a fancy name. So my mother had come to take her back to our house, warning her to stop the moaning or she would have to take care of herself. All of my grandmother's friends, of course, had heard of the accident on their police radios which they monitored in their kitchens to keep up with the latest muggings and heart attacks, and when they called she wanted to be too sick to come to the phone so that her friends would come to see her or at least send flowers or cards; but my mother was perverse enough to assure them that she was perfectly okay and not to worry, all of which only served to make Granny furious, so she had stormed out of the house one night into the snow, limping badly and raining curses on my mother's ungrateful head. "She was wearing her slippers, for chrissake," Joe went on. "So I went after her in the car and finally found her up by Centre Street, slush caked up to her knees. She didn't want to get in. She wanted to die right there in the snow so that the whole world would finally understand what kind of woman Ma is. I had to practically get down on my knees in the snow to get her to come home."

Joey laughed his high-pitched crazy laugh. "I managed to tuck her in and even brought her the evening paper so she could look over the obituaries, but nothing would calm her down. *God has eyes*, she kept screaming, *God has eyes to see.*" Joey shook his head slowly from side to side.

"So of course she got on the phone immediately to weep out her new tale of woe about Ma and the night, and it wasn't a half-hour before two of her buddies were over to see her. Ah, she looked fine then, propped up on pillows, moaning double-time, with the old girls at the bottom of the bed nodding their heads and clucking along with her. That was in January and it's June now, and she hasn't set foot in our place since, and she says if she so much as saw Ma peeking in her window she'd have the police out there so sharp Ma wouldn't have a chance to say a good Act of Contrition." He laughed again.

"And how is she?" I asked. "Joey?"

He shrugged, pouring himself a milk-glass of whiskey and throwing in an ice-cube to make it respectable. "Ah, not so bad, Jimbo. Still gets around, y'know. I'm not on the blacklist yet, so I see her about once a week. Chicken as always. I told her the last time, if I came for breakfast you'd have chicken and eggs. You know what she said? Stay home, there's steak there if you can put up with her."

"I'm sorry, Joey."

"Christ, Jim," he said, looking away. "It's not your fault. Damned if I can figure it out. What can you do?"

I looked hard at him. Joey seemed to have put on a lot of weight around his eyes since the last time I had seen him, and I wondered if he had learned he would never be president.

The following morning I went to see her at her new place. She had been one of the earliest supporters of James Michael Curley, the ex-newsboy who became Mayor of Boston and (what next?) Governor of the Commonwealth. She had wandered up and down the streets of Jamaica Plain calling on Democrats (for she wouldn't be caught dead in a Republican house) and sipping tea and complaining about the hard bed of poverty upon which they all lay. "Jimmie," she said to me when Curley died, "they may say what they will of James Michael but he was always good to the poor, right there with a handout or a job, and that was something they always begrudged, and it matters beans to me if he was behind bars at times, he was always Your Honor to me."

So it was only right that she should have gotten one of the new apartments in one of the yellow-brick buildings that the City of Boston had put up for the aged over by Jamaica Pond just up the street from the old Curley mansion. Some of the pensioners and widows out pruning rose bushes in the sun smiled at me and then followed me carefully to see whose visitor I might be. I could see my grandmother watching at the front window behind her window-box of pansies. She opened the door with a rush and pulled my face down to her. "Oh, Jimmie," she said, "thank the Good Lord."

I rubbed the back of my hand against her bristled chin. "Granny Bluebeard."

"You should talk," she said, slapping at my cheek, "and those the first words out of your mouth." She stood back to look me over, her eyes poring over me as if I were a mass card. "Still skinny as a rail, have you eaten lunch?"

"Twice," I said, pinching her arm, still unable to find the bone. She pushed me away and wiped her hands on her apron. "You always were a smarty-pants, sit and I'll get coffee."

"Don't fuss."

"And what else should I do," she said, already on her way to the kitchen, words trailing after her like the train of a gown, "ah, Blessed Peter, Jimmie, you don't know how cruel she's been to me with you away, one card on Easter and nothing for months, it might have been the moon for all I heard but I suppose you've been too busy like the rest of them, do you like the apartment?"

I looked around at the tiny glass cats and matching dogs, the seashells and saucers from Florida; at the dozens of gilt-framed pictures of the family, at one of myself on the mantle grinning out inanely from under my high school flat-top. On the walls hung brocaded prayers from the Sisters of Mercy and the Oblate Fathers, and a two-foot plaster-of-Paris Blessed Mother with a pink Jesus in her arms stood vigil by the door; beside two faded beige Louis the Something chairs she had dragged around with her for over thirty-five years; and there over in the far corner squatted the gigantic color console she had won at a raffle and never managed to adjust properly so that everything was purple and green. It was her place all right, and it made me smile. "You take cream of course," she said coming back in with the tray.

"Not anymore."

She held the pitcher over my cup. "It's no good to drink it black," she said, "it'll ruin your complexion."

Her hands shook as she poured the sugar. "I've lost my strength," she sighed, "Cancer of the fingers." She pointed to two long ropes that hung from the ceiling behind the couch. "They're for the end when you can't get to the throne. I'm sick and tired of looking at them every day as if I need a reminder, still and all I suppose they're good to have."

"Joey told me about the accident," I said, wanting to change the subject.

Her face lit up, all fire and fury in the old way. "Isn't it awful," she cried, "biting the hand that fed her and she the oldest. I want it carved into my tombstone: *This woman died of a broken heart.* She can think of it then."

She made the sign of the cross over herself. "I didn't want to write you and break your heart like she broke mine, I pray to Saint Anthony every night – she's mad you know, should have been put away years ago but I didn't have the heart – because he's the patron saint of lost souls and she's certainly that, it's my last summer anyway." She pulled her apron to her eye to wipe away a dry tear. "God forbid I should live through another winter like the last, I pray to Him to take me, I've got blood on the bone you know."

"Blood on the bone?"

"Didn't Joey tell you, it's from the fall, listen." She knocked her knuckles together noisily.

I nodded slowly.

She seemed relieved and stopped the knocking. "So everything's ready," she said, backing into a chair and her short legs shooting out straight before settling back. She edged forward, her feet still dangling inches off the floor. "Mother of Mercy, wouldn't you think I've seen enough of the grave already, Helen and the baby, then John." She stopped to sniffle. "And a woman never saw a better man, always home in the house before six and never more than three drinks at a single sitting." She looked about distractedly as if she had forgotten I was there.

I sipped my coffee noisily.

"So, Jimmie, it's all set," she said, looking back at me, "I've talked to Herbie Donahue the undertaker up on Huntington Avenue who's an awful robber by the way but what can you do, it's all paid to the last penny."

I got up and started toward her. "Sit down, Jimmie, you don't know, you can't know, I wouldn't trust it to her, and I only pray it'll be in my sleep, I don't want them carting me away some place where you lie around like a zombie like my friend Celia with nothing to do but take gloop through tubes, poor Celia, lying there dead to the world with bubbles on her mouth, what kind of life is that now? Do you want more coffee?"

I shook my head.

"Well," she said, struggling to her feet, "you ought to have something because you'll never be able to do a good hard day's work unless you get some meat on you, but, stay here, I have something to show you." She moved to the bedroom and returned holding in front of her a sheer pale-pink gown with lace frills at the bottom. "Do you like it?" she asked, cocking her head coyly.

"Yes, it's lovely."

"You don't think it's too much, do you – too much to be laid out in?" she said, coming out from behind the dress. "I mean if you can't be a little extravagant then when can you be, besides pink has always been my favorite color, it matches my coloring, and when they lay you out you look so waxy you need a touch of color, I wouldn't be caught dead in one of them black horrors I've seen on some."

"No." I shouted, standing stiffly and floundering with my hands. "You can't – "

She put the dress on the couch beside her, fluffing up the edges. "Oh, I know what you're thinking," she continued softly, "but when you get to my age, dear, you can't be worried about such things." She faced me, folding her arms over her breasts. "And I suppose I'm supposed to keep it in the closet and not talk about it, keep *me* in the closet she would if she had her way, I wouldn't be surprised if she forgot to bury me, God bless you but you're an innocent, you wouldn't know the Devil if you were sleeping with him."

"Come home with me," I urged her. "Come home – you know she wants to see you."

"Not for all the tea in China," she said, her face quivering with rage, "over my dead body."

Shortly after, I stumbled out of my grandmother's and went home to plead with my mother. "She can do as she likes," my mother said, her mouth twitching. "No one's stopping her, but I'm not getting down on bended knee if that's what you mean."

We all drank too much that summer – my father, Joey, and myself – I guess it was kind of an occupation. But no matter what we said my grandmother was determined to write her own last act with my mother cast as villain. The rest of us were just the audience. When Dad insisted my mother really was sorry, my grandmother just scowled, "What are you – her translator? Let her come herself."

When my grandmother died in her sleep that August, unreconciled, my mother sobbed through the night. "Some bluff," Joey muttered to me. "She sure to Christ lost that deal. Some bluff all right."

"No. I won't allow it," my mother screamed when Dad told her of the pink dress. "I won't be made a laughingstock. Show some respect for the dead. Whoever heard of being buried in a pink dress?"

"She wanted it that way," my father said. "That's what she specified."

"I don't care," she whined, her face streaked with tears, "she's my mother."

"You can't forbid the last wish of the dead."

"Holy Mother," she cried, reaching for her pills, "sustain me in my hour of need."

So my grandmother was laid out in a pink dress and brought into the front room of Herbie Donahue's Funeral Parlor in a mahogany casket with gold trim, her eyes closed down peacefully, her brow smooth and unruffled, her tiny mouth pursed into a Cupid bow. Against the white satin backdrop the pink dress made her look as modest and demure as a young girl on her way to communion, and through her fingers Herbie had strung the fat black beads of a rosary and settled the heavy silver cross on her bosom. I said a prayer. For her sake, I hoped it all was true.

At the wake that night mourners turned out in legion. All those evenings she herself spent shedding a lost tear and patting a disconsolate widower at many a funeral parlor had not been forgotten. Out of their solitary kitchens they filed slowly into the front parlor – old women shuffling along in blunt-heeled shoes and orthopedic hose, old men cradling canes and toothless dignity. Kneeling before the casket, their weak eyes strained to read the names on the cards under the horseshoes of roses and carnations and the lilies-of-the-valley in their delicate vases – then, looking down, they smiled wistfully, perhaps at the pink dress.

An old bachelor in a stiff old-fashioned suit sidled up to me and blinked in my face. "You must be Jimmie," he said, peering at me through thick bifocals. "She was always talking about you. I knew John as well and I'd have married her afterwards if she would have had me, but I drank you see." He blinked, his thin face tightening in remorse. "She made coffee for me and mended the holes in my pants," he sniffed, "and then told me to get lost with my whiskey breath before she gave me a foot in the rear of the premises." He tried to laugh but could only cough. "A grand lady – ah, she was the one all right," he said, tottering off.

And I found myself thinking then of my cousin Jack's wedding a few years back to which my grandmother came, tightly corseted, in a bright red dress with matching pumps and an enormous red hat topped with flowers. At the reception a three-piece band who billed themselves as the Killarney Kapers kept playing all of the old drippy stuff from "Peg O' My Heart" to "Danny Boy." My grandmother was in a fine mood, eyeing my highball. "Just a sip," she whispered, polishing it off in a swallow and flushing as scarlet as her dress. "Let's dance," she said, grabbing my elbow.

"What kind of fool are you," put in my mother, "at your age."

"What's none of your business," my grandmother said, "is none of your business, Little Miss Busybody, so change your face."

"How childish," humphed my mother, unable to change anything, least of all her face.

My grandmother rose. "Come on, Jimmie, I'm not about to live in a closet for her." And so we danced, the relatives gathering about and clapping rhythmically. I remember the song – the words.

> My girl's an Irish girl
> with the blarney in her smile.
> She's the fairest in the isle,
> sure she sets people talkin'
> when she goes out walkin'.

And my grandmother was up on her toes – one-two, one-two-three-four – and gliding, and how light and feathery she seemed in my arms. "Oh, Jimmie," she kept saying. "If it's the death of me, don't stop now."

And when the number finished she walked over to the Killarney Kapers and told them, eyes twinkling, "You're wonderful, boys, I wish I could take all of you home with me." She came back smirking, sixty-seven then, and my mother scandalized.

It rained on her burial day. The funeral home was a swirl of black silk and dying flowers. I went to her before they sealed the coffin. There was a faint odor, something strangely sweet like beeswax. As I kissed her briefly on the lips, I could sense my mother's shudder behind me. "It's all right, Ma," I wanted to say, "I'd do the same for you," but I just took her arm.

Then we were somehow at Saint Jude's, and I remember the Christ with the chipped nose above the altar and the Dies Irae rumbling down over us like heavy stones and the screech of a little girl whose toes caught under the kneeler. When the priest came down from the altar to march around the casket with the incense, my mother swooned. My father and I caught her, and she shuddered to life again as we trailed out together behind my grandmother.

We went to Mount Hope Cemetery where she was to be laid next to my grandfather right under a tall cypress on the side of a high hill, a lovely spot with the lights of Boston visible in the distance. "It looks peaceful, Ma," Joey said, but my mother's hands trembled in mine. We formed a circle around the open grave. A light rain was falling, running off the waxed surface of the casket onto the ground as Father Meagher, the old rector, offered up the final dust to dust. As I looked in the hole, I heard her scolding me after I had beaten her in a game of canasta. "*You* mister, if the good die young, you'll live forever. Dear Lord, forgive his black heart."

As they lowered the coffin, "It's the living who suffer," muttered a tiny lady at my side, Mrs. Callahan who had gone on the last Florida trip. "She's been planning this a long time," Mrs. Callahan smiled, "a long time, poor thing, and now she's to have some peace at last." She leaned up confidentially. "I wonder, Jimmie, if you wouldn't mind taking a couple of chances on an air conditioner for the Jamaica Plains Women's Club. It was something she dearly loved, she won the color set from us, and you never know, you know, they're fifty cents apiece."

I fumbled in my pockets for a dollar to slip her. "Don't tell a soul," she whispered and winked, squeezing my hand, "they might not understand."

"No," I promised, "I won't tell a soul."

I squeezed her hand back and walked away. Behind me, I could hear the clanking of shovels and the clumping of the dirt going in over the coffin and my mother's voice cutting through the rain. "Let me go with her," she was crying, "let me go too."

I kept walking. The rain was letting up, the sky brightening on the horizon, but I was still shivering and thinking only of how I'd be damned if I were ever going to have children myself – and clutching my raffle ticket like a talisman.

The Enemies of Rose

I AM WEARING A CELTIC COSTUME, A WHITE WOOL DRESS EMBROIDERED with Celtic designs, a matching cape and headband. It is March 17th, 1950 – Saint Patrick's Day – and it hasn't yet occurred to me that being the child of immigrant parents makes me a member of a minority. As I see it, practically everyone in New York City is Irish: the policemen, the firemen, the bus drivers, and all the sisters at Holy Name School. There's no school today, of course, because of the parade.

Dad and my brother will march with the Tipperary Men, and my mother with the Ladies Auxiliary of the Hibernians. I get to march *twice*, at the head of two contingents, a starring role I take for granted, veteran that I am, having marched every year as far back in my young life as I can remember. I have my technique down pat. I'll keep my back straight and take long strides, or march in place when the cops stall the line to let pedestrians cross the Avenue. And when I pass the Cardinal standing on the steps of Saint Pat's, I'll turn, smile, and do a little curtsey.

First I'll lead the Hibernian Ladies, but I won't go the whole route with them; before the end I'll fall out and double back to join the Offaly Social and Athletic Club, which doesn't march until later in the parade. Offaly doesn't have a ladies auxiliary, it's just one club, men and women both. My Aunt Rose is vice president and she says ladies auxiliaries are a crock – that's the way she talks – and since nearly every adult of my acquaintance speaks with a brogue, I consider her New York twang somewhat exotic. Every year she brings a thermos bottle to the parade, filled with coffee that's milky and spiked with Irish whiskey. When you're stamping your feet in the cold, waiting for the signal to join the line of march, a hot drink really helps. I know, because when nobody's looking, Aunt Rose gives me a swig.

Rose Lavelle isn't my real aunt, she's my godmother actually. She lives two blocks from us, up by Columbus Avenue, and she lives alone, although I've heard she was married once, but that's a big secret. She was born right here in New York but she says that her father back in Ireland was a hero of the Easter Rebellion. She wouldn't miss the parade for anything. When my father didn't march last year because he had to work, she was furious with him. "Mad enough to spit," she said. Aunt Rose works too, but says that working on Saint Patrick's Day is against her religion. She works in Schrafft's restaurant where she's the hostess and doesn't have to wear a uniform. All the waitresses there are Irish. "Right off the boat," Aunt Rose says. She says Schrafft's has a goon squad that goes down to the pier every time an Irish ship docks and they shanghai all the girls into service at Schrafft's. This makes my mother screw up her face and tell me, "Pay no attention to Rose." Rose calls Schrafft's "the dump" and her customers "the old farts" and says that when I grow up, I'll work there over her dead body. Schrafft's, however, is my idea of heaven: tuna sandwiches on toasted cheese bread and hot butterscotch sundaes served in silver dishes. Secretly I am aspiring to be a hostess there, just like Rose.

So the second time I march this afternoon, I'll be out in front again, with Aunt Rose behind me holding up her end of the ENGLAND GET OUT OF IRELAND banner. And when we pass the cathedral, Cardinal Spellman will think he's losing his marbles when he sees me going by twice.

When the parade is over we'll all meet at home and sit down to a meal of ham and cabbage. It's not my favorite, but my mother claims it's traditional (that means it's my father's favorite). After dinner Aunt Rose will leave to go home and change her clothes, and then there will be a lot of carrying-on about who's going to get into the bathroom first because the rest of us will have to get ready for the dance tonight, too. It won't be just a dance like one at the parish hall, but a real ball at the Essex House, which is a fancy hotel downtown, and everyone goes formal. Aunt Rose will probably wear a strapless. She won't have an escort but that won't matter because she'll dance with every man in the place and some of the women, too. But when the band plays the "Stack O' Barley" she'll dance with me. The "Stack" is *our* dance. It won't matter if she's talking to someone or clear across the ballroom someplace, she'll come looking for me. "Come on, kid," she'll say, "let's show 'em how it's done!"

❦

My mother was a neatness freak, partial to linoleum and formica, and maybe that's why I so fondly recall every detail of Rose Lavelle's apartment. Her living room was carpeted wall to wall, and the sofa strewn with pillows: a satin one, a velvet one, a needlepoint one, a fringed one with a painted palm tree that said "Miami." Bric-a-brac cluttered every surface. China dogs, cats, and flowers. Southern belles of spun glass. A statue of the Infant of Prague cloaked in red velvet with a border of sequins. In the foyer outside her kitchen a massive breakfront housed her good china and such treasures as a crystal dinner bell, a silver tea ball on a chain, and a clam shell from Atlantic City that sprouted a flower when sunk in a glass of water.

Rose was a tall woman with a great halo of stiff blonde hair, and her adornments were proportionately grand. In her bedroom there were jewelry boxes crammed with double- and triple-stranded necklaces with elaborate clasps, heroic brooches, earrings that dangled, and a solid gold bracelet so heavy with charms that I barely could lift my arm when I wore it. Of this stash of playthings, only one item was ever withheld from me – a large, square-cut emerald ring, which was never in a jewelry box but always on Rose's finger. "I never take this off," she said. "But someday this ring will be yours. When I die, I want you to have it. I'm putting that in my will."

I believed the ring had been a gift from a gentleman admirer. I don't know whether Rose told me that, though she probably dropped the hint. I imagined him to be a huge, husky man who laughed a lot and told jokes. He wore a pin-striped suit and a diamond stick pin in his necktie. He was very rich, maybe famous, and married, with about a dozen children. Why else would he not have married Aunt Rose? When I tested this theory on my mother, she said, "Oh, Deirdre, for goodness sake! Pay no attention to Rose." But my mother couldn't deny the emerald was genuine and hardly affordable on a hostess's salary.

"How big is it?" I asked Rose more than once. "Oh, about the size of a hippo's molar," was her usual tease. "Come on," I'd wheedle, "how many carats?" With a silly grin, she'd shrug her shoulders. That was Rose all over: she liked to be mysterious. In the neighborhood her past was the subject of rumor and speculation. I heard that she had had a child of her own – not her husband's – and that she'd given it up for adoption. My mother said that was nonsense. She said Rose once had a miscarriage. The husband had been a violent drinker, he knocked her down when she was pregnant, she lost the child, and after that he ran off and left her. It was anyone's guess which story might have been true. Perhaps neither, because Rose was capable of fabricating and launching such rumors herself. In this respect she was a bit peculiar, and inventing stories about herself wasn't the worst of it. She also invented stories about other people, a proclivity that earned her a legion of "very bad friends," as my mother put it, all former friends of long standing who had, according to Rose, "showed their true colors."

Now, if you were unlucky enough to find yourself on the wrong side of Rose, you were in for trouble. She would spread the word of your disloyalty far and wide. If you were popular, she would inform your best friends of disparaging remarks you had made against them. If you handled money for a club or charity, she would warn your colleagues to watch you weren't dipping into the till. If you were attractive, she would plant the general suspicion that you were vamping someone else's mate.

But Rose was no ordinary gossip. A choreographer of chaos and intrigue, her talent lay in her ability to convince Enemy A that the originator of the slander had been Enemy B, and vice versa. Then she'd sit back and watch the fur fly. Laughing. She had a lisp and laughed with her tongue stuck between her teeth. She snorted, too. It was wonderful.

"Poor Rose gets a bit peculiar now and again. Pay no attention to her." This was my mother's standard advice to the victims of Rose's machinations. "Rose just likes to stir things up," she'd say. When Rose would drop by for a cup of tea or a highball at our kitchen table, she stirred my mother from the tedium of her decorous existence. "A breath of fresh air," my mother said, although Rose was more like a gale blowing in to spice our afternoon with her boasting and prevarications. She made my mother chuckle, click her tongue, draw in her breath, whoop with laughter. I enjoyed my lively mother when Rose was around. I liked the way she excused Rose's often indefensible behavior. When occasionally she found herself on Rose's enemies list, she practiced what she preached, ignored her, waited for the tide to turn. In part, my mother's unflagging patience had to do with Rose's devotion to me: in the godmother sweepstakes, I had drawn the winning ticket.

From the moment she had held my bawling ten pounds over the baptismal font, Rose Lavelle decided nothing was too good for me. She took me to the circus at the old Madison Square Garden, to the rodeo, to the Christmas show at Radio City. Each spring she contributed some spectacular accessory to my Easter finery—most memorable, at age twelve, my first pair of two-inch heels—and in June, at the end of the school year, she whisked me down to Macy's to select the latest fad in bathing suits.

My family summered at Rockaway Beach (the "Irish Riviera" in those days) in a rooming house on Beach 97th Street, a block south of Playland Amusement Park. Larkin's Ocean View the place was whimsically named, a view visible only from its tiny single-rooms on the top floor, one of which Rose annually reserved for her two-week vacation from Schrafft's. For those two weeks, Rose and I would loll away our days on the beach—she slathered with Noxema, under the double protection of a wide-brimmed hat and a beach umbrella, regaling me with passionate and hilarious updates on the dastardly doings of her current foes. At night she'd go off to do the rounds of the Irish dance halls that lined both sides of Beach 103rd Street from the ocean to the bay. And the summer I was fifteen, she managed to bamboozle my parents into letting her take me along. The Dublin House, the Leitrim House, O'Gara's, and Gildea's: we did them all. Sipping seven-and-sevens (my mother would have had a conniption had she known) we were grandly entertained by the likes of Pete McNulty and by the Queen of Rockaway herself, Ruthie Morrissey, whose quintessential rendition of "Ireland's Thirty-two" never failed to bring down the house, the naming of each county setting off a pandemonium of cheers and whistles. Bouncers stationed at the doors to check IDs merely smiled and nodded as I sauntered in with Rose. With the younger stags who passed the muster of my rather lax chaperone, I danced my feet sore to the music of Timmy Cronin's band and Mickey Carton's. But when they played the Stack, I danced with Rose. We got up and "showed 'em how."

I don't remember if Rose and I danced one last Stack at my wedding, although I do recall attempting to teach the steps to my thoroughly American husband, while his thoroughly American relatives zanily bounded across the floor mimicking our example. Rose was resplendent in cascades of shocking-pink chiffon. She drank too much, which resulted in a crying jag. She cornered the groom several times to threaten he'd have to answer to her if he didn't take good care of me. A few of his guests mistook her for my mother. Perhaps she knew that the comforting old law about "not losing a daughter but gaining a son" might not apply in the case of a goddaughter about to be whisked away to Pennsylvania.

Bill Kirkland, the young man I married, had a passion for cars and a cousin with Volkswagon, Inc., in Philadelphia, who had maneuvered a job for Bill in their parts department. We bought a little house in nearby Norristown, Bill rapidly rose to manager of his department, our first son Christopher was born. Then the company insisted on transferring Bill to a branch in Jacksonville, Florida. I was pregnant again when we moved south, to a spanking new development of large homes, ours a stuccoed facsimile of a Spanish mission, fronting a man-made lake.

Bill was not welcomed with open arms by his southern colleagues. In a year, he scuttled the pressures of corporate politics and bought a dealership. He loved Florida. He thought the new Rabbits would sell like hotcakes. They didn't. To keep the business afloat, we got rid of the house on the lake and moved into an apartment complex, built around a pool.

I remember all this — the Florida phase — as a blur of palm trees and palmetto bugs. A blur because there were often tears in my eyes when I chauffeured our eldest to nursery school, or sat slumped in a lawn chair watching that our toddler didn't tumble into the pool, while in the meantime my husband was working up the nerve to leave me for another woman — the bookkeeper at his dealership.

I ended up leaving him. My priorities fell into place with a thud when my mother had a stroke. My father had died some years before, shortly after he and Mom had moved from Manhattan to Queens, forced out of the old neighborhood by an orgy of so-called urban renewal: the street on the Upper West Side of Manhattan, where I was raised, literally vanished, its brownstones and tenements replaced by high-rises. Now my widowed mother was in the hospital and needed someone to care for her when she got home. Bill and I never spoke the words "trial separation." He sheepishly kept his distance as I (by now expert mover) furiously packed the kids and our essentials into our shiny red Rabbit hatchback.

My mother rallied, quickly recovering her speech, and by degrees her mobility, progressing from a walker to a cane. She was so grateful to have us, she suppressed any inkling that all was not well with my marriage. My lies about late night collect calls to Florida were validated by the conscience money Bill sent each month.

"Whatever happened to Rose?" I asked her on one of those after-noons we sat together reviewing our lives over a pot of decaffeinated tea. I knew that Rose had stood her ground on Columbus Avenue until she saw the whites of the eyes of the demolition crews. Last I'd heard, she had moved farther uptown, to Washington Heights.

"We used to write," my mother answered. "Of course, Rose wasn't much of a hand at writing. But she'd call me off and on. And then . . . it was the strangest thing . . . one of my letters came back from the post office, stamped 'Addressee Unknown.' I rang her up but her phone had been disconnected. She must have moved again, but I never did find out where." My mother looked down at the pale brew in her cup. I remembered how she used to read my fortune for me when I was little and she steeped her tea dark and strong — Irish tea, from loose leaves. "Ah well," she sighed. "You know how it is . . . you lose touch."

Mom died at home in her own bed, when a second stroke took her in her sleep. A few of the old crowd showed up at her funeral, but Rose was not among them. Details of her whereabouts were sketchy and conflicting. Someone said she had quit Schrafft's. Someone else said Schrafft's was phasing out its restaurant operations and Rose had been terminated. She had gotten an apartment in the Bronx. No, she was living in Manhattan still. Considering her penchant for sub-terfuge, and the body count of enemies, it was no wonder that her cronies showed little interest.

Bill was there, looking tanned and prosperous. Also contrite. The dealership was finally paying off; the affair with the bookkeeper wasn't. He spent a week with me and the kids, begged me to come home. I said I *was* home: back in New York where I intended to stay. He said he loved us, couldn't live without us, all of that. I said prove it. It took another year, but he finally did. We opened a dealership in Queens, on Northern Boulevard. I do the bookkeeping. We bought a house in Bayside.

Saint Patrick's Day, 1978. It was the kind of morning that couldn't make up its mind, cloudy one minute, sunny the next, and I had a case of the blues. I was missing my mother, and had in my possession three tickets to the parade — V.I.P. seats on the reviewing stand — that Bill had gotten from one of our customers. I figured a dose of banners and bagpipes might be a good tonic for me, that a dose of their mother's heritage wouldn't do my kids any harm either. So I herded the boys onto the Long Island Railroad and headed for Fifth Avenue.

When the Army's 69th Regiment stepped off with their wolf-hound mascots, I cheered right along with the kids. We had third-row seats, directly behind the Grand Marshal, the Mayor, and various other notables. I recognized some other faces above us in the stand: a couple from the old neighborhood, another from the bygone balls at the Essex House. And when I spotted Rose making her way toward us, it did not astonish me at all. I was a backsliding time-traveler and Rose was right where she was supposed to be. Our reunion, though animated and affectionate, was no more extraordinary than if we hadn't met in months, rather than years.

"Aren't you marching today?" I asked.

"Nah. The old legs aren't what they used to be," she said.

"Do you mean to tell me that County Offaly can manage to find their way up the Avenue without Rose Lavelle?"

"That bunch of jerks," she said. "I wouldn't give them the time of day."

She was toting a huge shopping bag crammed with clothes. I could see a couple of sweaters and a knitted hat – and things wrapped in tin-foil. I didn't like the seediness of her appearance, but she had a pass for the reviewing stand where seating was by invitation only, so I presumed her Irish connections in New York were well intact.

I asked her where she'd been hiding herself all these years. She told me she had a job as live-in companion to a wealthy woman on the East Side. "Living the life of Riley," she said. She also described herself as "happy as Larry," an expression which delighted Michael, my youngest, and which he parroted, ad nauseam, the rest of the day.

Along about mid-afternoon, when the sky darkened and a chilly drizzle began to dampen the proceedings, Rose ransacked her shopping bag and came up with a thermos. "Here kids," she said, giving it a shake, "this'll warm you up." I made a grab for it. It wasn't that I was afraid to have my kids introduced to the taste of Irish whiskey. I just didn't want to chance their throwing up on the homeward-bound LIRR. "Don't waste it on them – we need it more than they do," I joked. Much to my disappointment it tasted horribly sweet. That was when Michael ceased being "happy as Larry," and announced he had to go to the bathroom, which seemed the perfect moment to call it a day.

"If we stay too late the trains will be jammed," I explained to Rose. Making her promise to keep in touch, I gave her my phone number. Wrote it out for her on the back of an envelope. I failed to get hers, though. I think she said something about not having her own private line where she lived.

Okay. Maybe I didn't press her for it. The truth is, not all of my emotional pistons were functioning. Several had become encrusted with the plague of upward mobility, that gummy, corrosive stuff that can clog the soul and cause it to misfire. I admit, too, that I noticed the patina on Rose's shopping bag was worn dull, and cracked, like old paint. Its corners were frayed. It had four handles instead of two, so there was a liner inside. The cache she was hauling in it was more than she'd need to get her through Saint Patrick's Day from dawn to midnight.

But let's not be maudlin. I didn't seriously fancy Rose had taken to the streets. Because when she had handed me that thermos of Irish coffee, one of the fingers wrapped around it was adorned by a square-cut emerald the size of a hippo's molar.

Several years later, on a quiet night in early December, I got a phone call. Bill already had gone to bed and I was lingering in the den, writing Christmas cards. It must have been well past eleven, so when the phone blared, I snatched it up on the first ring.

"Hello?"

"Is this Mrs. William Kirkland?" an unfamiliar female voice inquired. "Mrs. Deirdre Kirkland?"

"Yes?"

"My name is Agnes Mulvaney. I was a friend of Rose Lavelle's, and I thought you might want to know that she passed away."

I stared at the holiday clutter on my desk, trying to get my bearings. Not that Rose's death was such a shock—she'd have been well over seventy—but hearing the news from a stranger was disconcerting.

"Who is this?" I said.

"Agnes Mulvaney," she repeated. "Rose used to work for us—for Mr. Mulvaney and me. We have a little restaurant in Rockaway Beach and Rose was our cashier for a while. She died in her sleep. Very peaceful. We found her in bed, in her apartment."

"In Rockaway?" The last place I'd have thought that Rose would have been holed up. I'd once taken the kids there on an outing, and what I'd found was depressing. Its colorful hurly burly had been silenced. Its famous street of dance halls had been obliterated by a municipal parking lot. Playland was gone.

She went on to tell me that it had been some time since Rose had worked for her and her husband; that after she quit them, she worked only sporadically. "Rose was . . . *odd*, you know," said Mrs. Mulvaney. "She often had trouble holding down a job, or even keeping an apartment –"

"But you said she died in her apartment."

"Oh, yes, she was doing fine lately. She'd had her ups and downs, but she was living in this place over a year. I helped her find it – just a studio apartment, one room, but comfortable, you know? I was a very good friend to Rose. By the way, you're not related to her, are you?"

"No. She was my godmother."

"Oh. Well, that explains it then. Because we found a bank account in your name. That's why I'm calling you."

"In *my* name?" I was stunned.

"She had an account with me, too," said Mrs. Mulvaney, "but she never mentioned this other one. I mean, the only reason I had an account with her was to help her do her banking. She had arthritis in her knee, you know, and wasn't able to get around much in the end. So we had this joint account and I did her banking – as a favor – but there was hardly anything in it, just a couple hundred dollars. There's more than that in yours, though, and we thought she should have a nice funeral, you know?"

"Yes, of course," I agreed.

"She had a cemetery plot, in Saint John's on Woodhaven Boulevard. But there wasn't any insurance, which kind of surprised me. I mean, a woman like that – a retired school teacher and all – you'd think she'd have had enough to bury her."

"A what?" I piped. "Rose wasn't a schoolteacher, Mrs. Mulvaney. She worked for the Schrafft's restaurant chain most of her life."

"Oh, no . . . you must be mistaken," Mrs. Mulvaney presumed.

"No. Rose was like an aunt to me when I was growing up, practically one of the family," I let her know. "As you said yourself, she was rather odd. Perhaps odder than you realize. She had a tendency to make up stories about herself." It was Mulvaney's turn to be stunned. I took advantage of her silence to move on to the real business at hand.

"As far as her burial is concerned," I said, "I assure you I'll be happy to take care of everything. And since you and Rose were such good friends, I will of course appreciate your help with the arrangements."

"I already made all the arrangements," she informed me, rather curtly.

"I see. Will there be a wake, then?"

"She was waked tonight. She's being buried in the morning."

The woman was beginning to annoy me. "You might have called me sooner."

"Well, she'd been dead for two days when we found her. I'd been calling her on the phone and when I got no answer, I went over there. The landlady didn't have a key, so we got the police. I told them I was Rose's cousin — you know, just so they wouldn't hold the body in the morgue while they tried to find relatives. I mean, I knew she didn't have any relatives."

"No, she didn't."

"Well, I was pretty sure of that, like I said. I knew the husband was dead and the son, too."

"Rose had no son, Mrs. Mulvaney."

"Oh, yes she did. He was killed in Vietnam —"

I couldn't help it. I had to laugh.

Mrs. Mulvaney said, "I don't see anything funny about it."

"Please excuse me, of course it isn't funny . . . but the fact is Rose had no son. No husband, either. Although now that I think of it, she *was* married — briefly, in her youth — and since she was Catholic, I don't suppose there was ever a divorce. For all I know, he may still be alive."

"Alive? Oh, no, no . . . I'm sure you're wrong."

"Well, it's not important, really. The man disappeared over thirty, maybe forty years ago." I had detected a hint of alarm in her voice, which made me uneasy and just a mite suspicious, now. "We can talk about all this tomorrow at the funeral," I said. "Would you tell me what arrangements you've made?"

The drive from Bayside to Rockaway took about an hour, and when I pulled into the parking lot of the funeral home, a light snow was swirling on the wind. The final viewing of Rose's simple coffin was underway in the mortician's smallest parlor, where I found Agnes Mulvaney attended by two elderly ladies, tenants in the building where Rose had lived, and by Mr. Mulvaney, who stood by the closed casket, rocking on his heels like a wobbly footman. Lest there be confusion as to who was Chief Mourner, his wife was all in black: a black velvet pants suit and a matching hairdo that might have been stolen from Ann Miller's wig chest.

"Thank you for coming," she greeted me, batting her eyelids in a pained way. As if bravely bearing up.

"Traffic wasn't too bad," I casually replied. She took my hand in both of hers and I felt Rose's bank book sandwiched between our palms. The funeral director appeared; he cued us it was time to leave for the church. As I slipped the bank book into my purse, Mrs. Mulvaney squeezed my wrist. "We'll talk later," she whispered.

There was no limousine to follow the hearse, just my car, and the Mulvaney's. They took Rose's elderly neighbors in the back seat of theirs and I followed them in mine to Saint Camillus Church, where I had worshiped on countless summer Sundays, long ago. Sometimes with Rose.

Her requiem service was tedious. A very young priest officiated. His sermon had something to do with "the cosmic Christ," and nothing at all to do with Rose Lavelle. He seemed to be polishing a theme for delivery at some future date to a capacity crowd. We, the rehearsal audience, numbered eight in all, including the three pious souls upon whose private worship our cortege had intruded.

When at last we were liberated, we came out of the church to discover the world had turned starkly white. A couple of inches of snow had settled on Rockaway Boulevard and more was falling heavily. I turned to Agnes Mulvaney. "May I speak to you for a moment, please?" We stepped back into the shelter of the vestibule. "I won't be going to the cemetery," I told her. "I think I'd be wise to start home before the roads become hazardous."

"Oh?" she said. "Well in that case, we can go to the bank right now—I'll just tell the undertaker to wait. I have the death certificate with me and the bank is just up the boulevard a few blocks."

Go to the bank? What was she talking about? "That won't be necessary," I balked.

"Well, I assumed you'd want to close out the account . . . today . . . save yourself another trip, you know?"

Now I felt I was being pressured. Didn't like it one bit. "I really don't think you should concern yourself with that," I told her. "Just mail me the funeral bill. Or better yet, I'll tell the undertaker to send it to me directly."

"I already paid it," she snapped.

"I see. And what did it come to?"

"Twenty-three hundred dollars."

A preposterous figure, I thought. I removed Rose's passbook from my purse and took a look at the balance. Of course it approximated Mrs. Mulvaney's averred outlay. "I find that figure questionable," I said. "Do you have the receipted bill? I'd really like to get an itemization."

"Questionable?" she squawked. "What's that supposed to mean?"

"It seems too high . . . for the meager services rendered."

Her bosom rose and her chin retracted. With her jet black hair and eye makeup, she looked like an outraged vampire hen. "Where do you get off saying that?" she challenged. "It was a very nice funeral. It was a very expensive casket."

"Please. It's a very ordinary casket. The room she was waked in wasn't much bigger than a closet. It was a closed-coffin wake, so there was no cosmetic work done, no clothing provided. There are no limousines, no flowers —" I braced myself when I saw the way her eyes narrowed.

She took a step backward and sneered at me. "What gives *you* the right to criticize everything?" she said. "And just where the hell were you when Rose was alive? You should be ashamed to take her money!"

"Just a minute!" said I. "I'm simply trying to verify what it is, exactly, that I'm volunteering to pay for. And since we're being frank, I'd like to ask you what became of Rose's effects."

"Effects? What effects?"

"The contents of her apartment."

"She had no *effects*," Mulvaney scoffed. "Just a lot of junk."

"Oh?" I gave her a cold, knowing smile. "I wouldn't call an emerald ring junk."

Bingo! Her face reddened and her eyes were guilty as hell. "I don't have to stand here and take this from you!" she fairly shrieked. "You . . . you . . . bitch!"

With that, Mr. Mulvaney came bounding up the church steps. "Hey, hey," he said, putting himself between his wife and me. She tried to push him aside, telling him, "Stay out of this!" He gripped her shoulders and backed her up against a pamphlet rack. "Look Agnes," he pleaded, "I'd like to get this show on the road. It's snowing, for crissake." Over his shoulder, she glared at me. "I wouldn't take a penny from you," she snarled. "Not one penny! Go back where you belong, why don't you! You wouldn't even be here today, if I hadn't called you!"

She was correct on that score. "What *am* I doing here?" I asked myself out loud.

I was halfway home before I noticed the speedometer wavering a point or two over sixty-five — I was that distracted and upset. Seeing a blinking tail light ahead, I braked as gently as I could, afraid of skidding. The other car turned off at an intersection, leaving me with the road to myself. I felt abandoned.

I told myself I had bested Mulvaney. Had she not been underhanded, I would have covered all expenses gladly and made her a generous offer for the emerald, as well. I could almost hear Rose's voice: "When I die, I want you to have this ring." How many times had she said that?

And suddenly I understood why Rose had opted to leave me the money instead. Call it a crazy notion, but I will always believe that while Mulvaney and I went at each other in the church vestibule, Rose had been peering down from some celestial observation deck, laughing and snorting, with her tongue stuck between her teeth. Happy as Larry.

The Palace

AFTER THE WEDDING, I RODE TO THE RECEPTION IN A SHINY BLACK CAR. I sat in the back seat between two other bridesmaids. I was sixteen and light-headed with excitement. I had come up to Chicago on the train to be in my aunt's wedding. I wore a long satin dress, with an overskirt of yellow chiffon. The bodice was pinned in the back to make it fit in the bust. My high heels were of clear vinyl, through which I could see my toes, and I wore puckered nylon gloves that ran all the way to my elbows.

"What a beautiful ceremony," said the short bridesmaid on my left, whose name was Karen.

"Everything was so lovely," said the tall bridesmaid on my right, whose name I never quite caught.

"That's the kind of wedding we all want," Karen sighed. She glanced at me. "Your orchid is crooked, sweetheart."

I adjusted the smooth petals on my shoulder. I had never seen an orchid before this afternoon, and I was surprised that it had no smell.

"Where did you say you were from?" the tall bridesmaid asked me in a voice that was sweeter and higher than normal. Because I was younger, and a stranger, the bridesmaids all talked to me differently than they talked to each other.

"Peoria," I said. "But we're moving to Minnesota this summer."

"Oh, how nice," said the tall bridesmaid.

"Isn't that the land of ten thousand lakes?" Karen laughed. "You know, I've never been north of Milwaukee."

"Did someone say Milwaukee?" The groomsman in a black tuxedo, who was driving, glanced back at us. "Best city in the country. That's where I'm from."

The two bridesmaids laughed, as if they thought he had told a joke. I leaned forward. It was a sunny March day. I could see the gray turrets of the Lakeshore Palace Hotel in the distance and high against the sky the red roofed cupola where I had always wanted to climb. I had been taken inside the hotel once by my grandparents when I was eight or nine, but all I could remember was drinking a limeade at the marble counter in the hotel's drug store.

"I'll park in the garage," the groomsman said. "I'll let you girls off at the front entrance."

"It's quicker to go in the back," said Karen.

"Oh, let's go in the front," said the tall bridesmaid. "I love walking through the lobby."

We drove under the green-striped canopy, and stopped at the bottom of a monumental staircase. Bellboys in red uniforms were running up and down the stairs. Our door was opened for us, and we stumbled out. The marble steps were slick under my high heels, and I held onto the brass railing. There were three sets of revolving doors at the top of the staircase, and I twirled through the one in the middle. I paused on the other side. I tilted my head back, looking up at the three tiers of balconies. The lobby was dim and bright at the same time. There were slender columns of rose-colored marble, oriental carpets, leather chairs arranged in intimate groupings, and crystal chandeliers. I had never seen anything so beautiful. I wanted to walk slowly around, touching the little cherry tables and the lion's head finials on the backs of antique chairs, but the other bridesmaids were moving swiftly toward the row of elevators. They entered one going down, and I almost lost my shoes as I hurried after them. The blond elevator boy closed the doors with a flourish. He pushed his buttons, then stood staring at the floor, whistling softly, never once looking at any of us.

The elevator door opened onto a long, brightly lit corridor. I was a little disappointed. The floor was only speckled gold tile and the ceiling low. We went into a large, windowless room where rows of tables with folding chairs had been set up for the wedding reception. My aunt and her new husband had already arrived and were posing for the photographer in front of an enormous cake covered with silver roses. My aunt's lace veil had been thrown back from her face, and her cheeks were pink. Her dress was covered with little seed pearls that glittered under the bright lights.

"Oh, don't you look beautiful," my grandfather said when he caught sight of me. He put his arm around me. "Come take our picture," he called to one of my uncles, who had a camera around his neck. I smiled and blinked into the flash. My grandfather looked exceptionally handsome in his tuxedo; his pale gray hair was still thick and wavy. He had his picture taken with three of the other brides-maids, and then with my grandmother, whose new pink suit could not hide her painfully hunched shoulders.

I stood at the very end of the reception line while the guests arrived. The room filled quickly. I met cousins I never knew I had, from Gary, Indiana, or visiting from Ireland. Sometimes they asked about my father or told me how pretty I looked in my bridesmaid dress. Two nuns in huge headdresses admired my little hat of yellow organdy petals. I nodded and smiled at everyone. Finally I shook hands with an old priest, who suddenly leaned forward and hugged me.

"I bet you don't remember me," he said jovially. "I'm your great uncle Pat."

"Oh, Father Pat," I said.

"I haven't seen you since you were twelve," he said, stepping back to look at me with sharp blue eyes. He resembled my grandfather ex-cept that his skin was smooth and unwrinkled, and his voice had a more pronounced lilt to it.

"How are you?" I asked nervously.

"Fine, fine. And how's your pretty mother? I hear she's pregnant again."

"Yes," I said. "The baby's due any day now."

"And how many will that make?"

"Nine," I said.

"And isn't your father here? Did he drive you up?"

I shook my head. "He had to work. I came up on the train by myself."

"Well, well," he said, moving away. "It won't be long before you'll be a bride yourself, will it?"

Finally the bridal party was able to sit down. Waiters in white jackets began pouring the champagne. I held my breath until they had filled my glass to the brim like everyone else's. I lifted it to my lips for the first toast, and it was as wonderful as I had expected. I drank the whole glass.

"Well, you're Irish all right," said Karen, who was sitting behind me at the end of the bridal party table.

"What do you mean?" I asked.

She pointed at my empty glass. Her own was still almost full. "I bet you're not even dizzy, are you?"

"No, " I said. "I'd like some more."

She laughed. "So would the groom, but they're only letting him have one glass for the toast."

"Why only one?"

"Never mind," she said, putting a piece of wedding cake in her mouth.

I ate my chicken salad and had another glass of champagne. The musicians arrived, with their accordions, fiddles, and flutes, and began to play something that sounded vaguely like the "Blue Danube Waltz." The bride and groom danced cheek to cheek while everyone applauded. Then they sat down and the Irish music began. Some of the guests clapped and others began singing "Who threw the overalls in Mrs. Murphy's chowder?" in gay voices. The waiters were still bringing champagne, but there were bottles of whiskey on some of the tables now, too. I saw Father Pat pour himself a shot.

"Do you think I could go walk around the hotel?" I asked Karen.

"Sure," she said. "They're going to push the tables back for dancing. We'll be here for hours."

I took the elevator back up to the lobby. Now I had time to notice the little shaded red lamps on the tables and the distinguished men in suits sitting here and there, reading newspapers. The front desk was a long, mahogany counter, with heavy, carved pillars, and I told myself that someday, when I grew up, I would check in here as a guest. I walked down a wide corridor, where gold lamps hung on the paneled walls, to the restaurant. I stood outside the French doors, half-hidden by potted palms, looking in at the glittering tables where I would sit some evening in the future. There were silver ice buckets or small silver coffee pots on all the tables, and the diners — there were not very many at this hour — brought their forks or wine glasses slowly to their mouths, as if they were doing so underwater. The women had bare arms like swimmers, and their hands moved in undulating gestures when they talked.

I went up a wide, thickly carpeted staircase to the first balcony. I heard exquisite music, and walked toward it. I came to some felt-covered doors, one of which was propped open with a chair. A tall, gangly bellboy stood just outside, his face strained with attention. He seemed to be leaning in toward the music. I looked past him into the room. A string quartet was performing on a low platform in front of a small audience of men in tuxedos and women in evening gowns. I held my breath and listened. I had never heard music like this before. It was clear and exhilarating.

"What is it?" I whispered to the bellboy, who did not seem to hear me at first.

"Beethoven," he answered in a moment, speaking from the corner of his mouth. "It's the 'Grosse Fugue.'"

Just then a bald man in a white jacket got up from his chair and darted to the door. The bellboy backed away, coughing.

"Do you have a ticket, Miss?" the man asked me in a sharp voice.

"No," I said, stepping back with the bellboy. My face burned with embarrassment.

With one swift movement, the bald man removed the chair from the door and pulled it shut behind him. I could no longer hear the music.

"Dirty bastard!" The bellboy kicked the carpet as he walked away. His voice was choked.

I took a deep breath, then went up to the second balcony. I stopped to look at some large, dark paintings in heavy gilt frames. Some were portraits of dour-looking men, but others were huge historical canvases. It was hard to make them out in the dim light. I was left with an impression of twisted male torsos and chariot wheels. I had just paused to study the marble statue of a woman in a toga when I felt someone behind me.

I turned my head and caught a glimpse of a thin, jet-haired man in a rumpled sport shirt. His closeness made me uncomfortable, and I moved rapidly away. I went back down the two flights of stairs to the lobby, and decided to see if I could find my way up to the cupola.

I waited for an elevator, watching the numbers above the doors light up as the cars passed from floor to floor. When the first elevator going up arrived, I told the elevator boy the number of the top floor.

"I suppose you're going to a party in one of the penthouses," he said as he pulled the inner gate shut. "That's a real pretty dress." He smiled at me cheerfully. He had a bad complexion and a crew cut. His scalp showed in white patches above his ears.

"No," I said. "I'm at a wedding reception downstairs. But I want to go up that cupola. Do you know how to get there?"

"Sure. You're going to the right floor. There's a fire door in the middle of the hall. Just take the stairs. But watch out for the wind. Boy, is it windy up there!"

"Do you like working here?" I asked as the elevator jolted and rose. I pressed my hand against my stomach.

"It's great," the boy said. "You meet all kinds of people at the

Palace. Celebrities, too. I rode with Cary Grant once. It's too bad they're tearing the place down."

"Tearing it down?"

"The land must be worth a million a square inch. They're going to put up apartments." The elevator stopped and he opened the door. "There you are. Maybe I'll catch you on the way down."

"Thanks," I said.

The fire door was right where he said it was. I could feel the wind in the stairwell, and as I climbed up the spiral stairs to the level of the open windows in the cupola, it made a whistling noise. At first, I could hardly open my eyes in the face of it. My hair was whipped back from my forehead. But then I grew used to its steady push against my body.

The lake was dazzling. No real sea could have pleased me better just then. The plane of the water seemed to tilt upward toward a vaporous blue horizon, and across it ran foaming waves that broke on the rocks below me with stolid turbulence.

Then my eye caught the glint of the setting sun on the glass fronts of the apartment buildings along Lake Shore Drive. I felt a pang. I would never see this view when I grew up – when the future came, this hotel would not exist. I ran my palm along the rough stone window ledge. It occurred to me for the first time that the other solid objects with which I had furnished my future would soon not exist – my home, my high school, and even my friends would all evaporate this summer when my family moved, and I could not begin to imagine what might replace them.

After a few minutes, I think I began to be self-conscious about my sadness. I told myself that I was grown up, that this was the way you felt as an adult. I threw my head back, and looked up at some soft hazy clouds that were gathering as the sun dropped. I tried to hum the scrap of Beethoven I had heard downstairs, but the melody eluded me. I could only faintly recall its effect on me.

I went slowly back down the spiral stairs, trying not to stumble in my wobbly heels. As I reached the fire door, I heard a grunt. In the corner of the stairwell stood the jet-haired man I had seen up on the second balcony. As I stared at him, startled and immediately uneasy, he fumbled with his pants and opened his fly.

"Here, Miss," he said softly, grinning at me.

I gasped, and ran past him. It took me a few moments to get the fire door open, for in my panic I kept pushing against it instead of pulling it open.

"You want it, don't you, Miss?" the man said, coming closer to me. "You'd like to put it in your mouth, wouldn't you, Miss?"

I pulled the door open at last. I ran down the hall toward the elevator. I saw one open and waiting and I knew I had to reach it before the doors closed, or I would be trapped. My right shoe came off, but just at that moment the elevator boy, who was not the same one who had brought me up, reached out to close the door.

"Wait!" I called, abandoning my shoe.

He held the door open for me. I hopped awkwardly into the elevator with one stockinged foot. Before I had time to catch my breath and ask him to wait until I got my shoe, he had put his elevator in motion. He had a sullen face and bitter, twisted lips, so I did not speak to him. I leaned back against the back wall, fighting tears and hysteria. "Be calm, be calm," I told myself over and over like a litany.

"Where to?" the elevator boy asked in a harsh voice.

"The basement," I said.

He shrugged and pushed a button.

We shot down so quickly that I felt sick to my stomach. When the door opened, I stepped out immediately. I found myself in a gloomy area with rough stone walls, and I realized that I was in a real basement that must be below the level of the reception room. I heard the elevator door shut behind me, and I knew at once that the elevator boy had been maliciously literal when he let me off down here. I decided to find a stairway up, rather than call him back.

I took off my other shoe. I walked between bins that were piled almost ceiling high with coal, and came to a huge furnace. The door of the furnace was open, and the flames shot up wildly. A man in overalls, covered with coal dust, was heaving coal inside with an iron shovel.

I was afraid to let him see me and hurried past him. I went up three wide steps into another part of the basement, which was noisy with the roar of washing machines. The floor was wet and soapy, for some of the machines were overflowing. Three black women in white cotton smocks were pulling sheets out of the large commercial dryers that lined one wall. The next room was loud with the clank of ironing machines. Here there were about a dozen exhausted-looking women, some black and some white, feeding sheets through the big rollers. The women were plastered with sweat, and their shoulders seemed permanently hunched. A few of them glanced up at me when I passed, but their faces remained blank and expressionless.

I found a stairway up at last. I had to stop in a rest room to take off my stockings and wash my feet, which were covered with soap and coal dust. I flinched when I looked at myself in the mirror. My eyes, staring back at me, seemed furtive, and there was an unpleasant thinness about my lips. I tried not to think about the jet-haired man, but his ugly image was imprinted on my brain as if I had deliberately taken a photograph.

I could hear the Irish music coming down the hall. It struck me as tinny and garish. The reception room was so hazy with cigarette smoke when I entered that I coughed and gasped. Everything in the room was blurry, and the smoke drifted in waves. My aunt was smoking in her satin gown, and her face looked gray and drawn. Her new husband was scratching himself under his collar. My uncle had drunk too much, and his embarrassing laugh rang through the room. I sat down beside Karen and slipped my single shoe under the table. I noticed the sharp, envious expression on her face as she talked to my aunt. Across the room, the groom's sisters were whispering together in the corner, and I knew by the shape of their mouths that they were saying nasty things.

I looked around me in surprise. I seemed to have x-ray vision. The martyred expression on my grandmother's face was carefully studied. My grandfather, as he hopped about in his tuxedo, doing some kind of jig with a cousin from Ireland, was vain and self-centered. Everyone I looked at was pinched or mean or stunted in some way, and I knew I was no exception. I heard unkindness and jealousy in all the voices that rose around me in supposed merriment.

My aunt moved away. The back of her wedding gown, where she had been sitting, was all wrinkled. The tall bridesmaid came and sat down on the other side of Karen.

"I'm glad I'm not marrying into that family," she said in a low voice. "What a bitch his sister is."

"You'd think it was her wedding," Karen whispered back. "You know, she told me I ought to have gone on a diet. She said my dress was too tight."

"What a nerve!"

"Bitch."

I got up and went to sit beside Father Pat, who was staring at the empty shot glass in front of him.

"What happened to your shoes?" he asked. He spoke slowly, his words faintly slurred.

"My feet hurt," I said, flushing and looking away from him. I knew I would never tell anyone what had happened as long as I lived, but I would never be able to forget it.

"Somebody said you were upstairs."

"I was looking around the hotel."

"It's a grand place." He slid his empty glass back and forth along the tablecloth.

"They're going to tear it down," I said before I could stop myself. I knew I was speaking out of meanness.

"Are they now? I read something in the paper, but that was a long time ago. I thought it had blown over." He picked up the shot glass and looked at it curiously. "They tear everything down. By the time you're my age, everything you used to like will be gone."

I looked at the tablecloth, which was covered with bread crumbs and specks of frosting.

"When I went back to Ireland two summers ago," Father Pat continued, "they'd even torn down the church where I said my first mass. De-consecrated the building and torn it down." He sighed. He reached across the table for the whiskey bottle and poured himself another shot.

I looked at his profile as he put the glass to his lips. His hair was thinning over his temples, and I could see bluish veins through his fine, pale skin. The veins ran deep into his brain, where all the evil things he had heard in confession over the years must still be lodged, fresh and sharp as a packet of straight pins. Inside everyone's head, just below their pretty or bored or wandering eyes, the strangest and most frightening pictures must be permanently etched; yet the real world around them shifted and changed and disappeared.

I wanted to get up and go away somewhere and hide my face, but there was nowhere to go.

"Excuse me. You lost your shoe, didn't you?"

I looked up to see the cheerful bellboy with the crew cut who had taken me up to the cupola. He held my high heel in one hand.

"I found this in the hall," he said blushing until his ears turned red. "I thought it must be yours, so I came down here on my break."

"Oh, thank you," I said, taking the shoe from him. I found it hard to smile. He took a step backwards.

"Well, Cinderella, don't just sit there," said Father Pat with a sudden laugh. "Give the boy some cake. He might be a prince indeed."

"Would you like some cake?" I asked.

He hesitated. "Well, sure."

I got up, and led him over to the cake. The top two tiers were gone, and big chunks of the bottom tier had already been eaten.

"Do you like frosting?"

"That's the best part," the boy said, playing nervously with one of his gold uniform buttons. "You know, I thought of Cinderella, too."

"I didn't," I said.

"Didn't you always want to be Cinderella?"

"I'd rather be the fairy godmother," I said, cutting him a large piece of cake with a silver rose on top. "So I could change things."

"I'll just take this back with me," the boy said as I handed him the paper plate. "I've only got ten minutes."

"Thanks a lot," I said. "It was very nice of you to bring my shoe."

He swallowed. "Don't mention it," he said. He looked a little hurt, and glanced around the room. "It looks like a swell party. I'll have to get married someday just for the fun of it. See you later."

"Good-bye," I said. I wished I could have been warmer to him, but my throat ached. My heart was a lump of coal. I went back to join Father Pat, just as my grandfather stood up, waving his arms at the musicians.

"I've got a song to sing," my grandfather cried, his eyes shining. "Do you know 'The Lambs on the Green Hills'?"

"Sure we do," shouted the accordion player, putting down his beer and adjusting his keyboard.

Father Pat whispered in my ear. "He used to sing that when we were boys. We stood on the hill together, looking at the sea. We thought we could see as far as America. Your grandfather always had a fine voice."

My grandfather began to sing. His tenor voice was high and clear, transcending his age in a way that startled me. I leaned forward. I had heard him singing around the house, in the shower and in the car, but never formally like this. He held onto the lapels of his tuxedo, his eyes closed:

> The lambs on the green hills stood gazing at me,
> And many strawberries grew round the salt sea,
> And many strawberries grew round the salt sea,
> And many a ship sailed the ocean.

He opened his eyes a moment, and I saw they were wet. The song went on, telling the story of a bride and the man she had not married, who was going to die for love of her, and who wanted her to sprinkle his grave with flowers so sweet. I could tell that my grandfather really saw the strawberries and the salt sea, and every time the song returned to the refrain, I saw them, too. And for a moment I was up in the cupola again, with the wind on my face, looking at the lake, with no knowledge of the jet-haired man who lurked at the foot of the stairs.

Father Pat had shut his eyes, too. His lips trembled. When the song was over, he shook himself.

"It gives me the shivers," he said. "I'm over seventy, and I thought I was a boy."

I wiped my forehead, which was covered with cold sweat. I looked around the room at the other wedding guests, who were clapping and whistling and stamping their feel, trying to get my grandfather to sing again, which he refused to do. I felt as if a fever had broken. My grandmother touched my grandfather's hand when he sat down beside her. The groom had his arm about my aunt's shoulder and was whispering something in her ear which made her smile and look at her ring. People were laughing and having second helpings of the big, ruined cake, and it seemed to me that I knew even less about everything than I ever had.

The Greenhorn

I.

THE DAY COUSIN CHRISTOPHER ARRIVED, I HALF EXPECTED HIM, LIKE the figure of Saint Christopher in my old copy of the *Lives of the Saints*, to be carrying a lamb on his shoulders. Instead, he was carrying a smoked salmon under his arm.

As he walked down the ramp from the Aer Lingus flight, my father called his name through the glass that separated the foreign travelers from their waiting relatives. My father's voice sounded funny.

"Chris," my father said. "Chrissie, lad."

My cousin walked on, not noticing; his thin body was hidden in mud brown tweeds. He looked all messed up, like he'd been sleeping in his clothes. Which he probably was. In addition to the salmon, my cousin Christopher carried a paper shopping bag which looked as if there were rocks in the bottom. On the yellow bag were big black letters, SHANNON DUTY FREE PORT.

He was older than I expected, older than anyone I thought my father should call lad. Even from this distance, he looked like he needed a shave. His fine black hair fell over his forehead and he walked with a quick, sort of military step. Careful to avoid clipping the heels of the passengers ahead of him, he maneuvered through the revolving door. My father and I lost sight of him as he entered the Hall of Immigration and we moved on to the Customs exit. After we had waited more than an hour, he finally emerged; he looked startled by the hiss of the automatic doors. My father, his face twisted in a funny way, wordlessly embraced Chris with his long arms, pounding him self-consciously on the back. Dust flew up from my cousin's tweed jacket and I noticed that, under the clear plastic that covered the slab of fish, there was a shiny membrane. The fish looked spoiled.

"Chris, lad, it's grand you look," my father said, wiping his nose with a big handkerchief and stuffing it quickly into his back pocket. "The image of Jack. The blessed image of Jack, Lord have mercy on him."

"Uncle Seamus." My cousin set down his shopping bag and shook my father's hand. "It's grand I feel to be out of the sky."

His voice was deep, like he was talking from way back in his throat. I guessed he would be fond of singing.

"Chris, this is your cousin, Nora." said my father, holding me lightly by the arm. Since Chris and I were almost the same height, my cousin nodded and smiled into my face. His eyes were gray, dreamy. Country eyes.

"It is my pleasure and honor, Nora."

I held out my good hand and he took it. His hand was cool and strong.

The way home was cheerful, as if we were celebrating something. My father pointed out the sights along the Brooklyn-Queens Expressway.

"Red Hook is a place to stay out of. Hoods everywhere."

"Hoods?" said Chris.

"Mafia," said my father. "Italians."

We traveled cautiously, clinging to the right lane. The Ford Fairlane was an uneven black. My father had repainted it himself. With a powder puff, if you can believe it. He'd done it three weeks before, in honor of his emigrating nephew. The greenhorn, my father called him, trying to sound tough. He always tried to sound tough, even though he always carried a black and silver rosary in a small leather purse in his breast pocket, over his heart.

Below the elevated highway, the brick tenements of Williamsburg slipped by, each window framing an empty, dark room. Church spires rose at almost every intersection. Their brick clock towers were strangely neglected; the clocks had broken hands or missing numbers. Only the clock of the Williamsburg bank told the right time.

"That's the Army Terminal," my father said, pointing to the massive cement warehouse lining the Brooklyn waterfront. "Your Uncle Josie used to work there. During the war."

We drove on in silence for a mile or more. I thought of Uncle Josie, eighth in my father's family of seven brothers and four sisters. Uncle Josie always wore his best navy blue worsted suit at my mother's Sunday table. Silently, he would help himself to seconds of roast lamb and potatoes. Silently, he would chew his food and wipe his dark moustache with the edge of his dinner napkin. At Christmas, three years ago, Uncle Josie had, as usual, wiped his moustache with my mother's fanciest linen and risen from the table. He announced that he was going for a cigar. We had not seen or heard from him since.

"Whatever happened to Uncle Josie?" I asked.

My father cast a sidelong glance at Cousin Chris and laughed.

"Gone to the tin mines, *mavourneen*," he said. "Gone to the tin mines." My father liked to be mysterious. He was a cop. He used to say he was in law enforcement, so you might imagine he was a detective. But he was a patrolman. His beat was downtown, near the Courts. He spent a lot of time in the back of a barbershop on Fulton, shooting the breeze.

At the 69th Street ferry line, we pulled up behind a milk truck. Its cream-colored bulk blocked the view of the ferry shack and the Lower Bay. My father ceremoniously set the brake and we all got out, my father to buy the ferry tickets, Chris and I for a better view. Around the edges of the ferry slip, the green river surged and sucked at the pilings. The air smelled of creosote and salt spray. We stood near the heavy iron dock rails and watched the water traffic.

"Is it always like this?" Chris asked.

"You mean busy."

"Yes."

"Always. Sometimes more."

"And will we be near?"

"We are just across. On Staten Island."

He stared at the massed skyline of downtown Manhattan.

"Sweet Jesus," he said. "I didn't know . . . I didn't imagine it would be this near."

It was eerie, his voice.

My father startled both of us, sneaking up quietly from behind.

"That's the great lady herself." He raised his arm in the direction of the Lower Bay and the Statue of Liberty. It was just dusk. The statue was a dark shape, clearly outlined against the evening sky, the lamp upraised but unused for years. My father lit a Camel and offered one to Chris. My cousin accepted gingerly, careful not to touch any of the other cigarettes protruding from the torn pack. When Chris lit up, I could tell he wasn't very practiced at smoking. He didn't inhale, at least not much. And his hands shook.

"Looks a bit small from here, doesn't she, Chris?"

My cousin looked across the water at the imposing figure in the distance, his eyes soft.

"To me, she's big enough, Uncle Seamus."

"Ah, but you should have come in a great ship, lad. Up the bay, past the forts." My father drew on his cigarette and flicked the ash into the water below. "In those days, you picked up the pilot off the Sandy Hook. Stood off for the tide." He sighed, remembering. "A thrill, all right. Thrill of a lifetime." His face had become sweetly sad, his mouth with just the trace of a smile.

The pipe of the ferry whistle shattered the quiet, signaling the next boat into the slip. My father took another drag and dropped his cigarette into the sea.

"Time to trot," he said, pulling his fedora down over his eyes.

We got back into the car, this time with me squeezed between. Chris made room, putting his left arm across the seat backs. His tweed suit smelled of tobacco and ashes and his thighs were outlined under his trousers. I held my shoulders tight so the empty sleeve on my right side wouldn't touch up against him. We edged onto the boat, my father engineering between the dairy truck and a late model Buick.

On the ferry, we bought crullers, twists of dough deep-fried in fat and rolled in crystals of sugar. We bought coffee served in mugs. At the front of the second deck, we watched the lights coming on in downtown Manhattan and the port of Saint George getting bigger and bigger. The ferry terminal was newly painted, a blinding white. The greasy dock hands were vested in day-glow orange. Behind us, on the receding Brooklyn side, sulfur lamps tuned to the dusk lit up the ring of the Belt Parkway.

We were fifth off, behind the Buick. My father laughed and pinched me on the knee.

The house was warm and fragrant with the odor of roasting meat. From the back, the kitchen shone under its central fixture, the tone warmed further by the butter yellow walls.

"Mary," my father shouted. "It's home with the nephew."

My mother stood in the doorway, her body a slender form against the light. She was wearing a semi-dressy print outfit with a patent leather belt at the waist. Stepping forward, she flicked on the dining room chandelier with its twenty-five-watt bulbs in the shape of amber flames. Two of the six bulbs were unscrewed. To save on the light bill.

In seconds, her white printed apron was slipped off and rolled into a tiny ball. She came toward us and extended a hand to Chris. I looked at her the way Chris might have seen her, meeting her for the first time. She was beautiful, pale creamy skin with big dark blue eyes. My father stood just behind Chris, like he was presenting my cousin to royalty.

"Welcome to America, Christopher," she said.

"It's grateful I am, Aunt Mary."

"You must be tired," she said, holding on to his hand for an instant.

"A bit, yes."

"And hungry."

"A bit, yes." They both laughed and she tucked the ends of hair back into her old-fashioned french twist. Her hair was thick and dark reddish. She called it chestnut. Chris looked at her with bare arms raised and then looked down at his feet. Her arms were pale and round.

"Dinner is almost ready."

My father stood waiting for her kiss.

"Was the ferry bad?" she said, touching her powdered cheek to his face. She moved past him and switched on the small lamp at the edge of the upright piano. Pictures of my uncles, their wives, their children, smiled or glowered or gazed dully out of their dark wooden frames. A restored portrait of Grandmother Sullivan was in a special silver frame. The picture arrangement was like a memorial of some kind. Even the bronze statue of Rin Tin Tin at the other end of the piano seemed reverent. The red bow left over from Christmas was still tied around his neck.

"It was not. We were in the front, by luck." He winked at Chris.

"James," she said, as if seeing him for the first time, as though he were a visitor. "Your hat."

I remember my father's face when she said that, puzzled, like he wasn't sure of something. Then he gave a little click with his teeth and removed his fedora, placing it carefully in its space on the hall closet shelf, next to his service revolver.

At the time, all of this seemed pretty normal.

❦

My cousin gave my mother the salmon.

"This is for you, Aunt Mary. It isn't much, but it's fresh smoked."
My mother took the package without looking at it. She put it on the
dining room table like she was afraid the smell would get on her.

"Thank you, Christopher," she said.

"And this is for you, Uncle Seamus." My cousin lifted a heavy
bottle wrapped in tissue paper out of his Shannon shopping bag.

"Well, well," said my father, tearing off the wrapping. It was Old
Bushmill's. My father rubbed the side of the dark green bottle,
polishing it; then he set it on the sideboard. "Thank you, lad, you
shouldn't have." My mother took the bottle and shut it away in the
linen press, turning the small brass key. No one, excepting my
mother, ever opened the linen press.

For me, my cousin had a hanky, linen with lace trim on the
borders. It was in a tiny box with a cellophane window in the shape
of a shamrock. I tucked the hanky into the sleeve of my sweater.

II.

The ebony upright piano was in our front room as long as I could
remember, although nobody played it until Chris came to the house.
He would play the old tunes, "In the Good Old Summertime,"
"Daisy," "Sweetheart," tunes my mother and I knew. We would sing
together in the afternoons, the three of us, my mother sitting on the
sofa or standing behind him. His dark head bobbed in time to the
music and his strong fingers worked easily over the keys. Watching my
cousin play, I could see each day more sureness and ease in the way
he carried his body, the way he moved.

Sometimes he sang things we didn't know, songs from home. His
voice was dark and clear, lingering over the ending notes. He taught
my mother a song called "Eileen Aroon." Once, when I came in from
school, they were singing it together in harmony. My mother was
wearing a salmon pink blouse made of a soft, silky material. It was late
in the afternoon, and they hadn't bothered to turn on the lamp over
the piano. The color of her blouse and of her skin shone with a pale
interior light.

That spring, at my mother's suggestion, I read *The Citadel*. At
night after supper, after I had done my Latin translations and my Trig
and Physics at the dining room table, I went up to my room and read

about David and Catherine. First I would sit propped up on the bed pillows, my neck bent and the book balanced on my chest. Later, after my father came in to say goodnight, I would continue to read under the covers with a flashlight I had taken from the cellar.

It was a Saturday morning, very early, when I got to the part where Catherine goes out for the bread and is hit by a car. I thought I had made a mistake, so I went back and re-read the chapter to be sure. But it was true. I closed the book and wept, helpless. I imagined, not Catherine's violent death, but the pain, the remorse for David. Unending, never changing, unresolved. I went down to breakfast with a heavy step.

"What is it, Nora?" my mother asked.

"Nothing."

"Tell me. You look like a long, wet day."

She stood in front of me, waiting, her hand holding a full milk pitcher.

"It's *The Citadel*," I said, my face screwed up in a messy effort not to cry.

"Oh," she said. "You got to the part about the loaf of bread."

"Yes."

"Wasn't it terrible."

"Yes."

She came around to my side of the table and dropped her hand on my shoulder.

"It's hard," she said. "But that's what happens sometimes."

"What?"

"There's a tragedy. The woman dies."

"Oh," I said.

She looked radiant, almost happy when she said that.

My cousin Christopher got a temporary job as a stock clerk. He was hired for the Easter season, just to fill in. He left for work each day about four o'clock. He would be dressed in his tweed jacket and the khaki work pants my father got him from the Army Navy store on Fulton Street. He had put on a little weight, especially in the shoulders, and looked less and less like a lad. My mother often waved to him from the porch window as he turned the corner and walked quickly down the street to the subway station.

The week before Palm Sunday, Chris came home all excited. I was already at the dining room table, translating Cicero.

"Aunt Mary," he said, rushing past me. "I got the job!"

He stood in front of her and she dropped her hands to her sides.

"That's wonderful, Christopher. I knew you would."

They stood that way, looking at each other.

When my father came in from work, he unsnapped the metal studs in his leather holster, releasing the gun. After checking the safety, he placed it high on the shelf in the hall closet. Next to the gun, he placed his blue garrison cap with the silver badge in front. Walking through the front room, he shed his uniform jacket and loosened his dark blue tie. Under his arms, dark rings of sweat stained his oxford blue shirt.

"A scorcher," he said, sitting at the head of the dining room table and draining the glass of cold water that was always there at his place. Every day, he was home promptly at four P.M., the eight to four shift for twenty-three years. A little more than half his life.

"Christopher got a job. A real job," my mother said, laying the bread and butter in front of his plate. "With the Telephone."

"The Telephone," my father said, leaning back in his chair. "How did he do that?" His face was pale, his mouth set. Two lines extended from the corner of his eyes deep into his thin cheeks.

It happened in August, during a heat wave. It happened the night my cousin called my mother Moira, the Irish for Mary.

Outside the locusts were chirping loudly in the maple trees. Some of the neighborhood men were down at the sea wall near Sailor's Snug Harbor. There wasn't a breath of air. I could hear the mewing of the gulls as they circled over the exposed mud flats. From the front steps of our house, you could see the harbor half a block away, the water flat and oily. It was dead low.

Inside, my father was at the table, as usual, finishing his supper. On top of the linen press, a small electrical fan the size of a dinner plate spun crazily in its tiny cage. It moved from side to side, ruffling the leaves of the summer roses my mother had put in the center of the table. It was a Monday, a day off for Chris. We were all there, together.

"Will you have canned peaches, James," my mother called from the kitchen.

"A few. No syrup."

Chris was there in the kitchen with her. It was half dusk and the lights were off in the kitchen. To keep it cooler, my mother said. In the twilight, the two of them blended together in shadow, crossing in front of and behind each other as they began the washing up. Chris was scraping the plates into the sink. Through the semidark, my mother's round pale arms moved slowly as she drained the peaches against the edges of the tin. She arranged the fruit in a small white bowl.

"Christopher," she said. There was a sweetness in her voice that I had not heard before. My cousin turned to her and, saying nothing, reached for the dish and brought it in to my father. The peaches, edged with red, were slick with juice.

"They're freestones," my father said.

"Yes, Uncle."

"I don't like freestones." My father stared at the peaches, his square hands stretched flat on either side of the white dish. "Too expensive."

"You deserve them, Uncle Seamus. Moira says you deserve them." The four of us drew breath when Chris said her name. It was so personal. You could feel something turn, something in the air turn and close, like air being shut off. The three of us, my mother, Chris, and I, looked toward my father.

"Moira, is it." His head was lowered, the skin of his neck and ears a dull red. Slowly, he raised his right hand above his head and, with tremendous force, slammed his fist down on the table. The dish of peaches bounced an inch into the air. Half the fruit slid onto the white cloth. Again, my father raised his hand and slammed the table, this time with an open palm. He squeezed his fingers together, gathering the folds of linen in his fist. The bowl of roses toppled over in slow motion, spilling water and flowers onto the floor.

"Nora," he said in a strange, flat voice. "Go to your room."

"Yes, Daddy."

"And close the door."

"Yes, Daddy."

As I mounted the stairs, I could hear drops of water still dripping to the carpet. Neither my mother nor Chris had moved since my father's fist had struck the table.

"The Bushmill's," I heard my father say.

"James," my mother whispered.

I closed the door and lay down in the dark, fully clothed, my ears straining. I heard my mother's muted words overrun by my father's stronger voice. His tone was lifeless. All speech was muffled by my closed door, the jog in the stairwell and the portieres which had been drawn closed over the dining room archway. My cousin's dark mellow voice came through clearly only twice. Then I heard him no more.

I rolled to my side and pulled the chenille bedspread across my body. My teeth were set on edge, clenched tight, causing a nerve in my cheek to twitch. Soon, my shoulders, my knees, were shivering as if it were the middle of winter instead of a hot August night.

Suddenly, there were sharp steps on the parquet floor. My mother's high heels. Then, water running in the kitchen. Once I heard my father shout, "Jesus." Moments later, I heard more hurried steps, this time muted on the carpeted stairs to the second floor and then rattling up to the attic room. Chris was moving around overhead. A drawer squeaked, the third one in the warped oak dresser that used to be mine. Then, I heard my cousin's steps down out of the attic, along the upstairs hall, rumbling as he gathered speed down the stairs to the room below. There were no words. A chair was moved. I heard the back door screen squeal and thump shut. It had to be Chris, going.

I rolled off the bed and pulled back the covers. Stretching out under the light summer blanket, gradually my shaking shoulders grew still. Through the window of my room at the front of the house, I could see the summer night deepen. The crickets had fallen silent and the street settled into its nighttime quiet.

I awoke much later to the sound of a drowning, strangling noise, almost a bleat; it was punctuated with gasps for breath. Just outside my door, there was another sound, the noise of a heavy object being dragged or pushed along the hallway.

"James, I can't."

"You will, my girl." It was my father.

"It's too heavy."

"I hope so, woman. I hope so."

My mother, my father, moving something. A piece of furniture? Hair on end, I opened the door a crack. On the second floor landing, at the top of the stairs, was my mother, her dark hair loose and in confusion. She struggled under the weight of a mattress they were carrying. Lower down the stairway, my father bore most of the weight on his back. Light shone up from the front parlor lamps. His face was wet, his skin reddish gold, as if burned. When he turned to stare at me, his eyes were brilliantly glazed, wild looking. He swayed slightly. I suppose he was drunk. "Shut the door, Nora," he said. "Shut the goddam door."

I obeyed and leaned against the wall, my shoulders again beginning to shake. From the hall, I heard the sounds of effort, my mother's short gasps for breath.

"It's caught, James. On the corner."

"Push, woman. Push."

There was a bump as the mattress hit something hard, the tinkle of glass. Perhaps it was the cheap chandelier in the front hall as they passed beneath. I could hear the rasp of the bricks on the front stoop as the mattress went over the steps and into the street. From the front window, I could see them in the light of the street lamps, the striped mattress between them. My mother was in front, being pushed, helpless to disagree.

"James," she whined. "Please stop."

"For shame, woman," he said.

They moved slowly across the small lawn, through the summer flower beds, crushing a stand of zinnias and marigolds. Attaining a kind of rhythm, they moved toward the sea along the cement sidewalk, in and out of the circle of lights cast by the street lamps. Now out of earshot, their movements were dreamlike. I saw my mother release her burden at the edge of the wall and take a few steps backward. My father lifted his end of the mattress higher and higher until it toppled over the edge of the wall. The tide was on its way in, almost full. You could see that the water was close up to the sea wall, surging against the jagged pile of broken granite that formed the barrier.

Soon, my parents came back to the house and I heard my mother's steps on the stairs. She went into their bedroom alone, the room next to mine, and blew her nose. The bed made a noise as it received her weight. My father remained in the house below, moving about from room to room. As the sky began to lighten, he left the house by the back door.

I waited until the sun was up and then went down the street to the sea wall. Below was the green and white striped mattress, heavily weighted now with water. Floating just underneath the surface of the canal, it was a few feet away from the wall. I waited and watched. Gradually, the rectangular shape began to move in a slow arc toward the Lower Bay. As the time passed, I watched the tide turn and pick up momentum, bearing the half-submerged mattress faster and faster to the mouth of the river and the ocean beyond.

Nothing was said. There was silence in the house for days. When I looked into my cousin's attic room, the bedsprings were bare, not even covered with a sheet. The closet was empty, the drawers stripped of their paper liners. I searched for a handkerchief, a button, a paper. Nothing. It had been swept clean, as if he had never existed.

In my parents' room, the bed was neatly made, as always, the spread turned down just below the plumped up pillows in an inviting way. Like a hotel. The air coming through the window was fresh with the smell of the harbor. It had rained during the night. Over their bed, on the wall, the rosewood cross with its bronze figure of the crucified Christ made a dark mark on the blue-flowered wallpaper. The clock on the bedstand ticked comfortably.

Standing in their room, I knew they weren't sure how much I understood. That if we didn't talk about it, we could go on as if nothing had happened.

The Boat

When I opened the curtains, it was my face
that I saw reflected in the window.
Not the face of my father
and not the face of my uncle Roy,
it was almost nobody's face,
being only my own.

Past this face, if I forced the view,
I could see the small boat tied to the dock
and beyond it the choppy water of a lake
where clouds gathered and darkened.
Why had I put off everything till this morning?

The clock in the entry started to clear its throat,
preparing to chime the hour,
and I knew without looking that the time was already seven.
I crossed to the stove for another cup of black coffee,
to which I added all that was left of the whiskey.

The boat was a sweet little boat,
it was damned near perfect,
and I knew Uncle Roy had chosen it well.
But back at the window, I saw only a fragile craft
tethered to the dock of a large, threatening lake.
In front of it all was the face of a man
with his nerves up against the wall,
the face of a man turned inside out.

Hard-Won Gifts

Sometimes Father will just be standing there,
shoulders collapsed,
hands busy wiping themselves
on his vest,
eyes behind thick lenses
flat and ungrasping.

And sometimes Rose stands beside him.
She helps him into a chair
at the small table,
then places a hand on his arm.
Together, they are stationed to face down
the intrusion.

Mother is never there.
Or Jimmy, or Mark, or Uncle Peter.
Their existence itself is tentative,
their location unsure.

I don't know why I always
feel it this way,
why hard-won gifts weigh heavy
in my hopeless hands,
why select phrases, like fishbones,
stick in my throat.

Part Two

The Furies and the Silences

Edge Skool

I knew it was
dangerous going
back to the island
left behind,
flying forward
into past fire,
pissed families,
prayers & potatoes.
I sensed
at this scene
of gendering such
violence, such traps
of silence &
furious hospitality
& a sacred veil
putting all in
check, a crux
of codes
tongue for
tongue.
So much resentment
could only have
accumulated
very slowly,
year by year,
day by day,
century by century

the way our fathers
& Father Ireland
showered blows (but
don't you dare
tell) on
us — his disappeared
children.

To My Father,
Dying in a Supermarket

At first it is difficult
to see you
are dropping dead —

you seem lost
in thought, adjusting your tie
as if to rehearse

some imaginary speech
though of course beginning
to fall,

your mouth opening wider
than I have ever seen
a mouth,

your hands deep
in your shirt,
going down

into the cheeses, making the sound
that is not
my name,

that explains nothing
over and over,
going away

into your hands
into your face,
leaving this great body

on its knees
the father
of my body

which holds me
in this world,
watching you go

on falling
through the Musak,
making the sound

that is not my name,
that will never
explain anything, oh father,

stranger, all dressed up
and deserting me
for the last time.

My Brother Inside the Revolving Doors

I see you in Chicago, twenty-five years ago,
a tall kid, surprisingly sure of yourself.
You have just arrived from the goat farm
to meet your father, the god you invented
after he left you in childhood.
It is the sunniest day you can remember,
and you walk the wide streets
of the city by his side in the dream
you have had all along of this moment,
except you are beginning to see how different
he looks, and how he does not care
about this in the same way that you do.
Which is when it happens, you are taken
inside the doors. Just like that
you are shut off from him, walking
in the weightlessness of your own fear.
And when you push your door, it leads
to other retreating doors, and again
and again, it takes you to the voice of him,
the fat man standing outside who has nothing,
suddenly, to do with your father and shouts
let go! let go! and you cannot let go.

Kathleen Lynch

The Zoo Is Not the Zoo

CYNTHIA THOUGHT GOING TO THE DUMP WITH HER FATHER WAS AN honor, a thrill. Tom Conlan would elect one of his four daughters to accompany him on this mission, and most often he chose Cynthia. Perhaps he chose her because she did not complain about smells, the oily, sickly-sweet stench of garbage baking in the sun. Cynthia pretended she didn't mind being seen in their hulking, beat up station wagon, the wooden sides peeling and scarred, the back down to accommodate the stinking heap of her family's refuse.

Trash accumulated in their narrow side yard and seemed to grow with a force of its own. When it crept around the side of the house, up the little cement stoop and into the service porch, it was Dump Time. Always a Saturday. Always a morning with her father swearing and grumbling, her sisters' stifled whimpers, "icks" and "P.U.s." The girls helped Tom load the car with sodden newspapers, bags of decaying plant cuttings, and kitchen garbage that never made it into the battered, overstuffed can.

Cynthia took to the task energetically, without complaint. She left the easy things for her sisters, recent papers that still looked dry and clean, bags of countless crushed Lucky Lager cans. She chose more sickening things, sopping bags that had become habitats for snails, slugs, maggots. She chose heavy and dirty things, and bore them proudly in the procession from yard to car, hoping to catch her father's eye. Hoping he would see what she was willing to do for him. That he would choose her.

And when he did, they pulled away from the house, two six-packs and a can opener on the seat between them. Cynthia waved to the shadow of her mother, who stood behind the screen door, arms knotted across her chest.

Their journey always started with her father winking at her and saying, "Okey dokey, kiddo, pop one for Poppa." She opened the cold, sweating can and passed it to him, knowing that in minutes his face would slacken, become sweeter and playful, the sense of relief in the car almost as tangible as the smell of garbage.

Once on the road, her father sang, his voice deep, loud, lusty. Cynthia loved listening to him, even though he did not sound very tuneful or melodious. He had a wide repertoire: nursery rhymes, navy songs, jingles, love songs, Christmas carols. Even on a 103 degree Saturday in July he might burst into "Deck the Halls," and Cynthia joined in, her own flat little fa-la-las rising in the hot breeze and mingling with her father's.

Frawley's was the last gas stop before the long drive out past McClellan Air Force base to the county dump. Tom wheeled the stuffed, reeking station wagon up to the pump, leaned out the window and hollered, "Hey Sarge. Filler-up with gas-n-oil, okey-dokey?"

He called all gas station attendants Sarge. Cynthia thought he did so because they wore uniforms. The attendants seemed to like being called Sarge, and they definitely liked her father. Tom got out and followed the man around the car as he ministered to it. He asked "Sarge" about his family, his work, which team he wanted to win the ball game. As they huddled in front of the gaping hood, Cynthia heard the rumble of their conversation, punctuated by her father's occasional "Gee whiz," "No foolin" or "Son-of-a-bitch, Sarge." By the time they circled the car, Tom had always made the attendant laugh. Tom thumped the man heartily on the back and shook his hand.

Her father dwarfed most other men. He stood a beefy six-four. The gas station man beamed up at her father as Tom fished out his dollar bills.

"Take care, Mr. Conlan. Stop in again. Don't be a stranger."

Cynthia studied the expression on the attendant's face. He looked transformed, as if something good had happened to him. As if he had heard great news or just had a stroke of real luck.

Back in the car, her father tugged one of her dark braids and asked, "What say, little Cricket, wanna go dump some junk?"

Cynthia knew this was the cue for his next question.

"Afterward, does my gorgeous little girl want to go to the zoo?"

Cynthia wished he wouldn't call her a little girl and she knew she wasn't gorgeous. She also knew the zoo was not the zoo. They had a secret, she and her father. A pact. A sacred trust.

Gulls shrieked and criss-crossed, rising from and alighting on steaming hills of trash at the Sacramento County Dump. Cynthia wondered why they didn't seem to mind the putrefying smells of human garbage. They fought over slimy scraps and shreds of rotted food.

Cynthia helped her father unload the car, sliding bag after bag across the floor of the wagon onto the back door tipped-down like a ramp. Tom flung the bags, called "Heave-Ho!" with each toss. Between bags he took a swig of Lucky from the can perched on the roof. Cynthia watched his face to gauge his mood. This time was good. He looked like a happy man.

As they pulled back onto the main road in front of the dump site, Cynthia could tell right away where they were going. If they turned right, they were going straight home. If they turned left, they headed toward the river, to the house-boat people. But they crossed onto the two-lane road that seemed to make an endless cut through miles of flat farm land, on the way to visit Slim and Dag, in their little trailer out in the middle of nowhere.

Tom tooted the horn in short, cheery blasts as the station wagon crunched up the long gravel path to the trailer. All three of Dag's dogs charged out barking and wagging and loping around the car. Cynthia and Tom waited in the car until one of the women came out and herded the goose, "Gander," into his chicken-wire pen. Slim had warned Cynthia, "You won't catch any grief from those pooches, kid, but that bird'd make mincemeat out of you. There's only two humans he'll allow on this planet, and that's me and Dag."

Cynthia had never heard of a guard-goose before. She tried to make friends with it on the first visit by sticking some fresh green field grass into the pen, but the goose hissed and shrieked and charged the flimsy-looking wire so fiercely that Cynthia nearly cried. She gave up the idea that she could be friends with that creature, and never approached the pen again.

Slim and Dag seemed like they could be sisters, but they weren't. They looked about the same age, clearly older than Cynthia's mother. Once Dag said, "Shoot, kid, this old gal's seen more than half a century." They both dressed alike, in tight corduroy Levis, with neatly ironed, well-tucked-in tailored shirts. They had similar short-cropped haircuts, too, though Dag's was shorter in front and on top. Slim let her bangs and hair near the temples grow longer. Usually, when Cynthia and her father visited on a Saturday, Slim had a neat row of curlers rolled from ear to ear over her forehead, like a wreath of small metal flowers.

One time Cynthia asked Slim why people called her Slim when Dag was the thinner one. Slim laughed and smacked her belly with both hands. "Oh honey, I used to be a stick, a real Olive Oyl, I tell ya, 'til I moved out here with Dag. Too many brewskies, I guess. Too much good food." She rubbed her hands up and down her sausagey middle.

Dag told Cynthia that her real name was Dagmar. "Dagmar Dolby. Can you imagine a parent saddling a kid with that? A little girl kid? And then expect her to turn out right?"

Cynthia loved the inside of their trailer. Everything looked so cozy and cute and clean. Even though their whole dwelling was barely bigger than the Conlan's living and dining room combined, it looked neat, gleaming, cheerful.

The windows all had bright yellow curtains edged with orange rick-rack. Except in the bedroom, where pale pink dotted swiss curtains with ruffles covered the window. They matched the spread on the double bed that nearly filled the tiny room.

On the wall hung gold-framed pictures of Slim and Dag in their Air Force uniforms, and many snapshots were tucked into the frame around the mirror. One showed the women together at a picnic holding their beer cans aloft and laughing hard, leaning against each other. Another, taken indoors in a dark, crowded place, showed six people at a round table holding up gold filled mugs and stubby glasses of dark liquid. All their eyes glowed red from the flash. Cynthia knew only three of the people in the picture – Slim, Dag, and her father.

Cynthia liked visiting them because Slim fussed over her, called her Doll-face and Doll-buttons, made her salami sandwiches on rye. For a treat, Slim gave her Hershey Kisses or a gooey popcorn ball she made herself. Sometimes they all sat outside on folding chairs, the grownups drinking beer, Cynthia sipping a tall Coke with a lemon wedge squeezed in it.

Cynthia listened as Dag and Tom did most of the talking. They swapped stories about being in the service. Tom's Navy stories and Dag's Air Force tales were as familiar and soothing to Cynthia as the whoosh of summer air through surrounding fields, the clack of cicadas, the rustle of small creatures in the grass.

They laughed a lot. Her father's great booming holler and Dag's loud staccato honking rose and fell in the afternoon air. Cynthia giggled when they were funny like that, and Slim smiled broadly, shaking her head back and forth in little tsk-tsk movements.

Sometimes Slim unbraided Cynthia's hair and brushed it over and over, with long, gentle, rhythmic strokes until it shone and the hair rose up of its own accord to greet the brush. "I always wanted me a little girl like you, Cyn, someone I could dress up, fix real pretty, show off to people."

Cynthia wanted to ask Slim why she didn't get married then, and have a little girl if she wanted one, but she felt funny about asking, and never did.

When they stayed inside the trailer, Tom and Dag scooted onto the bench around the table. Her father looked huge in the little booth, like a giant in a dollhouse. Slim puttered nearby, or, when she smoked, stood at the door with her cigarette arm outside, every now and then poking her face out the crack to take a puff, hold it, and let it out.

After an hour or so of sipping beer, Dag said to Slim, "Hey hon, let's crack some of the good stuff." Slim took the whiskey bottle down from the high cupboard and got three wide short glasses from the one below. Cynthia liked the clunk and chink of ice in the glasses and the way the dark shellac-colored liquid swirled when Slim poured it in. She poured less in her glass than the others. "Just a dash," she winked at Cynthia, adding water to fill it to the brim.

As the afternoon wore on, Cynthia wandered around outside, threw sticks for the dogs, walked down the long pebbly drive and onto the road to see how far she could go before she felt too scared, too alone, and had to turn back. Very few cars passed her. Once she went so far down the road that when she turned to see the trailer she couldn't find it at first. A sick feeling rose in her belly and she thought she might cry. Then at last she sighted the trailer, so far away it looked like a bread box in the grasses, the sharp sun glinting on its aluminum roof.

When she returned, she found Dag and her father huddled low over the table, talking deeper, slower, their voices sloshy and trailing off. Slim got a concerned look on her face and said, "Okay, Chief, you better get this Doll-baby home before dark. Now come on, up-'n'-at-'em Tom."

As they turned back onto the road headed home, Tom stepped on the gas and drove real fast, fields streaking by, windows down to air out the car. Over the sound of wind and engine, he hollered to Cynthia, "Let's dance, honey, wanta hula?" and the car swerved and careened across both lanes, her father singing, "Oh we're going to a hukilau, a huki-huki-huki-huki-hukilau . . . " and Cynthia slammed into the door, then against her father, then the door, laughing, terrified, tears in her eyes, trying to find something to hold on to.

They did the cha-cha, her father jabbing the brakes then jamming the gas pedal, Cynthia jolting back against the seat then up to the dashboard, her hands held forward to thrust her back. After a while he slowed down, both hands up high on the wheel, leaning forward like he was concentrating on driving right, staying on his side of the road as they got closer to town, to traffic, to home.

"Don't tell your mom we went visiting, okay kiddo?"

Cynthia nodded. "Okay Dad, I won't. I won't tell."

"That's my girl, Cyn. My special girl."

They arrived home many hours late, as the purplish dusk darkened and cooled their small home. Her mother stood at the door watching for them, twisting her apron in her fists, her face pulled tight as if she had decided not to breathe anymore.

Tom approached carefully, his hefty hand braced on Cynthia's shoulder, trying to walk without keeling over against the stucco wall. "Sorry so late, Mar. Took my little helper to the zoo." He tried to sound lighthearted but his voice came out too high and tight, as if he, too, couldn't get enough air.

Her mother pushed the screen door open slowly and looked directly into Cynthia's eyes. "Did you go to the zoo, young lady?"

Cynthia tried not to look away from her mother's gaze. Her own eyes suddenly felt too big, like they were bugging out and starting to get dry. "Yes, Mama. We went to the zoo. I had lots of fun."

Marla looked steadily at Cynthia, held her stare until Cynthia looked away, then turned her eyes up to her husband's face and stepped back, admitting them into their home.

As Cynthia ran for the kitchen or the backyard, looking for her sisters, Marla turned and walked resolutely down the hallway to the back bedroom, Tom trailing after her, saying "Hey, Mar, you mad at me? You mad at me, hon? You mad at ole Tom?"

Abandoned

Gimme that lemon wedge, he says.
Wiggling, the child passes it over.
He puts down his glass, stuffs
the lemon into his mouth,
twists his body into alphabets
of agony, spits it out, stares—
eyes bulging—at the grin of
peel on the floor beside his foot.
She wiggles more, beams at him.
Gimme another, he says.
She runs to the kitchen bar,
grabs another and rushes back.
He pops it in and doubles
over, holding himself in pain.
His face twists like a corkscrew.
Again he spits it out, in
a gesture of angry voidance.
She roars with joy, runs for another.

When she returns he has walked
off, walked away, disappeared.
She runs outside, finds him
getting into the car. Tears form.
Gotta go, kid, he says. See ya.
Gotta go. No, really. Gotta go.
She holds out the lemon.
Hey kid, he says, give me a
break, I was just fooling
around, I was only fooling.

Full Military Honors
(June 1970, Contra Costa County, California)

dedicated to Anne Penn Chew Born Grady

CHRIST, ALL THAT WINE AND SMOKE. THREE JAYS THIS MORNING, HELL! Goddamn you, Keith Carlton Kinsella! Oh my God, oh my God, oh my God.

Michael Gorman dropped his fist softly on the roof of the car he'd borrowed. Triple K, you dumb son of a bitch.

Gorman put on his Air Force billed hat, checked his summer dress blues and wondered if God could hold this dreadful day twenty-four hours.

The stupidity of it all. Joyriding in a fucking Puff the Magic Dragon, then splattered all over the jungle floor. Keith, what the hell were you doing?

Gorman began to disconnect. He rubbed his forehead as if the motion would save him from his fears. It'd happened before, when the dam holding back the tensions ruptured, and the demons that ate at him rushed through his spirit.

There wasn't enough smoke in the world or booze in the universe to still this day's demons. Goddamned Kinsella, you son of a bitch!

The sergeant walked slowly to the door of the funeral home. He'd face it, as predestined as the world of Calvin and Knox.

A goddamned joy ride! The obscenity of it, the profanity of it. Fucking dead! One dead sonuvabith, who'd been my friend! Gorman snorted, like a bull.

The visitation rooms in McCallum and Sons' Funeral Home fanned out in a half moon from a sun-bathed lobby. Gorman shivered when he saw the names of the dead. The names. Each written in a fine hand, fitting for the Domesday Book, and enshrined on easels.

Gorman signed the condolence book, scanned the pages to see if any of the others had made it: Tom Kennedy, Mike Kopas, Barry O'Keefe. Kennedy was there. Kopas a page later. Gorman had hoped for strength in numbers. But no O'Keefe.

An American flag draped the closed casket. Gorman suddenly felt distances as if his eyes were a camera clicking off frames: mounds of floral arrays to the left; riots of reds, oranges, purples, and blues. Two unlighted altar candles at each end of the bier. Oh Keith, Keith, Keith.

"May I help you?" The tone was comforting. Gorman wheeled in an about-face. A large florid man in a navy blue suit, darker tie, with a white-on-white silk shirt and a white carnation in his lapel stood behind him, smiling slightly.

"Sergeant, I'm sure the family is glad that you could leave your duties to be with them at this time. When the others arrive, I'll explain what you'll need to do. I understand that an honor guard from the Presidio'll meet us at the church. It's the least the country can do for brave young men."

The words, "brave young men," pounded in Gorman's head like drums. Hendrix ripped through "All Along the Watchtower"; the joker talked to the king. The sergeant wanted another jay, another hit — anything to bring this day to an end.

"Have you had a chance to pay your respects?"

"No." Gorman's voice was cold as ice.

The disconnect started again as the funeral director took him by the arm and led him slowly to the kneeler.

Click, like the old Kodak box camera his mother Mary'd used to make a visual history of the family's birthdays, graduations, ballgames.

The reds and blues of the flag burned his eyes. He clumsily wiped a tear away.

Fragments of the Lord's Prayer stormed across his mind. "Hallowed be Thy name, Thy kingdom come." Gorman knelt in banked fury before the casket of his friend. "Forgive us our trespasses as we forgive those who trespass against us, and deliver us from evil."

"From evil." Ten days before, half a world away. The salvagers putting what they could find into bags to cart to Saigon for autopsy. So we'll know how each and every one died. There couldn't have been much left. What did they write? Traumatic injuries upon impact with jungle. "Death, where is thy string?" Through my heart, through my soul!

Eric Clapton ran off a guitar riff with Cream, an explosion of electric energy, like a cardinal act of mercy. Gorman dwelled on the central fact: It could've been me. "Forgive us our trespasses."

Gorman didn't hear the family, the priest, and the other mourners enter as he rose from the kneeler.

Pat, Keith's father, offered his hand. "Mike, thank God you're here. It means so much to Charlotte."

Another frame clicked.

"To Charlotte."

"To Charlotte."

"To Charlotte."

The waves kept pounding the rocks at Asilomar in the milky light of dawn.

Charlotte's face was hidden behind a thin black veil. She sat at the end of a row of reproduction Louis XIV furniture. A Celtic cross hung from a thin gold chain. A mourning queen in a palace with a slain prince.

Click.

His mind spun back seven months, basking in the delight of the Kinsellas' celebration. It had been of Charlotte's forty-fourth birthday. The huge cake, the tables groaning with Dungeness crab, sourdough bread, avocados. The wealth of California's valleys and waters. Dozens of their friends and Keith's.

The house of Pleasant Hill bounced with joy and music. Odd mixtures of Sinatra, Keith Jarrett, Otis Redding, the Kingsmen. How the world seemed to laugh. Even with the Modernaires.

Gorman tried to say something to Pat. "I'm, I'm, I'm glad, glad, I could, could . . . " He took a deep breath.

Pat touched him on the shoulder. "I know."

That night when it seemed the entire East Bay had come to celebrate Charlotte. Keith and Mike sneaked onto the huge sweeping deck. A little jewel of a valley twinkled before them.

Keith lay on his back, staring at the heavens. "The diamond in

Orion's belt," he said pointing to a star, low on the November horizon.

"How do you know, jock?" Gorman said with a wicked laugh.

"Cuz I did something other than throw a football, asshole." Keith took a swig. "Cowboy, you're a real fucker, you know that."

"Quit hogging the juice."

"Fuck off," Kinsella passed the bottle of chardonnay and laughed.

Gorman stood at the railing. "So different," he said. "So really different here." He wanted to speak, but how to describe the days that became so clear after the fogs burned away? Lovely, beautiful, awesome were too tame. Gorman had never felt this way before.

Keith kept searching the skies. "Isn't this the way everyone lives?"

Kopas was with Kennedy and O'Keefe in the back of the room. All in dress blues. They'd been scattered to the winds.

Cymbals crashed. Ginger Baker's arms were blurs on the Carousel Ballroom's stage. His Air Force was bombs away rock and rolling inside Gorman's head. And there was Kinsella with Mary Consuelo, the woman he wanted to marry, screaming into the night for more, more, more, more. The black light strobes danced around the room, filled with the lazy smells of alcohol, tobacco, hash, and dope. Oh, yeah!

The camera froze another frame. A short, gray-haired Italian priest stood before Charlotte. Pat's arm was draped across her shoulder, her hands enwrapped in the priest's.

"Sergeant." The funeral director's voice cut like an electric saw through bone.

Mary Consuelo stood with her father in the far right corner of the room, her face haggard and worn.

Gorman moved back to the others who were here to bury Keith Kinsella.

The priest put on a red stole, the symbol of martyr's blood and God's justice, blessed the casket with holy water and made a sign of the cross over it.

"Come my friends: Let us go to the church to celebrate the Mass of Resurrection." He spread wide his arms in embrace.

Little eddies of dust swirled around the parking lot. A Contra Costa County deputy, no older than the young men in this liturgy of life-after-death, slid behind the wheel of a turbo-charged Olds cruiser to begin the ten-minute journey to Saint Francis of Assisi Church.

"So different here," the words mocked Gorman.

"You get used to it," Kinsella'd said, pointing to another star and throwing off a name Gorman didn't catch.

"No. It's sweeter here," Gorman said.

Kinsella convulsed with laughter. "You've been too long in Indian country, cowboy. It's The World. The Big Exchange. That's all."

Gorman wrestled with himself that night, a struggle as fierce as Jacob's with the angel. "I see something here, with your folks and you." The land was an ambrosia, but the nectar Gorman thought he could taste was inside the bonds of this family. "It's so goddamned hard to talk about."

There was so little support. That's what he was trying to tell the dumb son of a bitch. Across the Great Divide was how Gorman explained it to himself: Big Jim, his father, and Mary, his mother, locked in a hell they couldn't escape, ever since his sister, Vee, had died. Damn you, Kinsella. Damn you, you son of a bitch.

The church's parking lot was terraced asphalt gouged out of hillock. Stairs and inclines led to the front door; the hearse and the limousine parked by the entrance.

Gorman looked at the Buicks, the Cadillacs, the Chryslers, the Lincolns, the occasional Triumph or Jaguar. Oh, it was different here. Not a VW microbus, chopped Harley, or Monza in sight.

The helmets of the honor guard gleamed in the sun. The soldiers stood at parade rest by the church door, ready to lead the way down the aisle.

The priest wore the red vestments of the martyr's Mass, and stood with two servers in black cassocks and white surplices in front of the church.

"May the Lord be with you." The priest's voice died on the warm wind.

"And also with you." The response from those gathered was like a cannonade. He watched, mute, as the honor guard snapped to.

"Detail!" the lieutenant's voice could've carried to Sacramento: "Ten-hut!"

The six enlisted hit a brace.

"On my command!" Gorman wanted to scream as he heard the first click of their boots on the marble, a solemn signal to the organist.

A voice filled with joy rose from a hidden spot behind Gorman and the others as they walked slowly down the aisle in lockstep with the honor guard.

> "God who raised Jesus from the dead
> Will give new life to our mortal bodies
> Through his spirit living in us, alleluia."

The joy of my youth. Michael Bloomfield and Muddy Waters wailing against the evils of the night. White and black, soul mates. Until Michael Gorman and Keith and Mary and sweet Jeannie Fontenot had boogied, really gotten down, smothered in the Carlos Santana Blues Band's "Evil Ways."

Click. The plaza in front of San Francisco City Hall alive with half a million people. He and Keith and Mary huddled together on a cold May day, listening to sweet Jeannie sing, "Amazing Grace." Song on the wind, voice bouncing off buildings.

"The Lord is my shepherd," the priest said, "there is nothing I shall want."

Stand in there, Mike. Put your game face on.

Big Mama Willie Mae Thornton wrapped her meat hooks around the microphone in Berkeley's New Orleans House and growled like the meanest tiger bitch that ever stalked the land. "Eat your heart out, suckers," she shouted, and the walls shimmied like my sister Kate.

Jeannie banged a tambourine on her hip. Mary waved her hands above her head. And Keith and Gorman yelled, "Get it on! Get it on! Get it on!"

"He guides me in the right paths for His name's sake," the priest said. "Even though I walk in the dark valley I fear no evil; for you are at my side."

Big Mama's voice, warm as fine whiskey. He glommed on the words like a caterpillar to a leaf. Silky threads of connection.

Cal Tjader worked the vibes in North Beach. O'Keefe had the smoke; Kopas was already blasted on drink and hash. And oh, how the black man worked the congas, even the Carol Dodas of the world felt alive when that man worked his mojo on the skins. Goddamn, man: it's fucking good to be alive. There sat Kinsella, at ease with everything about himself and life, nodding and bobbing.

The words of the psalm were sure; Gorman wanted to wash himself with them, cleanse himself in the repetition of the Mass's prayers. A knot built in the stomach when he saw Charlotte steal a glance at the casket.

Click!

Stopped forever was the quick jerk of the head to make sure all around here was not something she could run from. Oh, Keith's there, Gorman told himself. A presence, part of All Soul's Day.

"I am the resurrection and the life, says the Lord; he who believes in me will not die forever."

The sergeant lowered his head. The response, "Glory to you, Oh Lord," tasted like bitter herbs.

Gorman dropped uneasily into the pew as the priest began his homily. Charlotte. Keith! Damn you! For leaving us here!

The priest's tone was reassuring. Peace, security, war, sacrifice, redemption, body of Christ, arms of the Lord. All laid out in a familiar road, better marked than an interstate. Life after death, life after death, life after death.

Trane with Miles. An ax and a horn, two visions of life. Inchoate sounds. "A Love Supreme" and "Bitches Brew." They blew their brains out seeking something on the other side of life. Not In Country, not in The World. But out there in infinity, where the hungry hearts gather.

"May Keith Carlton Kinsella's immortal soul rest in everlasting peace." The priest bowed his head in silent prayer.

The offering of the bread and wine, the changing of these gifts into the body and blood of Christ became more frozen frames of film. Gorman, like the photographer in Antonini's *Blow Up*, expanded the images, over and over again, until he wasn't sure what was reality.

"Lord Jesus Christ," the priest implored an unseen deity. "You said, I leave you peace, My peace I give you. Look not on our sins, but on the faith of your Church and grant us peace and unity of your kingdom where you live and reign forever and ever."

"Per omnia saecula, saeculorum." A shout from the Darkest of Ages to this hideous time.

"The peace of the Lord be with you always," the priest extended his arms.

"And also with you," the gathering of mourners answered.

"Let us offer each other a sign of peace," the priest said.

Gorman watched Patrick Kinsella kiss his wife tenderly on the forehead and then frame her face with his massive hands and lightly touch each eye with a kiss.

The camera in his mind went click, click, click.

The priest now stood before the Kinsellas, offered each his hands. There was no hurry.

"Oh Father Joe, Father Joe." A scourging pain seemed to pour forth from Charlotte. "Give me the strength. Give me the strength."

Gorman couldn't watch any longer. Mary's sobbing continued.

The priest took a step back and made the sign of the cross over all in the front row. Then he went to Patrick, Mary Consuelo, and her father and said "God will give us the strength."

Then the priest and Pat took Charlotte by the arm and escorted her from the pew. The pallbearers came to her. She embraced each one beside the bier. "Thank you," she said.

Gorman's mouth filled with cotton when his turn came. He looked at the misty green eyes and the pale face for a clue. Her arms fell heavily around him, as poignant as the Pietá.

Gorman returned to his place in the second pew. Two of Keith's boyhood friends bit their lips, one rubbed his eyes with a handkerchief and the fourth hid the tears on his face behind his hands. Kopas, Kennedy, and O'Keefe weren't any better.

The glint of a silver cross was almost buried in Mary Consuelo's clenched fist. Like the old women in black who haunt the 6:30 weekday Masses, she fingered her beads.

Gorman ached to pour out his heart to her and to Charlotte. Mary and Keith. Lovers. Why this awful thing had to happen . . . He shook his head. There was no answer.

Miles Davis had his back to the audience. The trumpet was wired and notes poured out, crystalline clear until they turned to angry shouts of black electric noise, sending riffs into the heavens.

Gorman saw now so clearly the drunken rages and mad lusts he and Jeannie Fontenot had flung into the stratosphere. He couldn't concentrate on the Mass. Lovers? Not the same as Mary and Keith. Would Jeannie be here, if it were me?

"This is the Lamb of God," the priest said, raising the host. "Who takes away the sins of the world. Happy are those who are called to his supper."

Gorman flipped hurriedly through the paperback missalette for the response. Instead of prayers, he saw the charnel house of sins that were his alone. No pretense of commitment. That was the difference between Jeannie and him and Mary and Keith. At least on my part.

And Jeannie? I never asked, just took, like the nightly mind-numbing efforts to get blasted, wasted, fucked-up.

"Lord, I am not worthy." The words rumbled from the back of his throat, each syllable tinged with remorse: "to receive you, but only say the word and I shall be healed." Gorman felt shriven of his sins.

The Kinsellas and the Consuelos walked past the coffin to the altar. Each was given a host, the body of Christ. Each then drank the wine, the blood of Christ.

Trane's sax was so mellow. Each note led into another. Human communication at its most divine. McCoy Tyner smiled as he kept chording the piano for the long solo to round out the set.

Gorman took his place in the line of communicants. He had to be with the Kinsellas in this, their most awful moment. The Act of Contrition flashed across his mind like heat lightning. He closed his eyes when he accepted the host and with deepest care put the wafer into his mouth.

"I am the living bread from heaven, says the Lord," the priest declared, looking at the congregation and up at the ceiling of his church. "If anyone eats this bread, he will live forever; the bread I shall give is my flesh for the life of the world."

The celebrant looked directly at the Kinsellas before he said firmly, "Alleluia!" When there was a response from somewhere in the church, the priest looked at Mary Consuelo and repeated,"Alleluia!"

Trane's solo ended in an elegy of Africa, the islands, America. "A Love Supreme." "A Love Supreme." "A Love Supreme."

Tyner closed the piano at the Metropole, the Vanguard, the Gate.

Close by the cemetery gate rested the backhoe that had dug Keith Kinsella's grave. Over the gravesite with the rows of folding chairs with padded seats was stretched a robin's-egg-blue canopy. All but the gaping hole in the ground seemed more appropriate for a celebration.

The honor guard was assembled. The pallbearers' final duty was brought to them when the rear door of the hearse swung open.

"Present, HARMS!" the lieutenant commanded.

The pallbearers, following the priest, walked through the guard toward the lowering device stretched across the closed earth.

"Taps" echoed through the valley from a bugler who stood under a live oak several hundred feet away. Gorman's eyes misted. He felt drained of strength, of spirit.

Three volleys from the guard rent the summer stillness. Final. Killed in action.

The young officer waited until the echoes stopped before he and a sergeant unfastened the flag from the casket. Slowly, in the precise half-speeds of the military funeral, they folded it with sharp creases.

The lieutenant held the flag, for a moment, close to his chest – for all to see, an exposition.

"For having offended you, I detest all my sins. . . . " Gorman's head resonated with the words of contrition.

The officer took measured steps toward Charlotte. When he was directly in front of her, he bowed slightly. She struggled to her feet. She'd pushed the veil away from her face and extended her arms toward the lieutenant, received the blue-starred triangle.

"Thank you," she said with the saddest acceptance.

Gorman's ears rang.

The lieutenant took one step back, saluted her. She clutched the flag to her chest.

"All rise." The priest took an incense-burning thurible from the funeral director and for the last time blessed the remains of Keith Carlton Kinsella. The casket was slowly lowered into the ground.

Ashes to ashes, dust to dust. Oh Keith, Keith, Keith. You son of a bitch.

"Mike," Kennedy tugged at his shoulder. "We oughta go."

Pat and Charlotte had already returned to the limousine with the Consuelos. Only the four airmen remained.

"Cowboy, you with me?" Kennedy asked.

"Sweet, sweet Jesus," Gorman said, staring at the hole in the ground. "I don't wanna leave him, Tom. I don't."

"Cowboy, there's nothing more we can do," Kennedy said.

"Oh my God, my God! The honor guard. Jesus, sweet Jesus." Gorman slammed his fist into the palm of his hand.

"Let go, cowboy," Kennedy ordered. "It's over." Taking Gorman by the arm, he turned him toward the cars. "Are you going to the house?"

Gorman didn't answer, slid into the car without a word.

"Mike, you want some company?" Kennedy asked.

The sergeant shook his head, then looked at the blue of his uniform with disgust.

"We're staying at the Market on Lombard, cowboy. Really man, you oughta at least stop by." Kennedy patted Gorman on the arm.

The damned uniform. That's what killed him.

"In the beginning was the Word, and the Word was with God. . . . " Keith had loved that. They'd spent an hour musing on the Gospel of John, waiting for the flight out of The World. Kinsella had been swept up in the mystery that had surrounded the church of their boyhoods.

Gorman started the car. He'd drive to Tamalpais, climb that hill and watch the fogs from the bay marry those of the ocean. For Keith.

By the time he reached the Caldecott Tunnel, he was bawling like a baby.

"For God so loved the world, that He gave us His only begotten Son. . . . "

It Ain't All Bad

LOVE, THAT'S WHAT THIS WHOLE LOUSY LIFE IS ALL ABOUT. AND I AIN'T feelin sorry for myself, not this chick, I just can't figure it out – why everybody I ever loved, man or woman, has shit on me. And maybe if I knew what was so freakin wrong with me, I'd cut my throat.

You gotta cut your throat, you know, if you're serious. When you slash up your wrists all you're doing is makin a mess for somebody else is gonna have to clean up. Which ain't too thoughtful. And then you got scars on you, showing the whole world you ain't nothing but a crybaby coward. 'Cept in the winter, when you got gloves on and shit.

Give me a cigarette? You're gonna get me talkin, I gotta smoke.

My father was a drunk, still is, even though his heart's about to pop. Now he's goin early mass every day and prayin God'll give him a second chance. Way I see it, God gave him a million second chances but he just pissed them away.

Like I should be talkin. I still got my pipe and torch behind the second drawer a my dresser. That ain't news for you to be broadcastin neither. Not that I'm plannin on usin it no more. I got it broke in nice, that's all. And it's just a comfort knowin it's there. Like the crucifix over the bed. Or havin a bagful a money somewhere.

My cousin Raymond, he says, "Destroy all paraphernalia." He says I gotta make a commitment and that the only way to do it is to start by bustin up all traces of my former life. He talks about being reborn and shit. Not like the Jesus junkies, he hates them, and he says the Church ain't nothin but a corporation. And accordin to Raymond, God's a crutch like drugs. He ain't too brilliant. God's a fact, I know. Cause he's pulled my ass out of some close freakin calls. But anyway, he used to be a druggie himself. Raymond. Speed, pot, some acid, he says – and of course: booze. Everybody in this family's got or had a love affair with alcohol. But Raymond ain't never smoked a bowl a crack in his life, and only snorted coke a handful a times. So he don't know shit when it comes to that subject.

Am I boring you?

Maybe you don't like hearin junkie-talk, maybe you're too squeakin freakin clean to be sittin there listenin to somebody who don't live up in Northpoint Bay with all them trees and country clubs and shit, and all your fancy-ass parties. Well, I know all about your parties. I know a lot a shit you never will. More than one rich dude up in Stuck-upsville wanted dates with yours truly.

Here, take your cigarette back, phht.

You people make me sick. You people only got money — you ain't got no more love than any a the losers out there in the street. Only difference is, they'll cut your heart out if they get a chance — for your ring or your watch or five stinkin bucks. That's reality. I know, I been there.

Shit. I'm outa here. Why should I pour my guts out with you givin me them looks like I was covered with AIDS? Huh? I ain't, by the way. My father made me get tested, and I ain't, cause God has been watchin over my ass.

You're probably makin eighty bucks an hour sittin there. Hell, I should be a shrink — how do I get started?

Nah, I'm just toyin with your head. I don't want to be no shrink. Bet I'd be a good one though. I know how to sit back and take it all in. And I'm very understandin too. I don't go judging no books by their cover, like mosta the good citizens.

I'm gonna put just-the-edge a my boot on your desk. I like to be comfortable where I'm at, that's all. It ain't no disrespect to you or your office. Thanks, you're a sweetheart, darlin.

You know what I want? You know what I really want? — hell, if you're makin that much money offa listenin to me, I'm gonna make you hear the whole story: it ain't all bad. I want a coffee shop.

Yeah, a coffee shop. Your type's into the fine-dining bullshit. Well, I'm sure you pass by one now and then. There's a nice one down on Beacon Street, by the railroad station, right next store to a Fat Lady Boutique. Well, I'd like to get one just like it — or buy that one off the old woman that owns it. I can get up early, no problem. And I'd be fixin coffee for all the stiffs in suits like you and jokin and flirtin with the carpenters that came in. Butter some rolls, scramble some eggs, fry a little bacon, sausage. That's my big dream. Gigantic, ain't it?

And you wanna know somethin sick? The money I made sellin

coke and my ass, and just stealin it – I coulda bought that place ten times already. And what do I got? Three years probation. And you.

Hey, I'm sorry, okay?

You ain't so bad, least you listen.

Most people don't want to hear shit, especially if it can't help their bank accounts. All they do is babble. Everybody in this town is walkin around starvin their ass off for somethin. But do they talk about it? Nah, they just smile their shitty faces off and talk shit until they're so freakin bored they don't know what they want. Then they go to the mall, and buy somethin. Or to Blockbuster. Sad-ass people all running to Rent-a-Life.

That's why I liked Pauline. Pauline was deep. Did two and a half years of book-work at Northpoint College. Psychology. History. English – and she could talk real good too. She used to say "The world's a storm, and we're all gonna die. So get high, get by, and stay warm." Yeah. How many people you know can come up with shit like that? She wasn't the first woman I slept with neither, but she was the best. Pauline could love. I'm makin you hot, aint I? You men all love that shit – two women gettin it on. But you wanna know why we get it on in the first place? Cause men kick our freakin hearts out, that's why. Every man I ever was with, every one, cheated on me. I gave 'em all the sex they wanted, I babied them, cooked, cleaned up, wiped the puke off their chins, and forgave their asses every time they busted me in the eye – and they all cheated on me.

Pauline did too.

That hurt my heart, after all I did for her. I mean, I was a slave in that house. And I was always the one deliverin too. Always my ass on the line. She wasn't using me though. That woman loves me – you hear what I'm saying?

I remember this one time I was meetin this guy with a black Mustang. That's all I knew, a beard and a black Mustang, in the parkin lot back a Macy's. I'd been drinkin my ass off all afternoon and left the house without it, just plain forgot it. Only I didn't realize that until I was staggerin across the litter toward this guy in a leather leanin against his shinin, black machine. I walked right up to him and said, "You ain't gonna believe this, but I forgot somethin."

Guess who turned out to be a cop?

And he wasn't buyin my story neither.

Him and his partner shoved me in the car and drove up one of them dead-ends around Highland Avenue where all the factories are.

Made me strip and checked me all over. Tore up my clothes searchin the linin. Fuckin cops. Pardon my French. Some cops got their own laws, you know what I mean? One's screaming at me. The other's saying, "Come on, honey, cooperate. My partner's an animal, and I can't control him." Lame. And meanwhile I'm handcuffed, standing in the street, naked in the damn drizzlin cold. And the one keeps saying, "You're goin to jail, bitch, you know that, don't you?"

I said, "Do what you gotta do, officer."

They hate that when you say that. It's like spittin in their face with a smile. You know, I woulda been a ideal prisoner. Like in a war. All they'd get outa me would be a name, rank, and number – and not even the real name. Hell, I got a million names. And a million different looks too.

Anyway, they kept me standing out in the cold while they smoked cigarettes and listened to the radio and told jokes and shit and laughed like a couple a freakin clowns. But I kept sayin the Our Father over and over to myself. And they finally let me go. I couldn't believe it. They just threw my ripped-up clothes at me and split.

Pauline said later she knew somethin musta gone sour when I hadn't come back, so she put shade on everythin – stashed it all behind a secret panel we got in a wall a the basement.

But they never showed at the house.

I guess they knew they blew it.

I'm startin to think Pauline mighta known that guy mighta been a cop. I'm not sayin she took a chance with my ass. All I'm sayin is that Pauline knew I'd never rat. I can keep my mouth shut, that's a fact. But I got a little tape recorder, and about ten of those tiny tapes up in my father's attic behind the Christmas tree. I got admissions to bank rob'ries and a million drug deals and all kinds of shit, all on tape. And if anythin ever happens to my ass, Long Island's finest are gonna have hours a pure listenin pleasure. But I ain't a rat. I know how to keep my mouth shut. That's why I got friends in all walks a life.

They got her, Pauline, eventually, and she's gonna be doin some time at the farm. Seven years accordin to the sentence, but you know she ain't gonna do more than two. I keep prayin for her early release. I miss her, she's my bud. Riverhead ain't that bad though, from what I heard. Just a place to pass the time and plan your future. Hell, I'd rather be in jail than a nuthouse.

I was in one, you know.

No, it ain't in your records. They don't know about that. They signed me in Jane Doe. And I wasn't crazy neither. I was saner than I ever been the night they drove me up that long creepy lawn.

It started at this bar. Truth is, I was lookin to get laid. Nothin wrong with that, men do it all the time. But when it's a woman, bang, right away she's a slut. I just felt like bein with a man again. Nobody did it for me though. One guy with a Harley was pretty hot – bikes really turn me on – but he left with some sleaze-bucket blond chick, and that was that. I was gettin ready to split, and this kinda fat guy comes over, asks me if I want to get high. I told him I didn't smoke no more. Pot just makes you stupid, that's a fact. And he says, "No, lady – coke." Well, I ain't never turned it down, any form, any time. So we go out into the parkin lot to toot it off the trunk of his car, only he's parked by the bushes and the minute we get there his hands are grabbin me – rough, where hands should only be gentle. I punched his face and he punched back, like a brick. That's why I'm missing these teeth back here. And then he was on me, tearing away. I said, God, you ain't gonna really let him do this to me, are you? And then I got the idea to give up. He let go, but I could still feel his paws all over me.

"Do what you gotta do," I told him, and he ripped down my pants.

But while he was whippin down his own, I pulled the knife out my boot, and the asshole dove on it. Just dove on it. Then he staggers back into the bar, bleedin from his fat stomach, and before I even got all my clothes on right, the whole bar's in the parkin lot, like a mob. I thought they was gonna crucify my ass.

Somebody called the troops, and they come a course. The cops are always there when you don't need them no more – ever notice that? And the scumbag who tried to rape me said I'd stabbed him and tried to rob him. Four a his friends said they saw the whole thing. "She's fuckin crazy," one kept screamin. Pardon me – just telling you what was said.

And I said, "Yeah? You see any knife? You see any blood on me?"

Sometimes I got the gift of sayin the worst thing at the worst time. I looked down and his blood was on me like an abstract paintin. The cops put their flashlights to work, and found the knife in the bushes, and five dime vials. And they dragged my ass away.

I had no. I.D. on me – never do – and I wasn't about to hand over my name and end up havin a primo Dad-and-Mom scene. And then another one with Dad, later. And I sure as hell wasn't gonna tell them I lived at Pauline's. So they took me to Pilgrims Park!

You want to talk about scared, I was shittin. Man, that place is a whole 'nother horror-show. I started praying the minute I saw them creepy buildings, and I never stopped. Hail Marys, Our Fathers, Acts of Contritions, the works.

If you ever ever ever go crazy, blow your brains out before you let anybody lock you up in that hotel.

Took me seven months to get out. And by then I was so blown away on whatever they kept feedin me all day I almost didn't want to leave. I sure as hell didn't know who I was. They were callin me Jane, and I was comin when they called.

The Greek got me out.

That's a very powerful guy I know. Let's just say him and your upstanding mayor share some shit in common. Anyway, The Greek got word somehow that I was in loony lock-up land and he pulled some strings. Somebody got paid a ransom to leave all them doors open, you can bet your hour's salary on that. My file disappeared too. I'm a genuine American mystery. And I will do anythin for that man, any where, any time.

I made the offer plenty a times after that, but he wasn't interested no more. When I was fifteen, I was his little princess. I know, it's corny, but that's what he always called me. And he even bought me stuff—jewelry, you know. I don't have any of it now though. Sometimes you sell even the sentimental stuff.

Guess I got too old for him.

Hell, I'm only seventeen—you'd think I was an old lady on my last breath or somethin.

The Greek wasn't no pervert neither. He never did nothin that hurt me, and I never had to hurt him. There's some real sickos walkin around, case you don't read the paper. And from your parta the universe too. Scary. Makes me shake just thinkin about it. All The Greek wanted was to love and be loved. The only part I didn't like about him was he was always sayin I reminded him a his daughter. I guess that's why he bailed me out of that hell-hole though.

You know, you're only the third person I ever told that too. Guess I trust you. And I ain't a easy person when it comes to trustin. I told Pauline, a course, even though she'd got it off the street the day after it happened. And I told Raymond last week when he took me to dinner.

Howard Johnson's.

Hate to say it, but Raymond's got zero class.

He's an actor—an artist, he keeps sayin—and he's just waitin for his big break. Personally, I think half these stars get their big breaks on their knees on somebody's carpet somewhere. But Raymond says he's gonna make it—he's got all this positive-thinkin shit going for him. Hey, maybe he will. You got all kinds a people out there makin millions—actors that can't act, lame-ass rock bands. Land a opportunity, right? Maybe he will get his mug in the movies. And then I'm gonna hit him up for a little loan and get me a coffee shop. Not too big, I ain't greedy. Just one like that one downtown. And he'd do it, Raymond. He's a generous type. Not too brilliant, but pretty generous when he's got it. He's all right. He loves me, I think. He said so.

Hard to tell sometimes who does and who don't.

To tell you the truth, I think Raymond always wanted to get into my pants. When we were kids we used to play this game at all the family parties. Got-You-Last, we called it. When the parents were getting ready to leave, we'd run around the rooms, taggin each other and sayin, "Got you last." It was fun, you know, kidstuff. And then the tags started being in excitin places. Which was kinda fun too. My mom and his would always be trying to cut it short on us though. Both Catholics, and to a true Catholic anythin sexual is truly perverted.

Shit, I'd a been burned at a thousand stakes by now if I was born in another century.

Anyway, I liked it a lot, so did Raymond. "Where are they, where are they?" they'd be sayin, and we'd hide under a bed or real close together in a closet.

Never did nothin though.

I tried to show him my tattoo once, before he got engaged. I was shitfaced, and when I turned around and told him to undo the backa my gown, he chickened, said, "I don't know if we should." Like I was offerin him some free feels or somethin.

We were at my cousin Darcy's weddin then. I ended up makin out with this cute redheaded fireman down in the basement where me and Raymond just were. A married one, which I regret, but he didn't say nothin about no wife. I thought maybe she was somebody else's date—cause I don't go bustin up no marriages. That's a sin, big-time. Well, my father hunted me down. My father, my father. My father's been guard-doggin me since the day I could walk. And it ain't done nothing 'cept to make me hate him.

I don't hate my father. I just said that. Honor thy father and mother, that's like number three in the big ten. I love my father. Everybody loves their father. You ain't natural if you don't.

Anyway, he comes down, roaring like God Almighty Himself and the next thing I know they're beatin each other's brains out and I'm gettin into it and — boom — busted nose. That's why I got this hump here. Thanks a lot, Dad. I left the place cryin, my shiny blue gown all ripped to shit.

I looked beautiful in that gown before that. And I got the pictures to prove it. I'll bring them next time, you'll see. I can still turn a certain man's head, and I know it too. Some a the flicks though ain't so great, like the ones where I'm laughin too loud, cause it shows where I'm missin them teeth. That's why if you see me smile when I'm straight, I kinda put my hand up in fronta my mouth.

Raymond thinks I'm hot.

He told me, said I was "a beautiful woman." I ain't convinced he means it — I see beautiful all the time in magazines and TV — but it made me feel good when he said it. And it's nice to have somebody say it and not be handing you a twenty dollar bill.

Raymond.

I don't know how he did it. Got clean, I mean. He said he didn't go to no treatment or AA or nothin. And you know for shit-sure he didn't go to no priest — which is gonna be his downfall, if you ask me. Just beat it himself. That's strong. I never thoughta him as strong before, but if he's been straight for five years like he says he has, he's a freakin Hercules. How'd he do it?

He's married now, and his wife's pure gold. Sweet, pretty, and she don't know the first thing about drugs. How he hooked her, I'll never know. Raymond ain't too cute no more. He took a beatin. I told him if he ever cheats on her, I'm gonna cut his heart out. Cause he's got real love there, and that's what this whole lousy life's all about. He's lucky. And don't you know he knows it too. Damn straight, he does.

I kinda hated him for a while.

Yeah.

He stopped comin to all the family reunion bullshits and left me sittin there with all the uncles and aunts and goody cousins who were going to college and makin somethin a themselves. That pissed me off, and I told him so at Ho Jo's. He said he stopped goin because he was strung out and felt inferior all the time. Well, where did he think I was comin from? I was a freakin Martian with the family. Specially around Elizabeth and Darcy. They were your kind, at least they thought they were, all uppity and dressed like yuppies – like they were from Rockerfellers or something instead of this half-hick bunch of Irish boozers we all are. Yeah, they sipped their little white wine spritzers, made their jokes about my clothes, my hair. Hey, this is how I am. You like it, fine. You don't, fuck off.

Sorry.

But the worst part a every party was my father's dirty looks. He'd start giving me one a his famous hard stares that lasted forever. Right in front of everybody. It was embarrassin. Even if he wasn't smackin me around no more, he was beatin my heart out with them stares a his.

My old man's a builder, by the way, and business is picking up again, case you didn't notice. The economy's goin down the toilet, but everybody wants to live on Long Island. You know, you got your water, you got your malls, you got the city, all your culture shit.

Give me another cigarette? Thanks. I'll pay you back.

I don't like talkin about my father, okay?

The only thing I'll say is that if I ever had a kid, I ain't gonna do no number on her like my father did on me. but I don't expect I'll ever get to play Mommy anyhow. Last abortion I had, the doctor told me I prob'bly wasn't gonna be able to have kids. That's abortion for you. And I'm here to tell you, if there was ever somebody who'd be a good goddamn mother, you're looking at her.

That's what landed me in this chair, you know – getting pregnant.

It was dry. Pauline's man had got shot in Southampton. Some clammers found him. Floatin in the water. Somebody made off with a shitload of Colombia's finest that night. And it was dry, dry. Me and Pauline got so sick we couldn't even touch each other, it was like the slightest touch or bump was agony. Withdrawal's a bitch, believe it. I was losing lunch a lot but I just chalked that up to the shakes. Then I realized my nipples hurt, and that's when I knew.

I couldn't go to Social Services cause they make you give your name and prove it. And now, with all them passionate Catholics holdin up their pickets and coercin their congressmen – didn't think I knew that word, did you? Yeah, well, with all that goin down, I don't even know if you can get an abortion outa the Social Service clowns no more. And doctors ain't doin their good deeds for free. Which means I had to get rich in a hurry.

The Catholics are right, by the way. Abortion's a crime against God. And I know I'm gonna have to face the Lord and my two snuffed-out babies some day. I know it, and that's why I pray for them every night, Nathan and Jeremy, but I just couldn't bring them into all this shit, and strung out right in the incubator. I'm sorry, but I was willing to face God for it, still am, and I think when the time comes and I explain it to Him, He's gonna cut me some slack. Besides, like The Man said, when the big court appearance rolls around, the high ones are gonna take a major fall, and the low ones are gonna get exalted. I'm countin on that exalted shit.

But there I was, pregnant, again — and I had to do somethin. And quick, because the longer you wait, the bigger the sin gets. I wasn't about to start walkin the streets and hangin out in the bars, smilin at the greasy mechanics with their wallet's stuffed full of Friday's paycheck. I'm sorry, but it ain't right for a woman-with-child to have to go that low.

And I didn't know the first thing about hot-wirin a car. But I knew a guy who wanted a Lincoln Continental. White, if possible. So I stood around in the mall parkin lot one day and when I saw this lady pullin the keys outa her purse, I asked her how to get to the Post Office. I had an envelope in my hand with stamps on it and everythin like I was mailin somebody a message — maybe you know this already — and inside: a flat sheeta iron. I was shakin like a storm, but when she leaned towards me and pointed over my shoulder, well, that's when her lights went out. And then, just my luck, I had a miscarriage the next freakin day. Cried my eyes out. Another baby gone. But I should be grateful, cause that's one less mark against me in the book.

Thank God that lady only had a tiny concussion. Shit, I coulda turned her into a vegetable. And there ain't many people good enough to love a woman on wheels. I regret it. I really do. I want to pay her back somehow. I told Father Pete how sorry I was, and I wrote her a letter — you know that part. And since she was a Catholic too, well, that's how I got this deal, probation and you.

And you ain't cheap.

My father's shovelin out some major money for this shit. And he's being sued from a couple different sides on accounta some houses he built that ain't standin. Which ain't doin his heart too good neither. So you better cure my ass, you hear?

Only kidding.

That's what he said.

I don't want to talk about my father no more. That subject is officially closed.

What was I talkin about before? Raymond. Yeah, he took me to dinner. Said I could have anythin I wanted, but that he wouldn't pay for no drinks. He won't give the poison to nobody ever again, he says. I told him – lyin through my teeth, a course – that I didn't really drink no more, didn't care for it no more. He said, "Really?!" His forehead was wrinkled all the way up to his bald head – he lost all his hair to speed.

Anythin that gets you up does that to you, speed, coke. Hell, my hair ain't as thick as it used to be. Even in them weddin pictures I told you about you can see it was curlier, and more of it. But I ain't gonna be bald, I'll tell you that straight out. Losin teeth I can handle – if you hit the numbers or somebody croaks and leaves you some cash, you can always get a dentist to fix you up. But if I ever end up bald, like I had cancer or somethin', that's when I sit in the old man's garage with the car running. Serious. Aint nobody gonna love a woman without hair, not in this world.

Being bald don't bother Raymond too much. You know who he kinda looks like now? James Taylor. Not really, but the way James Taylor looks old and kinda skeletonlike in the face. He did some dope, that man, and you don't have to be Magnum P.I. to figure it out neither. I can always tell somebody who's been through it, they look like maybe they did time as a hostage someplace.

Anyway, Raymond was so excited, I had to keep it up about how I didn't drink no more or do crack or coke or even smoke pot, which, like I said, I don't. Truth is, I didn't know what to say to him. He'd been in California for years tryin to bust into the movies, and all he'd got was a commercial where he said, "Honey, my life is completely complete now that I have a Lawn-wiz lawnmower." I was embarrassed for him, it was one of the lamest ads I ever saw, and I guess the American public wasn't buyin it neither, cause it didn't stay on the tube too long. Raymond said he came back to New York to give it another shot here. He kinda popped into my face outa the blue. Maybe my mother called him, told him to talk to me, who knows? Raymond to the rescue. So I told him I was clean, and he bought it.

"That's great," he kept saying, "You can do it, just get mad at it, hate it for all it's done to you, for all the misery and shit. Use your anger, blah, blah, blah."

And I do hate it, but I love it too, if you know what I mean.

I told him about my coffee shop and he got all excited about that. That's why I mentioned it to you.

He said it was exactly what I needed, a life-goal. He calls it a goal, I call it a dream. He said he wanted to be my first customer, and a regular. That kinda made me feel good, you know. But he's a vegetarian — what am I gonna give him? A bagel? Maybe a bran muffin, half a grapefruit.

I see you lookin at your watch there. I guess my fifty minutes is up — yeah, I can take a hint.

Hey, it's okay. I'm kinda tired a blabbin anyway.

Never had nobody like me, did you?

Thanks for listenin to all a my sick shit. I love you for it, serious, I love you.

Give me a couple more cigarettes for the road? I'll pay you back. You can bank on my word.

Love, that's what this whole country's spinnin out of control for — don't have nothin to do with drugs.

Thanks, God bless.

You remember I said that. Maybe you'll write a book some day about words a wisdom from waste-cases, and you can quote me on it. No names though. Names don't matter. Just call me the one that believes in God and love.

Same thing, you know.

My father's got a sign made outa yellow yarn in his office that says that: God is love.

Kind of funny though, comin from him, Mr. Slap-Happy.

Is that love, huh, is it? — smackin your kid around because she didn't make the bed or because you get it stuck in your head she's back-talkin you? I don't think so, no. And you know what I wanna know? How come every man I end up with turns out just like him? Am I a magnet for shit? All I ever wanted, from anybody — I swear, anybody — beautiful, ugly, stupid or Einstein — was a little bit a love. And I've got it inside to give back, ten, twenty, a hundred times as much. That's all this lousy life is all about. And maybe my life has been nothin but shit, and still is, and maybe I hurt some people, but I spill it all in confession, and I'm still praying my heart out, and the world is gonna turn for me. It ain't all bad, it can't be. And I'm gonna have that fuckin coffee shop, you can bet your ass on that.

Darcy Cummings

Where We Searched
for the Fathers

In the lapsed doors of neighborhood saloons,
where gray men tilted to the flickering
square, to the man whose words were easy
as the belly beneath his canvas apron.
His face floated in half light and the smell
of wrapped pipes and spilled beer.
We searched the uneasy eyes of the neighbor
whose sandpaper face claimed our faces,
and we made a pact against him. It was
Holy Week, we rode our bikes out
Seventh Street to the Polish church
and stood before Pulaski's donated casket,
stunned by the polished white limbs
of the dead Christ. The rules and fasting
forced a lightness through our bones
and our hands were floating before us,
we were giddy with sacrifice, trying
to understand the language of men, which was
Polish, and Italian. The heavy vowels
and consonants dragged them to the factories,
to the clumsy early morning bouts with furniture,
to one hour of remorse on Sunday under the eyes
of the beefy priest who offered bread and wine
to the old God above the altar, the God
who would desert us for one small sin
of our bodies. We were searching
for the fathers in the men around us,
while across the wide center aisle,
rows of their sons watched us, baffled
by the Virgin and the saints, and their mothers,
by the search they had begun together.

My Father, Standing at
a Snowy Bus Stop

My father, standing at a bus stop in winter,
tries to forget his numb feet, to forget
the broken stove, the smell of Clorox and diapers.
He has pocketed his smeared glasses, so the red blur
blinking through the haze is only the stove's erratic
pilot, not a sign: Joe's Bar, Schlitz Beer.
He turns away and concentrates on his sleeve,
on each individual snow flake, as I wait for him,
as I turn the pages of his book,
Seven Keys to the Kingdom, the litany
of words falling away, melting on the page
like snow on sweating windows. My brother
mows down his tin soldiers, Ka-bloom, Ka-bloom,
Nazis, Japs, going up in a cloud the size
of Philadelphia, ashes falling on the crowded
bedroom, on my father, whose bus is late,
and who knows the red glow in the distance
is not the welcome blink of the bus, salvation
in a wheeze of fumes and headlights, the familiar
rumble and pok-pok of New Jersey transport.
Asleep at last, the baby mouths the red nipple
that is only memory, the cracked, sore breasts
dried, then swollen, waiting for his rival.
My sister rises and falls in a fever, safe
because she is his favorite, her black hair
and sweaty, sweet neck pulling him home,
the red daze of her fever in his pocket,
jingling on his keys. My mother dreams
of the baby pushing against her ribs.
The words begin to blur: Protect us from
temptation . . . from weakness . . . from the numb

chill of our ribs. Prayers and promises
falter beneath the seductive quilts, the slow
sigh of my brother asleep with his armies.
My father, standing in the snow, shivers
and turns away from the bus, pulled to
the sign that promises comfort,
friendship, a kind of prayer.

Speaking with My Father

When he came home late, stumbling on the stairs,
boozy and penitent, money crumpled
in his hands, I'd stay in my room,
heart clanging like the corner alarm box.
Sometimes, sitting drunk at the table,
he tried to stutter about love and give me
a half-dollar, but I'd pull away.
Sober, he simply watched me, or spoke
through someone else: "Tell your sister:
pass the potatoes," or "Tell your daughter:
be in on time." We spoke so long through silence
that even now without medium or table rapper,
fragments of conversation come back to me.
Once I walked up Seventh Street,
forbidden short shorts rolled high on my legs,
pancake makeup and gooey mascara
melting in the July sun. Suddenly,
on a workday afternoon, he was
walking toward me. I thought he'd beat me
in front of the guys on the corner
but when they began to whistle and call,
"Hey, honey," he simply stared at me
then looked away. That night I heard him say
to my mother, "If she gets pregnant —
out she goes." When I got my first pay
(I was sixteen, the noise of frantic machines
clattered in my head) I put money
on the table and said, "Tell him:
Now I come and go as I please."
That night I didn't get home until four A.M.
A car screeched from the curb.
He was sitting at the kitchen table

looking at the three five-dollar bills
curled in the circle of the pull-down light.
He said nothing.
Frightened by his crumpled shoulders
I stumbled up the stairs, wanting to take the money back,
or give him my whole pay.

Maureen E. Rogers

At the Lake

TESS ROWED AT A STEADY PACE, A NEAT CHEVRON CUTTING THE water behind her boat. At 7 A.M. the day promised to be sultry once again. Hazy, hot, and humid, the forecasters said. Hell-like, horrific, hideous, Tess added. She hated this weather, the boring way that everyone talked about it. Every night on the news there were interviews with farmers who shook their heads and held up dried, crumbling husks of corn. At mass each Sunday, they prayed for rain, like pagans, Tess thought. The parish was mostly farmers, joined for the summer by people like Tess's family, out from Chicago to their cottages on Green Lake.

From Tess's side of the lake, there was no easy way to get to the Green Meadows Lodge, where she was working as a maid for the summer. By road, it was most of the way around the lake. Until you got near the hotel itself, the roads were terrible – dark and rutted, so narrow that, if another car came by, you had to pull off into blackberry brambles that swiped in through the passenger window, or onto the soft mossy shoulder.

Anyway, Tess hardly ever got the car. She'd only had her license for a few months, and her parents never let her drive, except to run errands or go to church. Most days, she rowed to Green Meadows. The boat was heavy and wooden. Early in the summer, Tess had painted it a violent lime green, trimming it with a chain of day-glow pink flowers, and to irritate her father, a peace symbol and a marijuana leaf. Not that he knew what marijuana looked like.

Tess pulled in under a tent of weeping willows at the edge of a deserted camp. There was time to smoke half a joint. She lit the joint with the Zippo she had filched from her father's dresser when he quit smoking. Inhaling deeply, she held her breath, then exhaled, expelling twin plumes of smoke from her nostrils. She smoked grass the same way she smoked cigarettes. Most of her friends held the smoke in until the last second, exploding it from their mouths. They claimed that Tess couldn't possibly get high, the way she smoked. But it wasn't true. She liked the mild buzz, the slight disorientation that a few tokes gave her. The way it calmed her down. The way it made things seem less important.

It was cool and still. Most of the lake was still asleep. Gradually, the quiet would be pushed out by the whine of motor boats, the shrill cries of children, the boat wakes slapping against the piers. Tess thought about her work at Green Meadows. Although she hated housework at home, Tess liked her job cleaning rooms at the hotel. She liked the company of the other girls, as they sat smoking and chatting in the steamy, bleach-smelling laundry room where they gathered to pick up clean towels and sheets. The other girls were mostly from the town, trying to make a little extra money during the summer season. She liked the talk about husbands and boyfriends, the raucous, bold way women talked when there were no men around.

"And he asked me to you-know-what," Sharlyn said. "And I told him, not in this lifetime, buster."

The girls all laughed. Tess, too, although she was not sure what they were talking about.

"Don't knock it. At least you can't get pregnant that way," Bobby said.

They all shrieked.

That was it Tess thought. French. BJ. 69.

"Let's not shock our little friend here."

They knew that Tess was still a virgin. Girls had ways of knowing. Tess was only seventeen, but some of the girls at the hotel had been pregnant by then. They knew all about Tess's boyfriend. He was going to be a priest, so they couldn't do anything. She told them about the Miraculous Medal he wore pinned to the underside of his jacket lapel, there to protect him from "getting carried away." When Tess talked about Larry, she used a phony, exaggerated voice, pretending that she was horny and he wouldn't even French kiss. She talked about finding a new boyfriend. Tess felt disloyal to Larry, even as she was talking about him, ashamed at the mean way she was betraying her friend. But she seldom had much to share with the others, and she liked making them laugh about her dates with Larry. "Father L," they had started calling him. "Larry Libido."

The other maids were nineteen or twenty to Tess's sixteen. Two or three kids apiece, already, some of them. They wore their hair in stiff bonnets, set each week at Al's Golden Chateau. Tess wore her hair long and straight. It was a soft taupe, but she had dyed a defiant streak the color of margarine across the front.

"You look cheap, for chrissakes," her father ranted when he saw it. "I can't stand to look at you. My own daughter. You look like a street walker."

Good, Tess thought, although she cried when he yelled at her. Afterwards, she locked herself in the bathroom and stared at her reflection in the mirror, sucking in her cheeks. Cheap. Good. Everyone knew cheap meant sexy.

The other maids called her "our little hippie," but they liked Tess. She baby-sat for two of them, Kay and Sharlyn.

Tess glanced at her watch. Running late, she quickly wrapped the remainder of her joint in tin foil and shoved it in the cloth sack she had nailed under the seat board.

By the time work ended, a menacing thunderhead, the color of a bruise, filled the afternoon sky.

"You better not go out on the lake," Sharlyn told her. "I'll give you a lift home."

Tess shook her head, no. There had been other threatening clouds, on other afternoons, and nothing ever came of them. If she rowed straight home, she could beat the storm, if it even happened at all.

"You sure, hon?" Sharlyn asked again.

"Thanks, I'll be fine."

As she set out across the lake, the lightning started, luminous bolts that shattered the sky. Thunder rumbled closer. Tess was frightened. It was foolish to have tried to row home. She turned for shore, pulling in at Wolfie's Tavern and Picnic Grounds. The people on the beach were scrambling to their cars, mothers grabbing baskets, blankets, thermos jugs, yelling to their kids to pick up their shovels and pails, their inner tubes.

The clouds broke, sending sheets of rain down, just as Tess made it into the tavern. She had been in Wolfie's lots of times. Elmer Wolfe sold bread, popsicles, milk watered down to a strange blue color. It was creepy going into Wolfie's, although it hadn't been when Tess was little and she was sent to pick up something for her mother. Now the men hunched at the bar called things out, "Hey, girlie, we were just wondering whether them shorts are painted on or tatooed."

Once, a man asked her if she was one of the bra-burners, and Tess looked down to see that, although she had a bra on, her nipples were clearly visible through her thin T-shirt. She blushed and left quickly, forgetting her change from the dollar she had laid on the counter for the loaf of bread.

Fishing a dime from her pocket, Tess called home. Her father answered the phone. Damn, Tess thought. She had forgotten that he was coming out early for a long weekend. When her father was home, there was always friction, fighting. Things her mother was too busy to notice, or chose to ignore, her father picked on. What Tess was wearing, where she was going. "I just wanted you to know I'm stuck at Wolfie's until the storm stops. I'll walk from here."

Her father began to yell. "I can't believe that you were stupid enough to try to row home in this mess. I figured you'd have enough brains in your head to just wait it out. Guess I figured wrong." Tess held the phone away from her ear, her father's words still sharp and distinct. "You could have been killed, for crying out loud." Her father stopped for a breath. "Your mother says bring home two cans of tomato soup."

"Yeah." Tess answered. "See you."

Tess went up to the counter, asked Elmer for the soup, and paid him. "I'm taking a Coke, too." She left the soup on the counter, and crossed the floor to the ice chest for her Coke. There were a couple of tables by the window, and Tess sat at one, pulling the dingy checked curtain back to watch the storm. Wolfie's parking lot had turned into a pool. At the border of the lot, the poplars were bending in the wind.

"They kind of look like they're touching their toes, don't they?"

Tess looked up to see a man standing there, holding a nearly empty beer bottle, swaying it back and forth like a metronome. He was maybe twenty, handsome in the tough way of the young guys from town. Not clean cut, like the boys she knew from school, with their brush cuts and neat madras jackets, their pressed chinos and shiny loafers with nickels in the penny slots.

He had dirty blond hair, slicked back at the sides and curling from the top into a funnel than fell into his eyes. He had green eyes, the color of the lake, and eyelashes that her girlfriends would say were wasted on a guy. He was wearing jeans and a navy blue T-shirt. A pack of Luckies was sticking up from the breast pocket.

"Do you mind?" he asked, gesturing to the seat opposite Tess.

"It's a free country," she said, more sharply than she intended. She had meant it to sound light, sophisticated.

"You're the girl who rows. I seen you out there everyday."

Tess took a swallow of her Coke. What was there to say? "That's me."

"Pretty scary out there today, huh?" He was looking at Tess with a faint smile.

"Not that bad."

"Then I'd say you're the type of girl who likes to live dangerously."

Tess watched him as he took the final pull on his beer. It was a little scary, sitting there in Wolfie's talking to this man, but thrilling. She never talked this way with the boys she knew. It was always about what college to apply to, and who you knew from Queen of Peace or Saint Matthias. She wished that she could have a beer, but Wolfie's would never serve her. The type of girl who likes to live dangerously. That was a laugh. "I guess so," Tess said. "That's me."

"Pete Seiler," he reached his arm across the table.

"Tess Breen."

Pete drew a cigarette from his pack, shaking another out to offer her. She took it, although she usually smoked filters. He steadied her hand as he lit both cigarettes on the same match. "I bet you wished this was something stronger."

Tess flushed. What did he know about her? What could he possibly know? She thought about her stash in the row boat, hoping that it did not get flooded out. "What are you talking about?"

"You know what I mean. I seen you out there, pulling into those trees. It doesn't take no genius to figure things out." He leaned back in the booth, grinning. "Is your shit any good?"

"Pretty good. I get it in the city." *You're crazy,* Tess told herself, *don't say anything more. He's probably an undercover cop.*

"Maybe someday you'll share your little stash with your friend Pete."

It took Tess a moment to realize he was talking about himself. She glanced out the window, the sun was coming out. "I've got to get going."

"I'll give you a lift."

"That's okay. I'll walk."

"Well, then I guess I'll take a rain check."

He walked Tess to the edge of the parking lot, then took her elbow and turned her toward the water. A full rainbow arced across the lake. "Bet you don't see many of those down Chicago."

She shook her head.

"I'll be seeing you, Tessie."

She walked a bit, then turned to see if Pete was still standing there, half hoping that he had disappeared. He was leaning up against a car, arms folded, a Lucky dangling from the side of his mouth. He raised his hand, giving her a mocking wave. "Bye-bye."

She had gotten a few more yards before she realized she'd forgotten the soup. Embarrassed, she walked back into Wolfie's, but Pete was already gone.

Three days later, as she was rowing home from work, Pete Seiler came by in a big outboard, circling her boat, rocking it in its wake.

"Knock it off," she yelled to him. She saw that the boat was called *The Fury*.

"Only if you'll go out with me."

"My parents won't let me. You're too old."

"My parents won't let me," Pete mocked her in an exaggerated, nasally whine. "I suppose your folks let you smoke dope and drink beer?"

She thought about what her father's reaction would be, if he saw Pete talking to her like this. She thought about Larry, and the awkward dates they had, holding hands and talking about the poetry of Gerard Manley Hopkins. She thought of the girls at Green Meadows, egging her on. "Look, there's a CYO dance this weekend at Holy Redeemer. I'm going with my girlfriends."

"I'm hardly going to go to a kids' church dance."

"It's where I can meet you."

"I'll be there." He revved the engine and spun away, leaving Tess in her rowboat, surrounded by his churning wake.

Tess's father drove Tess and her girlfriends, Barbara and Ellen, to the church hall. "Now, are you sure Ellen's dad will pick you up?"

"At eleven-thirty."

"Have fun, kids. Don't break too many hearts."

Tess leaned over to kiss her father good-bye. Why was he sweet like this, sometimes, and other times so terrible? She got out of the car, and, as her father pulled out of the parking lot, turned to her friends. They already knew the plan. "You won't tell. Swear on a stack of Bibles?"

Solemnly, Ellen signed on the front of her sweater. "Cross my heart and hope to die."

"Me, too," Barbara said. "Scout's honor. I just wish some hunky guy was after me."

Across the parking lot, Tess saw the lights come on in a black and white Bel Air. Slowly, it rolled up next to them. "Hey, girls."

"This is Pete," Tess made the introductions. "Barbara. Ellen."

Barbara grabbed Tess and pulled her aside. "He's old. I bet he's twenty-two. Are you sure you know what you're doing?" she whispered.

"He's only twenty," Tess answered. "I'm sure." She crossed in front of the car, the lights hitting her like foot lights. "I'll see you at eleven-thirty."

As Tess got into the car, she heard Ellen say, "Well, I think it's exciting."

They drove out past the town, out into the country, on two-lane blacktop roads that ran for miles, straight as rulers, through cornfield after cornfield. Pete said very little. He fiddled with the radio, trying to get a station to come in clearly, and drummed along on the steering wheel with snatches of songs that faded in and out. He sang in a toneless voice, behind the radio by a beat. He pulled off onto a dirt lane that ran through corn rows.

"I thought we were going on a date," Tess said. They had been driving for nearly an hour.

"Well, this is the date. Nice ride. Nice car. Nice girl." Pete killed the engine, turned off the lights and coasted to a halt. "But I hope not too nice." He reached in front of Tess, opened the glove compartment, and took out a bottle.

It was too dark to read the label, but Tess could see that the liquid was clear — vodka or gin.

Pete took a swig, then passed the bottle to Tess. "Dr. Seiler's Love Potion Number 9."

She tilted the bottle, taking a long swallow. It burned her throat, and seemed to go straight through her. She was like one of those baby dolls you fed the bottle to, she thought.

Pete took the bottle from her and spread his arm around her shoulder, drawing her close.

Tess felt her stomach tighten. She had made out with boys before, but no one like Pete. She thought of the tiny, bright blue Miraculous Medal in her pocketbook. She made fun of Larry for wearing one, but Tess had never gone on a date without hers. All of her friends took them on dates, pinned to their slips, on thin gold chains around their necks, slid in with the "I Am a Catholic" card in the picture fold of their wallets. What was it for? To protect you from what?

"I've got something to tell you. Don't get mad." Tess was mad at herself. She had gotten herself into this situation, half wanting it, half afraid. "I'm not on the pill." Tess pulled herself slightly away from him. She was staring straight ahead, out the window, at the road that seemed to run forever, to nothingness. "I've never done it before. Not all the way." First base. Second base, depending on how you counted.

"That's, okay. Everyone's got to have a first time. That's a fact of life."

She closed her eyes, hoping that would stop the tears from coming. *Baby*, she told herself, *cry baby. You've gotten this far.* She knew she did not want to go back, but she was not certain she wanted to go any further. She covered her face with her hands and wept.

"Jesus H. Christ," she heard Pete say.

Gradually, her crying stopped. Tess fished for a tissue in her pocket and blew her nose. "I must be a mess."

"You look fine."

Tess turned to Pete. He was not even looking at her.

They sat for a few minutes in silence. Tess wished that she had brought a joint along.

"Maybe we should go."

"Maybe we should go." He mimicked her, the same way he had that day on the lake. "Well, maybe I think we shouldn't go just yet."

Tess felt Pete pull her towards him, this time more roughly than before. He pressed his face against her, and began kissing her hard. Her face, her lips, her neck.

He pulled away and tugged her blouse out from her skirt. His hands were on her breast. "Does this feel good, baby."

"I don't know," she whispered. "I guess so." It did feel good. "Yes."

❦

It was after midnight by the time they got back to the church hall. There were no cars in the lot, no lights on in the rectory.

"My father will kill me," Tess said.

"I'd better get you home."

"My father will kill me."

❦

"Stop the car," they were nearing the road that pulled off to the Breen's cottage. "I'll walk from here."

"You sure?"

"Positive."

Pete rolled the car to a stop. A blackberry bramble scratched Tess's face and arm as she got out of the car. She walked around the front of the car, and leaned in the window to kiss Pete good-night. When will you call, she thought, but said nothing.

She heard her father before she saw him. He was coming up the road, yelling, "What the hell do you think you're doing? Don't you think I know what's going on? Don't you think I know this punk wants just one thing?" He was holding a flashlight, brandishing it like a weapon, shining it back.

"Daddy," Tess cried.

"Christ," Pete said. "He's nuts. Get in the car." Pete opened the driver side door, leaned forward, and tried to push her into the back seat. She was half in when Pete jammed the car in reverse. Stuck in the soft shoulder, the wheels spun. The car stalled. Pete tried to start it, but the engine was flooded.

Tess watched from the back seat as her father stood in front of the car, shining the light through the windshield, pounding with his fist on the hood.

"Get out of the car, Tess," her father called.

"No," Tess yelled back.

"I'm not asking you, I'm telling you."

"No."

Pete rolled up the windows, snapped the locks shut and leaned on the horn. "I hope someone calls the sheriff."

"There's no one around here to hear."

"Come out, Tess."

Pete hit the horn again.

Tess' father came around the side of the car, directing the flashlight beam onto Tess, crouched in the back seat, leaning against the front head-rest.

"Is this what you want, Tess? A big belly from this punk? Some dead-end life in this shit-hole town? Is that what you want out of life?"

Tess could hear a dog barking, an aimless yapping that stopped after a few barks. She could hear Pete's cadenced breathing, and her own. Muffled through the windows, she could hear her father's relentless question, "Is that what you want, Tess? Is that what you want?"

More, she said to herself, but made no move to get out of the car. She saw the taut muscles in Pete's neck, his tensed shoulders, his hands gripping the steering wheel. She could smell the Brylcreem in his hair. *Doesn't everybody know, I just want more.*

Hit or Miss

THE PROBLEMS STARTED AFTER MY FATHER LOST HIS JOB AND MY mother took the tap-dancing class. Every Tuesday night – the night she, in a jaunty mood, took the train from Hoboken to the Westside with her new tights and tap shoes – he called me up at college to complain. "Whatcha up to?" I said.

"Nothing." He sounded mopey.

"She's moving away from me, Jenny," he said.

"It's just a class," I said.

"It's the first class she's taken in thirty years – don't you think that's weird? I mean, the timing."

"She has talked about this for a long time, Daddy," I said. For years she'd said she wished she knew how to tap dance. Her legs were good, and people told her from a certain angle she looked like Cyd Charisse.

"It's probably not another guy, right?" he said, only half-kidding.

"Don't be ridiculous." I did think the timing was weird, though; but maybe she couldn't stand to see my father moping around the house. I didn't want to think about it, either.

"Maybe it's the tap dance instructor . . . maybe his name is . . . Maurice. Or something like Maurice. A suave name." I couldn't imagine my mother feeling sexual about anyone; although I did remember that when I was little she used to listen to "Blue, Blue, My Love is Blue" in the living room with all the lights off.

"You're just torturing yourself for no reason," I said.

It was spring. I was twenty and in love for the second time – the second made the first not count. Snow was still on the ground; I'd learned that in Chicago it never melted until it was too late – until you had forgotten all about the ground. I didn't want to think about my father. I had my own things to worry about: my classes were going badly, and my boyfriend Danny had dropped out of school. He'd lost his apartment and moved his boxes into my living room. My room-mate Elaine was not pleased about this. "It's temporary, Elaine," I stalled her. "He's just looking for another place." But Danny was not looking for another place; he had no money to do that. He had a part-time job writing class notes for the alumni magazine, but lately he'd been calling in sick a lot. I didn't want to press him about anything, but the whole thing had become – a problem.

When we met Danny was on an upswing. He was manic-depressive, but I didn't believe that at first; I thought he was just . . . special. I thought no one would ever know me so well, or like me so much. He was the first boyfriend I'd ever had who was as good as a girlfriend. We used to leave each other notes in a tree.

My godfather, Beebop Minerva, was arrested for running a chain letter ring out of Coney Island. This was after my baptism and we read about it in the papers. Beebop and my father used to work in a pool hall together in the fifties. After the arrest he moved to Montana and we never heard from him. Maybe he was sheriff. Maybe he joined the CIA. I decided he never married, though. I used to wonder about him, what he was like. I had only one picture: of my father and Beebop horsing around in a park. They were nineteen, twenty. In the photo they were pretending to be gangsters. My father was holding a fake machine gun, and Beebop was crumpling to the ground. I thought it was a great photo; the zootsuits, the cigarette dangling off Beebop's fingers. I thought what a great day that must have been, in the park, being nineteen.

My godmother, Maggie, my mother's cousin, had once been a nun. When I was younger I used to imagine that my parents would die, and that Beebop and Maggie would have to adopt me. That's the way it would happen in a movie. The judge would say, which one do you want to go with, and I wouldn't be able to decide, and so they'd have to struggle to make a go of it together for my sake. In the movie I'd be a cute kid with freckles who'd charm everyone, like Little Lord Fauntleroy. At first their differences would keep them apart; but then Beebop would come to appreciate Maggie's gentle hands and fine cooking. And his gruffness would make her feel like a real woman. They'd fall in love without even realizing it.

Before he lost his job, my father drove a hearse. This was for McNamara's Funeral Home in Hoboken. He was laid off after nineteen years because – enough people weren't dying. This was true. This was what his boss Leo told him. Leo said, Some seasons are good, Joe, and some seasons are bad. This is a bad one, he said. I knew, from my father, that winters were always a good season. More people caught pneumonia. Diseases worsened. This was the kind of thing we used to talk about at the dinner table. It didn't seem weird to me, though. It seemed like a normal job. I knew my friends' fathers did other things, but that – their jobs – just seemed more ordinary. At school if people found out, they'd crack jokes – you can imagine – but I thought they were just being silly. Someone has to do it, I'd say. I thought they were just being immature. I didn't think it was weird when my father brought home the leftover flowers from wakes. He'd say, "Here honey" – as if it were a dozen red roses – and my mother would crack up. His delivery was good. He always made her laugh which is why, I guess, things worked out.

I didn't wonder then why my father never got depressed about his work. He concentrated on the life part of it: the families he drove around, what they talked about on the way to the cemetery. What they looked like and what they were wearing. What they remembered about the person who'd died, the memories. Who cried and who didn't. He told us this at the dinner table. Sometimes I'd be moved almost to tears by the stories; my father was a good narrator. He'd amplify, and comment, and impersonate voices. He'd add humor when it was necessary. We'd all be moved to tears.

I first saw Danny at a poetry reading on campus. He got up after the main act, Nick Kass and the Creamers. All my friends wanted to sleep with Nick; one girl in my writing class even wrote a poem about him, "The Nick Blues." Nick chanted words – *evil, destruction, greed,* and so on – while the Creamers played loud punk music. There were some slides, too. Nick wore eyeliner, no shirt, a black leather jacket and silk pajama pants. Half the crowd left when he finished. Then Danny got up. He had flushed cheeks and bad skin, and his hands wouldn't stop shaking. I couldn't really follow the story. He was on a mountain somewhere, maybe Norway, and there was a girl, though maybe it wasn't a real girl but a fairy. But something about the way it was written – scrawled loopily on dirty yellow note paper – and the way he read – unevenly and passionately, with his voice making swoops – hit me. I wondered if he might truly be brilliant. No one was really listening to him; I had never seen such nervousness before. I wanted to just touch his hands.

My father had always had hobbies. He used to say the job fueled him up, gave him good material and time to think. He could drive on automatic pilot, he said. Not many jobs give you time to think, he said. It's a luxury. Mainly, when he drove the hearse around, he thought up new plot ideas. For years, since I was little, he'd been writing a series of stories – the Mickey Willis series – murder mysteries set in New Jersey. What state has more evil, hate, muck, and toxic waste, said my father. What better state for murder. Mick was "forty-ish" with "salt-and-pepper" sideburns. He was a cabdriver/detective and an ex-pro baseball player. My father used to play baseball. "You could say the guy had it all," said my father. Women loved Mickey; he'd been married three times, but he "swore never again." Each story was basically the same: Mick drove his cab to the scene of the crime (he had a shortwave radio in the cab, so he could pick up police reports), met a good-looking, dangerous sort of brunette who was somehow mixed up with the victim or the bad guys, got into trouble (car chases, deflected gunshot wounds), fell in love and solved the crime. In the end he left the brunette on a street corner and drove off in his cab. He always glimpsed her once in the rearview mirror – a handkerchief held to her eye – but he never turned back.

Over the years my father had written thirty-eight of them, all in longhand, in notebooks piled on his bookshelf. He used to ask my advice about the plots. "When I die, will you try to get them published," he always said. We didn't know where books, or movies, came from; they just appeared by some mysterious law like everything else – a kitchen table or a bottle of ketchup. Everyone we knew had a job that was only a job, and wasn't involved in the process; who were the process people?

When he was sixteen Danny spent a year in a mental hospital. His parents admitted him. This was one of the first things he told me when we met. It didn't faze me; I thought it was just a bad mistake, an accident, something that could have happened to me if things had been different. It was a hospital for what he called messed-up suburban kids in Evanston, Illinois. We used to see ads for it in the paper in Chicago. In the ad, a long-haired teenager with a bottle of beer in his hand is standing – shouting – outside a big, well-lawned house. It's night; all the lights are off in the house except one on the top floor. Heads poke out the window. The ad reads: Is this your child?

In Danny's stories, that year was always the turning point: before the mental hospital, after the mental hospital. The hospital happened after his parents' divorce, when he was living with his father and his father's new wife in Lake Forest. He didn't get along with either of them, but he couldn't live with his mother, either, because she had her own problems. Danny said he was acting crazy then, and his father didn't know what to do with him. Not crazy crazy, but wild: staying out all night and then sleeping on his best friend Peter's floor because he didn't want to go home.

In the mental hospital they let him keep a guitar, so he wrote a lot of songs. They told him he was a paranoid schizophrenic, but he didn't believe it; later they said they made a mistake, he was just a manic-depressive psychotic. He didn't believe that either. He said he never worried about being crazy then, all he worried about was being ugly. His acne was so bad that people used to stop and stare at him on the street. I couldn't believe that. "You're exaggerating," I said. "I know you were always cute." He wouldn't show me the pictures, though. "You might feel differently," he said.

I called my mother. She said your father's been bugging me about this, about the class, but it's something I want to do. She said she was fifty-eight and her legs were still good and if she didn't do it now, well – when would she? When would she? She said, I can't worry about him *all* the time.

"Will it always be like this?" I said to Danny. My apartment was on the third floor, and the leaves were always right outside the window. At night they seemed ominous, even mocking. I didn't feel twenty – a happy, free twenty – but heavy and laden and much older. The city was gray and windy and cold, and the walk to campus never seemed worth the effort. Chicago made you want to stay inside and never move. We were sinking, sure nothing would ever work out for us. We had big plans – that I would be a famous academic and he'd be a poet. But then, in bed, that all seemed ridiculous and we feared we'd never be anywhere else – that our window would always look exactly like this.

"Tell me it won't always be like this," I said.

"How's school," my father said one Tuesday.

"Okay."

"You working hard?"

"Yeah."

"You taking good courses?"

"Yeah."

"How's Danny?" he said. My parents loved Danny; they used to say they wished they could adopt him. If I was out and Danny answered the phone, my father would ask his advice about his stories, too. But then my father would complain to me later that Danny always led him astray, wanting to introduce supernatural forces and fairies to his storyline. "He doesn't really understand my style," my father would say.

I asked my father how the job search was going – this was a painful question but I felt I had to ask – and he said, "Not too great. Basically, no one wants to hire me."

"Maybe you could take a class," I said. "Now that you have all this time."

He told me that now that he had all this time, he found he was wasting a lot of it. He didn't know what the hell he did with all of it. Hobbies, he said, were only good as long as they were hobbies, and not, you know, the main thing.

"Did you ever notice that our names would be the same if you take away the first two letters?" said Danny. And our eyes were both small, and our birthday was the same, backwards. We could wear each other's clothes, and our last name had exactly the same number of letters: six.

When I was little and my friends and I played the game, "If Jesus had to kill one of your parents first, which one would it be?" it was always my father. I couldn't think of him alone; but my mother, though—I could imagine her picking out vegetables, going to church, being hardly slowed down at all. I could see her outliving plagues and wars—living, like her own mother and grandmother, past ninety-five, leaving behind husbands and brothers. But my father I imagined growing smaller. The folds on his bathrobe would multiply. His nose would loom, like an exotic bird's. He'd be eating hot dogs with no mustard—with just ketchup.

After the poetry reading I saw Danny three times on campus. Each time he stopped whatever he was doing—if he was walking with a friend on the quad, or checking a book out of the library—and stared at me. It wasn't a casual stare, I thought. It seemed significant. His eyes—which were blue and painful to watch—fastened on me in a peculiarly intense way. I wondered if he remembered me from the reading. I wondered whether, if he didn't remember me, he could detect something distinct about me that I was unaware of. I mean, it didn't seem random.

Later on, months after we'd met (casually, at a party), Danny didn't remember any of these meetings. I was furious. "You mean, you don't remember staring at me?" I felt our relationship had been based on a fraud. "What, do you just stare at everyone like that?"

"No . . . God, I don't know what to say to you," he said. "If you remember it, then I guess it happened. I'm sure I stared at you. What difference does it make now? We're together now, right?"

"It makes all the difference," I said. I was sounding whiny. "I thought you chose me, and I chose you, and that it was special. That we both somehow knew. But if only I knew that, then it doesn't matter—then it wasn't special. Then we both could have been anybody. Don't you see?"

"God, Jenny, you're getting hurt over nothing."

"I thought you were a pure starer, but you're not – you just stare all over the place."

He laughed. "God, why are you so upset?" I was upset; I practically curled into a ball on the bed.

"Okay, wait a second," he said. "I think I remember it now. I think it's all coming back to me."

"I want to be mad at you," I said. "Don't make me laugh."

When my father was nineteen, he played shortstop in the minor leagues. This was in Philadelphia. Something happened: a knee injury, or a back. That part wasn't relevant. Another time his cousin Eddie got him an interview for a job drawing cartoons for a newspaper in New Jersey; my father had some talent in that area. He was twenty-one then. Something came up. His aunt died and he had to go to the funeral. Or there was a blizzard in New Jersey that week.

"Didn't you reschedule?" I said.

"No. I can't remember why," he said.

A couple of other prospects arose over the years. They fell through. In his telling, the whys were always obscured; just the loss came through. They became myths of disappointment he held over all of us. I was still haunted by them: I told Danny about them, in bed. In my head I tried to change the facts, rearrange them into happier conclusions. I thought up new combinations of fate. If only, I thought. If only he hadn't slipped and hurt his knee. If only his aunt had died the following Thursday. "People make choices," said Danny. "There's a pattern here. Maybe he wanted to fail. Maybe it's that simple."

At night Danny told me stories of the mental hospital. Once, when he was in the bathroom stall, he heard two boys, mean boys, talking. One said, "Isn't that boy Danny ugly?" And the other said, "He's the ugliest boy in the whole ward." I had my own ugly story like that; that when I was fifteen and hurrying to my friend Margaret's house, I had to walk past a park where a rough crowd hung out. Usually I avoided it, but I was late. And though I hurried, I knew this gang of guys who had grown quiet was just watching as I walked – watching my ass and breasts move – and I prayed I'd get by before their words reached me. And then it came: Man, you are the ug-liest bitch I've ever seen. And then from another, Don't worry, honey. God loves you.

Then Danny and I hugged each other, said, no, you're beautiful. Really.

One Tuesday my father called with a new idea for a story. It was called, "Love When You Least Expect It." He said that now that he had all this time on his hands he wanted to dip into the romance genre. In the story, two car-crash victims – bandaged and bleeding internally – find love in the recovery ward.

He said, "What I want to know is – do you think it has potential? Do you think it's worth pursuing, I mean."

I told him I could see it as a TV movie.

"That's just what I was thinking," he said. "I think maybe if we could get Stephanie Powers –"

"Or Michelle Lee," I said.

"You're right – she *would* be great. She has that fragile quality – fragile but strong. And I was thinking for the guy, maybe Tony Franciosa. You know, the swaggering type but inside a softy – Michelle would catch him by surprise. You see, what I like about this," he said, "is that these two strangers fall in love before they even *see* each other. It won't be till the end of the movie that they get to take their bandages off. It's powerful. Don't you think?"

"Yeah," I said.

"But what I want to know is, how would I get something like this on TV? I mean, what's the procedure?"

"I don't know, Daddy," I said. "I don't know."

At night in our room, Danny played the guitar. The songs he wrote were usually sad – mournful, twanging songs about being alone, on the street, without a family. Some of the songs were about our breakup. Almost as soon as we started going out, he wrote songs about it. In one, years in the future, he's waiting on the sidewalk – rain pouring on his head, ten cents in his pocket – outside my office building. I stare right into his face without recognizing him. He calls my name and says, "I wish I had an umbrella so we could walk under it together for most of the night." I think he's a bum – it's been weeks since he's shaved – and tell him to get lost.

"I have never, in my entire life, said 'get lost,'" I said. "Or 'bum.' That's not the way I talk."

He was insulted when I didn't like the song. "This isn't healthy," I said. "Why do you dwell on sad things? We're happy now, right?"

In another song, "Straitjacket," he's trapped in a mental hospital, calling my name; "but you don't come," is the refrain.

"God, Danny, would you stop being so morose," I said. "Can't you write a happy love song – something peppy. Where we're running in a field together."

"When I start to feel too happy," he said, "I always get that scared feeling – that it will go away."

I didn't think it was as simple as what Danny said, about my father, about why he'd missed all his chances. I thought some people had luck or fate that was worse than others, and there was no reason to it. Like Danny or my father. Sometimes I looked at it the way my father looked at it. "You get one chance at the plate," he used to say. He always talked in baseball metaphors. "And you hit or you miss, but the game keeps going."

"We haven't had sex in two weeks," Danny said one night. "Why don't you want to sleep with me anymore?"

"It's not that I don't want to sleep with you, I'm just not in a sexual phase right now," I said, though the truth was, after eight months he was starting to feel like my brother. My mentally ill brother. We were so close and bound-up and alike, and all I could do was rub his head and want to go back in time and take away all the bad parts. It seemed somehow wrong and impure to want to sleep with him.

"You're not attracted to me," he said. "You're still thinking about Eric. Or maybe it's that other guy – Michael."

"That's ridiculous. I don't want anyone but you, Danny."

But when I tried to imagine us together anywhere else, in a future that was better or easier, I couldn't. I couldn't see anything but that room.

One Tuesday night I was busy and couldn't talk. "I don't have time to shoot the breeze with you," I said.

"I *have* to work this out," my father said. "Look — listen," he said. "If Miranov gave her the poison, would he still have time to get to Newark Airport to deliver the jewels?" Miranov was the Russian agent in the latest Mickey Willis installment.

I sighed, "I don't know, Daddy."

"Well, you must have some thoughts on it."

"I don't really have time . . . okay, maybe he has a girlfriend," I said.

"Yeah . . . "

"She's a singer at the airport lounge."

"Hold on, let me get this."

"She hides the jewels in the piano bench, and during the big number — "

"Wait, wait, I'm not getting this down."

"She has good legs — give her good legs."

"Okay, okay."

"I wish we could sleep at the same time and die at the same time," said Danny.

In the mental hospital Danny had a girlfriend named Maria. She was fourteen. They used to sneak out of their rooms at night, down the back stairs, and sleep under a tree. Or else in the kitchen — it didn't matter where. Maria had a Snoopy sleeping bag they could both fit in. Danny said if he didn't sleep with Maria, in that *exact* sleeping bag, he couldn't sleep. It was more than just longing, he said. It was greater than longing. For years after that, he had trouble sleeping. Maria was a special case: she was from a bad neighborhood in Chicago, but they let her in for free. A kind of financial aid scholarship, said Danny. Before that she'd been in the state hospital. Danny met her in the lounge — it was called the *entertainment* lounge, said Danny, even though there was only one TV. Maria sat down next to him on the couch — right next to him. There was at least six empty feet on the couch, he said, but that's where she sat. There was no one else in the room. She was beautiful, he said, and he was shy. He couldn't believe how beautiful she was. He'd never been with a girl before, not really, and especially not one this beautiful. There was Carrie Lewis in seventh grade, but that was – nothing. They'd just kissed once, no tongue. Maria took out her notebook – it was like a child's notebook, with big, girlish script. She was blowing bubble gum. He was scared. He asked her – at first his voice cracked, so he had to clear it – if the channel was okay with her. She didn't say anything. He said, Because I could change it if it's not. She was writing in the notebook, making loopy swirls with one of those pens that had five different colors of ink in it. Then she handed him a note and walked away. The note said: I think you're the cutest boy I've ever seen. I love you. My name's Maria.

My father called. He said Uncle Al had found him a job selling advertising space for the Saint Ignatius church bulletin. This was in Dumont, New Jersey. He had to commute an hour and the money wasn't great; he worked by commission. But it was a job, he said. And he could work out of the office, which was important. "Cars free your mind up," he said. "There were lots of great jobs I could have had in the past, but they just didn't give me the same freedom."

"That's great, Daddy," I said.

I used to think about other ways of meeting Danny. Before the hospital. I would've turned a corner in New York and Danny would be there. We'd be sixteen. He'd have a frisbee and we'd go to Central Park together. Or maybe I was in Evanston, and he was the boy who had the locker down the hall from me. The shy one I'd told my friends about. He didn't paste anything up in his locker except one picture, a special one. He'd been saving it for years. One day – it was late, after classes, after even the track team had gone home – we were walking down the same corridor. It must have been fall, because the light had changed; it was nearly dark already and I wondered if I'd missed the last bus. He caught up to me – it wasn't planned, but he'd been practicing.

Leaving Home

The steel door of her husband's silences . . .

There are continents, she thinks,
between the blue calm of solitude
and cold planet of mute rancor
masquerading as a different quiet.
This stillness bellows.

Late now, she repeats old motions
like the sleepwalker whose body knows
the dark scenery by heart.
So she lays good-byes like talismans
on her children's sleeping eyes,

Wills them nerve and tenderness enough
for their blonde mysteries to unravel on their own,
then turns and feels again the abstract past
like the rough and pitted jug of sand and weight
it is. And lets it go. Lets go.

But the delicate hook of marriage
lodged just beneath her throat,
the double-edged **S**-curve of family –
that fine and helpless metal,
tensile as love, as hate –

Has planted deep prongs in her,
and will tighten its clutch
with every dimming of the lights
behind her, each practiced closing
of the outside door.

Sleeping in Conor's Room

How peaceful to lie among bright dinosaurs
on a child's bed. Conor breathes his musky sighs
from the crib across the room and the striped tiger
nightlight keeps its watch nearby.

It doesn't smell like whiskey here
among these yellow ducks and other gentle animals,
no sour fog of alcohol suffocating air
as sure as any pair of hands around the neck.
No, this room is clean, exempt, and kind.

So does it smell like mother-love,
the tranquil perfume of a Norman Rockwell
summer's night?

Actually, it reeks of compromise:
the first-born son sold off to daddy's bed
and gagging snores, while mommy, like a fugitive,
chips another gold nugget

from her three-year-old's childhood,
hugging cool dinosaur sheets
in Conor and his absent brother's room.

Nosebleed Portrait Series:
Plague of Inc.'Est

1.

Commitment
& coils of silence
burn to the center
like insect repellent:

We love this son
who sleeps with his mother
in the grave
whom I hold like a heart
to my ear
who hugs me in the dark
& wraps
the herbal scent
of my freshly shampooed hair
around his face
as he kisses you:

No wonder your nose bleeds
as we watch
incredulously
a box of yellow Kleenex
wadded to roses
collapse
in a clumsy mess,
a blood-heavy bouquet
saturated,
unstaunching.

2.

Your Florence Nightingale
for a moment

we witness me
hurl a chair
from over my head.
We leave the smithereens
of that skeleton on
the carpet of the Graduates'
Common Room
& head outside
through the rain
across cobbled stones.

3.

We didn't sleep
that night. That night
we didn't touch.
The next day I left
for Paris & Pamplona.
On the boat
from Rosslair to LeHavre
I drank until I had heaved
the pearly sea of my father
out of my guts.
I drank to the dead —
center of my dread,
past my deepest denial
to a long avoided
mourning.
I drank until I could touch
that starfish
hacked into a nightmare
of reproduction: incest
thriving from every lopped
limb until I connected
my terror with these
distant, untouchable
twinklings.

Eileen Hennessy

Electra in the
Kindergarten Bathroom

In that slag-heap
of peach plastic babydoll bodies flung
into the toy bassinet near the bathroom door,
there must be three who look like us,

my sister strangled by her cord,
my sister killed by a hole in her heart,
and me,

three blood-covered turds pushed out
in duty to a husband. Surely my mother's body
wrapped the cord around the neck,
drilled the hole in the heart,
pushed to kill, with a whirring
and a blueing and a convulsing
of our lips and limbs. Surely she knew,
from the way I kicked the walls of her womb,
that I would not be a friend to her.

Advice on Preparing for a Role Not Often Performed Here Anymore

Shrouding yourself
in the winding white summer curtains
and standing
downcast-eyed and window-framed
while your playmates sing
Here Comes the Bride

is easier done

when you have watched your mother's back
arch over the washtubs under the cellar window,
when you have helped her
haul the basket of wet curtains up the stairs
and hang them on the nail-studded wooden stretcher frame
leaned against the back wall of the house,
when you have left pearls of fingertip blood
around the nailholes in the edges of the curtains.

The Irish Cop's Niece

I OPEN MY EYES. THE SLANTED DORMER CEILING OVER MY HEAD REMINDS me that I am not home. I hunch up to avoid hitting my head as I get up. The room is filled with morning light filtered through the limbs of an old maple tree outside, coming through three small windows set at floor level. I count the panes every morning – twelve each times three, and say "thirty-six," like a prisoner counting months of confinement. I have been here twenty-one months. I don't know how many more I will have to endure. The worst part is having nobody to talk to – safely.

My twin bed is a mattress set on stubby steel legs. The other twin bed is empty now, where my little sister Deirdre slept till nine months ago. I have a quilted coverlet left over from my real home. The card table beside my bed holds my school books: Latin, English, French, geometry, and history, and my zippered leather notebook separated into these categories by colored plastic tabs. The card table is very heavy, made of cherry wood with inlaid green leather. My parents used to play bridge on it with their friends. It is the only survivor of our household furniture.

Gram has already left for work by the time I have washed my face and brushed my teeth. I go to my big low closet cut into the slope of the eaves opposite my bed and pick out my favorite suit, brown checked wool with a circle skirt and fitted jacket. My stepmother bought it for me at Lord and Taylor's on my last visit.

I take out the bobby pins that hold my pincurls and comb my thin brown hair into a curly long bob. My hair is hopeless, just like my mother's. It will be stringy and flat by lunchtime. I wish I could wash it every night, but *Seventeen* says it's bad to wash your hair more than once a week. Especially when you're having your period. Mary Martin washes her hair every night and twice on matinee days for the shower scene in *South Pacific*. *McCall's* says her hair might fall out, even if she uses special conditioners. Martin cut her mousy hair short, like a man's. I'd like to try it, but my friends would think I was a lesbian.

I eat my breakfast of chocolate milk and cinnamon toast. If it weren't for milk, I'd starve to death. Mom used to cook me oatmeal or scrambled eggs. I don't have time. I drink milk for lunch, too, because I have only twenty minutes. After school, I walk down the street to the drugstore and buy a double chocolate milkshake in the drugstore. That's where I have to buy Kotex and acne cream. I hate to ask Adelaide's dad for Kotex, but there isn't anyplace else to go.

I wash the glass and knife and leave them on the drainboard, then go down the wooden stairs to the cellar. It's nice and warm down here. I close the damper half-way to bank the coal fire in the furnace. It will stay warm till lunchtime. I'm the first one home after school, so I'll open the damper again. By then, the house is freezing. When the coals begin to glow, I will add a shovelful of greasy coal and coax the fire back to life.

I put on my winter coat, pick up my books and hold them close like a shield, and lock the front door behind me. The high school is three blocks away, past Betty Carol's house. Betty used to wait for me at her corner, but she leaves an hour earlier for cheerleading practice. I didn't make the squad. The tryouts — doing flips and splits and high jumps — left me so sore I couldn't walk for three days. Betty Carol looks so cute in her short, flirty skirt — maroon on the outside, white satin on the inside, our school colors. "Maroon and White, Fight, Fight!" I'm the only one, besides her parents, who knows Betty Carol had an abortion last summer.

In history class, I argue with Mr. McKenna about the New Deal. I heard Mrs. Roosevelt talk at State College. She is the only woman I know who is as famous as her husband, and smarter. Marie Curie was even more famous and smarter than her husband. Mr. McKenna likes to get the students excited so they'll talk. He says I'm the only girl who ever could beat the boys in history and basketball. I play left forward on the girls' team. We can't play boys' rules, so it's a pretty dull game. My best friend Elly is center, so she can run to both ends of the court. She and her brothers and sister are the only Negroes in our school. She calls me Brain. I call her Slick. We don't talk much, but we understand each other.

In Latin, there are only six of us. I sit next to John and squirm while he struggles through Caesar. He's such a brownnose, but I go all sweaty when he winks at me. Mrs. McKenna smiles when it's my turn. She's Mr. McKenna's mother. Her husband was gassed in World War I. She's had to work ever since. The six of us, says Mrs. McKenna, are the cream of the crop. We are all in the College Entrance program, getting Regents' Diplomas. Only Harold Anderson and I weren't born in Huguenot. Harold's father, a professor at State College, brought his family from Minnesota. They fit somehow in Huguenot. Betty Anne is my other best friend. I don't talk about my parents, though, or Gram. We talk about Eleanor Roosevelt, and I tell her that I'm going into politics one day too. Betty Anne and I were sitting on the rug in her living room when President Roosevelt died. We heard it on her father's big floor model radio. We cried and hugged each other. FDR had been president ever since we were born. Dr. Wilson, another college professor, always says grace before dinner. My father says that religion is for dumbbells. Everybody in Huguenot goes to church except me. John's father is the principal. His mother acted on Broadway before she had John and Roland. Janet's father is descended from one of the original Dutch Huguenot settlers. Adelaide's father is French Huguenot. He's the pharmacist. Betty Anne was born in Huguenot, though her father came from Ohio, and he changed from Baptist to Dutch Reformed.

Betty Anne takes me to choir practice on Wednesdays, but I never go on Sundays. I can sight read and I love the hymns. John's mother plays the piano and organ. Betty Anne and I giggle because we can see her breasts jiggling under her dress – she doesn't believe in brassieres, she told Betty Anne's mother. John, singing baritone solo, winks at me in the soprano section. I wish he'd ask me out. He has blond hair and brown eyes and wants to be an actor, like his mother used to be.

Betty Anne wants me to join the Youth Fellowship. I've been helping her with catechism, learning the Beatitudes and memorizing the books of the Old Testament myself: blessed are the sorrowful, for they shall find consolation. Genesis, Exodus, Leviticus, Numbers, Deuteronomy. I love the sound of these words, but I have no idea what they mean, except for Genesis – the Beginning. Betty Anne says that the Dutch Reformed Church is for everybody, not just the Dutch. You just have to be a Protestant. Whatever that is. The Reverend Doctor Bronck is a liberal, she says. He voted for Roosevelt the last time.

I don't know what I am. Religion fascinates me because my father says I'm nothing, like him. I crave religion, like anything forbidden or considered bad for a child. Everyone else is something, Catholic or Protestant. Protestants seem quieter, more certain of their superiority. Catholics are more interesting – the boys loud and wild and getting into trouble for smoking and lifting up girls' skirts in the playground; the girls red-headed and smiling demurely with mischief in their eyes. When I was younger, I envied the Catholic girls in their white organdy dresses, white stockings and patent leather shoes. This fairy garb was donned only once, like a wedding dress. I didn't know what Confirmation was and didn't care. I just wanted the clothes that went with it. I finally talked my mother into buying me black patent leather shoes, like my Catholic friends wore to "Mass" every Sunday. I wouldn't wear any others. One day, while I was skinning the monkey bars, my mother, who'd been sitting on a park bench reading, saw holes big as quarters in the soles. That's as close as I got to being Catholic.

When school is over, I run home because it's downhill and I'm hungry and want to put on my blue jeans and drop my books. As I jump up the porch steps of Gram's rented house, I spy the white envelope through the mailbox slit. I set my books down and take out the mail – a letter for me, from my mother. My heart thumps and tears well up, no matter how I harden myself. Before I let myself open the letter, I go upstairs to my room, put my books on the card table, hang up my coat, and then go downstairs to the cellar to open the damper on the furnace. The house is like an icebox. I pray the fire hasn't gone out. Once I closed the damper too much and it did. Gram said I was dumb for a Jewish kid supposed to be so smart. I open the damper wide, open the furnace door, and throw a shovelful of coal atop the gray coals. I watch anxiously, fanning them with a folded newspaper, until the coals finally redden from the increase of oxygen.

I go back upstairs to the kitchen, my stomach growling, waiting for a milkshake. My allowance has nearly run out, and Gram will be late tonight, doing food shopping after work. I fix a peanut butter and banana sandwich and make a glass of chocolate milk. Finally, when I've finished the snack, I go upstairs and sit on my bed, opening Mom's letter, slowly and carefully. I don't want to tear through her perfect gradeschool penmanship. I've worked very hard to write like my father – sharp angular letters and artistic printed capitals. Mom says my sister Deirdre loves first grade and is at the top of her class. Deirdre made her enclose a crayon drawing of a horse, a palm tree, and the ocean. The horse has a dotted penis – optional. The palm tree has two big coconuts, like testicles. Deirdre has drawn herself in a blue bikini, swimming in the ocean off Miami Beach. Mom says Arthur is working seven days a week. The pay in Florida is much less than in New York, but Arthur loves hot weather and never wants to come back north. Mom enclosed a snapshot of them, all darkly tanned. My mother's left ankle is bandaged, as always. She was in the hospital again, for a month this time. She isn't allowed to walk for six weeks. Arthur does all the cooking, shopping, and cleaning. Once a week, Mom and Arthur, who always win, play bridge with neighbors. Arthur once made the finals of a bridge tournament. Deirdre got badly bitten by fire ants. The grass is full of them, so the kids can't play barefoot. If they win the lottery, Mom says she'll send me a plane ticket to visit them in June when school gets out. She says to look for a package from Burdine's for Christmas. Mom doesn't ask where I'm spending Christmas.

I leave Gram's mail on the enamel kitchen table – the electric bill and the coal bill. There's a letter from my father. I know what's in it – my weekly allowance. Sometimes he writes on a piece of torn paper, How are you? Give us a call one of these days. Sincerely, Bill. This time, there's only the check wrapped in a piece of blank paper. I'll have to run to the bank to cash it before closing. I hate to ask Gram to cash it for me. I heard her tell Mrs. Brennan, who drives her to work in the dress factory and to bingo almost every night, that my father is a rich kike. My father pays Gram a lot for my room and board. Gram does piece-work in the factory, and she's really fast. She taught me how to sew in one day on the Singer Mom bought for her. My mother refused to learn; she won't even sew on a button. On nights when there's no bingo game at any of the Catholic churches, Gram crochets doilies out of thin thread. The color is ecru, she told me. It looks like dirty white to me. Ecru doilies cover the backs and arms of the easy chair and sofa. Gram is making a tablecloth now. She has a shopping bag full of ecru snowflake-shaped circles crocheted together. She wants to finish it by Christmas.

I do my Latin and French homework while Gram gets supper. She's hurrying because there's a bingo game. I helped her put away the groceries and set the table. She complains about the cost of the taxi she has to take when she shops, but I know Dad's check covers the rent, the coal, and the food, with plenty left over for cigarettes, bingo, and taxis. The smell of roasting meat makes my mouth water. We'll have baked potatoes and frozen peas with the eye-round roast. When my mother cooks, she prepares fresh vegetables and meats in delicious sauces, wearing slacks and a blouse with the sleeves rolled up like Katharine Hepburn. Gram wears a flowered apron with a U-shaped collar over her good dress. She has already put white powder and rouge on her freckled face. Her brownish-gray hair is rolled over a ribbon in a continuous bun along the back. Her left eye is light hazel; her right eye is dark brown. After nearly two years of living with Gram, I am still afraid of the light one — it looks like the jeweled eye in a cat left in an Egyptian tomb.

After dinner, I clear the table and dry the dishes for Gram. Then a horn honks and Gram leaves. The house is quiet as a tomb. My dog Roger disappeared last April, a month after my mother and sister left. Roger was alone all day in the house until I got home from school and let him out. He'd rush right back in to play with me. One day, he didn't come back. I looked everywhere and called the dogcatcher the next day. He'd just disappeared, like my father and mother. Good riddance, said Gram.

I change my clothes and put on my warm green sweater and tweed skirt and green tights. It's twenty-one degrees and Theodore and I will have to walk to the movies. He rings the doorbell at seven. The walk down Main Street is a mile. The movie theatre is crowded and warm. Cornell Wilde as Chopin plays a Prelude for Merle Oberon, who is George Sand. It's a piece I love to play, and I cry silently, wanting to be alone. Theodore has his arm around me, feeling my breast. He puts my hand on his fly so I can feel his erect penis. Mom bought me an old upright piano before she left. I can't play Beethoven yet, and my new music teacher, appropriately named Mrs. Upright, is terrible. She tries to teach me popular music, thumping the keys with fat hands.

After the movie, we have hot chocolate in the College Cafe. It warms me up and I feel better. I go to the ladies room, pee, comb my hair and put on fresh lipstick. The cold hits my face like a slap when we leave. Theodore puts his arm around me, and I put my arm around him. We walk slowly, blowing clouds of frozen breath before us, winding the long way back to Gram's through the darkened State College campus. An occasional streetlight makes a yellow circle on the hard snow. The college is closed for the long Christmas break. Theodore finds a dark corner and presses me against a brick wall of the main building. He kisses me. Our lips are cold as ice. Gradually, they warm, and he unzips his fly and opens my coat. It's too difficult standing, so he takes off his jacket and spreads it over the frozen snow.

I shiver putting on my underpants and tights again. Cold has penetrated me. I think I shall die of it.

Mrs. Brennan's car pulls up just as Theodore leaves me on the porch. Gram is smiling. She must have won at bingo. Across the street, the curtain in Mrs. Riley's front window twitches. Mrs. Riley is responsible for my freezing with Theodore. She called up Gram to tell her that Theodore stayed alone in the house with me when she went out to bingo. Gram told me she didn't care if I got knocked up, but she couldn't have the neighbors think she was running a whorehouse. I would have to cat around somewhere else, just like my mother used to.

Theodore is my steady. All the girls who count have steadies, but mine is the only college student. I don't like Theodore that much, but it's better than being alone. He's very smart. He was high school valedictorian last year. We argue a lot about politics. He's a Republican. He wants to get married as soon as he graduates from the State College. I don't have to go to college, he says. I have the highest average in my sophomore class.

On Saturday, I sleep till ten. Betty Carol, Betty Anne, and I are going ice skating this afternoon. I have to wash my hair and do my laundry first. The indoor back porch has two big galvanized iron tubs. Gram pours in bleach and soap powder and washes her sheets and towels and underwear. She hangs the wet sheets and towels on the pulley line out back with wooden pegs, then drapes her corset and underpants on a wooden clothes rack on the back porch. I strip my bed, collect my towels, underwear, and blouses and carry them to the porch when she's done. Gram is sitting smoking a cigarette and waiting for the kettle to boil in the kitchen as I pass through. She never speaks to me unless I speak to her. She never looks at me when I come into a room. I tried to have a nice chat with her after Mom and Deirdre left. She was sitting at the kitchen table, playing solitaire, slapping the cards down. A cigarette dangled from her lips, sending smoke up past her dark, squinting eye. All at once, she grabbed her spoon and stuck it into the steaming kettle, pulled it out, wiped it dry on her apron, and held it against my bare arm. See – it don't burn if it's dry, she said, grinning. My mother had said my grandmother was cruel. I didn't believe her till Gram burned my arm – for no reason.

I dump my dirty clothes and linens into the tub, add warm water, soap powder, and a little bleach. Gram's things smell strongly of bleach all week. She takes a bath once a week, so the bleach smell, mingled with stale sweat, smells dirty. Gram complains when I shower too long every day, says it costs a fortune to fill the tank with hot water. Washing clothes is easy, even fun, sloshing clothes around in the warm, sudsy water. Rinsing takes longer, getting out the soap scum. Wringing out the heavy sheets and towels makes my arms ache. I hang my sheets and towels on the clothesline after Gram's, then drape my underthings on the rack. By four o'clock, when I pull in the sheets and towels, they will be frozen stiff as boards; but they will have the fragrance of fresh air I love. My freshly made bed smells like the outdoors for two days.

Betty Anne and Betty Carol are already waiting on the bench beside the flooded soccer field. Boys are playing ice hockey at one end. Small kids in bulky snowsuits, looking like teddy bears, scratch across the ice on double-bladed skates that strap onto their shoes. John isn't here – he's working in the grocery store. No college students either. They've gone home, mostly to Long Island, for vacation. Local college students work on weekends and vacations. Theodore is a waiter in his uncle's diner, and anyway, he can't skate. He isn't very athletic.

Betty Carol wears a twirly skating skirt, red velvet lined with white satin. Her legs are bare to her fluffy socks and white skates topped with red tassels. She says her legs aren't cold, but the skin on her thighs looks like measled chicken skin. Betty Anne and I are wearing sensible, bulky snowpants. I hate them. They make me look like a fat baby, even though I weigh only 102 pounds. Betty Anne looks worse because she weighs 125 pounds and is 5'2" like me. We practice our twirls and try skating backwards. A hockey player, a rough Italian who sneaks smokes in the hall, whistles as Betty Carol raises one leg and shows her red panties. Her dimpled, rosy cheeks are set off by rabbit fur earmuffs. I wish I were as cute as her. She ignores the hockey player, a dirty wop. Betty Carol's latest steady is Buzz, a salesman who used to be a teacher. Buzz pals around with Betty's parents who like to go to bars on weekends. That's how she met him. Her parents don't seem to mind that he's thirty and Betty's only fifteen. After the abortion, Betty Carol dropped her other boyfriend, Luke, the star basketball forward.

Betty Anne's father won't let her have a steady. But she's going secretly with Skip. When Betty Carol's parents are out at the bar, we go to her house with our steadies, turn out the lights, and neck. Dr. Wilson would kill Betty Anne if he found out. They think Mr. and Mrs. O'Shea are home when we're "having a party."

Betty Anne asks if I'm going to Youth Fellowship tomorrow. Betty Carol is Catholic, so she can't go. She thinks we're snobs anyway, because we're in the A-track class for kids going to college. She's in B-track, for kids who aren't smart enough. I guess so, I tell Betty Anne. John will be there, she says.

I have to write a paper for English this weekend, so I call Theodore and tell him not to come over Saturday night. Miss Genevieve said we could write something creative if we wanted, based on Macbeth. I have an idea for a story, set in the present. Macbeth is a vice president of a big corporation who wants to be president, but he has to get rid of better-qualified rivals first. It takes me all night Saturday and all day Sunday. I copy the final draft in blue ink, writing more like my mother than I wish. Tears run down my cheeks. I hate it, but it's too late to write anything else.

Sunday night the Dutch Reformed Church is all lit up and even more beautiful than in daylight. The Youth Fellowship meets in one of the basement rooms. The Reverend Dr. Bronck wears a dark business suit with a white clergyman's collar. He asks us what the difference is between pagan and Christian beliefs. Hands shoot up. Harold Anderson gives a lecture on the blending of Anglo-Saxon pagan ideas with Christian values. He learned that from his father, who made Harold read *Beowulf* before any of us had even heard of it. John says we should respect other beliefs and religions, even if they seem ridiculous; pagans are converted anyway once they see the superiority of Christianity. The contradiction doesn't seem to occur to John. I raise my hand for the fifth time. Reverend Bronck stares at me momentarily, then slides his eyes towards Betty Anne and nods. He won't call on me.

On the way out after the meeting, each Youth Fellowship member shakes Dr. Bronck's hand and says Goodnight, Doctor. When it's my turn, he frowns and doesn't reach out his hand. Betty Anne tells him my name and says I'm her guest and hopes that I'll join because it's so much fun. Reverend Dr. Bronck suddenly recognizes me. "Your family doesn't belong to our church, Miss Dichter. I doubt if they'd want you to take instruction to become a member so you could join the Fellowship." We don't shake hands.

2.

Gram says Aunt Audrey and Uncle Lou are coming for Christmas dinner. And Grampa? I ask, since she so rarely tells me anything.

Gramp has to work. We only see him when he's on vacation for two weeks from his bartending job in a resort in the Catskills. Last time, he came home in a taxi and had to be helped into the house by the driver. Gram fed him canned beans and scrambled eggs, and then he fell asleep in her easy chair. He sat there all night, waking at intervals to scream and curse. I couldn't sleep, afraid he would kill Gram or me. But the next morning, he was sober as a churchmouse, frying potatoes and onions in bacon grease, humming cheerily. He hadn't shaved, and he reeked of stale alcohol coming out his bare armpits. Huge plantar's warts hung under his arms, jiggling as he broke four eggs into another pan for sunnyside up. Tasting his potatoes, he shook his head and grabbed a can of chilipepper, shaking it liberally over them. He tasted again. Ah! Then he served himself at the kitchen table. He dipped bread into the runny egg yolks and stuck it into his toothless mouth, dripping yolk on his sleeveless undershirt and chin. My mother's table manners made you think she'd been raised in a palace. She liked Gramp better than Gram because he took her fishing when she was a little girl. He cleaned their catch and cooked the fresh fish for her – her only happy memory I ever heard her tell.

It was nice at first having Gramp home after school. I sat down and practiced my Chopin waltzes. Gramp came up behind me and rubbed my back. Then he asked me to give Gramps a nice kiss. I gave him a grandaughter kiss, but he pulled me close to his fat belly and 'scratched my face with his grizzled beard. His penis was soft, so I wasn't scared, just disgusted. When Grandpa Dichter kissed me, his chin was shaved and he smelled nice. Dad didn't like him. Playing casino, they fought about Communism and capitalism all the time when we visited, slamming the cards down and yelling. But Grandpa Dichter always was nice to me, slipping a ten-dollar bill in my pocket when I kissed him good-bye. Buy yourself something nice, chickadee, he said. Gramp looks like a white pig and says He don't and You wasn't.

The rest of that week, Gramp sat in Gram's easy chair and tied flies out of bright silk thread, wearing Gram's reading glasses. He sells them to rich customers at the resort. Gram yelled at him when he was sober, and he got drunk again. Gram called a taxi and sent him back to work a week early. Gram got her easy chair and glasses back so she could crochet her tablecloth. Gramp came home once more, when he had a kidney stone attack. Nobody could get him to go to the hospital, so Doc Reid gave him pain killers and said he hoped he wouldn't die this time. Doc Reid belongs to AA. He got my mother to join. That's how she met Arthur.

I don't remember Aunt Audrey and Uncle Lou very well. My mother took me to visit Gram and Gramp only once when I was little. They lived in an apartment in Inwood, next to Audrey who had married Lou, a cop. Audrey had thick, auburn hair and white freckled skin like Gram. She giggled and smoked and coughed all the afternoon we visited. Lou was so big I was afraid he'd hit his head on the door lintel. His round pumpkin head was covered with carroty hair, and he stood with meaty hands on his hips, sneering at my mother and asked how the Jew was. Mom had brought expensive gifts for everyone. Gramp was out of work again, but he'd bought the biggest tree he could find and covered it with precious antique ornaments left to him by his mother. I sat on the smelly sofa covered with doilies, marveling at this giant tree and the snow village skirting its base. Gramp had a folding red picket fence that surrounded the cotton snow, and tiny metal figures on skates and sleds, mufflered men and women, and tiny houses and a church lit from inside. Mom warned me not to eat anything. It was no problem to say, No, thank you, to the strong tea and hard biscuits.

Audrey and Lou still lived in Inwood. They had two children, but Donald, the older, was killed last year when he ran in front of a car. His mother was watching out the window when it happened. Lou said he was a dumb kid; he should have known better. Being a cop on the beat, Lou has had plenty of experience with dumb, dead kids. Bobby, their younger son, is a choir boy and goes to parochial school. Gram has an eight-by-ten hand-painted photograph of Donald and Bobby on her vanity. I don't know what she did with the photograph of Deirdre and me my mother gave her.

The day before Christmas, I am happy because Gram lets me help with the cooking. I tear bread into small pieces for stuffing, chop celery and onions, slice apples for pie. She sniffs when I say Mom doesn't use much sugar in her apple pie. Gram dumps in a whole cup and sprinkles on too much cinnamon.

The smell of giblets simmering on the stove and stuffed turkey roasting in the oven fills the house on Christmas day. It almost seems like home. I put on my new blue sweater set my mother sent and my tweed skirt, then set the dining room table with the dishes and silverware Mom bought for Gram last year. Gram's crocheted tablecloth is covered with a long sheet of transparent plastic. While I wait eagerly for my aunt and uncle and cousin, I want to play the piano, but I know Gram will get mad. Instead, I peel small white onions and soak them in cold water, but my eyes fill with tears all the same. I am making white sauce when Aunt Audrey, Uncle Lou, and Bobby burst into the house. Cold air whooshes in, mingled with cigarette smell and Audrey's perfume – I recognize it as cheap Emeraude. Lou's head nearly touches the low ceiling in Gram's living room. His hair is just as orange as I remember, as is Bobby's. Audrey is plump under a fat fur coat my mother gave her a long time ago. My mother hated it. Audrey says hello with a weak smile and brushes my cheek lightly with bright red lips. Lou doesn't look at me or say anything to me, like Gram. Bobby smiles a girlish smile.

Uncle Ed comes in a few minutes later, bobbing his head and grinning. He lived with Gram till last year. He's bobbed his head continually since he had rheumatic fever as a child. Ed was engaged last year to a college girl whose father owned the local hotel. Gram invited Lois to dinner to see the ring. Lois had blonde hair, draped in a silky page boy like Veronica Lake. She spoke to me as if I were a college girl too, and looked really pleased when I said I wanted to teach. Lois brought a box of milk chocolates for Gram. Ed must have told her they were her favorite. After Lois left, Gram threw the chocolates in the garbage. A few weeks later, I was listening to Jack Benny on the radio in the living room when Ed got home from work. Gram, snapping her crochet hook, said that Mrs. Brennan said Lois was a whore – slept with half the salesmen in her father's hotel and had an abortion last year. Ed's head stopped bobbing for a whole minute. He and Lois broke up just before she graduated. Lois took a teaching job in Westchester. Uncle Ed moved into an apartment his boss gave him for practically nothing. He works for the local Mafia, servicing pinball machines. He says the pay is steady, he don't work too hard, and he's got free rent and protection when he needs it.

Lou slaps Ed on the back and asks How's business, winking. Audrey hugs her brother and giggles. They look like twins, giggling, bobbing, and coughing together. My cousin Bobby is dressed in a blue suit, white shirt, and navy tie. His orange hair is slicked down over his freckled forehead, his eyes an empty blue. He walks mincingly towards Gram and kisses her on the cheek. Audrey and Gram smile upon him as if he were already a priest.

Lou and Ed talk about the track. I sit on the floor in a corner, listening to the strange, lilting accents, the strange grammar, and the strange topics. Ed takes out a small spiral notebook and writes down numbers Lou whispers in his ear so Audrey won't hear him. I am so hungry, I feel nauseated. Last year, at Daddy's, we didn't eat Christmas dinner till 9:30 P.M. My stepmother can't cook, so my dad did it all. He didn't know it took so long to cook a fifteen pound turkey. It was still a little bloody at 9:30 P.M., but they were too drunk to care and my baby half-sister and I were starved. This year they have another baby, so it's too crowded for me to come, they said.

Gram finally calls us to the table. Lou proudly carries in the twenty-five pound turkey, roasted to a turn, and sets it in front of Ed at the head of the table. Audrey and I carry in the steaming vegetables and potatoes, the warm rolls, and the bowls of cranberry sauce. Gram brings in the brim-full gravy boat. I wonder when they'll serve the wine. I've set the wine glasses at each place. What the hell mucky-muck is *this?* says Lou, holding up a wine glass. Everyone laughs. Gram and Audrey remove the wine glasses and bring in tumblers and bottles of Budweiser. Gram, Bobby, and I get water. Lou raises his foaming glass, Here's to food, lots of food. Audrey and Ed giggle and sip their beer.

Ed picks up the carving knife and fork my mother left (the wine glasses were hers too). He rips off a leg and a wing, then slices thick chunks, clumsily, piling them on the serving platter. While Uncle Ed carves, Gram grabs the bowl of turnips and puts a mound on Bobby's dish. She passes them on to Audrey, then takes the mashed potatoes and plops another mound on Bobby's dish. Gram starts circulating each dish in this way — cranberry sauce, stuffing, gravy — while Ed passes the turkey. Audrey and Bobby dig in before everyone has filled his plate. I sit with my napkin open and my hands in my lap. Lou's napkin is tucked under his chin. Everyone else's napkins remain folded and unused beside their plates throughout the meal.

I pick up my fork when I see everyone eating, savoring the first bite of turkey and gravy. It isn't as good as Mom's, but it's better than Dad's. Lou hands me the basket of rolls, and I turn and see his plate for the first time. Audrey catches me staring at it: mashed potatoes and turnips dripping with buttery glaciers form a double peak six inches high on one side, turkey and stuffing form twin peaks dripping gravy lava on the opposite; in the middle are two lakes — a red one of cranberry sauce and a white one of creamed onions, blending into each other, like water in wine. Around the edge of the whole plate, carefully balanced, are celery sticks, olives, and four buttered rolls.

Audrey giggles and nudges Ed. She ain't never seen nothin like the way my Lou eats. They all laugh at me, except Bobby who is daintily munching a black olive with chipmunk teeth. Audrey giggles again, washing down potatoes with a sip of beer. She says Lou's mom said she'd go to the poorhouse trying to feed him and his big brother – Lou's brother is an inch taller. So she made a rule: only *one* helping of each dish at meals.

When the apple and mince pies are brought out, Gram cuts them in half, then quarters and eighths. Lou takes the spatula and helps himself to four pieces of apple pie and two of mince. I'm a little full – I'll have another piece of mince tomorrow. He takes a slice of apple pie and shoves it into his huge pink mouth.

That was the last time I saw my Aunt Audrey, my Uncle Lou, and my cousin Bobby. Eighteen months later (three more months than windowpanes in my cell, counting the twenty-one months I'd already spent there), Gram said she couldn't afford to keep this big house anymore. I had to move out the day after I graduated as valedictorian from high school.

My Irish relatives disappeared from my life like all those impoverished and envious souls – Murdstone, Bumble, Mrs. Jellby, Bill Sykes, Ralph Nickelby, Fagin – who have no sympathy for a hapless child thrown on their mercy for an indeterminate sentence. My father's generous room and board payments kept them at bay, but one hazel eye and bright red hair often return in a bad dream where I am imprisoned once again in a dormered room with three small windows, and I smell my flesh-burning – damned as half-Jew, half-Catholic.

In this imperfect world, I had to make a choice to be *something* to end the war in my blood. Gram, Gramp, Lou, Audrey, and the Reverend Dr. Bronck made the choice easy.

Catherine Brady

The Custom of the Country

LAURA AND I SET THE TABLE FOR CHRISTMAN EVE DINNER. THE TABLE-
cloth was patterned with red poinsettias, and the matching napkins
were rolled inside Christmas tree napkin holders. In the center of the
table Laura had arranged angel candlesticks and draped a garland of
cranberries and popcorn around them.

I tried to stuff a loose cranberry into the mouth of one of the
angels.

Laura slapped my hand. "You've got no Christmas spirit. You
mind your manners, or I'll put on my Andy Williams album – the one
with Hawaiian love songs."

She not only had Andy Williams – originally my father's album,
salvaged by Laura in a fit of kitsch – but also owned Bing Crosby,
Peggy Lee, and Johnny Mathis Christmas albums. The Bing Crosby
Christmas album was already on the stereo when I went into the living
room to join our parents and our husbands.

Tom and Jay knelt by the fireplace, crumpling newspapers onto
a stack of logs, playing with a box of oversized matches, in general
pretending to male competence. I felt a twinge of pity for them. Both
would rather have been sitting on the sofa with me, having a beer, but
Laura didn't serve drinks before dinner, a concession to my father's
hard-won abstinence. He had quit drinking for my mother's birthday
three years ago, a surprisingly sentimental gesture.

My father sat in the armchair poking a screwdriver into the in-
nards of a hotplate – Laura's husband Tom was hopeless at fixing
things, and she saved up repairs, from broken toasters to leaking
shower heads, for my father's visits.

My mother was on her hands and knees on the carpet with the
baby, stacking plastic blocks. "Bama," Emily said, thrusting her fat
hands in between my mother's. *Bama* was her name for my mother;
whenever my mother came on a visit, Emily went right to her. But

with my father she was hesitant, as if she had inherited the caution we had had to learn as children.

When my father came home at night, we never knew whether we'd receive a casual hug or be pinioned in a drunk's sloppy grasp. Often it was the drunk's embrace we preferred, even with its short-comings—the sickly sweet stale breath, the sometimes rib-cracking fierceness of his hands. Sober, he was often either irritable or in-different, but drunk he was lovely, chatty, willing to join our games, full of ideas for pranks we could play on our mother. He'd rig the fuse box so she'd blow a fuse every time she turned on the washing machine, or move everything around in the kitchen cupboards, or pretend the steak she'd made for dinner was so tough he couldn't cut it. And we were always in on the joke. He invented a game called Mess Up the House. It would start out with Laura and me throwing sofa cushions and pillows around the living room and end with him jump-ing out at us from behind the curtains or under the kitchen table to wreak The Terrible Punishment. Sometimes he'd knock the table over jumping out of his hiding place, and he'd laugh with us at the mess it made, the broken plates and spilled food. He'd stick his thumb in a glob of jam oozing from a broken jar and encourage us to do the same.

Emily tottered to her feet and made for the Christmas tree. Her outstretched hands opened and shut in time to the blinking lights on the tree. It was a magnificent tree, a five-foot-high Scotch fir laden with ornaments, lights, tinsel. The red-and-green felt skirt at the foot of the tree used to adorn our Christmas tree when we were kids, and in among the expensive verdigris and fragile paper ornaments on the tree were faded and battered remnants of our childhood Christmases —angels with silver paper wings and Santa Clauses and reindeer Laura and I had made ourselves from construction paper.

Laura must have taken those ornaments when my parents moved from Chicago to the apartment in Florida. All our Christmases were at Laura's now. Jay and I flew to Chicago from Boston and my parents drove up from Florida. Laura put Jay and me up on a sofa bed in her den and my parents stayed at a motel. On Christmas Eve Laura and I baked cookies in the afternoon, a tradition she'd invented out of thin air, just as she'd manufactured a tender attachment to the styrofoam ornaments stuck with sequins, the product of our elementary school art classes.

I didn't understand my little sister's fondness for these mementos of our childhood. The holidays had been the worst times for us, because my father drank more heavily then, and my mother was usually present to suffer over it. I remembered too many Christmas mornings when my father had stayed in bed, nursing a hangover. By afternoon he feebly marshaled his strength and took us off to a round of parties at the houses of his friends, where he'd quickly recover his vitality. So many Christmases I fell asleep in the crook of my mother's arm in somebody's bright, noisy living room where his voice boomed louder than that of any of the other silly drunks.

Emily took another step toward the tree, put her hands up to the hot bulbs. "Lye," she said proudly. Laura claimed that light was her daughter's first word, that as a baby Emily would hold her hands up and turn them, fanning the fingers, so she could study the moving shadows they cast.

The baby wobbled forward, reaching for the lights of the tree.

My mother, who was nearest her, put out a hand. "No, no."

The baby shook her head. "No no," she repeated, struggling to get past the barrier of my mother's arm.

When Emily started to cry, Laura came rushing in from the kitchen to scoop her up in her arms.

"You'll spoil her," my father said.

"Oh, Dad," Laura said. She poured the child into my father's arms. "Here, you spoil her instead."

Both Emily and my father appeared stunned for a moment by their sudden proximity. Then my father stuck out his tongue at her and she laughed.

Laura turned to go back to the kitchen.

"Laura," I said. "I want to know what possible explanation you could have for this." I fished out from between the sofa cushions a holster with two matching ivory-handled revolvers, the kind of things that little boys got complete with cowboy outfits. Definitely not Laura Ashley enough for my sister.

"Oh, those horrid things. Hide them again before you-know-who sees them. They're a Christmas present from Tom's brother. He's twenty-three." She shrugged. "The men in that family all need work, including the one I got."

"Hey!" Tom said. "I never heard any complaints before —"

"That's because you can catch more flies with honey, sweetheart," Laura said. She gave him a wink before she disappeared back into the kitchen.

My father jogged Emily on his knee. He jerked his knee under her so that she'd fall backward, only to be caught just in time. Her laughter when she started to lose her balance skated just this side of fear.

"Don't be too rough with her," my mother said. She was still sitting on the floor, her legs drawn up awkwardly to one side, her attention fixed on Emily and my father.

"She won't break," my father said.

"She's pretty tough," Tom said. "Those little pistols are only the beginning. I'll have her out on the firing range before she's five."

My mother looked over at Tom. "They were terrors in Joe's family. Terrible for teasing. I used to dread the Saturdays when he'd take me out to the farm with him. He was working in Dublin when I met him, you see, but he'd go out to the country every Saturday to be fed. His mother baked her own bread every day, they had fresh cream, eggs, and they'd even slaughter their own lambs for the table. You couldn't eat like that in the city. His brothers — five or six of them, and big, so tall they had to stoop to go through the doorway — they didn't leave you alone from the time you crossed the threshold. We'd be sitting having tea and one of them would reach over and press a hot spoon down on the back of my hand. I'd jump ten feet. They were terrible."

My father laughed. "Could have done worse on you, you know."

He held his wrist out for Emily, who was trying to remove his wristwatch.

Jay came and sat beside me on the sofa. "So what's the story?" he asked my father. "Were they just miserable bullies, or did they mean no harm?"

My father snorted.

"Go easy on him, Dad," I said. "He's innocent about the ways of the world."

"It's the custom of the country, don't you see?" my father said. "You had to make your own amusement. We even used to play tricks on the ol' fellas in church. They'd be kneeling in the pews, napping with their heads on their hands, and one of the boys'd go down the pew behind and tie the laces of their shoes together. So they'd be hobbled, like. They'd fall all over themselves when it came time to stand up for the offering of the Eucharist."

I smiled at my mother. She stole a glance at my father before smiling back. He was waxing professionally Irish on us — his pub Irishman's accent, which always had a taint of falseness even though it was genuine, perhaps because when he told the stories he lapsed into the expressions of his youth, *a dollar for bread and a dollar for daisies, you can't get blood from a stone, looking like the wreck of the* Hesperus.

"And we'd give my sister Nellie a run for her money," my father said. "She'd be after doing all the sewing for the day, and when she went up to bed we'd take the shirts from the basket and cut off the buttons and lay them all back neat for her to find in the morning. The buttons'd spill all over the floor when she went to put the laundry away, and she'd have a devil of a time figuring out which buttons went back where."

Laura appeared in the kitchen doorway, her face flushed, and mouthed "help" at me. In spite of her fierce pursuit of housewifely perfection, she could not learn to cook and had to be babied through the smallest dinner party. I followed her into the kitchen and surveyed the damage. Four pots were bubbling away on the stove and the oven door was opened on a turkey that wasn't turning brown on schedule.

"Can we do anything, Lee?" Laura said. She wrung her hands.

I laughed. "Turn the oven up." I basted the turkey and poked at the joint with a fork. "I'd say another hour."

"But everything will be burned by then," she wailed.

I shrugged. I began taking the pots off their burners, trying to repair or postpone the damage.

"I've eaten more than one burnt dinner and so have you," I said. My mother used to try to keep dinner for my father, only she never knew how long it would take him to wend his way home from the bar, and as often as not dinner was a sorry affair, spoiled food and accusing silences.

Laura set her mouth. She reminded me of our mother when she did that but I didn't tell her so. Laura did not want to be like our mother.

I mimicked her grimace. "It didn't hurt us then and it won't hurt us now."

I started to shake some dill on the peas, but she stopped me. "Dad doesn't like spices."

Laura always cooked to my father's tastes when my parents were visiting, and she always stocked her refrigerator with things he liked, salami, chocolate mints, 7-Up, as if he were a kind of invalid. Her solicitousness toward my father annoyed me. If I ever slipped up and reminded her of any of the minor inconveniences of having a drunk for a father, she'd set her mouth and cut me off with, "I remember the good things."

And I'd always be astonished at that, at Laura's apparent ability to distill what she wanted to remember from the more random mess of things. When we were little kids I was as much in love with my father as she was. Once he had had to take a week off work to take care of us when my mother had a hysterectomy. He had his friends over for poker every night, and they littered the kitchen table with beer bottles, glasses, overflowing ashtrays, and candy wrappers, and in the morning we had to eat in the living room on our laps because the table was never cleared from one party to the next. My father had us serve the drinks and make sandwiches — inedible, gloppy messes — and let us stay up long after bedtime, even though we had school the next day and we knew he would make us go — his nerves couldn't take our staying home, not when he had a hangover to cure before the next party. We feasted on potato chips every night, rubbed my father's belly for luck whenever he requested it, and shrieked with delight when he jumped up from a winning hand to gives us each a piggyback ride — a victory ride — around the table.

For most of the week Laura and I enjoyed the holiday. But by the end of the week I was worn out, I would cry for no reason other than the vague sense that my mother wouldn't like this if she knew. My father was puzzled by my tears. He had let us stay up late, have as much soda as we wished, and here I was making trouble in front of his friends. Always his bewilderment gave way to anger. "Your sister's not crying. What's the matter with you? Go to your room if you can't be civil."

My mother came into the kitchen. "Can I help?"

"We're all set," Laura said.

My mother went to the stove anyway and looked into the pots. "You might boil the vegetables a bit longer. Your father likes them soft."

"I know," Laura said.

"The baby's a bit cranky, honey," my mother said. "If it's going to be much longer, maybe you want to feed her first."

"And have her miss her first Christmas dinner? I'll give her a bottle," Laura said. She reached into the fridge for milk.

"You'll spoil her appetite," my mother said.

Laura didn't miss a beat. She filled a bottle for her daughter, capped it tightly, and set it in a pot of water to heat. In anything that had to do with her baby, her movements were practiced, serene, and when she brought the bottle out to Emily and took the child in her lap, her grace seemed perfected, madonna-like, and I envied her her transformation.

My father brought her the hotplate and showed her the loose wire he'd repaired. He spoke so softly that Laura bent her face close to his, to his blunt hands, her face tender, receptive. I pictured all the possible things one might say to draw out that expression and faulty wiring wasn't one of them.

"I wish I could get your father to do the same for me," my mother said to Laura. "I've a list as long as your arm of things to be done around the house. He's too busy fixing things for the neighbors to get around to fixing them for me."

That was like my father: he was a regular hale-fellow-well-met, fond of dallying over the fence with neighbors, always ready with practical advice, and ferociously insistent on proffering his help. "Everything for outsiders," was how my mother put it.

My mother shook her head. "My car is a wreck."

"Nothing wrong with your car," my father said. For someone who could be so garrulous, he was surprisingly capable of delivering terse, unforgiving judgments. It was a tendency I always associated with his sober state, which may have gone a long way toward explaining Laura's and my preference for him when he was sauced.

"It doesn't start —"

"You floor the gas pedal every time you turn on the ignition and you ruin the starter. No point fixing it for you."

"Oh." My mother folded her hands in her lap, the picture of the chastised little girl. "Well, I don't know about these things."

"Neither do I," Jay said quickly. "It's a good thing it's not a criminal offense."

"You couldn't be as bad as me," my mother said. "Poor Joe's forever losing patience with me."

"Oh, but I'm worse," Jay said.

He wasn't, of course, but he was probably her equal in wanting to smooth things over. When we were first married, I had headaches every day for two years. Jay dragged me from doctor to doctor, suffered with me the side effects of all the migraine medication that didn't work, all the panic. Sometimes I would come home from work and curl up on the bed, and Jay would come in to find me in the darkened room and hold me. Even when the last specialist gave up on me—"Try therapy," he'd said, unable to keep from his voice the contempt that was an inevitable consequence of his failure to succeed—Jay kept on believing we'd find a pill that worked, a cure, a cause. Eventually we settled on allergies as the culprit, tore up our carpeting because bare wood floors didn't trap dust and mildew. It seemed to help.

I would never have told Jay—it would have seemed like a betrayal of his loyalty—but for me the headaches came to represent some allegiance I owed my mother for all her uncomplaining years. I had to learn to remember her, standing in the kitchen, peeling apples for a pie, the skin spiraling over her fingers as she worked with her characteristic haste and gracelessness, her tears leaving wet spots like freckles on her floured hands. The year my father quit drinking, her birthday followed by only a few weeks a car accident—miraculously his only one ever—in which mother had had her nose and three ribs broken.

Twice during dinner my mother complimented Laura on the meal, even though the vegetables were dry by the time we got them to the table. But the compliments went unheard, because my mother couldn't stop herself from remarking, when the baby wouldn't eat, that Laura should have fed her sooner.

There was a war between them that I didn't understand; Laura seemed to be so like my mother, just as devoted to mothering and housekeeping, and yet they bristled at each other. My mother wasn't terribly interested in my work as a graphic designer, she didn't like the "spicy" way I cooked Creole, Mexican, and Chinese food, and she pitied my taste in decorating, which ran to folk art and Oriental carpets. But she and I could sit in my kitchen for hours laughing and talking over old times. We would laugh together at things that hadn't seemed funny then: how she had had to pin up the shredded hem of a raincoat because she couldn't afford a new one, how she'd once thrown a fistful of mashed potatoes at my father and later had to scrape the hardened stuff off the floor with a knife.

Over dessert my father announced that he wanted to spend Christmas afternoon visiting the Johnsons and Kearneys, at those parties he had so often taken us to when we were kids. Everyone drank at those parties—no one thought anything of it then, especially when the men got drunk. It made them so cheerful; they tossed the children up in the air, teased their wives, burst into impromptu renditions of Irish songs, managing to be maudlin and irreverent at the same time.

"Can't we stop in on them later in the week?" my mother said. "I want to spend Christmas with the family."

"We used to go every year," my father said. "All of a sudden, you object."

"Why do you have to be so stubborn?" my mother said. "Don't you want to spend Christmas with the kids?"

My father's face went red. "Did I say I didn't?"

"Why don't you compromise?" Laura said, her voice bright, bell-like, false.

"I'll have to spend the entire day out with you when I want to be with the baby," my mother said. She couldn't let him go alone, not to those parties. He might have quit drinking, but she would never be able to quit her surveillance.

"It's just a few hours," Laura said. "We'd still have the rest of the day, Mom. It's all right."

"It's not all right," my mother snapped at her. "Why do you have to make excuses for him?" She had tears in her eyes, as if Laura had betrayed her. When those parties had reached the point where my mother started to nag my father about leaving, Laura always pleaded with her not to, as if her nagging were the cause, not the consequence, of his state.

"There's no need for you to bite her head off," my father said, willing to be reasonable now that the damage was done. "If you don't want to come with me, say so."

She couldn't say so.

After dinner Jay and Tom volunteered to do the dishes. I knew that when they got into the kitchen they would sneak a bottle of Scotch from one of the cabinets and pour shots for themselves, because Laura didn't like it if they drank in front of my father.

Laura knew it too. "Just leave the dishes," she said.

"We'll only be a minute," Tom said.

"*Leave* them," she insisted, but her husband gave her a smacking kiss on her forehead as he cleared her plate and headed for the kitchen with Jay.

My father got up from the table. "I'm going out to the garage to get some things," he said. When they'd arrived, he'd been carrying a big green plastic trash bag, and he'd ostentatiously refused to divulge its contents and taken it out to the garage. He had to go through the kitchen to get to the garage, and Laura watched him go with a grim expression that meant that Tom and Jay had just better not have broken out the Scotch yet.

My father was gone for a good fifteen minutes when the doorbell rang. Laura went to answer it, and Tom and Jay came out from the kitchen, Jay with a dish towel still in his hands.

Laura opened the door to Santa Claus.

"Ho, ho, ho," he boomed. He came into the room, tugging a little at the pillow that gave him his big belly. This was what had been in the plastic bag. The red felt suit, the black patent leather belt, the flowing white beard. He even clutched a shopping bag stuffed with gift-wrapped packages, and there were bracelets of jingle bells on his wrists.

"You're early, Santa," Tom said. "Haven't had a chance to put out the milk and cookies yet."

"Early bird catches the worm," Santa said. "Ho, ho, ho," he said again, awkwardly advancing on Emily. She sat slack-mouthed and stunned on the living room floor, never taking her eyes off him.

"Who's been a good girl this year?" he said, putting his hands on his knees and crouching before her. "Did I hear that Emily was a good girl?"

I think it was his voice — so loud, so familiar and yet issuing from this strange creature — that scared Emily. Her face puckered and she burst into tears, wails of a kind that would make any mother fear she'd been maimed. And at first Laura held back, she stood where she was by the door.

My father must have decided that force had to be met with force. He spoke more loudly to Emily in order to be heard over her screams. "Santa will be handing out lumps of coal if you go on like that. Be a good girl now." He put out his arms to pick her up and she nearly toppled over backwards in fright.

My mother rescued her. She picked her up in one smooth easy gesture and held her out of arm's reach of Santa. "It's Grandpa, honey. It's only Grandpa."

"Whisht up, woman," Santa said. "You'll give the game away. Don't be listening to that woman, Emily."

My mother put her face close to Emily's. "I'll not have you frightening the child."

The true cold shoulder, that's what she was giving him, turning away from him so that Emily's view of him was obstructed. Something like stubbornness set in the lines around my father's mouth. But after all, what did my mother owe him?

My father's hand scaled the barricade of my mother's body and he shook his bracelet of jingle bells next to Emily's ear.

Emily struggled to wriggle away from him, her cries coming in hiccups. Laura had to take her then. My father stood watching them, one finger rubbing at his hairline, where the fluffy white wig must have scratched at his skin.

"She's overtired," Laura said.

His trick had gone bust. I couldn't help but think, finally, he gets his just desserts. For making my mother the butt of his jokes, and doing that to her through her children. And we didn't know better. We didn't know that that life in him when he gave us those wild piggyback rides was all thanks to Johnny Walker.

I thought even Laura couldn't contrive a way out of this. She stood rubbing Emily's back as the baby slowly calmed down, afraid to glance up at my father. Tom went to her and nuzzled the baby. But when he leaned toward Laura to give her a kiss, she pointedly turned her face away, as if the smell of liquor on his breath were a novel and unpleasant sensation for her.

But then Laura did come up with something. She went to the stereo cabinet to put on a CD, still balancing Emily on one hip. "Time for rock 'n' roll Christmas," Laura said.

Guitar chords thrummed from the speakers. Bruce Springsteen singing, "Merry Christmas, Baby." Maybe Laura didn't have even a limited sense of irony. Maybe all she had was pathologically indiscriminate taste.

"This is the lowest blow of all," I said.

"You can be such a party pooper," Laura said.

Laura started to dance, holding one of Emily's arms out as she waltzed with her. Emily smiled, tears still wetting her cheeks.

Jay tugged at my hand. "Come on," he said. "You're not going to take that from Laura, are you? You're not going to go down without a fight?"

I didn't want to help cover for my father. But Jay put an arm around my waist and cupped my hand in his and started dragging me around the room. Jay was a brutal dancer; he stomped and pulled and yanked and hoped for the best while I fought to keep my feet under me. He moved so quickly and switched directions so suddenly that it would have been malicious if it had been intentional.

Watching us, my mother began to laugh. She had to make an effort to catch her breath before she could speak. "Oh, Jay, stop! You'll have her bloody and bruised before you're through."

Laura danced Emily over to my mother and handed the baby off to her. She went to my father, bumped her hip against his in some version of a seventies disco dance. He resisted her, steady as a rock.

She bumped harder against him. "Come on, Santa, baby, wiggle that tush."

He looked at her with something like disapproval. Under the fuzzy Santa wig his face was the face of a hanging judge. Laura gave him a good poke in the ribs before twirling away from him.

Maybe it wasn't that he'd lost his touch. Maybe he never had the gift, at least not as I remembered it. The gift that was to compensate us, him, for the damage his weakness did.

As Jay whipped me around I caught another look at my father's face. I saw what I wasn't meant to see, a look of bewilderment and fear that I could have called loneliness if I'd had a more forgiving heart.

I wrestled free of Jay and scooped one of Emily's revolvers from the sofa and advanced on my father with the hammer drawn.

"Dance, Santa," I ordered. I pulled the trigger and the gun made a satisfying pop. I clicked the trigger again and again.

My father faked a smile. He put up his hands in a sort of grim surrender to the fun.

"Oh, come on, Joe," my mother said. With the baby still in her arms, she did a little skip to show him how.

I gave him a shove on the shoulder. "You can pick up those feet or you can start saying your prayers."

He caved in to us finally. He did a hasty little tap dance, jingle bells jingling, the big old rubber boots slipping up and down on his feet when he lifted them from the floor. Not a bad effort, really.

My mother clapped time for him, one arm awkwardly prisoned around Emily. Then, forgetting the baby's fear, she went to him and yanked on that fluffy cotton-ball beard, exposing his chin.

"Oh, for Christ's sake." My father batted her hand away.

I blew imaginary smoke from the barrel of the shiny nickel-plated revolver.

"I guess I'll let you live after all," I said.

Ethna McKiernan

Theft

from the "Alzheimer's Weather" suite

Last night I stole her blue beaded necklace,
the one I'd given her some past Christmas.
While she sat in her favorite flowered chair
tracking dust motes under the table lamp,
I slipped the string of beads
into the zipper pocket of my black purse.

When the dead leave, what is left to clutch?
All the rough intangibles becomes so much dust,
flour sifting downward from a torn bag.
Some raw material thing becomes necessity,
an article which owns the memory of perfume
or holds the far remembered cry of a voice
calling us in summer on the fevered afternoons
we'd stray too deep into the lake.

She won't miss it now, the necklace,
a minor theft when bumped against this largest loss
of all. I watch her press her hands to her head
asking where in God's name it has disappeared,
who has sacked her life and carried off her very mind,
who the robber, what theft, when the larceny occurred,
Jesus, why.

Absences

from the "Alzheimer's Weather" suite

Cell by cell my mother is leaving us.
No one can stop the memory leaking
from her body in such helpless cupfuls,
the way flecks of dead skin disappear
and scatter into air like loose dust gone wild
when brushed from sun-dried flesh.

The lost language in her eyes,
my face before hers like a question mark,
her vision blank with Haldol
or bright with terror,
a terrible incomprehension
stuttering through her body —

I hear the doctors say her brain
has atrophied a few degrees
beyond the CAT-scan of last year,
and I see a border of gray air
circling that unprotected, shrunken mass,
empty spaces wind could rattle through,
small animals could chatter in.

The howl at the door. Each day, every night.
Down the road, a gravesite beckoning.
My body like a fetus, curled in mute rage
on the floor near her bed. Selfish
as an infant, wondering who will know us now,
where we were children.

My mother in all her Irish beauty,
singing suddenly at 3:00 A.M.:
"The flowers only bloom in the spring, Maggie . . .
When I first said I loved only you,
Maggie, and you said you loved only me."
My father, weeping.

Savage, Minnesota

In the spring the streets would flood so deep
we could swim naked.
And when we slept three to a bed you kept
your hand curled around my ear.
If we were poor I don't remember.
Outside our window was a field filled with horses.
We spent hours drawing their faces
and dreaming them our own.

When you are gone for a long time
I drive back to this town to save you.
I sit on the steps of Saint John's where once
you hid a wet communion host under your tongue
and handed me half in the back pew.
You told me we were angels. I owe you.
I'm trying to settle a vendetta with this town
so you can look back and believe that we were happy.

I wear a fur coat.
No one recognizes me.
You could come too
and kill the bastards with your beauty.

Against the angry eyes of small town strangers
I invent a life you won't be ashamed to share.
We wear matching caps and gloves
and carry so much money
it falls from our pockets as we walk to school.
The neighbors fight over quarters.
We are the envy of everyone.
We are even a good family.
Now you can go on living.

Joseph Gahagan

Island People

1.

INSIDE MY MOTHER'S LIVING ROOM IT IS ALWAYS 1962. THERE IS NO changing that fact. The furniture is arranged so that it appears to have been once part of some forgotten ceremony. To a stranger, to an outsider intruding upon this scene for the first time, the discovery would seem startling, as if he had come onto a place stranded and cut off from the flowing stream of life all around it.

"You never tell me the truth anymore," my mother's voice says, trailing down the hall stairs.

I stand registering the scene, seeing it again as I have over all the years I've been away, this scene which is so deeply rooted in my memory. I cannot answer her pleas. She already knows everything she wants me to reveal. It has always been that way.

"Go ahead then. Don't answer me. I guess that's just part of the thanks I get for raising ungrateful children."

I sing "I would cross over the deepest ocean . . . " hoping the phone doesn't ring, hoping my mother stays upstairs, hoping I don't give in to the temptation to walk out the door this minute. "But the sea is wide and I cannot cross over . . . "

Lace doilies enfold the arms of the stuffed chairs and couches. Lace from her grandmother's hands, embroidered in another place and another time. In the late afternoon the sun seeps in through the cracks of the venetian blinds, catching the dancing specks of dust whirling in endless circles like miasma from a distant epoch, rising in protest against this foreign intrusion. The stranger plods carefully across the room, his clumsy feet sinking deeply into the carpet, sending more particles upward into the whirling dance.

On the walls are a crucifix and two pictures. The crucifix on the west wall divides the room with its holy sentiment and tidings of things to come. To its right, on the north wall, is a portrait of John Kennedy: young, virile, majestic, as he will always appear in this room. A votive candle is kept burning in a silver tray resting on a drum table beneath his picture. The flicker of devotional light plays off the picture in perpetuity. Inside the drum table are an endless supply of candles along with a vial of holy water and a box of stick matches.

Directly across from this, on the south wall, is a portrait of Sean Lemass, the great Taoiseach, prime minister of the moment. Outside this room the two great chiefs are gone now, but sometimes I think they will always live on here in some wistful stubbornness, unwilling to recede into the past, unable to come to terms with the present. I think the world outside this room ceases to exist, not just for my mother, who's been alone now since my dad's passing last year, but for all who enter under its spell of gloomy serenity, a serenity that promises eternal stasis rather than mere nostalgia.

"Kevin, are you still down there? Why don't you answer me?"

I hear her voice but cannot answer. I find myself grabbing at the dancing specks. When I was a child I believed they were stray pieces of sunlight which had turned to gold dust. I start to run through the living room, grasping handfuls of air.

2.

When I left here, I was going over seventy. I would have gone faster but that's all I could coax out of the old Ford Galaxie I had. There was no fear of my turning to a pillar of salt. I was already half-calcified by something I couldn't articulate — some unspeakable racial sadness that manifested itself in the tribal self-hatred, blind loyalty, and fierce territoriality so traditional to the hosting grounds of Chicago's Celtic South Side. Any more than that I cannot say now, even to Liz to whom I've tried to explain everything these last two weeks.

Sadness, I tell her. That's what was driving me away faster than the old Ford could carry me. And yet it was never fast enough. In the end it always overtook me.

"That woman you live with rang up here again. You better ring her back. I can't be worn out running to the phone every five minutes."

"Mom, I told you. I don't live with anyone."

"She probably wants to know how soon she can have you back. Tell her that it won't take that long to be rid of me and the old house." She stoically butters a cold piece of toast looking as if she's about to break down any second. It's an old game, but I try not to play along.

"More tea, Mom?" I ask, reaching across the table for the pot. She's not answering now. She's truly offended by my feigned indifference. It's all part of the game and I realize that by getting me to lie, she already has me playing it.

I don't know how she found out Liz and I are living together. Instinct, I guess. But it goes deeper than that. And I really don't know why a thirty-four-year-old man should have to deny how he lives. Even to his mother. I'm certainly not ashamed of Liz. Quite the contrary, I'm more than a bit envious of how easily she deals with life, how the pitfalls and snares I struggle to avoid are already smoothed away for her. I complicate where she simplifies.

For three years now we've shared an apartment in Connecticut. I met her when I was doing the Capitol beat at Hartford. She was involved in putting together a housing bill for a legislative committee. She told me she always wanted to be a writer and I told her I was always expected to be a lawyer. She just looked at me puzzled and that's about the closest I ever came to trying to explain myself. At least until now, these past two weeks we've been apart.

To her, being Irish was shamrocks, leprechauns, and green beer on Saint Paddy's, Bing crooning some awful sentimental slop, good cheer and drunkenness, and I've always been content to spare her the truth. Where I grew up, pain was something you only inflicted upon those you loved, and I did what I could to spare her that.

She thought that my taking a leave of absence to help my mother sell the house and settle my dad's estate would be a vacation of sorts, that I would be back in two weeks time. I tried to explain. Gently at first. Nudging her toward some kind of understanding.

"It sounds wonderful to have such roots like that, to have such memories. You don't get that growing up in the suburbs. I mean really, there's no sense of neighborhood, no sense of history where I come from."

"You're the lucky one then," I tell her. "History has a way of taking hostages of those who won't quit its company."

She laughs, telling me I should have been an actor with my flair for the dramatic.

"Drama is all part of the Exile."

3.

We've lived here on Claremont for as long as I can remember. And for just as long, I can recall the sadness, the sense of never being really home. Yet the old house was alive with the warmth of family motion: my father playing his concertina in the dining room, the smell of boxty and Winston sausage frying in the kitchen, the cries and squalls of my little brothers from the nursery, the constant chatter with neighbors about friends and relatives I did not know, the whispers and nodding glances with each new letter from back home.

Back home. With all the music, talks, sounds, and smells that inhabited this house, there was always that phrase, back home. If this wasn't home, then where was it? The place my parents had come from in the years before I was born? Then what was this life I was growing into? Was it somehow fractured, incomplete? Was my birthright being withheld because I was born in the wrong place at the wrong time?

The latest letter, the holiday phone call, photos of faces that were only vaguely familiar: all these had to do with back home, all these contributed to a sense of displacement, that somehow my journey got off in the wrong direction, that somehow there was always "back home" to return to.

4.

The summer is nearly over and my mother has not packed a box. She has not called a real estate agent. She hasn't even bothered to make any plans about where she is to live. Three months now since I set foot in here. Three months of watching her tend to her living room vigil, her daily mass, the routine of everyday life.

I don't say anything because that's part of the game. I know what she wants but I have her stubbornness inbred in my nature and I refuse to be the one to crack first. But I know she's wearing me down.

Right now she's on the phone to her friend Rose Duffy, whom she's called every month since as long as I can remember. Rose is her one reliable link to back home. Even though letters arrive all the time from the family and even though she made several trips back home with my dad over the years, things were never the same there. Rose makes things the same. She grew up with Rose near Ennis. They went to the nuns' school together, ran the hedges together and now, even though Rose and her husband have lived in Blackrock for the past thirty years, my mother still calls every month to get the gossip from back home.

"After all, Rose stood up at our wedding," she told me time and time again over the years. When I was little I thought this was because they ran out of pews in the church. Now I suspect it was to get a better view of what everyone was wearing.

I walk into the kitchen where I expect to find her chatting away. This is usually a good time to make my escape out of the house. But this time I find her sitting quietly in her favorite chair next to the phone, looking very pale.

"Did Rose finally run out of things to say or is she busy getting ready for the Ennis market?" I say, getting a beer out of the refrigerator. My mother says nothing, just sitting there being very quiet.

"Mom? Are you all right?"

She looks up startled, as if she has just become aware of my presence. "What? Ah, Kevin. Have you called in on Mr. Callinan yet today?"

Mr. Callinan has been our next door neighbor all these years. He's been widowed for some time now and had heart surgery a little while ago. My mother's been bringing him over his meals and she has me take him for a walk every day.

"No, not yet. He's not expecting me till four." I see she's pre-occupied with something, looking off into some distant corner of her world, fidgeting with the phone cord. "Are you sure you're all right? What did Rose have to say?"

"Rose? She's a bit under the weather. I didn't want to wear her out talking."

"I didn't think that possible," I say, waiting to hear how someday, when the elderly and obscure Mr. Duffy (no one in our family has ever met or even seen him) passes on to his reward, Rose is going to have my mother come live with her in Blackrock, how she's going to bring her back home to live in glorious Dublin suburban comfort. I think even my mother knows that's an old joke by now. Instead she gets up and slowly moves across to the sink and runs the water.

"Mom . . . " I start to say as she shakes two pills out of a prescription bottle she's pulled from her pocket. "Mom, what are those for?"

"Just something Dr. Sullivan gave me for my nerves," she says.

Then in a low voice, as if someone might overhear, she says "Your dad's estate came through the probate court. I received the letter yesterday."

"Then you're free and legally clear to sell the house," I say, hoping I'm not giving too much away.

"Yes, you can go back to work soon and . . . " I expect her to say that woman, but instead she just slumps back into her chair by the phone. ". . . and get on with your life."

There is no mistake about it. The resignation in her voice is something I've never heard before. At first I suspect this is another way of keeping me here, but something tells me otherwise.

"Mom, you know that's not important. I came home to make sure that everything gets settled right, that you'll be looked after." Both my brothers live right outside of Chicago, but I knew she wanted me back to stay when she called last March and said she was putting the house on the market because she couldn't stand living here all alone anymore.

"You better look in on Mr. Callinan. His heart is so weak and he shouldn't be left alone," she says, closing her eyes as if to put an end to the conversation.

I stayed four days here for my dad's funeral and I knew then that if I was ever to get away from the sadness, I had to end this life of perpetual exile. I walk out the back door and cross the yard to Mr. Callinan's, knowing that soon, no matter what my mother has planned, I must leave. *By the rivers of Babylon we wept when we remembered thee, O Zion . . .*

5.

The day John F. Kennedy was shot in Dallas, the bells of Saint Rita's rang in endless mourning all through the afternoon and into the night. Here in the Claremont neighborhood, as in Bridgeport and Beverly, he had been more than president, more than just an elected leader, more than even a symbol of who we were. He was our chief in exile, a living testimony to that unspoken bond of long remembered suffering and fear that made us huddle into urban clusters, cultural islands, long and far away from the stony gray soil and bogland from which most of us had come.

And long into that Friday night we knelt in front of what was to be the first of an eternal series of vigil lights: My mother calling out the rosary and the rest of us responding in tearful answer, as much from the pain of our bleeding knees as from heartfelt remorse.

The thing I remember most vividly from that day is coming home from first grade and finding my mother weeping, sitting alone in the quiet of the living room. She looked up, her mouth open and gasping sobs and then, in a horrible voice, saying "They've killed him. Damn them forever, they had to go kill him."

Today the clock on the side of Saint Rita's steeple is stopped at 3:10. I ask Mr. Callinan how long it's been that way, but he doesn't recall ever noticing it before.

"And you know, this whole heart business hasn't affected my mind. Not one bit. Mayo men are born with long memories," he says, laughing at his own joke.

I believe him though. For as far back as I've know him, Leo Callinan has been a flowing well of knowledge, a self-educated man who proved he had a good enough teacher. I always remember him as being old, even when I was a kid and his wife still alive. His white hair, however, was a cover for a man filled to the brim with life and curious facts. On Sunday afternoons he'd come over and teach us how to swing a *sloitar*, giving us not only the history of every Mayo team that ever took the field, but the very history of hurling itself. He certainly had me convinced that he'd taken the field with CuChulainn himself, he knew the game that well.

On Christmas Eve, he would bring over a bottle of Powers, and he and my dad would sit in the kitchen smoking cigars and talking the talk of back home. It was the only time whiskey was drunk in our house and the half-finished bottle would spend the rest of the year in the back of the bathroom shelf, waiting for a medical emergency.

Later that night, Santa would wake us all with a delivery of presents and I guess it wasn't until I moved away that I realized that the old fellow in the red suit had a definite Mayo accent.

We stop and take a look at the old church. I realize I'd never seen Mr. Callinan at mass the whole time I was growing up. I know I would have spotted him when I was an altar boy since I had to hold the patten under the necks of every receiving parishioner at the communion rail. I guess I just assumed we went to different masses.

"Ah, I remember my Margo and your parents gallivanting down to the old parish hall here every Friday night."

Margo, his wife, did come to mass and every Friday night she also came to the parish hall where the games of 26 were played.

"Didn't you ever play 26 here?"

"I did not. I was never one for the cards. All my luck, and a lot of it I have, is marked bad."

"That's an odd sentiment coming from a respectable self-educated man."

"Self-educated *chulchie*, you mean. We're allowed the bogman's sentiment and superstition. It's like playing Paddy for the foreigner."

This is his way of talking around something he doesn't want to talk about. Acting out Handy Andy for the Castle Rackrent crowd and their band of undertakers. Appearing like they expected you to. Every old Irishman of country origin knows how it's done.

I tell him anyway of the nights we kids would hang out on the playground, sometimes stopping our games of King Rory or search-light to listen to the strange talk of grownups – our parents – and the babble of accents and rules. *Put some meat on those bones, you pup* or *Down the boreen and over the water* or some other strange epigram would come floating up from their card games.

"Ah, 26 is an immigrant's game. It's not for the likes of you to learn it. Being born on this side of the water, your mind's too clear to be cluttered by the ill-bred nonlogic of such games." He turns and starts to walk away, as if he's suddenly tired.

I want to ask him what he meant by that, about those born on this side. Did that mean he could understand why I could no longer stay here? But it would have to wait for some other day as we walk the eight blocks back to his house.

Climbing the front steps he suddenly becomes very bright again. "Do you know, you're really down in the mouth for such a young man. You look like you could do with a bit of the *craic*."

"I suppose I could, but I don't know anyone here anymore."

"And what am I? King Richard's wardheeler on election day? You wouldn't have a jar with an old friend?"

"But I thought . . . I mean with your health, well . . . "

"Damn my health, lad. It's winter fodder for a winter I'll never see again. You give your ma the slip next Tuesday night and we'll hit that old place I used to see your da at over on Kedzie."

"Thanks. Sure, Mr. Callinan."

"None of that Mr. Callinan. It's Leo to you. It's Leo to all my friends. You tell your ma that a man can't wait forever for the cows to come home. If you wait until she settles on the house, you'll end up a Pioneer, and a monkish one to boot." He laughs and climbs the final step, giving me a wink before he disappears inside.

6.

One dreary December day in 1976 didn't work out so well for Richard J. Daley. After cutting a ribbon and making several speeches, hizzoner spent his lunch hour dedicating a gymnasium for his old pal Ed Vrodlyak and sank an underhand set shot with his first try. He had a way of coming through in the clinches. That shot was to be his last. He had his limo driver take him downtown to his physician's office where he collapsed on the floor.

The funeral at the Nativity of Our Lord's Church rivaled that of any earthly king. Dan O'Connell himself never got such a sendoff. We commoners stood in the sleety snow for hours just to pass a brief second in front of his casket. The night before the funeral the Secret Service kept vigil in the Church, like medieval knights for a fallen king. I suppose it was to be sure no bombs or snipers lay in wait for the president's visit, but the gesture of their presence was the sort of ritual and pomp the Old King would have loved.

Cardinal Cody invited the elect and powerful to be seated in the sacristy while Daley's right hand man, Colonel Jack Reilly (One-eyed Jack as my dad called him because of his black patch) handed out pew tickets to the yeomanry and ward heelers that made up the machine. We humble peasants lined the streets with our loyal sorrow, watching with mixed regret the passing cortege, watching the passing of something that had outrun its time.

They buried him with all the glory and splendor that befitted his office. Buried him in a plot in Holy Sepulchre Cemetery in the middle of the Republican suburb of Worth, the final slap at his enemies. A week later I loaded my Ford Galaxie and began my journey to freedom.

The 6511 Club isn't much to look at. A plain drab building with a short bar and a back room with sawdust on the floor. This evening there's a small *sessiuns* going on back there: a fiddler, a couple of tin whistles, and a bodhran, along with a few punters, hangers-on, listening in and quietly spitting into the sawdust.

An outsider might think he fell through some hole in time and space and come out in some mountain shebeen on the other side. There are only a few old ones sitting at the bar when Mr. Callinan orders up the pints and Powers. I settle down on the stool and take the place in. Not much has changed over the years I've been away. The dusty plaques, yellowed mirrors, banners proclaiming the same old county slogans, the GAA benefit posters, the wooden harps, the deflecting shades of the various bottles and the portraits of Jim Larkin and Padraig Pearse, each one flanking the ends of the bar. Both men, lifelong teetotalers, watching guard over their lost tribes. I point out the irony to Mr. Callinan.

"Ireland sober is Ireland free, is what my dad used to say."

"Your da was a good man, and many a lesser man has made that same observation," he says, handing me my pint. "That's our people all over again for you. The only logic they can muster is in contradiction."

I let him talk on. He seems like his old self tonight and I realize he needs this night out as much as I do. He tells me about things he shouldn't know – the Synod of Whitby, the fall of Persia, Ciceronean verse, the Clan na Gael and how poor Dr. Cronin was killed by his own people, political rivals, right over on Lake Drive back in 1889. It would seem like an odd assortment of disconnected facts coming from anyone, much less an immigrant pipefitter from Claremont. I want to ask him how and why he has come to know such things when he notices my whiskey.

"You haven't touched your Powers. Don't tell me you don't care for it, the Waters of Life?"

I tell him how I self-medicated myself when I was twelve and left alone in the house. I swallowed half of what was left of the Christmas bottle and nearly got sick.

He laughs. "Perhaps that was your problem. You weren't sick enough to begin with." He reaches for his glass when from behind a big red paw slaps itself down on his shoulder.

"Leo Callinan. It's good to see you up and about, lad. Did'ja get the flowers I sent to the hospital?"

I turn around and see Martin Dunne, King of the Irish in Claremont. That's the name given to those Irish who looked out for the newcomers from back home. The King of the Irish is the one who can set them up in a job, find them a place to live, tell them who to vote for. Each neighborhood has their own King and Martin Dunne's been ours since he became a ward boss for the old party machine years ago.

Mr. Callinan suddenly goes silent and nods his head, almost as if he's afraid of this well-fed back slapper. "And who's this?"

Now it's my turn to feel his hand on my shoulder and the hot perfumed paw makes me dizzy like when I was sneaking a drink at twelve. I want to move because suddenly I feel that I am being made to sit here against my will.

"Don't tell me. Kevin O'Neill. Kevin Barry O'Neill. You've turned into a real man."

I ask him how he knows my middle name.

"Why shouldn't I know it? I was there for your baptism at Saint Rita's. And your parents new to the neighborhood and all." He laughs and slaps me even harder on the back. "And how is your mother, God bless her? Has she recovered from your poor father's passing? I hear she has the house on the market."

I want to tell him to fuck off and mind his own business, but then, this is his business, so to speak. "I don't know, Mr. Dunne. The way things are going she might never move."

"Ah, waiting for a seller's market. A wise decision. And what about you? Has the prodigal son come home to his own to stay?"

"I'll be moving on soon, Mr. Dunne, very soon." I turn back to the bar and drain the whiskey glass. Now I know what Leo meant by sick enough.

Leo Callinan, I'm told by the very same man, is someone who became good at fooling himself. "I was twenty-three when I left Mayo, and I swore I'd be back to stay, my fortune made, before I was thirty. Well, it didn't work out that way. It never does. Sure, when I landed in Chicago I didn't have a tosser to me name and it being the Great Depression. But I worked hard and by the time I reached thirty I had married Margo and we already had two little ones. I guess I still planned on returning, but the letters from home sounded like they were talking to me from another world. Nothing specific, mind you. The old heifer that was still calving, the electrification tax, this or that neighbor passing on. But I got the sense that just in the act of leaving,

I had violated some trust, broken with the land like a child leaving home for good. It's as if you become dead to the place you left."

I tell him I know the feeling. The feeling I get when I look at the oil-cloth-lined shelves in my room at home that my mother has covered with pictures of me over the years – a picture of me in my surplice and cassock, in my hurling outfit, in my graduation picture – and so on. And the rows of track medals and GAA trophies. "I looked at that shelf when I came home and said out loud to myself 'That's not me. That's not who I am.' If I were to fall over tomorrow though, that would be my gift to posterity – my mother's record to the world of someone I'm not."

"Ah, but it was you once."

"Taken out of context. Sure. But it doesn't say anything about what I've become, who I am now."

"And that is my point, Kevin. After all the procrastination about returning home, I finally reached the conclusion that I was to be buried here, among strangers and not in the rocky churchyard back home. You see, back there I was already dead. Back there I only lived on in the island of my home parish as a twenty-three-year-old lad with a sack flung over his back and a hurling stick in his hand. That's how I'll always be thought of as long as anyone there might remember me. And that's how it is with we Irish. We've forgot how to forget and so we've learned how to cast a spell over history, to keep it from dancing away, to infect the present with the past. We say 'Nothing is gone that remains in the heart.' The world changes, we don't."

It begins to make sense. My mother, this place, the last fourteen years. I tell him about this feeling of sadness that makes me sick with remembrance.

"It's true, lad. You've been caught between two worlds, one that's forever changing and one that will never change. You've got to choose one or the other. I warn you though, if you stay here, you'll end up alone. Even the new Irish won't be here in twenty years' time."

"You mean they've figured all this out?"

He laughs and finishes off his pint. "No lad, I mean when you give up what you call your sadness, when you let all the past escape from your heart, you set yourself free. But you give up who you are in return. It's the price you pay. You can't have both."

"But the Beverly Irish, my brothers in the suburbs – they've broken away from the old neighborhoods."

"Ah, and they've paid for it. You see, we're not good winners."

"I don't understand."

"It's like your mother with her vigil lights. With Kennedy we won and by winning we lost. Lost it all. Lost who we are and who we've been. Lost. Everything. And that's the sadness you feel."

I can't deny it. Everything falls into place and now I feel even worse.

Mr. Callinan gets up and shakes his left leg as if it's asleep. "I'm for the jakes," he says grinning and hobbles off to the back of the bar.

7.

Liz says she knows I'm not coming back. I may be fooling myself but I'm not fooling her. Of course I deny it. Of course, I say, it's been over six months now, but my mother's been packing boxes for the past couple of weeks.

"Really? And how many has she packed?"

"She's getting there." I don't have an exact number, but I know it's only a few, three or maybe four. "But at least it's a start. We micks have a hard time packing up the past. It's a big burden to carry."

"Oh stop it, Kevin. I know you think you're joking now, but I've heard all I want to hear about the past. Let the past be the past. You've got only one decision to make, come back to me and your career now or be forever stuck in that place you claim to hate so much."

I try my best to assure her I'll be back by the first of the year, at the latest. "And you know that's a firm date. I don't make those kind of commitments unless I can keep them. And I called my editor last week. He was very understanding. Said that a leave of absence in family matters is understandable and that my position is still there for me."

"Don't be sure of that lasting for too long. The world won't wait just because you have to stop and catch your breath."

I tell her she doesn't get it. I tell her this isn't my decision but something circumstances have forced upon me. I tell her that the last thing I want is to become stranded in a world where I no longer belong, if I ever belonged there in the first place.

"I hope so. I hope for your sake, Kevin. Don't think you're the only one who's had to make decisions about the direction of their life. Remember, there's no going back. I can't say 'Suburban Girl' and suddenly everything is Bullet Park all over again. There are no more smoky cocktail parties, no bickering parents, no more acres of swimming pool culture, no more restrained angry voices in the night. Not that I miss it, or should miss it. It's just gone. I have no wish to inflict pain upon myself for things I can't help."

"Nothing is gone that remains in the heart," I find myself saying.

"What is that supposed to mean?"

"I don't know. Nothing. Just something I heard once. It's nothing, really."

I hear her draw a deep breath. "Take care of yourself, Kevin. Don't get caught someplace from where you can never return."

My mother has stopped calling her that woman. Now she just asks how is my friend. The fight seems to be draining out of her and I can't tell whether it's from the final resignation to moving or if her health's gone bad. She's become so morose lately and looks so tired I suspect it might be both. For that reason I don't want to rush her. I worry about her health. I don't want to lose her too.

"Mom, maybe you better take a break," I say as we wrap some old beleek in wads of newspaper.

"No. No, it's all right. It's just that I haven't been able to sleep nights the past month, even with the new pills Dr. Sullivan gave me."

"I wish you wouldn't take any more pills. Maybe if you saw another doctor."

"Ach, my headaches are bad enough at night even with the pills. And besides, Dr. Sullivan is an old family friend. Don't forget that."

"Well, keep him as a friend. I'm just saying get a second opinion."

She stops wrapping and turns a chipped plate over, examining the chip. "I've got all the opinions I need, thank you. I'll be fine if you just let me be."

8.

Most of the faces are old. The younger ones speak without any trace of an accent and have a look of smug self assurance. They bring their drinks into the viewing room, although Mr. Taughty, the proprietor, warns them they'll have to dispense with them once Father Farrell starts to call out the rosary.

The crowd is sparse. Not even enough to fill half the folding chairs set out in neatly spaced rows. I find that I'm trembling in spite of myself. I don't want to see him, but I've got to take one last look. He said he knew long ago that he was to be buried among strangers, but I like to think I'm the one exception in this crowd.

The copper-colored casket stands out among the few floral sprays and wreaths. As I wait for two old ones to finish their coffin side assessment, I notice one wreath from the Pipefitters Local 230 and another from his Beloved Children.

"Doesn't he look awful well," says the first old one with her Mayo accent.

"Old Taughty made him up good. Quite natural. Looks better now than he has for years," says the other in an accent I can't identify. Probably Cork. Cork women love a good wake.

"Old Leo Callinan who never darkened the doorway of a church and now Father Farrell saying the prayers over him."

"I heard he made a deathbed confession."

"He never did. They found him slumped outside a bar on Kedzie. Said it was his heart, but I know it was the drink that killed him."

"Still and all, it doesn't hurt to have a priest doing the burying."

"Well, me and my old one are from up in the same part of back home as he was. Different parish, mind you – he was west Mayo, the mountainy type, pagans one and all – but you could tell anyway what he was about with his politics. Blackhearted socialist, gun-toting Republican type, always the secret whisper and handshake, rubbing elbows with communists and freemasons."

"You don't say."

"It's true, God forgive him. I think that's what broke his poor wife's heart. She died on him a good twenty years ago. His heavy drinking and waving the red flag is what did her in."

"Now who would have thought that?"

"Ach, I have my sources among the County people. Mind you, I've said nothing, but his type are better off alone than pretending to be respectable by marrying a good church-going wife."

I watch the two of them shuffle off to the spread in the next room, thinking about why my mother keeps those pictures of me sitting on the bedroom shelf. Concrete evidence of a life well lived, I suppose.

It's true. Leo looks none the worse for all the verbal abuse and all the primping and powdering of the mortician's cold art. The final cover up. He's laid out in a blue suit with his white hair all combed back and his hands folded over. At least they didn't try to force a rosary into them.

I stand, knowing what Leo might think if I knelt. On one of our walks he told me that once he knew he was never going back home, he made up his mind to live in the world as he found it. That meant severing all the bonds that held his heart in place, including shunning all visits back home and even walking away from the church.

"It's not that I ever gave up anything I believed in. It was more a matter of letting go of that which would stop me from living in the here and now."

He began to read everything he could get his hands on so that he might, as he said, know more than where the home parish boundaries begin and end. "A foolish pride, I suppose," he had said. "Even my children think me odd, always trying to rid me of my books. They tell me to enjoy life more, as if it's just a matter of chewing it over and digesting it easy like a cow her cud."

When I found him two days ago sitting in his easy chair, he had a copy of General Humbert's memoirs spread out across his knees. His eyes were wide open and staring up at the ceiling. He had a little grin on his face. All around him in his living room were the mountains of books he had collected and read during all his time in exile. The books nobody else wanted.

Taughty sees to it that no one is buried from here with a smile on their face. I heard he cements the lips shut into that tight grimace just in case one of his clients should be shocked back to life by the bill and sit up and start talking.

I reach for his stony cold hands and rest one of mine there for a second, wondering if there's anyone left back in that windswept parish in Mayo who remembers Leo Callinan. I wonder if there's anyone these days who looks over the unnavigable waves of the western sea and sometimes thinks of a twenty-three-year-old emigrant who left the parish years ago with a canvas bag on his back and a heart full of awe. I wonder if anyone notices his name missing in the family plot of the church yard and asks of the silent stones what's become of him.

Father Farrell is in a hurry tonight. He rushes through the Sorrowful Decade like there's a K of C banquet he might be missing somewhere. Nobody seems to mind. The young ones keep on drinking and whispering while the old ones dutifully respond in kind to Father Farrell's call. Just another old paddy to be seen on his way with the usual ritual of dignity and respect.

I find I can't even pretend to pray along. I'm worried about my mother. She seemed to be getting on better the past week or so and then, when I found Leo, she just collapsed altogether. Took to her bed and stayed there.

I called in another doctor, but he says there doesn't seem to be anything wrong besides nerves and the usual toll of age. Still, it's not like my mother to miss something like this, especially since it's Leo Callinan.

I'm standing at the back of the parlor and I can feel the blast of the cold November night every time someone opens the front door. It'll be December in a few days and I'll have less than a month to finish up here. I try to keep my mind on the wake, but there are too many worries.

Another cold blast runs up my back and I'm about to move up to one of the folding chairs when I feel the hot touch of his hand.

"Poor Leo," he hisses in my ear. "It'd be a pity to be late for the old fellow's sendoff, but that's how business is."

Martin Dunne has his overcoat and muffler hanging over his arm and somehow he's already got a drink in his hand. I half nod in his direction, hoping he'll go away. Strangely enough, he reminds me of a cunning raven, with his heavy hand perched on my shoulder, all perfumed and manicured, and his black bushy eyebrows that sink lower and lower down his face whenever he speaks. His hand slides from my shoulder to my forearm and just as I think he's about to move off, he leans over and whispers in a warm wet breath, "Stick around. I've got something I'd like to talk over with you later. Something I'm sure will interest you." And then he's gone, working the crowd, shoulder-slapping and hand-shaking, wagging his head, the bushy eyebrows rising and sinking from person to person.

As Father Farrell finishes up with a makeshift sermon, I suddenly realize that most of the people here are strangers. In fact, the person I knew best is on his back with his lips glued shut. No one else from my family or any of the other exiles from the old neighborhood. Leo was right, I think. We've won what we've always wanted: respectability. And that's made us dull. No room for the South Side tribal passions in the suburbs. They've cut loose the old ties to the heart and in doing so, they've learned once again how to forget. I walk into the side room and pour out a whiskey. Powers, the kind Leo brought every Christmas. Maybe my mother isn't the one who's wrong after all. I raise the amber stuff to my lips and whisper, "Slainte Leo, I won't forget."

I swallow it quickly and head for the cloakroom. I can hear the chairs creaking in the viewing room and know the prayers are over. I want to get out of here before the party really begins. I rip my coat from the hanger, ready to head out the door when I find my path blocked by the King of the Irish.

"O'Neill. Not running off already, are you? The night's just begun."

"My mother's ill and I have to look in on her."

"Is she? I'm sorry to hear that." He smiles like he's never been sorry about anything in his life. "I hope it's not serious."

"Everything about my mother is serious."

He chuckles and extends his hand toward my arm. I quickly move away, but I find that I've blocked myself into a corner and I'll have to hear him out.

"Listen, O'Neill. Kevin. I don't want to hold you up, but like I said I have an offer to make to you."

Don't tell me he wants to put a bid in on the house, I think.

"I've heard that your mother's mood is not the best these days. Now never mind where I've heard that. We all have our sources. But as I said, it's knowing that your mother's sick that makes me sad." He rubs the end of his pointed nose and runs his eyes over the cloakroom as if he wants to be sure no one else is listening. "And do you know why she's sick? Because she has an ungrateful son."

King or no King. I'm about to break his royal beak when he starts waving his hand and tut-tutting. "Now I don't mean that personally. I'm sure you think you've done everything a son can do for his widowed mother. But I've been around longer than you have and I know mothers."

I'm about to rush by him when he takes out his pocketbook and shoves a card into my hand. "What I want you to do is give me a call first thing Monday morning. We have a place for a bright young man like you. College educated, a writer, someone who really knows the neighborhood." He waves his hands now like he doesn't want to be thanked for this great honor.

"Just think it over, lad. There's a future for you here. We can use your type. We'll even see to it that you get a law degree. Pay for your night classes. You're almost required to have one these days in politics. Not like when I was getting started."

"Mr. Dunne, I'm not interested in your offer. I think you better step aside because I have to leave."

"Just think about it Kevin. And you can call me Martin."

"Mr. Dunne, my family and my life doesn't concern you. Now if you'll excuse me . . . "

"That's where you're wrong. They do concern me. This whole neighborhood concerns me. When more and more of our own people leave the city, that concerns me. When we can't see our own good, that concerns me. When the new Irish, so young and bold with their *Glor an Deorai*, walk all over everything we worked so hard to build up, that concerns me. And it should concern you, too. And if it doesn't, at least think about what your mother wants."

I push him out of the way, surprised at how easily he yields. I hear him call out after me to think it over, but I'm already out the door and running full speed down the street.

I come down the stairs fighting my necktie. I've overslept and I've just got time to make it over to Taughty's for the start of the funeral. I slept like I was the one who was dead, a deep dreamless sleep that left me numb all over, only faintly hearing my alarm clock ringing, like it was trying to reach me from some distant place.

I rush to the kitchen to rinse out my mouth which is all dry and dusty from my long sleep. I begin to run the water when I realize I'm not alone. My mother's out of bed, sitting up in her chair by the phone, not saying a thing. Her face is all twisted and frightened in a way I've only seen once before.

"Mom?"

She looks up at me but says nothing.

"Mom, what's wrong? Are you sick?"

She begins to turn and bend her fingers from one hand to the next, almost clawing at them.

"She's gone."

"Who's gone, Mom?"

"She's gone. She's not there anymore. I tried to tell her husband, but he pretended like there was nothing wrong."

I took over at the phone receiver sitting on the counter and then it hits me. "Rose. Is she dead?"

"She's gone. She doesn't remember me anymore. I've had to re-mind her the past few months and then it would come back eventually, but now she's gone. She doesn't remember me at all."

"How do you know that?"

"I called her early this morning. She said she doesn't know who I am but that maybe her husband would." Her eyes looked up at me frightened and helpless. "She said that her name was Rose and that she'd like to meet me sometime."

"And what did her husband say?"

"He said she was just having one of her spells. But I know better. I knew Rose Duffy like no one else ever did. And this time she's gone for good."

She reaches up and pulls me down to her, clinging and sobbing like a frightened child. "I've got no place to go now. You understand? No place left to go."

I kneel down and throw my arms around her, feeling her deep heavy sobs breaking against my shoulder. I feel her heart pounding against my chest and I hold on to her tighter than I've ever held any-thing in my life. She's home now. There's no other place to go.

Monday morning I will call the King of the Irish and tell him what he wants to hear. I will tell the King of the Irish that I'm home to stay. And then I will go next door and start packing Leo Callinan's books.

Controlling Mother

"I'M AFRAID WE'LL HAVE TO SEAT YOU NEXT TO MOTHER AT THE reception. Sorry about this, Kathleen, but your sister and I have been over the list a hundred times and we haven't come up with any other solution."

"You don't need to apologize, Mom."

"I thought you might be bothered."

"No. Of course not. Why would you think that?"

"Good. Because Mother will be safe with you and Howie. It would be an absolute disaster if she got out of control again. Not after what happened at Joe M'Gurk's wake."

"Yeah, I heard all about it."

"That's right, *you* weren't there. Let me tell you, Kathleen, you have no idea. It was extremely upsetting for everyone present, especially your aunt Patsy. I thought she was going to have another stroke. And to think it was all because no one would take responsibility for watching Mother. Mark my words, Kathleen, she could spoil your sister's wedding."

"She won't, Mom. I promise."

"Good. Lorrie will be very relieved to hear you're going to help out. I kept telling her we could count on you."

"Well, sure . . . but what about Mrs. Washington?"

"Oh, that woman – ! Don't even ask. After about a dozen phone calls back and forth I thought I'd finally convinced her to come and sit with Mother in the church. Well, somebody has to. We'll all be standing beside Lorrie at the altar. But Mrs. Washington refuses to stay for the reception. Saturday's her afternoon off, and it's written in stone. You should have heard us begging and pleading. Your father even offered her a generous bonus – too generous if you want my opinion."

"You're positive she won't change her mind?"

"The woman is as stubborn as they come."

"Then, can't you stick Grandmom with one of your sisters or brothers?"

"Well, no. I told you: Lorrie and I went over every possibility. We can't seat her with Dot's family because that would mean moving Grace to Rita's table, and everyone knows that Grace doesn't speak to your great-aunt Colleen anymore after that terrible scene at Jackie's wedding between Hugh and Joe Junior. And Jack and Mary Frances aren't even coming, from what I can tell, because one of *her* nieces is supposed to be getting married in Torresdale that same day. At least, that's what she was saying when we saw them at Joe M'Gurk's funeral, which was ages ago and we haven't heard from them since. And you know Bernie and Denise never go anywhere without Jack and Mary Frances. And, of course, since Joe M'Gurk and my brother Danny passed away I *have* to put Patsy and your aunt Rita together, which means sticking them at my aunt Colleen's table. And Patsy's wheel-chair takes up two spaces. So when you add Rita's Jimmy and Joe Junior and Jackie and his wife and Mary Pat, and my cousin Lorraine and her husband, where does that leave us?"

"I have no idea."

"I'm sure it comes out to ten at each table. Wait, I'll find the diagram —"

"Never mind, Mom, I'll take your word for it."

"You're upset about this, Kathleen. I can hear it in your voice. And after Lorrie was *so* concerned about not hurting your feelings. You should have seen her going on and on about it last night."

"I'm not upset."

"Good, because there really wouldn't be room for Howie and the girls at the head table, anyway."

"You mean, we're not even sitting at the head table?"

"Well, no, we thought we'd put you on the, ah, periphery. That way when the children get bored they can get down and run around without disrupting traffic. You know, the waitresses. And people will be getting up to dance."

"Oh, terrific. And while you're at it, why not put us between the swinging kitchen doors behind a six-foot potted fern? Maybe you'll get lucky and no one will notice us at all."

"Don't be dramatic, Kathleen. You know perfectly well it isn't anything like that. As a matter of fact, we put your table in the garden."

"Well, excuse me. That changes everything. My family is now banished to the great outdoors. Tell Lorrie not to trouble her pretty head – I am thrilled to sit with Grandmom. At least she can bear to be at the same table with my children."

"Oh, please. Lorrie and I had your best own interest at heart. We figured you'd be happier outside. Howie can keep an eye on Caitlin and the baby, which will leave you more-or-less free to deal with Mother. And you're so good with her, Kathleen. Everybody says so. You're one of the few people she really responds to these days."

"Mmmmp. Who else is at our table?"

"Your father's relatives."

"At the same table with Grandmom? Whose brilliant idea was that?"

"Well, where else could we put them? Anyway, it's not the way it used to be. She'll *hardly* know who they are, and by the time we all sit down they'll be pretty deep into their bourbon or whatever it is they're pickling themselves in these days."

"Oh, fine. So Howie and I will babysit everyone. It's the least that we can do for Lorrie and Josh on their big day."

"You're impossible."

"I'm not."

"Your sister is counting on you, Kathleen. If I'd had any idea that you were going to be this difficult –"

"I'm not difficult. I said I'd be happy to sit with her."

"Kathleen, I'd put her at my own table if I were able. But even if I felt I *could* manage to keep an eye on her – I'll be so preoccupied with all the guests! – we couldn't possibly squeeze her in. There'll be, let's see: Lorrie and Josh, your father and I, and Josh's parents, his grand-father, Father Fenster, and the Vatican ambassador –"

"The *what?*"

"Oh, you haven't heard? Well, it seems that Josh's mother has some old school connection to the Vatican ambassador, of all people, so she's invited him to the wedding. Poor woman, she's desperate to impress us."

"The Vatican ambassador to what?"

"To the United States, of course."

"You mean, a priest?"

"No, well, that's just the problem. He's married to Josh's mother's college roommate's friend. We just got the reply card last night, and that's what it says: Mr. and Mrs. Suchandsuch will attend."

"Suchandsuch?"

"Something Italian. I don't remember. But the point is, there goes the tenth place at our table."

"But—why are you seating *them* at the head table? They aren't relatives. We don't even know them."

"Kathleen! After all, he *is* the Vatican ambassador. Now, if only I could get your sister to change her mind about not having an 'Ave Maria.' I don't understand Lorrie, really I don't. First it was 'no Mass.' Who ever heard of not having a mass? And now this. You know what I think? I think it's really Josh who's causing the problem. He didn't even want to have the wedding inside the church, you know."

"Well, Mom, I mean, can you blame him? He's Jewish."

"Half."

"Still—"

"He's been putting pressure on her, I can tell."

"Maybe he's worried about making his relatives uncomfortable."

"Honestly, Kathleen. Do you feel uncomfortable at a bar mitzvah?"

"No, but . . . "

"When I married your father it was the same way. 'Have a mass if you must, Peg, but no Ave Maria.' He was afraid his WASPy family wouldn't approve! Of course, Mother went ahead and told Danny to sing and he did a lovely job, and—the truth of the matter is—your father's family has never approved of anything I've done in thirty-five years. Not before the wedding, during it, or since. So what difference would a single hymn have made in the course of our lives?"

"None, I guess."

"And you and Howie were the same. You didn't want the 'Ave Maria' at first, either, but in the end you both were glad I talked you into it. Danny was in terrific voice that day—it was before they found the spot on his lung, remember?—and Howie's family loved him. I guess just about everybody loves an Irish tenor. Howie's mother was so moved she came up to us afterwards with tears in her eyes."

"Howie's mother? She did?"

"Besides, the marriage ceremony itself if entirely too short when you cut out the mass. The fact of the matter is, we *need* an 'Ave Maria.'"

"Yes, well, but actually, when you add in all the other music . . . "

"Kathleen, this is the only wedding your sister will ever have—at least, we have to *believe* that will be the case if it's to take place inside the walls of this church — so, honestly, what's the sense in barreling through it with just a couple of readings and a quick Exchange of Vows? Why is everyone in such a rush?"

"Mom, I really don't think that's the point here."

"No, I'll tell you what the point is, Kathleen: your sister is so concerned about not offending a bunch of strangers that she's willing to compromise the integrity of her own wedding. All right, fine. That's her perogative. But what about her *own* family's feelings?"

"Do you really think anybody cares much?"

"Kathleen, I'm positive my brothers and sisters are expecting her to ask Danny's son to sing. You know, to honor his memory."

"What? *Which* son?"

"Bernie."

"Mom, come on. Isn't Bernie in some kind of heavy metal band? I mean, it was embarrassing enough when Uncle Dan use to belt out hymns like a night club singer."

"You're missing the point again, Kathleen, in addition to being totally misinformed about my brother Danny's singing. You never did have much of an ear for music — that piano nun at Saint Bartholomew's was right."

"Wait a minute, which nun?"

"Sister Seraphine."

"Mom, how could you even consider repeating anything Senile Serpentine told you? The woman was tone-deaf and you know it."

"Oh, calm down, Kathleen. You over-react to everything."

"That's not true!"

"You've always been thin-skinned. Why do you think Lorrie was so worried about telling you about the seating arrangements?"

"I already said, *I don't give a damn where anybody sits at Lorrie's wedding!*"

"Besides, there's no point in arguing because it's too late."

"Too late for what?"

"Kathleen, I've been trying to tell you this, but you never let me get a word in. It happened on the way out of the church after Danny's funeral. Of course, you and your sister were both too busy that day to come —"

"The kids had chicken pox, for Christ's sake, Mom. And Lorrie had to work."

"Don't swear, Kathleen. Honestly, you have no idea how much it bothers me. Besides, *you* weren't there, however, for your information, I will say it was one of the most depressing funerals I've ever attended."

"And I said I was sorry."

"Your Aunt Rita was so sedated that her daughters had to hold her up. Then, when Bernie started singing 'Danny Boy' as his brothers carried the casket down the steps – "

"What? You never mentioned this part before."

"The instant he started singing – Oh, Kathleen, that kid is his father all over. It's like a miracle. Everyone who heard him said so. I just wish you girls could have been there to see it. We were all in tears, all of us, even Mother, though I'm not sure whether she knew what she was crying about."

"Oh Jesus. I know what you're going to say next. Mom, how *could* you?"

"You'd have done the same thing in my shoes, Kathleen. Yes, you would. It was the only decent thing. I asked Bernie on the spot if he would take his father's place at your sister's wedding."

"I knew it! But, Mom, Lorrie never asked Uncle Dan to sing."

"Of course she didn't. Danny was too sick."

"Oh boy."

"All right, so I'll admit maybe I did let the moment get the better of me. But what's done is done and I can't go back and change it. So what am I supposed to do now? Just answer this: would you have me go back and *un*-invite him? Is that what you and your sister want? Well, how would *you* like to be the one who calls the poor boy up and tells him we don't want him to sing at Lorrie's wedding? It would break his mother's heart."

"Has Lorrie heard about this yet?"

"You girls, you know, the both of you are so utterly insensitive. Really, sometimes I have to ask myself where you came from. Excuse me. I do know. The *Spock* generation. The 'me-society.' As I was say-ing to your father the other day, 'God help us, Al, we have only ourselves to blame for their selfishness.'"

"I gather you told her already, then. How did she take it?"

"How would you expect her to take it, Kathleen? You know as well as I do when your sister gets her back up there's no talking to her at all. She's downstairs in the kitchen right now, banging around my good pots and pans."

"You mean you told her just now, just this minute? Is this why you called me in the first place, because you just had a fight with Lorrie?"

"I have no idea what you're getting at, Kathleen. The reason I called was to talk about controlling Mother during Lorrie's reception."

"Well, if you want me to be honest—not that I'd believe for one minute that you would—well, okay, here goes: I think Lorrie and Josh have a right to choose the music for their own wedding. I really, really do. And, what's more, I refuse to play any role in pushing Lorrie into something she doesn't want. I won't do it, Mom."

"Kathleen, Kathleen. What am I going to do with you? You've got yourself all worked up over nothing—in addition to missing the whole point of this discussion. The point here is that Lorrie gives in to Josh entirely too often. Now, I know how much we all love Josh, but you have to admit it's a problem. Your sister has always been a bit of a pushover with men, ever since that awful boy with the leather dungarees—you remember, when she was in ninth grade."

"Who, Gordie Watkins? He was cute."

"Cute, my foot. He was selling drugs in the recess yard."

"No one ever proved that."

"Oh, I never should have let that child go to public school. I worry about Lorrie. This business about Josh's family—you can see what they're trying to do."

"What?"

"They're trying to take over. I can see it already. First this business of trying to manipulate the wedding; next thing you know, the kids will be moving to Connecticut. Lorrie's been talking about Yale Law, you know."

"It's just graduate school."

"In Connecticut. In *their* state. Doesn't that seem a little suspicious to you? What's wrong with Villanova, if I'm allowed to ask? Too *Catholic* for her? Well, it wasn't too Catholic for your father, of all people—though, Lord knows, his mother did try to scoot him out of there the minute he set his eyes on the likes of me—"

"If Josh's family really felt that way about Catholics, then why on earth would his mother invite the Vatican ambassador to the wedding?"

"God only knows what motivates that woman. All I can tell you is that *I* didn't invite him, or half the names on the list, for that matter. Have you *seen* Josh's mother's list, Kathleen? It's not to be believed. Twice as long as what we asked for. I mean, who *are* these people? Friends of friends of friends. People they met in the supermarket. She

invited their mailman, for God's sake. Have you ever heard of anything so pushy?"

"Josh says he's known that mailman all his life."

"And to think, we didn't even have enough space for most of your
cousins – "

"Mom, we have so many cousins, half of them wouldn't even recognize Lorrie on the street. She didn't want them at her wedding – "

"And what about this business of half-a-dozen groomsmen plus
their *dates?* Who ever heard of such a thing? They're all Josh's friends
from growing up. I don't think Lorrie even knows them. I can't imagine why she didn't put her foot down. Not that she ever asks my
opinion. After all, I'm just the one who does the work and writes the
checks."

"But, I mean, really . . . you're tickled he's coming, aren't you?"

"Who's coming?"

"The Vatican ambassador."

"Well, *Kathleen*. Look, you and your sister can mock me all you
want, but he's still the Vatican ambassador and that means something
to me. As well it should to you – but I guess that's my fault again.
Spock generation."

"Okay, you made your point, Mom."

"*And* he's bringing a Papal Proclamation. At least, that's if Josh's
mother knows what she's talking about. I wonder – do you think we
should list it in the program? I wonder whether he'll make some kind
of speech."

"I have no idea."

"You know what I've been thinking, Kathleen? I've been thinking
how much Mother would have enjoyed sitting beside him at the head
table. She used to love John Paul. Remember how she'd make us all
sit down and watch him on TV?"

"Yeah, what about those Papal spoon things she was always
polishing?"

"Your grandmother paid a fortune for that spoon collection – one
of those 'Limited Editions' from the Franklin Mint. And, to answer
your question, I'd imagine your Uncle Jack and Mary Frances made
off with them the time they 'tidied up' her house after we fired that
awful Mrs. Gonzolez. Mary Frances always went in for that kind of
kitsch. She took the cuckoo clock, too."

"Oh, no, I loved that clock – "

"What I'm *trying* to explain to you, Kathleen, if you'll please stop interrupting, is that a moment like this—the Vatican ambassador at her own granddaughter's wedding—would have been one of the high-lights of my mother's life. Just imagine, if only this whole business could have happened six or seven years ago, when your grandmother was still herself."

"Mom, seven years ago Lorrie and Josh were in high school."

"It kills me to put Josh's grandfather in her seat. It really does."

"Okay, okay, so if you feel that way, why not seat Josh's grand-father someplace else?"

"Kathleen, I spent *three* hours on the phone with Josh's mother on Sunday night—honestly, that woman never winds down—and I specifically promised her I'd seat her father at our table. I couldn't possibly call her back about it at this point. You know how difficult she is."

"Yeah, you said."

"A woman like that one, you eventually just give in to her out of sheer exhaustion. It's the only way to deal with her. She's impossible."

"Right."

"She'll talk you in circles until your head spins. Though, I must say, a conversation with her certainly provides a lot of insight into understanding Josh."

"Right."

"So, we'll just leave it as it is. Unless . . . "

"Unless what?"

"Never mind."

"*What?*"

"Unless maybe you would want to call her."

"Oh—I don't think so, Mom."

"I have her number right here. You could say you were calling, ah, about flower arrangements for the hall. Did you know it's the respon-sibility of the family of the groom to pay for those? I just found out myself."

"Where did you hear that?"

"Well, you know I never read those silly magazines, but I happened to glance at an article last night in a copy of *Modern Bride* that Lorrie brought home."

"Any chance Josh's mother might have read the same article?"

"I thought you could mention it. Just work it into the conversa-tion casually and see what she says."

"No *thanks*. I mean, you're the one who understands how to handle her."

"Oh, forget it, Kathleen. I don't know why I even bothered bringing the subject up. I should have known you'd be like this. You can be so utterly unhelpful sometimes. It's true. Everybody says so."

"Wait a minute, who says so?"

"Well, just last night your sister—No, never mind, I really shouldn't have said anything. Just forget I mentioned it."

"Oh, really? So what's Lorrie saying about me now?"

"Don't tell her I told you this but, she says, well, she wishes you'd be more cooperative about the dresses."

"Cooperative! I'd say I'm being about as cooperative as I know how, considering I'm expected to pay three hundred dollars for dresses that make me and Caitlin look like a couple of fish."

"Salmon is your sister's favorite color. I certainly can't do anything about that. We all have to live with her choice."

"Well, between you and me, she has lousy taste."

"So, you see what I mean about the music."

"What?"

"Honestly, Kathleen, for a bright girl you can be astonishingly dense. I've been trying to tell you for the past half hour that there's nothing vulgar whatsoever about Schubert's 'Ave Maria.'"

"I never said that it was vulgar."

"Then talk to your sister, will you? Please. Before she dents my Calaphon to bits."

"You mean, she's *still* in the kitchen banging pans?"

"Abusing gourmet cookware has been her favorite form of protest since she was a teenager. That's why we double-registered her for stockpots and dutch ovens at Wanamaker's and Strawbridge's. Talk to her, will you? Remind her about how Howie's mother loved your wedding—she's part Jewish, isn't she? Be sure and mention that. I mean it. Lorrie won't listen to another word from me."

"Okay, okay. I'll talk to her."

"Good, because you *do* understand the position she's put me in with your cousin Bernie. I mean, it's his mother I'm worried about, really. I heard they've still got her on Xanex. After all she's been through, Rita would be just devastated if we asked him not to sing."

"Okay, okay."

"Because we absolutely cannot afford to have another disaster like Joe M'Gurk's wake. Not at your sister's wedding. Not on her big day."

"I guess you have a point, Mom."

"It would spoil everything for Lorrie if Aunt Rita made a scene."

"I can imagine."

"So you'll talk to your sister for me?"

"Well . . . "

"Good. I'll just dash downstairs and put her on. You know, she might not appreciate what we're doing for her now, but I can promise you, Kathleen, someday Lorrie will thank us for keeping things under control."

New House

ON FRIDAY MORNING THE DULL GREEN PONTIAC PULLED INTO REN AND Nick's driveway. Ren watched from the upstairs window as her mother and father and brother and sister-in-law popped out of the rusting car like things that had been compressed too tightly, for too long a time. One of the car doors made a deep, cranky groan when it opened, and another replicated a loud yelp as it was slammed shut.

Ren peered over a hedge of forsythia in full bloom at her family stretching and looking over the Connecticut property that she and Nick had bought just two months before.

"They're here," Ren called to Nick, who was in the shower.

"I thought they had a six-hour trip. When the hell could they have left?"

She heard the soap hit the porcelain as it slipped from her husband's hands.

Ren's mother wore a large, pale-yellow dress that Ren had never seen before, and held a cigarette in her hand, extended as if she were taking an oath. Careful not to jostle the long, tenuous ash, Ren hugged her mother. Next she squeezed her much smaller father, who, as usual, was dressed in varying shades of brown from hat to shoes.

"Where are all these deer we've been hearing so much about, Renata?" Ren's mother asked, smoke coloring her voice.

"Oh, we're sure to see a few before the weekend's over," Ren assured them. As she pointed out the boundaries of the four-acre property, parts of the outline of the stone wall visible from where they all stood, Ren noticed Tammy teetering on three-inch red heels sunk into the newly-laid crushed stone driveway.

"Hey," Kevin said and kissed Ren on the forehead. Ren and her brother had reddish hair and green eyes, and whenever Ren saw him she felt the same comfort of familiarity she got when she looked into a mirror.

"When I was a young man, I ran into a poor little deer. Over on Greenspring Avenue," Ren's father said, looking down at his tan shoes rapidly losing their luster as he swiped one, then the other, back and forth across the stone and dirt.

"That was a dog," Ren's mother said. She was twenty years younger than her husband and constantly corrected his memories and perceptions.

"How the hell do you know? I wasn't even married to you yet."

"I know," she said and lit another cigarette. "It was a golden retriever."

As if on cue, as she had all of her life, Ren directed her family out of an argument and toward a distraction: today her home, the stone and dark wood country house that she'd dreamed of, but never truly imagined owning all those years that she and Nick moved from one cramped apartment to another as he wrote play after play and she auditioned in other people's plays for every part she imagined she could pull off. When one of Nick's plays was adapted and sold to the movies, they were delivered from the ten-year stream of dank basement apartments, sixth-floor walkups, studios in boisterous neighborhoods, to this place of light and space cleared out of a tree-covered landscape. The circular stone flower gardens and front of the house were colored with purple and yellow crocuses, hyacinths, deep green, leafy promises of tulips and lilacs, and sprays of forsythia.

The first weeks after they'd moved here, Ren felt she'd spent whole days walking through the rooms, the echo of her steps on the oak floors following her, placing her somewhere entirely new. She looked into the huge empty closets and out the floor-to-ceiling windows at hundreds and hundreds of trees in all stages of development. And, every so often, she felt she was acting the part of some wealthy, fortunate woman, she was that out of her element. Ren still couldn't accept the concept of owning trees, many of them far older than she was at thirty-three.

"We made pretty good time," Kevin said. "Ma closed her eyes while we went through New York City."

"I was sleeping," she responded, but not even Tammy believed her.

Ren's father said, "She was nervous as a cat."

"I was tired. We left Baltimore at four o'clock in the morning, for god's sake."

Ren pictured her family's two-bedroom house in a landscape of identical capes, each with a square of yard bounded by chain-link fence. Within the last three years, white vinyl siding had spread through the neighborhood like a blight, obliterating the colors of the houses. Even with this alteration, and even though she hadn't lived there in twelve years, the house that Ren had grown up in was still the first thing that came to her mind when she heard the word "home."

"We left early," Kevin said patiently, "so we would avoid hitting New York City at a bad time." Kevin had driven the entire way.

Years ago on car trips, that was the exact logic her father had used. While her father was normally an easy-going man, he grew frantic, even reckless, in traffic. And, as he aged, his panic had unfurled into areas other than congested highways.

Now he seemed disoriented by the new surroundings. He rubbed at his upper lip with the back of his hand. "Whatever made you decide to move way the hell up here, Renata?" As Ren put her arm around him, she felt his small, bony shoulders. She had her father's facial structure, and sometimes she found herself absently rubbing the edge of her ear as she'd seen him do so many times when he was thinking something over.

"Because, Dad, you know we had to be near New York. And it beats living in the city." Ren had to keep reminding her family that she was an actor and her husband a playwright. Besides her work in stage plays, Ren had made two television commercials in the past six months. And last week she'd done a voice-over for furniture polish.

While she once again explained the obvious – that she and Nick didn't work in a hospital or a cafeteria where they could pick up and put down anywhere her family wanted – she heard her own voice. It felt as calm and confident as when she'd promoted the long-lasting effects of a certain lemon wax. But even as she spoke, she knew she was only fooling herself. Around family, it was impossible to act professional for long.

When they stepped into the living room, its walls covered with dark panels of natural wood, Ren noticed that the thick main beam above their heads stretched across the ceiling in a direct path to Nick. His hair was still wet from the shower. He was dark and ruddy and strong. Ren thought that if you looked at the six of them standing there in the living room and had to circle the one who didn't belong—like all those comparison tests she'd taken as a child—you'd have to pick Nick.

She and Nick looked nothing alike. When they'd first met they hadn't been able to keep their hands off each other, they appeared so exotic to one another.

"So," Nick said, "how was your trip?" And they all began talking at once.

Ren hurried into the kitchen and set up the coffeepot. It was way too early for the lunch she'd prepared—an array of their favorite cold cuts (boiled ham, smoked turkey roll, and, for Ren's mother, olive loaf), a potato salad she'd made herself with plenty of eggs and mayonnaise, and, for dessert, thick, chunky brownies. As she dipped slices of bread into an egg mixture for French toast, she heard her husband answering questions about New York City. Her family considered New York City a foreign country and Nick one of its natives.

"Didn't I read somewhere that Manhattan had more muggings last year than all of the rest of the country combined?" Ren's mother's question snaked into the kitchen.

"She's always reading something," Ren's father said and laughed, still, after all these years, attempting to buffer her bluntness.

Ren quickly called the family to breakfast over the rumblings of her husband's reply.

"Don't we have a few things to get out of the car?" Ren's father asked as he wiped his mouth of syrup. He seemed to have become more comfortable in Ren and Nick's house after eating.

"Bring in your camera, Kevvy," Tammy advised. Like a child, she yawned widely, without covering her mouth. Tammy was fifteen years younger than Ren's brother.

"Yeah," agreed Ren's father, "you never know when we might spot one of the deer."

"Kevin, the two coolers," Ren's mother called. "We'll have to get that stuff into the refrigerator."

"Ma, we have plenty of food," Ren said, but her mother strutted ahead, ignoring Ren on her way back into the living room.

"This is a very nice house you have, Renata." She lit a cigarette and studied the walls and ceiling. Ren imagined the smoke her mother exhaled filling in the ceiling cracks and spaces between the strips of wood. Then, as if finding the inconsistency – a task she'd always been committed to – she said, "Renata, you never liked pink."

For the dark wood walls and beams, Ren and Nick had selected mauve couches. A large photo in a pink frame highlighted one side of the room.

"Well, now I like it," Ren said a little defensively. While she thought the light color made a feminine claim on the generally masculine quality of the house, she didn't mention this idea to her mother who would call it mumbo jumbo.

"Pink and orange. You never liked either of those colors."

Ren's mother went on about a pink voile dress she'd made that Ren had "turned her nose up at," until Ren said finally, "I was eleven." Even as Ren spoke, she saw that families held up the past as something you had to conform to for the rest of your life. Sort of like religion.

Kevin came through the front door with his camera bag slung over his shoulder, a cooler through his left arm, and a large object wrapped in crinkly white paper in his arms. He set it down carefully in the middle of the room.

"For the new place," he said and stepped away from the gift as if it might be alive. It was a foot-and-a-half taller than the end table nearest Ren.

Ren's father followed Kevin with two full-size suitcases which he plopped on the floor. "What in the hell you got in these cases, Arlene?"

"Lead," she said. "I packed them with lead." And then she lit another cigarette.

Nick was loading the breakfast dishes into the dishwasher and Kevin was focusing on a pair of cardinals at the bird feeder outside of one living room window. His shutter clicked.

"I can't wait for you to open it," Tammy practically squealed. "I just love presents." Ren's mother rolled her eyes at her daughter-in-law's enthusiasm.

Before he noticed the present, Nick spotted the two large suitcases situated between Ren and him. He gave her a subtle, questioning look, squinting his eyes ever so slightly, which said to Ren, "How long did you say they were staying? I though this was just a weekend visit."

"Why don't you open it, Ren?" Nick said. Nick had always been suspicious of gifts, of intentions.

"Go ahead, Tammy," Ren said.

"Really?" the girl asked. Kevin made a gesture to hold his wife back, but Ren assured him it was fine for Tammy to unwrap the gift. She was twenty, but she pulled at the paper as eagerly as a child.

Ren noticed gray and white, something that looked like an animal's ear, a red nose, a large bowl . . . She shot Nick a bewildered grimace, far less subtle than the one he'd given her over the suitcases. Ren recognized an animal's face. A cat. Tammy stood back from the four-foot sculpture of a gray-and-white striped cat standing on its hind legs and holding a large, shallow bowl.

"That's something," Nick finally said.

"It's a birdbath," Tammy explained.

"A lawn ornament," Ren's mother added. "Elaine down the street made it in her ceramics class and I bought it off her."

"She charged you?" Ren's father asked.

"Of course, she charged me. She can get good money for something like this. She only charged me for materials, though."

"Tell them about the turtle," Tammy said. She clasped her hands together. Her fingernails were long and colored the same deep red as her lips.

"Elaine had a turtle, too. He's so cute. He stands on his back legs and holds his shell up for the birds to wash in. Now you think about it, Renata. Because if you want the turtle, it's no problem for us to ex-change it," Ren's mother said.

"I've been hearing about this damn turtle ever since she got the cat," Ren's father said.

"I was going to take them both and keep whichever one you didn't want for our own yard," Ren's mother said.

"Aw, Arlene, we've got enough damn junk in that yard. I don't want to look at some turtle with his shell off whenever I go out to mow the lawn," Ren's father said, rubbing at his chin.

Despite her edge, Ren's mother made a job out of pleasing people. "Maybe I should have asked Elaine if she thought about creating a deer. You know, to attract other deer," she said.

At Tammy's insistence, Kevin heaved the birdbath into his arms and carried it out onto the lawn. From the kitchen window, Ren watched her family arguing over where the birdbath looked best. Kevin focused on the monstrous cat, then tried to get Arlene to stand beside it while he took a photograph, but she refused.

"Why don't you go help them decide?" Ren asked, coming up behind Nick, putting her arms around him.

"Not on your life," he said and flicked on the dishwasher.

"We're ahead of you," Ren's mother said, pointing at the forsythia and green-tipped trees. "Baltimore must get spring a good two weeks before Connecticut."

After only six hours of the visitors, Ren was a little testy. She wanted to say, "Well, I'm sorry you're getting a rerun," but she held her tongue the way she had as a child.

The six of them sat on the grass in webbed lawn chairs. Ren's mother launched into a discourse in praise of the advantages of a full-size freezer. As she exposed her whole-hearted belief in "stocking up," Nick stood up to get himself another beer. Ren's mother sliced a cheese log she'd brought from Baltimore and passed it around on a plate of crackers.

Ren tilted her head far back and looked deep into the trees. Spring had touched the Bradford pear trees with tufts of flowers resembling cotton from her distance, and a mist of green hung on others. The trees surrounded and protected Ren and Nick's house like giant hairs. Ren sometimes imagined the tulipwood and maple and ash and oak and evergreen all pulling together to screen the noises and curiosities of her wealthy neighbors.

Ren had grown up in an area far from four-acre zoning. The houses were so close to one another you could smell your neighbors' breakfasts and dinners cooking and hear your neighbors burp after eating them. And, on the other side of the house, you could actually watch another neighbor's television if you got the right angle by standing on a kitchen chair. Ren remembered that most of the time she'd lived there she'd stayed deep in her room, shades drawn on the brightest day, and dreamed of getting out, escaping scrutiny.

"Renata," her mother called, startling her. "Still daydreaming when someone's talking to you." Ren had been accused of excessive "drifting off" from conversation ever since she'd learned to tie her own shoes.

"I asked you what your neighbors are like."

"I don't know. I haven't met them," Ren said.

Ren's mother and father stared at her the way they had ten years earlier when Ren announced that she was getting married and they wanted to know about Nick's parents. Making major decisions without knowing all the people involved was unimaginable to them.

Because they suspected marriage would settle her down, maybe make her forget her crazy ambitions for acting, Ren's parents didn't put up too much of a fight about the wedding. But instead of reinforcing their conventional life, Nick encouraged and nurtured Ren's talent to the exclusion of every responsibility she'd ever been taught to respect.

"I can't understand living next to somebody and not knowing who they are," Ren's father said, reaching his right hand across his face to scratch at his left ear.

"We don't know that woman on the second floor, Kevvy," Tammy said.

"That's because she's a schizophrenic," Kevin said and patted his wife's hand which was searching out four-leaf clovers.

"We like the privacy," Nick said and shrugged. "That's why we moved here."

"That and no income tax," Ren added, to get them onto another topic. But Ren's mother wasn't going for a switch in the conversation.

"Call me crazy, but I have neighbors I can count on, even in the middle of the night," Ren's mother said, raising her eyebrows in a sharp angle. Ren considered that her mother had prepared all her life for one emergency or another that had never materialized, especially not in the middle of the night.

"We have 911," Nick said and smiled.

"What if your telephone's out?" Ren's mother persisted. Ren could see that her mother still did not respect Nick, although she accepted him a little more now that he'd written a movie that she'd seen in the movie theater and had a house as an emblem of his success.

Nick threw up his hands and walked off toward the front of the house where the birdbath cat stood out as a blatant reminder of childhood – hers and Nick's. Neither of them had ever found comfort in the endless rows of identical houses in Baltimore and on Staten Island. Ren preferred the haphazard boundary of trees.

Nick made his way back to the blanket and the cluster of webbed chairs just in time to hear Ren's mother say, "They're not niggers are they?" Nick and Ren stared at her. "Your neighbors. They're not niggers are they?"

Ren couldn't speak. Nick looked at her as if demanding that she make them stop fouling the air on their property, but Ren couldn't say a thing. Ren knew that Nick didn't feel he had the authority to criticize her family openly, but she sensed that he expected she should. Mouth open, she looked from him to them, but not a word, not even a sound slipped from between her lips. She was certain that if she let them know she was bothered by their language, by their beliefs, the rest of the weekend would be filled with challenges, all picking at her weaknesses, all reminding her of her youth and how far she thought she'd departed from it. They were capable of finding holes in the life she and Nick had made for themselves, of tearing her apart and then reassembling her as their own once again. All Ren could do all the years she'd lived at the little tan house was to keep the peace and change the subject, protect herself.

"Last week, Nick and I saw twelve deer under the crab apple tree over there," Ren said, immediately taking a hearty swig of vodka and tonic. The look Ren got from her mother was one she'd expect if she'd just relayed spotting a UFO.

"You're kidding," Tammy said then blew a huge bubble of purple gum. Ren could smell the synthetic grape flavor.

Ren looked to Nick to verify the deer story, but he had his back to her. She felt somehow compelled to show them proof of the wildlife in much the same way that she'd once tried to justify her career in the theater. Although her family had never seen her on stage, she dutifully sent home playbills and favorable reviews.

"Thirteen," Nick said simply. His voice sounded deep and disappointed.

"All I'm asking for is one," Kevin said, not looking up from the lens of his camera.

"I feel like the damn visitor," Nick said. He lay on his back on a blow-up mattress in an empty room with Ren.

"I know. But it's just for one more night after this," she said. She knew that the bed was only a prop for what he was really feeling. Her family's visit was a challenge to his faith in himself, and a reminder of his own discomfort as a son and a brother. When his father died, two years before, his mother had moved to Florida, and within six months, his younger brother and sister had both moved to different parts of the West Coast.

"Can you picture my parents on this thing?" Ren asked. She giggled, mostly out of nervousness. "Besides, my father needs to be near the bathroom."

Ren remembered her parents visiting years ago when she and

Nick lived in a studio apartment. To Ren's surprise, the large, opinionated woman hadn't issued a single complaint when she'd had to squeeze between dresser and bookshelves to get in and out of bed. Ren imagined her mother had to be relieved and amazed to see where Ren and Nick had finally ended up.

The night after Ren and Nick moved here, the moon was full and moonlight spilled across the unpacked boxes of clothes in the bedroom as Nick confessed that he was proud to have broken out of the tradition of factory and construction workers in his family and to have been able to make a down payment on a house without taking up a collection from his hard-working relatives. When his father died in an accident at work, Nick had been enraged at the factory for swallowing him alive.

"I refuse to work my ass off for some company that doesn't give a damn," he'd said.

When Nick turned on his side, the movement bobbled her into him. She waited for his regular deep puffs of breath that meant he was easing into sleep, but all she felt was a tightness in his body, even in the air between them.

"It will be all right," she said. She'd meant to whisper, but her voice nearly echoed in the unfurnished room.

As Nick pulled the blanket up around his neck, half of her naked body became exposed to the chilly night air. The other half, pressed against him, felt soft and almost too warm.

The next morning Kevin was patrolling the lawn before Ren had even made coffee.

"I heard somewhere that you have a better chance of seeing deer in the early morning," he said as she came upon him, "when they're feeding."

"Oh, I don't know," Ren said. She could have gone on to say that the animals were always eating whenever she or Nick spotted them, but instead she pointed out a woodpecker, high in a hemlock.

Without her asking him about work, Kevin said that he was thinking of quitting his job. He'd been driving a liquor truck and making deliveries to bars and retail liquor stores for more than ten years. A fellow union driver had told him about a need for drivers for a movie to be filmed in Baltimore.

"Wilgus has worked on two movies already. The money's terrific. If you get on two movies, you end up making more money than working all year for a liquor distributor."

"What would you do, drive the actors to the set?" When Nick's movie was shot in Texas, a local guy had picked her and Nick up at the airport in a van the movie's producer had just purchased. The guy had insisted on carrying Ren and Nick's bags, although they would have been more comfortable carrying their own.

"Yeah. And sometimes you drive the actors' trailers. You vacuum the trailers out a little in the morning. Some of the drivers bitch about vacuuming. I don't know. It wouldn't bother me."

Ren and Nick had stayed in a trailer for a couple of nights when filming was going on in a remote location. The trailer was always spotlessly clean.

"Remember the little Matchbox trailer I used to have? God, I haven't thought of that in years."

Ren remembered it well. When she and Kevin played with his Matchbox trucks and cars, they divided them up evenly. Kevin was very careful about being fair. He routinely selected the dump truck, fire engine, and crane, while Ren took the sports car, ambulance, and station wagon to push along the elaborate roadways of Golden Books spread all over the living room and down the hallway to the bathroom. But the trailer attached to a red car was the favorite of both of them. Kevin had timed their use of the trailer — Ren got it for fifteen minutes, he got it for the next fifteen. Ren looked at her brother straight on — his hair was receding, and tiny lines branched around his eyes. When Ren and Kevin were very young they watched as the forest behind their house was felled and scraped clean for another row of houses.

"You know," he said, looking off into the trees, "this reminds me of the Valley."

Ren laughed. When she thought of the Valley she thought of a party she'd once gone to where she'd felt totally out of place. She thought of lush, rolling horse country broken up by distantly-spaced homes of privilege.

"Ma said so originally," Kevin said.

"Ma said 'the Valley'? When?"

"Last night. After you and Nick went to bed."

Ren was used to hearing most of her mother's approval relayed second-hand. It was diffused that way, but still Ren felt a warmth spread through her and comfort her.

"I've been checking this house out," Kevin said, looking toward the roof. "You know, it would really look great if you stained it a dark brown. Almost a black."

Ren felt Nick come up behind her. Of course, he'd heard Kevin's last comment, the one he'd later call meddling, not the reference to the Valley. He had a habit, sometimes she could swear it was willful, of not seeing the whole picture. In fact, they all did, coming up on the tail end of one another's conversations. Sometimes Ren felt she was the only one unlucky enough to stand squarely in the middle of one situation after another.

"We kind of like it this weathered look, don't we, Ren?" The elements had turned the shingles a silvery gray. She felt his breath against the back of her neck and nodded.

Last night she'd woken up after two when he'd slipped off the blow-up mattress. Nick had whispered to her that his father had died before ever seeing how his life had worked out so far. Then Nick had gone on to say what she knew was true – that her family had never pardoned him for taking Ren off from her hometown. They'd never truly believed that he'd be successful in his career until now that there was physical proof: a house on four acres, in one of the most expensive areas of the country, a house nowhere near their own. Nick had gone on to remind Ren that for years she hadn't even told her family that she was striving to be an actor. Ren's defense was that they would have questioned her instead of supported her before each performance with, "What makes you think *you* could do that?"

Now Nick put his arms around Ren, claiming her, pulling her back to the life they had made completely out of their own ambitions and belief in one another, against incredible odds, with no precedents in either of their families. Nick needed her to reinforce this life.

"What's for breakfast?" Tammy's high voice broke across the cool, damp air. Standing behind her was Ren's father with his hands sunk deep in his pockets. A light breeze whipped up Ren's mother's peach-colored nightgown as she stepped out of the doorway. With her arms close to her sides, not crossed against her chest in her usual stance of defiance, Ren's mother seemed to admit that she felt out of place.

"Is that a poor, damn dog laying in the woods out there?" Ren's father asked. They all turned in the direction of his outstretched arm.

"It's a log, for Christ's sake," Ren's mother said, handing him a tissue to wipe his glasses.

"I think you're wrong, Arlene," Ren's father said softly. "It might be hurt."

Ren looked into the shades of brown and beginnings of green that could camouflage many things.

"It's a log, Dad," Kevin said. He walked toward the place Ren's father pointed out, and reaching it, kicked the wood for emphasis. "See?" he called.

On Sunday afternoon while Ren and her family were exchanging good-byes, Ren's mother produced a small brown bag and quickly handed it to Ren as if it were of no more significance than a litter bag.

"I meant to give you this earlier. But, well, I guess it slipped my mind," the older woman said with uncharacteristic embarrassment.

Ren immediately reached inside this bag, and before her mother could get into the car, Ren pulled out the small, framed sampler. Ren's mother had cross-stitched in purple threads, inside a green and pink border of flowers, "Wherever you wander, wherever you roam, be happy and healthy, and glad to come home." The car door made a cranking noise then slammed shut.

Ren's mother used to give Ren old towels or pans or knickknacks she no longer had a use for and which Ren couldn't afford to buy herself. "It's between you and the garbage," Ren had gotten used to hearing.

Ren squeezed her mother's fleshy hand through the window. Ren recognized the purple as a concession that had finally taken form. When Ren had been a teenager, she'd wanted to buy a purple felt skirt with her birthday money, but Ren's mother had overruled the choice. Ren had put up a fight but, in the end, settled for her mother's selection: a pale, blue-checked polyester.

Kevin turned the ignition in the old rusty car and called out the window, "Maybe next time we'll see the deer."

Ren's father, sitting in the back seat next to Tammy, looked smaller than when he'd arrived.

Tammy said, "Maybe they only come out for Ren."

Ren watched the car wobble off down the driveway. Her brother gave her a short, loud honk just before he hit the road. Ren imagined her mother and father and brother realizing that this wasn't a temporary stopover place, some phase, as her mother called so many of Ren's convictions, but a house she and Nick owned. Ren and Nick would never live in Baltimore. Ren imagined her family thinking, She doesn't belong to us anymore, and Tammy blurting out something like, "Ren must have bought those pants in some place like New York City. I've never seen people wear pants like that back home." Ren wished she could have eased all their minds by telling them that there were ties, thick as cords. And there were deer. She'd take pictures.

"Ren," Nick said, coming up behind her as she heard the car backfiring in the distance. "I couldn't have taken another day of it, I'm sorry. 'Why don't you do this?' 'Why not move the couch over there?' 'I don't want to interfere, but . . . ' How many times did you hear that one?" Nick paused. "Who do they think they are?"

His words came at her like sudden rush of cold air. She softly answered his question. "My family."

"I'm your family now," Nick said. He paused. "Why go out of your way for them? They never believed in us. Nobody even asked about your acting or my writing all weekend." He sighed. "They didn't even think we'd stay married."

For so long Ren had wondered if she and Nick would ever reach the place they strived for, if she had enough faith in herself and in what the two of them could do together. So many times they'd asked one another, "Do you think we'll make it?" and that meant so many different things. And now they had the beginnings of careers and a mortgage for a home so far from what Ren had ever anticipated that she felt a little lost in front of her own house.

"You're like mush around them," he accused.

Ren thought, Nobody but your family could make you go mute in front of injustice. Nobody but your family could threaten your most essential relationship.

"You could have seen them off," Ren said.

He ignored her reprimand. "What the hell are we going to do with that?" He pointed to the giant smirking cat holding a birdbath that not one bird had gone near since it had been positioned on the lawn.

"They thought it looked cute," she said, picturing her mother checking over the workmanship before deciding to pay for it.

"It looks horrible."

"But . . . "

"They want to make our place look like their damn white trash house. And then what happens when my mother gets in the act? It'll look like goddamn Coney Island up here."

Nick's eyes were wild, frightened. Ren recognized the look from when actors were running off with one of his plays, changing lines, forgetting intentions, disregarding all his weeks of writing and rewriting.

"They're just afraid, I don't know, that they're losing their hold on us," she said.

"That's a laugh. They just want us on their own terms." He took the cross-stitching from her and threw it against the huge oak in front of the house. When she heard the glass frame shatter, she thought, for a moment, that she'd screamed.

The sun was just starting to set when Nick came to her. She put her arms around him more easily than she'd anticipated, and, for an instant, every thought went out of her head.

He felt small, almost fragile, after her mother. She smelled his aftershave, rubbed against his smooth face. He sighed into her hair and she found herself going weak behind the knees like after she'd had two or three drinks. Then she sensed hunger, a rumbling in her stomach that she'd ignored for hours.

As she looked up, out the windows of the sun room, she saw the deer, three feet from the glass, head and neck lowered to the ground to eat. She'd never seen a deer come so close to the house. Its dusky coat practically hid the animal in the end of the day. Then she stared beyond the deer, and, as if she'd just put on her glasses, she saw two, five, a whole herd of them emerge from the dull background as they fed and crept noiselessly around the property. It almost seemed to her that they'd been there all along.

When Ren opened her mouth to tell Nick, she made a slight sound, barely a coo of amazement, but the first deer she'd noticed instantly raised its head. Its eyes sought her out; tail flickered. She imagined it could hear anything, maybe even what she was thinking. Her arms tightened around Nick. She breathed shallowly, carefully. At her slightest movement, they would bolt away.

Part Three

Lost, and Found Everywhere

Home

My father lies
at the back
of the house,
huge bed hoarding
his room, arm outstretched
as if to embrace
a stranger
or a friend, the door
he likes always open

and my mother sleeps
in front, surrounded
by photographs, jewelry,
lavender potpourri beneath
a peach pillowcase: two
loved ones cornering

the house
where I learned
to listen

and I, in between,
sleepless
at 3 A.M., stars
dot the sky
and all seems
calm.

Judith Ferguson

Love Song

Back before I remember knowing
much else, I curled up
in my mother's lap
and placed my head on her chest
as she sang to me.

I listened, through the melody
of her skin, to the soothing
muffled music of her body.

I could not make out the words,
but the humming deep in her throat,
the rocking of her body,
spoke clearly a promise
she could not possibly keep —

you will not come to harm.
you will not come to harm.
you will not come to harm.

Holy Places

OH, HONEY, DON'T HURT ME. I'M TOO OLD. THIS IS WHAT MY MOTHER used to say to me all the time when I reached the age when girls become smart alecky to their mothers. I realize now that she wasn't old then, just prematurely gray, early silver, my father used to say as he held on to a hunk of her waist length hair. But it worked. I wasn't unkind to her like my friend Sally was to her solidly brunette mother and Anne-Marie to hers. I figured Mom just couldn't take it, the old being much more fragile than the young.

And she wasn't unkind to me either, even when I broke all the rules and got pregnant at sixteen. I should have been smart enough to figure out that if she could handle an out of wedlock baby she could handle an unkind word or two. But by that time I'd lost the urge to be smart alecky. Being pregnant made me calm and content. Besides, I had other things on my mind.

Mainly Jeff. Jeff in his white Spitfire, one hand on the steering wheel, the other somewhere on me. He'd turn on the Motown station and if the top was down and we were on a country road he'd turn the music up loud and sing along with Jimmy Ruffin or the Four Tops or Mary Wells or Smoky Robinson and the Miracles. When we reached our cornfield all the sounds would stop and it would seem for a minute that we'd entered a church. And after a while the cornfield always seemed like a holy place to us, even if there hadn't been any noise on the way there.

It wasn't our cornfield, though, neither his nor mine. It was almost an hour away from our neighborhood and it was farmed by people we never even saw. We only went there at night. Jeff loved the drive there, the long straight road lined with tall trees and farms. When the night was bright enough, we could see the outlines of old silos. He'd go way too fast, seventy-five or eighty, but I didn't have the heart to tell him I was scared.

Sometimes there'd be straw in my hair when I got home. My mother, who'd have been reading on the couch or playing backgammon with my father, would pick some of it out and say that I'd missed curfew again, that she couldn't help worrying when I was late. And that little car is so flimsy, she'd say, it would protect you no more than a tuna fish can, what if a truck hits you. I told her once that Jeff was saving up for a Cadillac that would protect us, but I said it nicely, the old being unable to handle sarcasm.

My sweet father, for the most part, stayed out of these conversations. Sometimes he would nod and say, "Your mother's right, honey," or echo something she had said. He figured it was some mother-daughter thing. Or he figured sex was involved. Or maybe he just saw my mother as wiser than he.

She was wise. She knew I was pregnant before I did and before any test had been done. She could tell by my face, she said, by the way it puffed out a little. I was horrified and expected her to be but she said she knew I loved Jeff and that Jeff loved me and that out of such love babies are born. She was so calm. I relaxed and figured she would take care of everything. But no. The next day she said she'd support me in any decision I made. But she had no advice. She'd help me find an adoption agency or she'd hold my hand through an abortion. She'd drive me to the Florence Crittenton home for unwed mothers. She'd buy a new silk mother-of-the-bride dress for my wedding. She'd let me live with her and dad and be a single mother but she wouldn't take care of my baby for me. And she insisted on this: I had to tell Jeff. The baby was half his. I promised her I would but I couldn't. I was afraid it would spoil things and I couldn't stand that.

Three months passed and Jeff and I kept driving down country roads and I pretended to be carefree. By then it was too cold to lie in the cornfield. The loamy soil had gone hard. But sometimes we'd bring blankets and lie there anyway. We'd point out constellations and tell stories. Jeff liked to point to the east and tell me about Andromeda who, in Greek legend, was the daughter of an Ethiopian king. For some offense, some boast about beauty that her mother had made, Andromeda was chosen to be sacrificed to the gods. She was chained, naked except for some jewels, to a rock at the edge of the sea. Jeff told me about Andromeda's rescue by Perseus, how Perseus beheaded a sea monster to free her, he told me how that was nothing compared to what he would do for me. Perseus's love for Andromeda was nothing compared to Jeff's love for me. I'd stare at the stars, trying to see the configuration in the shape of a much beloved woman, and believe him. I'd imagine him slaying some monster for me, protecting me, freeing me, loving me forever.

And then one night he found my pants unbuttoned and made a joke about too many french fries. That was the night I told him. We were all wrapped in blankets.

After I blurted out the truth of it, he grew silent. He was silent for days, he pretended he hadn't heard me. This was unlike him. We always talked. We'd talk about constellations or we'd talk about his past or we'd talk about our future together. We didn't know when we'd get married but we knew that we would. We'd talk about which tall tower of apartments we wanted to start our life out in and how we'd decorate our kitchen. We'd talk about names for our babies – Laraine, Melanie, Sabrina. The first would be a boy, he'd be named Jeff. I showed him bits of leftover yarn my grandmother had given me. I showed him the pattern in her knitting book for a many-colored baby blanket, "for your trousseau, dear," she'd said and she'd promised to teach me to knit. We'd plan our wedding. Anne-Marie and Sally would be bridesmaids in fuchsia dresses. The best man and ushers would wear cummerbunds to match.

A few days after I told him I was pregnant, he told me this: he couldn't face it, he'd enlisted in the army, his father had signed for him, he'd leave for boot camp on his eighteenth birthday, only a few months away. He wouldn't even wait for graduation. No, I screamed, what about my yarn? What about our wrought-iron kitchen table with matching chairs? What about the map of the stars that would hang in our baby's room? What about me, your beloved, the one you'd kill sea monsters for? What about the Magnavox stereo in our living room where we'd play Temptations albums and Martha and the Vandellas and the Supremes? I begged him and beat on his chest with my fists but he was steel. He didn't even say he was sorry. Or ask me what I was going to do.

"There's a war going on. My country needs me," was his answer. He turned into a stranger. He was no longer the boy who sang into the wind. Suddenly he was all involved in the Vietnam war and stopping communism. It was a subject that had never come up, all those nights in the cornfield and in the car. All that talking we did, that incessant talking, and he'd never mentioned the war or patriotism or serving anybody but me.

For a week I grieved. For some reason I spent most of that week with Jeff's mother, not with mine. We'd sit on her couch drinking Cokes and eating potato chips and she'd promise me he'd come to his senses and "do right by you, honey." And if he didn't, well, then, "God would punish him." He was acting more and more like his dad, she said, stubborn and selfish. I don't know if Jeff was more afraid of me or of his mother but he spent the rest of the time, before he went in the army, at his dad's efficiency apartment, a sordid little place full of overstuffed used furniture. It didn't even have a radio. Losing Jeff like this was a heartbreaker for his mother. She didn't even get to be with her baby before he went off to war.

I wanted to die that week but then something happened. I started to feel calm and I gave Jeff up in my mind, his music, his pain, his Greek legends. I didn't throw his picture away but I took it off my dresser and put it in a drawer, under my scarves. I ceremoniously laid all his gifts, the opal ring, the cameo brooch, the gardenia corsage from his junior prom, in a box covered with quilted ivory satin and stored it high on a closet shelf.

By then, by the time I was free to think about my baby, it was too late for an abortion so at least I didn't have to picture what that would entail. That's what my mother said anyway. Perhaps that was her way of expressing the opinion she claimed to refuse to express. Another kind ploy in her bag of parenting tricks. Another refusal to pose as the authority in my life. Another chance for me to take responsibility for myself. And I was relieved that I could check off another option, to shorten my list of choices, a list I didn't want to face.

But I did. I faced the list. I decided to give the baby up. I decided it one morning after I'd had a dream about being a mother. My brown hair was bleached blond and stringy in the dream and heavy black eyeliner was on my eyelids. Me and the baby lived with no radio in a small efficiency full of used, overstuffed furniture. The event of the dream was this: I was using a knife as a microphone and doing an imitation of Diana Ross singing "Baby Love, My Baby Love." My hips were swiveling and I felt real cool and my baby started to struggle. I had laid him face down in a big chair and he started to sputter. The blanket under him had gotten all wadded up around his face and he couldn't get his breath. I knew he might die and I planned to get him but I wanted to finish my song first. I woke up before either the rescue or the death but I took the dream as a sign that I wasn't ready.

I stayed in school until my stomach got ridiculous. Then I made an appointment with Sister John Gabriel, the principal. I told her that my family was going to be moving because my father had been transferred. She put her hand on mine and her eyes went soft and understanding and she said she knew the truth of the matter, she had eyes to see and she was sorry. She knew this was a painful time for me. I hadn't expected her to believe me, I had eyes to see too, but I had expected her to be cold and cruel. I had expected guilt and shame. Her kindness took me by surprise and tears washed down my face. She took me in her arms and held my head against the side of hers and I felt how stiff her starched white cap was, under her veil. It scratched my cheek. I cried and cried and she just held me. When I was done I said thank you. I said I hoped my tears hadn't wilted her habit. She offered me a bar of the World's Finest Chocolate, with almonds, which we sold every year as a fundraiser.

That was my last day at school. And it was the day I told Sally and Anne-Marie the whole truth. The story I had made up, and that they had believed, was that Jeff and I had broken up because I'd seen a cheerleader from the public school riding in his Spitfire. I had explained that the loss of him made me feel so empty inside that I was filling up with food—hot fudge ice cream cake, onion rings, Milky Ways, cheeseburgers, whole jars of olives. I couldn't stop eating. They'd give me their pity and understanding. Both confessed that grief made them overeat too. They were just lucky they hadn't blown up like I had. They were both on the basketball team. I was the sedentary one. We talked about it quite a lot. Almost every night on the phone I'd produce a litany of the food I'd consumed that day. They tried to help: when you get the urge to eat, drink three glasses of water to give you the sense of fullness, scotchtape pictures of fat people onto the refrigerator door, always have peeled carrot sticks on hand. They were into my story.

The truth floored them. Anne-Marie kept covering her face with her hands and saying she couldn't believe it. Sally called Jeff a shithead over and over. Neither of them had known a pregnant person before so they had lots of questions. Sally wondered if they should get everyone in our class to sign a petition begging Sister John Gabriel to let me stay in school.

No, I said. Just don't forget me. Without Jeff, without school, I'll really have nothing to do. I'll just be home watching game shows and soaps, I said, and reading Victoria Holt and Mary Stewart.

But that's not what happened. Our television broke and my

mother said we couldn't afford to have it fixed. Even then I knew that was a lie but I accepted it. I didn't like TV that much anyway. She probably broke it herself, got a screwdriver and took the back off, unscrewed a bulb or a tube or unhooked a small wire. "Well, no use sitting around here," she said, I'd feel better if I exercised, she said, a radical notion for those days I realize now, but I obeyed her. Every day but Sunday we went swimming at the YWCA pool. I'd move slowly through the cool blue water and imagine that my baby was doing the same thing, moving slowly in the water in my womb, waving his tiny arms, kicking his tiny legs, holding his tiny eyes closed tight. My little swimmer.

We didn't have *in utero* photographs in those days like we do now. But there were sketches. I checked out a book from the library called *Expectant Motherhood* that fascinated me. I learned the words for all my parts from that book, words I'd had introduced to me in sophomore biology but that had seemed to belong only to married women: fallopian tube, cervix, vaginal canal, uterine lining. I learned that my bones were going to loosen up, I'd be split, sort of like an earthquake, when it was time for my baby to be born.

Our library didn't have books on how to put your baby up for adoption. I don't remember where we got the phone number that led me to Mrs. Quinn who told me all about a Catholic couple one state away. She didn't say which way. The man was a member of the Knights of Columbus and the woman was active in the Sodality. I bet the number came from Sister John Gabriel. The man was a lawyer and the woman a homemaker who loved to bake and do needlepoint. They'd been married for seven years and God still hadn't given them a child. I thought they sounded okay. I thought about it for a few days and then I called Mrs. Quinn and told her they could have my baby. I filled out forms.

I got down my bag of yarn and asked my grandmother for the knitting lessons she had promised me. Knit one, purl one. It was soothing to sit in the wing-backed chair in my mother's sewing room and knit. I thought the least I could do for my baby was to give him a many-colored blanket for a birthday present, a going away present.

My mother's sewing machine was across the room from me and as I knit, she sewed, humming away, making me maternity clothes. My mother made a ridiculous number of dresses for a person who hardly ever went anywhere except the library and the YWCA. But she kept buying great swaths of flowered material and designing me these tents. She didn't want me to get depressed.

My father brought me something everyday, just something from the newsstand by his bus stop, a box of lemon drops, a bag of salted peanuts, a strawberry twirler, a *Time* magazine. He'd ask me how I was feeling and smile kindly but he never mentioned the baby directly. He taught me how to play backgammon and let me help him build a birdhouse down in the basement, at his workbench.

Sister John Gabriel had implored me to keep up with my schoolwork, "to keep your mind alive." I had planned to do a little algebra every day, a little chemistry, some French, religion, and English but I got lazy. I remember I read some French plays, one by Corneille and one by Racine and one by Molière. I read each one out loud, alone in my room. The rhythm of their verses put me in the same mood as swimming did. For some reason it made me feel close to my baby. I felt like the poetry was a lullaby for the baby. It was soothing for me and I thought it was soothing for him.

My English class that semester I dropped out was British Literature. The only entire novel we were assigned was *David Copperfield*. I read that alone too, in my room. My class hadn't gotten to it before I left. When I first began novels in those days I always had a dictionary and a notebook at my side. Once I got hooked I never bothered to look up a word but for the first thirty pages or so I was alert for words whose meanings I was unsure of. "Caul" appears on page one of *David Copperfield* and that was my first entry in my new vocabulary notebook.

So when my baby was born with a caul I knew what it was, I wasn't shocked or appalled in any way by the bubble I first saw him in through the haze of the drugs they had given me for the delivery. The doctor pulled it away, the veil, the membrane, and I could see him more clearly. He didn't look much like the graceful swimmer I had pictured during my pregnancy. He was much more wrinkled and red-faced and greasy.

The next day my mother made me visit him. She walked me down the hall to the nursery and made me look at him through the glass. His eyes were closed, his lips parted in a smile. His hair stuck straight up. My mother motioned for the nurse to meet her at the nursery door. The nurse wasn't happy with what my mother said, I could see, but she complied. She handed her a gown and a mask which my mother then handed to me. I put them on. Then she led me into the nursery and told me to sit in the rocking chair. The nurse was mad. She told my mother she was cruel, the baby was being adopted out, what was she trying to do? punish her daughter for getting pregnant in the first place? My mother didn't seem to hear her, she just took the baby from the nurse and gave him to me. She unwrapped his blanket and told me to feel his skin, his hair, and to be sure I was ready to give him up. "Kiss him on the forehead when you're ready to say good-bye," she said.

I put my finger on his arm and moved it up and down. A petal. I touched his black hair and studied his toes. I laid my hand on his stomach and closed my eyes. I tried to conjure up the girl in the efficiency pretending to be Diana Ross. I even hummed her song, "Baby Love, My Baby Love," but I never saw the girl with the heavy black eyeliner and bleached stringy hair. She just wouldn't appear, even though I'd written about her vividly in my journal.

I kissed him on the forehead but I didn't say good-bye. I held him for most of that day and stared and stared at his face. I called Mrs. Quinn the next day and told her the deal was off. My mother got my old bassinet out of the crawlspace and put it next to my bed at home and she went to a department store and bought him kimonos and diapers and rubber pants.

A few days after we got home I called Jeff's mother and told her my news. She was shocked. I had been so firm in my resolve to give him up. She wasn't at all prepared to deal with having a grandbaby. But she was kind and told me she was sure I'd done the right thing and the next day she came over to visit. She brought a little blue sweater and hat and bootie set for David — I had decided against naming him Jeff — and she brought a nightgown for me. She brought along Jeff's last letter. It was full of the rigors of boot camp and included a photograph. I barely recognized him, his head was almost shaved. And that day, for the first time in three years, I felt no love for him. When he looked like a soldier, he was a stranger to me.

But the love came back in a few months. I even put his picture back up on my dresser for David to look at. And I kept imagining that he'd come to his senses, that a grenade would explode in front of him in the jungle outside of DaNang and knock him to his senses and he'd come home and marry me and move us into our favorite tower of apartments. On Sundays the three of us would picnic in the cornfield.

He did come home before his tour of duty was completed. He was wounded by "friendly fire" — a buddy's gun had gone off accidentally and the bullet got Jeff in the leg. His mother called me in secret to tell me he was home. She had written him everything. She was trying to persuade him to at least visit me. He didn't have the courage, it seemed.

David was walking by then. I polished his white hightop shoes and dressed him cute in a sailor outfit and took him over to meet his father. I had my body back by then and my hair was still long and I thought the two of us would be irresistible, sort of. My mother said later maybe I should have left David with her, if I really wanted Jeff back.

I don't know if I really wanted Jeff back that day. But I climbed the steps to his mother's door with David on my hip. I saw through the picture window that he was there, sitting at the kitchen table with his mother. He looked anguished. His chin was in his hands. His eyes were closed. His hair was still short. I guessed that they were talking about me.

He didn't kiss me but he was real nice to me. He told me he was sorry and he even wept a little. He kept staring at David, looking for himself I guess, and trying to make contact with him but David had found the cupboards with the pots and pans and was much more interested in making a racket than in making a relationship with his long lost father.

So Jeff wasn't the man of steel he had made himself be when he'd said good-bye to me all those months before. But he wasn't the same as he'd been in the cornfield, that's for sure. I could see it on his face — faraway eyes, set teeth, a line beginning between his eyebrows. I guess war changes a person, the way having a baby does. So by the time I said good-bye, by the time I threw my arms around his neck and told him I'd always love him and told him that having his baby was the best thing in my life, I knew that it was over, I knew that there'd never be a wedding with Anne-Marie and Sally in fuchsia.

And having his baby is still the best thing I ever did, nineteen years later. I tell my mother that, and I ask her if she had known it would be, if that's why she insisted I hold and touch his newborn self. But she swears not, she shakes her head adamantly, and says no, she thought that giving him up was the right thing to do. She thought I should have my own life. She didn't want me to be tied down at sixteen, tied down by love and obligations.

My mother is old now but there are hardly any lines in her face. Her hair is a bright white. She braids it and winds it into a bun at the back of her neck. He skin always looks tan with her hair so white. Her eyes are a clear blue, like the water in a swimming pool. We sometimes go together now to that YWCA pool where I first pictured David inside of me. We do laps side by side, slowly. It seems more meditation than swim sometimes. It seems like a holy place, the swimming pool, like a cornfield, like a church, like a room where a baby is born.

Pat McKinnon

Walking Behind My Breath

suddenly i am
walking behind my breath
with devin who's 3 & laughing.
says his feet are cold but
let's not go back yet.

so we pretend we are a train
churning down old track
the d.w.p. used to plow
but does no longer.

the blood in devin's cheeks
sings like some animal
taking its time being born
& his choo choo choos
go a long way out
before they evaporate.

James Griffin

To My Daughter

I will be in a farther star
burning still
for you,
my daughter,
when you pine as sweetly
as the sweet earth
breathing clouds
that glow above cracked lightning.
I know you in the years of thunder
and am not afraid
for you.
You can see
my love
as light rain
pattering simply
on the pond we once fished,
renewing
not a faith
wrested from fear
nor even sad love
between the planets
of the first sun,
but a dazzling reality,
the charged air
you breathe
as I breathe in you and of you
as you in me and of me,
in the dark that we have seen
swirling upward
from the stippled pond,
the line held taut

between us,
gripped by the sure feel of it
the surprise and delight of it,
neither of us seeing the other
but knowing beyond all grace
we are bound and boundless.

Maeve's Medicine

Last night,
my children and I
sat talking,
the topic: Indians,
not East Indians,
or West Indians
but those who
the more sensitive
modern schoolbooks,
for want of more
accurate language,
have lumped together
as "Native Americans."
They liked the idea
that a name
is a shield
and a shield
is both protection
and a sign
of who or what's
inside, and how
a name can change
as your medicine changes
in the changing world.

"What would your
name be, right now?"
I asked Helen,
at eight, my eldest.
She didn't pause,
even for breath.
"Quiet River." "And
Maeve's?" I replied.
"Dancing Fire."
"Who am I?" I asked,
"And who's your brother?"
Again, she had no problem.
"Why, you're 'Crazy Bear'
and he's 'Little Crazy Bear.'"
"And Mommy and baby Fionnuala?"
"Fionnuala's 'Little Big Spirit,'
and Mommy . . . " For some reason,
here she faltered.
The best she could
come up with
was "Cleaning . . . Woman."

Maeve seemed upset
in our laughter.
She said she really
knew her *real* name
but she wouldn't tell us.
Hard as we might
we couldn't tease
or coax it out of her.
"Singing Flower?"
"Light as Feathers?"
"Mutton Head?"
"Stubborn as Mule?"
"Sit and Pout?"
She just bowed her head

and hugged her ribs
and smiled. She knew,
but she would tell
no one:
not her parents,
nor her siblings,
not even herself.
Maeve's a child
who needs her secrets.
If you guess one
she invents another.

And I, who have called myself "poet";
I who have called myself "father"
will willingly let her keep them,
forget the consonants and vowels
we have lent her
and spend her life mouthing sounds,
watching for the earth
to shake its head
or the sky to nod,
listening always
for some fragmented sign
of the shining word
her tender arrangement
of flesh and bone embodies
but no lips could ever say
and remain living.

Finding the Curves
of Love

The summer of my twelfth year
I found a short piece of wood,
piece of a limb broken
from one of these trees,
elm or silver maple,
eight or ten inches long.
I began to whittle.
Sitting on the grass,
wandering around the yard,
I began to carve.

Surprised to find
the naked body
of a woman emerging.
Without arms. Crude.
Quite lovely.

Worked on her,
on and off, for weeks.
With my dull knife.
Searching out the curves
of that woman   emerging.
I was not bored.
I liked the feel of her
turning in my hands.
Just the right length
and circumference, hard,
in my fingers. Sweat
from my hands entered
her wood.

When I was finished,
Dad came upon her
and liked her.
Without a word to me,
he found a place for her
at the center
of the tool rack
on the east wall of our garage.
Pierced by a fish hook
at the end of a length
of old gut leader,
she hung there for years,
caressed by the shadows
of our passing.

Now and then I took her down,
held her in my hands,
put her back. Can't remember when
she disappeared. Believe
she must be someplace
around here yet. If I just
searched hard enough
I'd find her dusty
in one of Dad's old boxes.

But the memory stays
close and clear: age twelve,
bent around my small woman
of wood, finding the curves
of love, with a dull knife.

Catherine Clarke

In Your Poem, You Protected Someone Else's Child

As example of accident,
I think of how, at nineteen,
working with a horse, I struck my head,
slept deeply for three days,
and lived, much afraid I wouldn't last;
that was more than twenty years ago.

So now the accidental includes the chance
that better fortune happens. Contentedly,
as in the tune "The Gander at the Pratie Hole,"
a lucky creature happens on a store of pleasure,
small to us but, to the bird,
a roomy world of joy.

My father had his father's violin —
bridge broken, wood seams opened in places —
and took it to a stranger for repair.
He bought a bow; as gift, brought them both
to Ireland, where he had never lived.
His cousin there, another Clarke,
had a friend who played, a champion fiddler.

The tape of that playing carried home,
my father asked to have it heard downtown.
And who walked in when the pub door opened
but the man who had restored the violin —
his first visit there,
the last my father saw him.

As you lost a young son to accident,
my father lost a daughter to disease,
in Brooklyn, almost fifty years ago.
Riding in the car, I told him the story of your poem,
how later you protected someone else's child.
As we rode, my father cried, tipping his head back
to keep the water in his eyes, and sniffing.

That's another accident, isn't it?
I'm counting it —
on my list which, too, includes
the ugly sow, huge, raising her head
just as my small brother
shouldered his head above her fence.

The ugliness of hurt actually hurts — the thought
that the world would really be this way.
Love helps then — a squeeze, a kiss,
lips buried in beard and curling neck hair:
the pratie hole in a tiny store of what is —
and sometimes articulately honking,
aren't we the lucky ganders?

Boat Ride

for Galway

Since my girlhood, in that small boat
we had gone together for salmon
with the town still sleeping and the wake
a white groove in the black water, black
as it is when the gulls are just stirring and
the ships in the harbor are sparked with lights
like the casinos of Lucerne.
That morning my friend had driven an hour
in darkness to go with us, my father
and me. There'd been an all-night party.
My friend's face so tired I thought, *Eskimo-eyes.*
He sighed, as if stretched out
on a couch at the back of his mind.

Getting the bait and tackle. What
about breakfast? No breakfast.
Bad luck to eat breakfast before fishing, but
good luck to take smoked salmon to eat
on the water in full sun. Was my friend's coat
warm enough? The wind can come up.
Loaning him my brother's plaid jacket.

Being early on the water, like getting first
to heaven and looking back through memory
and longing at the town. Talking little, and
with the low, tender part
of our voices; not sentences but
friendlier, as in nodding to one who already
knows what you mean.

Father in his rain-slicker — seaweed green over
his coat, over blue work-shirt, over cream-
colored thermal underwear that makes a white V
at his neck. His mouth open so the breath
doesn't know if it's coming or going — like any
other wave without a shore. His mind
in the no-thought of guiding the boat.
I stare into the water folding
along the bow, *gentian* — the blue with darkness
engraved into its name, so the sound
petals open with mystery.

Motor-sound, a low burbling with a chuckle
revolving in the *smack smack* of the bow
spanking water. *You hear me, but you don't
hear me,* the motor says
to the fish. A few stars
over the mountains above the town.
I think *pigtails,* and that the water under us
is at least as high as those mountains, deep
as the word *cello* whispered under water —
cello, cello until it frees a greeting.

We pass the Coast Guard station, its tower
flashing cranky white lights beside
the barracks where the seamen sleep in
long rows. Past the buoy, its sullen red bell
tilting above water. All this time
without fishing — important to get out of
the harbor before letting the lines
down, not time wasted but time
preparing, which includes invitation and
forgetting, so the self is occupied freely
in idleness.

"Just a boat ride," my father says, squinting
where sun has edged the sky toward Dungeness
a hazy mix of violet and pink. "Boat ride?"
I say. "But we want salmon."
"I'll take cod, halibut, old shoes, anything
that's going," says my friend. "And you'll get
dogfish," my father says. "There's enough
dogfish down there to feed all Japan."
He's baiting up, pushing the double hooks
through the herring. He watches us
let the lines out. "That's plenty," he says,
like it's plain this won't come
to much.

Sitting then, nothing to say for a while,
poles nodding slightly. My friend, slipping
a little toward sleep, closes his eyes.
Car lights easing along Ediz Hook, some
movement in the town, Port of the Angels,
the angels turning on kitchen lights,
wood smoke stumbling among scattered hemlock,
burning up questions, the angels telling
their children to get up, planning the future
that is one day long.

"Hand me that coffee bottle, Sis," my father
says. "Cup of coffee always makes the fish
bite." Sure enough, as he lifts the cup,
my pole hesitates, then dips. I brace
and reel. "Damned dogfish!" my father says,
throwing his cigarette into the water. "How
does he know?" my friend asks. "No fight,"
I say. "They swallow the hook down
their gullets. You have to cut
the leader."

No sun-flash on silver scales when it
breaks water, but thin-bellied brown, shark-
like, and yellow-eye insignia
which says: *there will be more of us.*
Dogfish. Swallower of hooks, waster of hopes
and tackle. My father grabs the line, yanks
the fish toward the knife, slashes twice,
gashing the throat and underbelly so
the blood spills over his hand.
"There's one that won't come back," he says.

My friend witnesses without comment or
judgment the death and mutilation
of the dogfish. The sun is up. My friend
is wide awake now. We are all wide
awake. The dogfish floats away, and a tenderness
for my father wells up in me, my father
whom I want my friend to love and who intends,
if he must, as he will, to humor us. to keep
fishing, to be recorded in the annals
of dogfish as a scourge on the nation of
dogfish which has fouled his line, which is
unworthy and which he will single-handedly
wipe out.

When the next fish hits my friend's line
and the reel won't sing, I take out my
Instamatic camera: "That's a beautiful
dogfish!" I say. "I'll tell them in New York
it's a marlin," my friend says. I snap
his picture, the fish held like
a trophy. My father leans out of
the frame, then cuts the line.

In a lull I get him to tell stories,
the one where he's a coal miner in Ottumwa,
Iowa, during the Depression and the boss
tries to send the men into a mine where
a shaft collapsed the day before. "You'll
go down there or I'll run you out of
this town," the boss says. "You don't
have to run me. I'm not just leaving
your town, I'm leaving your whole goddamned
state!" my father says, and he turns
and heads on foot out of the town, some
of the miners with him, hitching from there
to the next work in the next state.

My father knows he was free
back there in 1935 in Ottumwa, Iowa, and he
means you to know you don't have to risk
your life for pay if you can tell the boss to
go to hell and turn your heel. What
he doesn't tell is thirty years on the docks,
not a day missed — working, raising
a family.

I unwrap smoked salmon sandwiches and we bite
into them. It is the last fishing trip
I will have with my father. He
is ready to tell the one about the time
he nearly robbed the Seminole Bank in
Seminole, Oklahoma, but got drunk
instead and fell asleep.
He is going to kill five more dogfish
without remorse; and I am going to
carry a chair outside for him
onto the lawn of the Evergreen Radiation
Center where he will sit and smoke
and neither of us feels like talking, just

his — "The sun feels good."
After treatments, after going back
to my sister's where he plays with her baby —
"There's my gal! Is the Kiss Bank
open?" — in the night, rising up in the dream
of his going to say, "Get my billfold," as if
even his belongings might be pulled into
the vortex of what would come.

We won't catch single salmon that day.
No strikes even. My friend and I
will share a beer and reminisce in advance
about the wonderful dogfishing we had.
My father wipes blood from his knife
across his knee and doesn't
look up. He believes nothing
will survive of his spirit or body. His god
takes everything and will not be
satisfied, will not be assuaged by the hopes, by
the pitiful half-measures of the living.
If he is remembered, that too
will pass.

It is good then,
to eat salmon on the water, to bait the hook
again, even for dogfish, to stare back at
the shore as one who withholds nothing, who,
in the last of himself, cannot put together
that meaning, and need not, but yields in thought
so peacefully to the stubborn brightness of
light and water: we are awake with him
as if we lay asleep. Good memory,
if you are such a boat, tell me
we did not falter in the vastness
when we walked ashore.

The Persistence of Rivers

In the still pool above the weir,
   anchored to her reflection,
the swan of my eighth year
   is the core of light on dark water
holding my eye; the left sleeve
   of my cardigan unravels.
Farewell is a word with no meaning
   in this snapshot
where I'm the apple of father's eye.

What has cast off the stitches
   in my green sleeve?
With the persistence of rivers
   my right hand plucks
the tight stitches of home,
   its pastures and pear orchards,
though I still play with dolls,
   tented under the kitchen table,
listening to voices:
   her father would give her the moon.

Later, I'll hunt the moon
   on the rivers of summer,
a boy's hand cupping my breast
   and mother's voice will begin its nightly task
of pulling words from my dreams.

But for now, it's dolls,
   pictures of the American West
torn from magazines, pinned to my bedroom wall
   and simple squares I learn to knit
in school; when I drop stitches, the nun's cane
   hisses across the back of my hand.

Leave, the verb of longing
   starts to chant in the winds
of November and *Quest,*
   a new word, billows like a green sail
in flames of peat fires
   father builds with care each morning.

Stillness of my face in a snapshot,
   my sleeve unraveling
in an Irish town where roads
   fly between avenues of oak and alder.
Quickness of my fingers
   picking at threads until *Venture forth*
becomes a phrase to utter
   over and over like a dreamer walking on water
as rain pelts the windows
   and homework's the tracing
of Ireland's map on transparent paper;
   my blue pencil wavers
along the eastern coast
   where the vowels *exile*
repeat themselves in the long, curling waves.

Little mother of years
   standing watch by the river,
I have carried you through doors
   where the word *exit*
burned a sign on your forehead.
   I have purled swans,
dark cables of rivers into new sweaters.
   In my landscape of maple and pine,
I blaze with the core of your being,
   a beating of wings above the weir.

The Map Reader

WHEN HE GOES INTO THE KITCHEN FOR BREAKFAST AND SEES THE TWO thermoses, the neat piles of sandwiches in wax paper, he knows it is a traveling day. Just as well: he has math homework that he didn't get to last night.

"Want an egg? Or cereal?"

"Where we going?"

"Oh, you think you're so smart you know everything, huh? The country, sport, the country."

His father is wearing his usual outfit, brown workshoes with what were once dress cotton pants—they still have cuffs—now faded and stained and patched. But on these occasions his father puts on one of his plaid flannel shirts. He loves them, always pulling out the ironing board while they watch TV and spending a lot of time getting the collars to lie down just so.

"Dad, Sister Gertrude is not too keen on this. She made kind of a face last time."

"Didn't I hear you sneeze this morning?"

"Yeah."

"All right then, you have a cold. Remind me to put that in the note."

The boy is smiling. He sees that they are going to have a fine time today. His father is already in his wise-cracking way. They walk past their nearly brand-new '65 Chevy Impala and climb into the rusty '54 Chevy step-side—the finest truck ever made, his dad boasted—and pull out onto Kenefick Avenue. Steam is rising from the sewers and some drivers still have their headlights on. His father shifts, the cold transmission makes clunking noises, and they head down Abbott Road. He sees the other kids from school walking toward them on both sides of the street. He always wants to wave and smile, but he doesn't want to push his luck and so keeps low. Sister Gertrude will find out somehow. She always does.

"Where's the map? You're sleeping on the job."

In the glove compartment, compliments of the Sinclair Oil Company, is a New York State highway map, which includes Street Maps of Major Cities. There is a smiling dinosaur holding the Sinclair Oil Co. sign on the cover. The boy wonders what the connection is between the dinosaur and gasoline. "Where we going today?"

"Thought we'd head toward Franklinville, maybe see what's going on in Cattaraugus County today. Stay on Route 16, right?"

His father knows the way. They always start their drives heading out of South Buffalo on Seneca Street, flying along in an empty lane, smiling at the line of traffic heading into the city in the opposite lane. With his father on shift work the last two years, they have a habit of taking these occasional mid-week drives to make up for, as his father says, the many weekends lost to work.

Lately his father doesn't say too much about it, the Niagara Mohawk Power Co., except that he prefers the old days, when everyone climbed poles. Now he works in a building somewhere. Wherever they go, the boy is often shown places his father has worked on. They just pull over and he starts pointing things out.

"Right or left?"

They've come to a junction. The boy recognizes it, sort of. He looks at the map opened on his knees. He quickly glances at his hands. He eats with his right hand, so that is right. And then he imagines himself on the map walking down that blue line, coming up to the junction, and then turning. "Left."

"And what direction is that?"

A trick question, don't be confused. Everything on the right, on the map, is east. Easy. "East."

"Great. You got it, sport."

He and his fifth-grade class spend a lot of time in geography working on maps with sharpened colored pencils. They worked their way down Central America – lots of close coloring here – and now are moving in on South America. They'll be doing Bolivia today. They have dry cool winters and warm rainy summers. Their main export is tin. The capital is La Paz. There you'll find llamas and Lake Titicaca. That last one always got a couple of laughs from the guys in his row.

"Want to pour me some coffee?" There is coffee in one thermos, hot chocolate in the other. The boy holds his cup close to his face to feel the steam. He swears he can feel it all the way behind his eyes. They water a little.

"Springing through Springbook." His father likes to call out the names of towns. He is always more restless in the spring – no football to watch, no more snow to shovel, no grass to cut yet. They don't go fishing much, either, though they tried it a couple of times. Too much waiting around, his father says, and the boy has to agree. When they are biting, it is great. Otherwise, you sit for a long time and stare at water. Kind of dumb. They both admit it is at least a good excuse to get outside.

More and more farms pass on the right and left. Some are prosperous – "Just count the silos; that guy is doing well" – but most have peeling paint and lots of junk like old refrigerators and cars lying around. His father often talks about getting a farm. Especially since the boy's mother died. The Sunday paper has ads for these places; they are listed under "Acreage," "Lots," or "Farms." They have to look carefully for them. His father pencils a star near the good prospects, and then they go "scout 'em out."

That gives the boy another job besides the map. He has to call out directions, and run a mark through an ad if it turns out to be no good. Most of the ads exaggerate, but his father is polite to the owners. When they climb back into the truck, though, his father can't help but say something. "Stream with view? What's that guy been drinking? A generous man might call it a ditch. And did you see any view? I didn't. Christ." After the disappointment, they laugh good about stuff like this.

"How about lunch in Arcade? How many miles is that?"

He counts on the map and adds in his head. He guesses about eighteen miles. His father then figures about thirty minutes to downtown Arcade, population 7830.

They usually drive as far as they can in the morning, maybe three, sometimes four hours, have lunch, and then return by a different route to the city. It is always dark by the time they get to eat dinner.

They now pull over near a neat square of grass in the center of town. The tailgate is lowered for a seat and table and they eat baloney and cheese sandwiches. His father cuts chunks from a dill pickle onto the wax paper. For desert, they each have an apple, a hard, sour one.

"So anyway, this guy worked on the trains. He was a conductor." The boy was waiting for this. His father always tells a good long joke or two on these drives. Some are very funny, others have to be explained a little. All are true stories, his father claims. The jokes that are about idiots or morons, the ones he has heard at work, are usually Polish or Negro jokes. The boy's friends at school let him know which group goes with which joke.

"He worked all day and night on the trains punching tickets because of a broken heart. You see, his wife left him for another guy." The boy throws his apple core at a tree and quickly turns to his father.

"You ready? Okay. Then one day he recognized a man on the train as the one who took his wife away. He lured the man between the cars and threw him off the train, killing him. He was, of course, arrested, found guilty, and sentenced to the electric chair." His father speaks louder and slower here for effect. He also does stuff with his eyes to help out the words. "The night before they took him to the electric chair, the prison people asked him what he wanted for his last dinner. 'A banana,' said the killer."

"A banana?"

"Yes, and when they put him into the chair and threw the switch, nothing happened except for a few sparks. The man was still alive."

"How? How could he be alive?"

His father holds up a hand and goes on. "The prison guys got ready to try again, this time doubling the power. When asked what he wanted for a last meal, the murderer said he'd like a half-dozen bananas."

"More bananas?"

His father continues, looking out over the trees. "When the switch was thrown this time, there was a little smoke, a few sparks, but no, the man was unharmed." The boy just eyeballs his father, trying to give him a big look of disbelief without smiling.

His father says the warden is in on it this time, making sure everything is right. "They tripled the power on the chair. The warden himself asked the man for his last meal request. The murderer said he'd like one dozen bananas. The warden granted the request, but checked out each banana and made sure he ate every one. As you can imagine," his father says in his best story voice, "this attracted lots of attention. There were reporters from all over to see this. The warden was very nervous. When everything was ready and the man was strapped in the chair, the warden himself threw the switch. There was a whole bunch of sparks and smoke and the lights even dimmed for a second or two. The man was slumped in the chair, so the prison doctor examined him. The room was very still. The doctor announced that the railroad man was alive. The warden was awfully upset; he knew now that the man would have to be set free because of a law that said you could only try to execute a man three times."

"Really?" says the boy.

"Really," says his father. "The warden went down to the man to tell him this, but the warden was so shocked and angry he instead asked the man how he did it, how did he beat the electric chair?" His father smiles now and the boy knows it is coming.

"The murderer said to the warden, 'I guess I'm just not a good conductor.'" His father's eyes get real big for a second, and then the boy lets him have it. "Aww, that was terrible." They both laugh good now, the boy punching his father's shoulder. He tells his father that that is really dumb, one of the dumbest ever. He tries to remember most of it to tell his friends.

"A bad conductor. I love it." His father laughs some more.

"But what did the bananas have to do with it?"

"Nothing."

"Nothing?"

"Yeah, that's the point. They're put in the story just to throw you off the track." His father laughs again. The boy exaggerates a groan. They both laugh.

"Do you have another one?"

"No. It's getting late. What do you say we check out that place I have marked in the paper?"

They clean up and get back into the truck. Shifting out of first, his father hands him a scrap of paper with some scribbled directions. The boy looks down at the map, rereads the directions, and returns his eyes to the map.

"Head south out of Arcade?"

"Yes, on Route 98 for about seven miles."

His father looks at the odometer. "Okay."

After snaking along the hilly paved road, they travel for a good bit on a dirt road with many ruts. The truck goes from one side to another looking for the easiest path. Lots of short trees grow in what once could have been pasture on both sides of the road. The boy cannot see any houses or barns ahead. "I wonder if we are going the right way."

"You're the navigator. What do the directions say?"

"That there should be a farm, a house at least, here, soon."

"Well, let's keep going then."

When they round a wooded bend in the road, they see it. It is a white house with a few red sheds, maybe barns, behind. There is a dog chained to a tree at the edge of the yard. An arc of dirt extends around as far as the dog's chain reaches. The dog's head stands about as high as the boy's belly, he guesses. His father rereads the ad.

"Forty-two acres, some wooded, with house and barns. Handyman special. Make offer."

The dog barks and stretches his chain as they walk up the driveway. When no one comes to the door, his father sends the boy back to the truck to hit the horn a few times. A short man appears from one of the red buildings. He is stocky, moves slowly, and seems to squint. The boy can't tell if he is friendly or not.

His father gets the guy talking. He always does this. The man grew up here, had twenty-five milking cows at one time, does carpentry work on the side to keep busy in the winter, and yes, the water is good, but no, the furnace needs some work. The boy can tell the man is trying to be enthusiastic about the place. But they won't buy it, the boy knows. The roof on the house sags, and the same goes for the small barns, if they can be called that. His father always notices this kind of thing. He won't touch a place that doesn't have "good lines."

"Why are you selling?" The boy was waiting for his father to ask this. He always asks that question. It is his way to get at the real story. You can learn a lot with that one question, his father says. It makes them into people, not salesmen.

The old man seems quiet about this. The boy sees that his eyes are real yellow and sort of wet. He wonders what makes eyes go yellow like that.

"My wife died two years ago this spring, and though it ain't the same, I still like poking around the place. But last winter, you know, we had some good snows. And with the arthritis getting on me, I could barely dig myself out of here. Had to call a neighbor-friend of mine a few times. I have a daughter in Rochester, too, so what the hell. I'm nearly eighty."

The boy's father asks the old man for his exact age. He says he is seventy-nine; in fact today is his birthday. His father shakes the old man's hand and congratulates him. The old man grabs the boy's hand, too. The boy sees his father doing a good job of making the old man smile, even laugh, with cracks about still looking like a kid, that sort of thing.

The old man insists they take a "tour of the castle." They go through all the rooms in the house, smelling dust and walking around boxes of stuff in the halls. When they finish, the man brings down some glasses and a bottle of dark purple, almost black, liquid from a shelf.

"Might as well have one here. Okay for the boy? It's only a little blackberry wine I make every year. It's pretty sweet."

"Sure. A little will be fine." The boy clinks his glass with the others and puts a little in his mouth. It tastes a little sour on his tongue. He remembers to smile when the old man looks to see if he likes it.

"Give it some thought. If you're still interested in the place, give me a call. I'll be here. I'm in no real hurry."

They thank the old man, shake hands again, and walk out past the barking dog. His father is quiet and does not pull out onto the road yet. The boy wonders what is wrong or if maybe he is just tired or thinking. He knows he should just wait. Sooner or later he will know what his father is up to.

The boy tries to fill the time by looking at the map, trying to find a new way home. He's never been to Attica. There is supposed to be a big prison there. He's never seen a prison before, except in movies. It is a little out of the way, but maybe he can talk his father into going through there. His father is looking out the window, but it is hard to see exactly what he is looking at. The old man is out there, walking around between the buildings. The dog keeps barking.

"Well, navigator, what do you see you like?"

"Huh?"

"On the map, what do you see you like?"

"Well, we can go back through Arcade, and then maybe north through Attica and then home."

"Pick something else, some other place. What looks good to you when you look at the map?"

His father is acting different. Maybe he is setting up another story or joke. The boy plays along. His eyes immediately trace the line between the two states. He has always wondered what is actually there—a fence, or maybe some police, or a path cut through the woods. How do they actually mark it?

"The border, here, between New York and Pennsylvania."

"Want to go?"

"What?"

"Want to go see it? We'll drive down there and look it over."

"It's real far though."

"We can sleep here, in the truck, or even get a room in a motel. We can do the whole works. What do you say?"

"What about school tomorrow, and work?"

"No problem. I can make a few phone calls."

"Sure then, okay, let's go."

By the time they hit the paved road, the boy is sounding out new names – Sugar Town, Knapp Creek, Allegany – tracing the new route south in his head. His father looks out over the steering wheel, getting ready for the next turn, the next junction.

John McFarland

Accepting Rides

THAT MORNING IN AUGUST I WAS SWIMMING IN SWEAT BEFORE I EVEN got out of bed. On the radio, Medium Al, Beantown's Morning Voice of Choice, forecast that we'd see the mercury break 100 with humidity in the low nineties. Moving over into wishful thinking, he said that this was going to be one day you wished you were in the Hudson Bay. Who knew if it was any cooler in the Hudson Bay than it was in Boston, but it had to be quieter there than in our house.

Up the back stairs from the kitchen, I could hear pots being banged around and Little Eva belting out "The Locomotion" from the radio. These were the unmistakable sounds of Dad up and racing through the preparations of one of his rare, stupendous breakfasts. In his book the meal didn't earn its name unless the table was groaning under the weight of curried scrambled eggs, country sausage, biscuits, fresh-squeezed grapefruit juice, and pots and pots of coffee of the gods. And, like everything else in the kitchen, it had to be done in a flash.

When I worked as a potwasher at his restaurant one year, people watching him fly from one crisis to another would ask me if he ever operated at a slower pace. "Relative to what? A tornado?" I'd reply, staying within the party line without going into any details about his summer mode. During July and August when the place was closed for painting and cleaning, he became a slug like everyone else. He slept late with a leisurely wake-up round about noon, followed by a call to his bookie to place bets on numbers he was going to play that day. Then, and only then, would the blinds be thrown open to the blistering afternoon reality of Boston's summer. Between two and three o'clock, he and I would head over to the restaurant to take up painting where we had left off the day before. He never altered the summer's lazy routine once until that particular day when he was up five hours early and cooking up a storm.

"Looks like another scorcher, huh?" I chanced as my opening contribution to the clatter of the kitchen.

When all the response I got for my effort was a grunt or two, I shuffled to the kitchen table and took a seat facing the window. Outside, the lawn was burned a honey brown. Its border of petunias was parched beyond repair. That was one summer we took the drought very seriously.

"We're going for a little spin today. I want to open up the jalopy on the Pike," Dad said, at last acknowledging with real words that I had arrived and was welcome. "Want to come along?"

"What about the painting?" I asked.

"The painting can wait."

"Where?" I asked, still keeping it simple.

"West," he said.

"The turnpike west," Mom piped up, standing at the sink bravely trying to keep up with the hail of pots flying her way from the stove.

"We'll be back by sundown. It'll get us away from this wicked heat for the day," he guaranteed, watching the sausages come up to snuff.

"After one the sun's at its worst," I argued as the voice of reason.

"We're leaving in half an hour," he said, now checking the biscuits in the oven. "Might as well, I can't play any numbers today."

"What?" I stammered. Not playing the numbers was incredible news, like the moon crashing into the harbor, or the Sox taking the pennant.

"Don't you listen to the radio, boy?"

"They caught somebody running a betting operation out of a State House elevator yesterday," Mom explained and pushed one last pot into the sink's soapy water. "The State House! An elevator! What next?"

"Nobody'll be fool enough to take any bets today," Dad said, not bothering to pick up on Mom's question. "We might as well go for a ride. Your loss if you want to stick around here and sweat your brains out."

"If you put it that way," I said, joining the crowd.

"Good," he said, heaping the amazing breakfast onto plates, "we'll see how the old tank handles a full load."

Up for the enormous challenge before us on the table, we three ate in humming silence.

For the entire time it was being built, people had placed bets that the Mass Pike (as the Massachusetts Turnpike was always known) would never be finished. "Look," they'd argue, "who's going to be better off if you finish it? You keep building it, it's a gold mine for construction, for graft, for right-of-way deals, for everyone. You open it, it'll be just an empty strip from the Harbor to the Berkshires. Sure it'll make it easier to get to Hartford, but who in his right mind goes to Hartford?"

Contrary to the smart money, though, there it was finished and open for business. And we were on it, the Impala clipping along at the speed limit with not a traffic jam in sight. Smooth, flat, and straight-ahead, the Pike was dotted practically every other mile by an orange-and-blue Howard Johnson chateau. Exit signs flew by advertising towns we never knew existed. Fiskdale, Bondsville, Woronoco, and Blandford, places some people must have called home.

Before you could say Holyoke-Springfield-Chicopee, we had driven through the toll booth at the western end of the Pike and moved on to the New York Thruway. Not one of us could believe that we had covered the whole Bay State that fast, and without a single traffic light. It was like a report from deepest California. Next thing we'd know everyone in Massachusetts would be blond and nineteen, like me at the time.

"We have all day," Dad said, "let's just go. We're that close to Albany."

Albany! Not Albany! I had to choke back a laugh.

For as long as I could remember, bringing up Albany got nearly as many laughs as Hartford. "Albany," they'd say, "where there's not a decent chop house!" before launching into yarns about the ne'er-do-wells who had been shipped west to clot up towns just over the state line. Once wagging, the tongues of the old neighborhood would resurrect rogues named Skipper, Buck, and Southie, and run down their ancient offenses. "Knowing Skipper," a typical teller would begin and quickly work around to the outrages against God, man, Ireland, the flag, and the memory of his dear-departed mother, rest her soul, that were fated to happen west of the fabled state line once the rogue got the lay of the land.

From the tales we'd heard, we all but expected a brawling cluster of prodigals and reprobates as far as the eye could see as soon as we crossed that line. Instead, by taking a wrong turn off the Thruway, we got Troy. Named after a city destroyed, it seemed to have slid right into its destiny, to be in ruins without a single rogue left alive.

After that disappointment, Dad got us back on track and brought us to Albany. We circled it at breakneck speed and dismissed the town for its lack of alleys and chop houses. Albany was an even bigger let-down than Troy, which at least had been in ruins.

With no time for apologies, Dad switched from the Thruway to Route 20 to continue our journey west, and bucked us up with the promise, "I'll show you where I ditched the Model A."

Years ago, when he was returning from a summer job as a resort butcher in upstate New York, he was lured onto a car lot. On the spot he picked out a spiffy Model A. Before he laid down the $150 for the car, though, he insisted they throw in a patch kit because, with the roads in those days, you'd need to patch a tire long before you'd have to refill the tank. The dealer forked over the patch kit and they closed the deal. Dad drove the car off the lot and the dealer had the season's wages he'd walked onto the lot with.

For the first five miles, the Model A was a dream, like all first cars. Then, on the first downhill stretch, he had stepped on the brakes when he was rounding a hairpin turn, and the pedal shot to the floor-boards. Acting fast, he'd downshifted and sheered over to the cliff side of the mountain road to bring the Ford to a stop.

The first thing he did after he climbed out of the car was to slide under and check if the brake cylinders had been split by a flying rock. He didn't spend one extra minute under there when he saw a piano wire wrapped around the axle, holding it together.

Back then, running five miles uphill meant you had serious mat-ters to discuss. The salesman in the showroom, seeing Dad arrive on foot sweating and carrying the Model A's jack handle, kept edging away while he went through the standard "as is" spiel, with all that "once a car leaves the lot" malarkey.

Skipping over the condition of the brakes, Dad zeroed in on why most people preferred a simple steel bolt over piano wire to hold an axle together. He offered to demonstrate the superior strength of solid steel for the salesman by hitting the showroom's plate glass window first with the jack handle and then with the piano wire.

"But, I was thinking," he had said to the salesman, his butchering arm holding the jack handle high above his head, "what if we turned back the clock? And you get the car, and I get my $150? No hard feel-ings. A brand new day, what do you say?"

As he began the downswing, the salesman peeled bills off a roll in a real hurry and flung them at his feet. The demonstration ended there without having to touch the plate glass window with either the jack hammer or the piano wire.

And now we were closing in on the territory. As we left Route 20, heading south through tree-shrouded mountain roads, the temperature dropped ten degrees. Ascending the road of legend, Dad pointed out the precise spot where he abandoned the Model A. Without slowing down, much less stopping, we marveled at the incline of the hill, the narrowness of the road, and the sheer drop on the far side.

Before I could say "jack handle," we'd crested the hill and careened into town. On the corner where he had bought the Model A now stood a gigantic Ford dealership. We circled the block twice to get a good look at it. Because he couldn't recall the name of the lot back then, we couldn't be absolutely certain that fraud with murderous intent had found rich rewards here. "It wouldn't surprise me one bit, though," Dad said and roared off, heading into the main part of Cooperstown.

We couldn't have covered the town more quickly if it had been laid out on a ski slope. The National Baseball Hall of Fame and Museum, the original diamond of Doubleday Field, the home of James Fenimore Cooper, the Indian Museum, the Farmer's Museum, the entrance drive to the resort where Dad spent three summers breaking down sides of beef, the view of Lake Otsego from the south, we saw them all as successive flashes from the car. Once the sights had been exhausted, we made a spectacular U-turn in front of the police station, and headed back.

We sank into a daze until Dad suggested, "Let's stick to back roads for the return," at the point where he could choose between the Thruway and the Old Post Road. You could see within a few miles on the road why it took an age to get a letter from Boston to Cleveland if this had been the express route.

As soon as we crossed the New York/Massachusetts line heading east, Mom started to talk a mile a minute. Only then did I realize she hadn't said much of anything while we zoomed in and out of New York. Back in her home state, though, almost anything was worthy of note.

Focusing on the road sign declaring we'd entered the town of Lee, for instance, she sang the praises of the Jacob's Pillow Dance Festival,

Ruth St. Denis, and Ted Shawn. According to her, the biblical Jacob's Pillow was the rock on which Jacob laid his head when he had his dream-vision, the one in which the ladder ascended to Heaven. Isaac, Esau, Rachel, Leah, all these names danced into the story as we sped through Lee, buried in green, the winding road tunneling through the million and a half trees of the Berkshires.

"The steering on this crate is not the best," Dad butted in as he worked the wheel on curve after curve, on reverses and inclines.

"You can *feel* the sublime grace out here. The *air* dances," Mom went on, not interested one bit in steering challenges. "Edith Wharton," she began, but stopped before getting to the dirt on Edith. Her eye had been caught by an imposing billboard, also the first one we'd seen on this stretch of road sunk in trees.

In letters two feet high, that sign announced, "5 Miles to Tony O'Dwyer's Flame Broiler!"

"Ha!" Dad said then. But when we rounded another curve farther along to see another billboard, even larger, proclaiming, "3 Miles to Tony O'Dwyer's Flame Broiler!" he simply spit out the window.

"Is Tony O'Dwyer *the* Tony O'Dwyer?" Mom asked.

"Who else would it be? If you weren't that bum, you'd change your name before you did anything else," he said. "I'd sooner call my restaurant 'Ptomaine Death' than have that name anywhere on it, and that includes the toilet."

Tony used to work for him until the night somebody took a close look at the liquor inventory. To this day, Dad holds a grudge against him tighter than he holds his carving knives.

While Dad raged on about how this dumb location, on a deserted road in the middle of nowhere, was the final proof that Tony O'Dwyer was not only a bum but an idiot, the curves flew by even more quickly.

"Maybe he's changed. He could want a quiet life now," Mom offered, the soul of generosity and forgiveness.

"When that moron wants something besides a blond with bazooms out to here, it won't be a quiet life," Dad cried into the wind as we approached the billboard that proclaimed, "500 Yards to Tony O'Dwyer's Flame Broiler!"

100 Yards! 50 Yards! 25 Yards! The signs came faster and faster until the promise of "Around the Next Curve! Tony O'Dwyer's Flame Broiler!" made the tension close to unbearable.

We rounded that last, agonizing curve. And there it was.

Who could have predicted what we saw? A lone brick chimney

dominated the blackened and still-smoking site. All around was a smoldering mass of wood, leveled to the ground. Two men with their heads bowed wandered through the rubble, kicking an occasional charred beam.

"Bad wiring," Dad concluded, as he made an exception for this total disaster and lightened his pressure on the gas pedal.

"This is beyond belief," Mom said.

It was five miles before we came to a roadside stand that would feed the hunger we'd found ourselves with after seeing the Flame Broiler, burned to the ground, completely self-grilled.

While we waited for the sullen counterman to rustle up our order, Dad tried to lighten the gloom by filling him in on the smoldering Flame Broiler down the road.

"It was a grease fire waiting to catch, that joint," the man said, shoving the cardboard box with our eats across the counter.

Dad picked up the box and we headed back to the car.

"You should have felt that counter," Dad said, grabbing a hot dog from the box. "I practically had to pry my fingers loose after I touched it. That guy has a lot of nerve talking about anybody else's grease fires."

"Isn't that the limit!" Mom agreed, between bites of the slice of yellowish pound cake she had picked out at the stand. Her energy was starting to flag and she was throwing out a phrase only every so often.

I could tell that even Dad was wearing down when he asked if I wanted to take the wheel. He gave up the driver's seat less often than he cooked breakfast.

As I drove east, they got more and more relaxed in the back seat. Their peace grew so profound that not even nighttime Worcester — the lights magically transforming the wasteland of Route 9 to which I had switched — merited a single comment. And these were the two who held very strong opinions about Worcester at any time of the day or night.

In blessed calm our morning-to-night trip to Cooperstown and back glided through its last hour on our approach to home. I could have thought about almost anything then, but instead I watched the mercury vapor lights fly into the dark behind us in the rearview mirror.

"Well, that's over with, isn't it, cross it off the list," Mom said at home when Dad brought up the fact that now she couldn't complain she'd never been out of New England in her life.

First thing in the morning Dad was on the phone, not in the kitchen at the stove.

On the radio Medium Al had already announced that the heat wave was history, "like yesterday, let it go, baby, you won't be seeing the likes of it again."

"He's calling the cemetery," Mom whispered when I arrived in the kitchen. "He had a dream."

"Jacob's ladder?" I asked, teasing her.

"Don't I wish," she said, as she took up her station at the sink. "His mother . . . "

"He'll call back," Dad said, joining us in the kitchen.

"I had a dream," he said to me.

It's in the air, this phrase, I thought but bit my tongue.

"An old woman is roaming in our yard. Her back is bent, but she's going around pinching the petunias. She's making clucking sounds and repeating under her breath, 'This place has gone to hell!' I go out to see what her problem is and when I get near her, it turns out she's my mother. She says to me, 'This place has gone to hell, Billy!' She looks around some more, pretty disgusted, and then says, 'Play the number on my gravestone, Billy!' Then I woke up."

"That's . . . different," I said, relieved it was a straightforward message from somebody who had been dead for fifteen years. I sat down at the kitchen table and looked out the window at the yard. Old Gram was right, the place had gone to hell, and you didn't have to have been wherever she had been for all those years to see it.

"So, I jumped out of bed," Dad continued, "and called the cemetery. I bet you didn't know the stone carvers, not the cemetery, put the numbers on the gravestones. So, anyway, the cemetery doesn't have a list of the numbers in the office." He paused to take a drink of water from the tap. "The groundskeeper, though, is going to get the number off the stone and call me back."

He approached the stack of clean pots and pans to start preparing another elaborate breakfast. For her part, Mom turned on the hot water faucet and started to fill the sink. I figured we would all gain twenty pounds if this didn't stop soon.

"So, nobody get on that line for a while," he warned, in case we didn't realize we were messing with death if we did.

The call came right as we were digging into breakfast, and Dad abandoned his plate and raced to the phone. Saying almost nothing on his end, he wrote down the four digits from the gravestone. Breaking that connection, he dialed his bookie and put two dollars on the front three numbers and two dollars on the whole four.

At seven-thirty that night, on our way home from painting at the restaurant all afternoon, we picked up the late edition of the newspaper. Dad went wild when he read the news that all four numbers from the gravestone hit in exactly the right order. When we got home, he was on the phone immediately to his two sisters and sole surviving brother about the phenomenal betting tip.

Kate, Sal, and Fred all agreed this kind of thing was right in character for their mother, but Kate was the one who said, "Ma was always telling us what to do when she was alive. It's just taken her this long to figure out how to do it from beyond the grave, that's all."

Into our lives the winnings brought a half-dozen air conditioners and a Mercury station wagon. I got the trusty Impala handed down to me. Out of her cut, Mom sent a cool hundred (it seemed like a fortune in those days) to the Jacob's Pillow Dance Festival. I thought then, as I still do, that if the people out there in Lee had known how that money had arrived in their mailbox, they would have taken up the tale for one hell of a dance.

Supposedly When
My Father Was Young

Stewart's Cafe, 1936

Before I will believe you, Uncle,

I will need a wireless mike, a powerful one,
that can thrust through decades of my father's truth
to transmit evidence indicting him and his friends
placing them around a huge oak table
Sunday mornings in the back of Stewart's Cafe,

a mike alert to a clink of what you say are whiskey glasses,
to loud last slurps,
to their crowd of footsteps leaving over red brick street,
before I will believe you, Uncle,

I will need a wireless mike, a tiny one,
that can tug to my father's lapel like an invisible leash
to transmit evidence indicting him and his friends
rushing up church steps as if propelled by a huge oak table
Sunday mornings swirling in the back of Stewart's Cafe,

a mike alive to the grate of clearing throats,
to my father's bass voice amidst a high mass hosanna,
to a devout choir bluff above the altar of Saint Thomas,

before I will believe you, Uncle.

White Sneakers

IT'S ONLY A MATTER OF TIME, DANNY TELLS HER, BEFORE THE MEN IN HIS family mess things up. They marry young and marriage doesn't change them. They still do exactly as they please, when they please — like children. They play basketball three nights a week, they go out drinking. They fool around. He knows this from the stories he's heard about his dead grandfather, Big John McKay, and from personal observation of the sons that followed. Wait long enough, he tells her, and the male McKay will do his thing.

Ellen squints green eyes in the sun. "What is that, some kind of warning?" It's Sunday afternoon and they're sharing a park bench behind their apartment in Syracuse, New York. She's a second year graduate student in sociology at the university. He's in his sixth as an undergraduate in journalism. They're both twenty-four. Not married.

He shrugs. "Just the facts, ma'am."

"Well, go to it then. Have fun. Maybe you'll have so much fun messing things up you won't come back." She watches two children swing in unison. Danny watches through the lens of his Nikon.

He passes on the shot. "You know, it's been over a year since I was back." He manages to say this with sincerity, though the truth is, having spent most of that time with her (studying, eating, shopping, arguing, going to bed and getting up) he doesn't know what he needs more — to go back to Iowa or to get away from New York. Coming here he never expected anything like this.

Ellen, it seems to him, expected exactly this.

"It's just for a week," he reminds her.

"Yes — Thanksgiving week. And don't tell me I can go with you, because you know I can't. *I've* got papers to write."

"They'd love to meet you." He blows invisible dust from the filter.

"I'd feel like I was knocking on the boys' clubhouse."

"Nonsense," he tells her. But the image is amusing — reminds him somehow of his grandmother, her purse full of silver dollars, going to fetch Big John from the Tripoli Saloon. A story he heard long ago.

Ellen turns her face to the sun, closes her eyes. "Still, I would like to see it – how you are amongst your . . . *clan.*"

"I'm exactly the same."

She smiles, but he knows he's said the wrong thing.

"I'm completely changed."

She laughs. A moment later she points to the swing set. "I think those two are twins."

He lifts his lens, zooms in on two boys sharing the same small cherubic face.

"You're right." Then, "Wouldn't that be strange, having a twin?"

But Ellen just stares, vacantly, before remarking in the flat, trance-like voice she sometimes uses, "They're only whole as a pair. Their future lovers will suffer vague, relentless jealousies. It's so beautiful. It's so sad."

Somewhere over Illinois the story comes back to him. A short one told to him before he was old enough to understand, really, what his grandmother was saying – about herself and about Danny's grandfather, a coarse and cussing man who, *somewheres near 1950, suddenly acquired a taste for nightcaps.*

Friday nights, just after dinner, he'd hop in the old Ford pick-up, take the bridge across the frozen Wapsipinicon into Tripoli. Back then the town boasted a population of two-hundred-and-ten. These were not great odds for Big John, and within a week Danny's grandmother knew it *weren't nightcaps pullin him across that river.*

One Friday night after Big John had gone, she put the boys to bed (she put them in the same bed, covered them with most of the blankets in the tiny house – it was a bad winter), and headed toward town. She walked two miles in her church shoes (*only shoes I had didn't let air in somewheres*), crossed the river, and found Big John where she knew she would, belly to the bar, sharing a beer with the woman she'd heard all about. By now Danny's grandmother was so cold she couldn't feel a thing but the dead weight of her purse in her hand – full of the silver dollars she'd been saving since she was a girl.

At first she thought she'd killed him, the way he slumped face-down to the bar. The woman he was with didn't scream; she simply cleared her throat and made for the ladies' room. The bartender gave Big John a couple of pats on the cheek to bring him around. Everyone who knew him liked and respected Big John, despite a fierce, unpredictable temper. Most times, though – Danny's grandmother let him know – most times Big John was *near as dangerous as a sleepy old dog.*

Big John lifted his head, shook it briefly. He adjusted his glasses and swiveled to get a look at who'd busted him blindside.

"You never saw such a look your whole life!" Danny's grandmother laughed. "All that fire and anger dropped in his lap like peanut shells when he seen me standing there with my purse!"

Big John rubbed the back of his neck. He pulled on the whiskers of his face. Finally, he turned and paid his tab. "Reckon I'll be heading back, now," he told the bartender, as though it were any other night.

Danny's grandmother waited for her husband in the Ford. They drove home together, and after that Big John never crossed the Wapsipinicon past sundown. He died ten years later – about the time his son, Danny's father, began running wild in the Waterloo public school system.

They can't be sure, it occurs to Danny in the airplane, they have no *proof*, but he and his brothers consider it a good bet their father, Big Frank, crossed a few rivers of his own before their mother divorced him.

He looks out the window onto a quivering wing, a sea of clouds below, the Midwest lurking deeper – and feels the speed of the plane like a boat.

Weren't nightcaps pullin him across that river.

A great silver hydroplane, he thinks, skimming waves.

By the time Danny and Martin finish basketball and walk downtown, Ray, the oldest, is snug in the gloom of a booth, a half-empty pitcher of beer and three glasses in front of him. He wears a black leather jacket, his long hair blown back from high speeds on his Kawasaki. Danny and Martin wear sweatclothes damp from basketball. Martin is not as tall as Ray – in fact, he's shorter than Danny – but heavy, a lineman in high school. Combined, his two older brothers make a pretty fair replica of Big Frank, while Danny, skinny as the day he graduated from high school, adds little to the equation. But he has the family chin: deep-clefted and prominent as elbows. Big Frank's new wife took one look at the three of them and said, *My God. The chins of the father*. They laughed hard. They'd never heard it before.

"So, *Boss*," Ray says to Martin, "how bad you get beat tonight?" Since losing his bus driving job two weeks earlier, Ray has been working at Martin's car lot, as a mechanic, until he gets back on his feet. Ray's two little boys live with their mother.

"Kicked ass," Martin answers.

"I drug it," Danny adds. "No gas."

Ray laughs. "Too much nookie for the rookie these days?"

Ellen is a thousand miles away, but Danny looks at his brother now – at his eyes, his grin, the gleam of malice in both – and feels as though she's right here, in this bar, taking notes.

"You got it, Ray." He gets up for more beer.

At the bar Danny shimmies his way past elbows to hand over the pitcher. Next to him, a woman's denim hip bumps his thigh, and without seeing her face he knows – by the hair, the perfume, the laugh – that it's Lois Liuski. He watches the bartender fill his pitcher: half full. Two thirds. He's got his money ready –

"Danny? Danny McKay."

He turns. "Hey, Lo. How's it going?"

"Fine! My God. What're you doing here?"

"I'm with my brothers. What about you?"

"Friends." She stares at him, smiling, until Danny manages, "So, where are you these days?" Collecting the pitcher he learns that Lo is down in Missouri, much happier since the divorce, finishing her undergrad, raising her kid. To Danny, watching her lips, her eyes, the tiny chip in her front tooth, she is still seventeen, and only the night before, following one brief, surprising jolt, he'd lain humiliated in the grip of her thighs.

"And what about you?" she asks. "Married?"

Danny fills her in on the basics, including Ellen and the apartment in Syracuse – but even so Lois Liuski implores him, before they part, to give her a call. "After Thanksgiving," she says. "I'll be in town for a few days. At the old homestead."

Purple curtains, he remembers, to match the purple quilt on her bed. Springsteen curling from the wall.

Taking a step away, toward his brothers, he asks, "Same number?" and she, nodding, waves good-bye.

"Christ," Ray growls, "took ya long enough."

Danny fills his glass and the two of them let the jukebox do the talking until Martin returns from the bathroom. When he does he boxes Danny in, and says, "So what about this Ellen, anyway? How come she didn't come with you?"

Danny refills Martin's glass. "Didn't want you goons scaring her away." He glances at Ray, for his comeback – but Ray isn't listening: he's watching, his back rigid, his eyes locked onto something across the bar, his smile pure ice.

Danny follows his glance to a huge bearded man in a driver's cap plowing through the bar. He wears black leathers and a black T-shirt with a faded Harley insignia, all standard biker apparel except for the cap, which Danny recognizes from Ray's days as a city bus driver.

"Ray . . . " Martin says. "Easy."

The biker wades past their booth without seeing Ray. Ray takes a swig and rises.

Martin sighs. "Here we go."

"What?" Danny says.

The sound of Ray's hands slapping the biker's back turns faces – turns them just in time to see the monster falling headfirst into a booth of women sipping margaritas. The crash ripples the beer in Danny's glass.

Martin stays put, blocking him in.

"Mart, for Christ's sake, let me out." He pushes at his brother's bulk. "That guy'll kill him."

Ray waits for the giant to free himself from the fists and fingernails of the four women.

"No he won't," Martin says. "But *that* sucker might," and like that, Martin is gone too, head down and digging in for the tackle, digging in, Danny thinks, for Ray himself – until he sees the other one, a second biker holding a full pitcher of beer high in his black leather hand, closing in on Ray.

Martin hits this biker low, bends him so far backwards he could grab his own ankles. The pitcher goes straight up and, somehow, comes straight down, still full, before shattering.

Danny gets out to see what he can do.

The fat bearded biker is up, ready to charge, when fluorescent lights whitewash the bar. Two burly bouncers give everyone a shove. Danny stumbles into another booth, is roughly shoved back out. The bouncers have Ray and the fat biker pinned.

Ray spits, "Back-stabbing, ass-kissing tub of shit."

The fat biker's face is the red of suffocation. "Fuck you, McKay. Motherfucking lowlife fuck-up."

"Come for it, shit-for-brains."

The bouncers hold them in place. Martin sits on the biker he's floored. Then, everything under control, the owner walks over wiping his hands on his apron. "Okay —"

"Hey, Joe," Martin says, as if he's just pulled up a chair in Joe's bar. Joe looks confused until Martin adds, "How's that Mustang running? A beauty, right?"

"Marty?" Joe says. "Jesus, you know these guys?"

"These two are my brothers."

"No kiddin?" He checks for the family resemblance. "Well," he says, "get 'em outta here, will ya? You too," he tells the bikers. "And if I catch any of you guys in here again I'll kick your asses out personally. Okay, Marty?" he adds. "Keep 'em outta here, I mean it."

The bikers go out the front, Danny and his brothers out the back. In the alley Ray slings a leg over his Kawasaki and sits back to light a cigarette. "That's the sonofabitch told my boss I was drinking."

Martin says, "Hey, Ray, forget it," and Ray stares at Martin for a moment like Martin is the fat guy in the bus driver's cap.

He grins. "Well, it's pussy time, anyhow — ain't it, boys?" He looks at Martin in his basketball sweats. "Whaddaya say, Kareem? Think the missus could tell one kind of sweat from another?"

Martin shrugs.

Ray mocks him. "How 'bout you, Mr. Syracuse? Or has Ellen got a cross-continental grip on your wally?"

Danny thinks of Lois Liuski — *Give me a call* — but says nothing. He wants only to be out of this alley, away from the shadows and the grime and Ray's relentless grin.

Looking from one to the other, Ray shakes his head. "Who do you fuckers think you're foolin, anyway? Think you're better than me, 'cause you keep your peckers in your pockets?" He looks from one to the other. "Shit, you're just young is all." He stands, jabs the key in the ignition, gives a vicious kick. Over the rumble of the engine he says, "But it's like Big John himself told me when I was six. 'Those sure are white sneakers, Raymond,' he said. 'But you know what?'" Ray raises his eyebrows high. "'Ain't no way to keep 'em white.'" He flicks his cigarette at their Nikes. "'Ain't no way, son. Sooner or later, dirt finds 'em.'"

He pops the bike into gear, scatters gravel, and is gone.

On the way home Martin says, "You know, I love that guy, but he can be a tremendous pain in the ass."

"Funny," Danny answers. "He says the same thing about you."

Danny follows his brother up the porch steps. Inside, Kate is folding laundry and watching the news. Martin slumps on the couch beside her (*think she could tell one kind of sweat from another?*) while Danny, half-drunk, goes upstairs to make a phone call.

She answers after six rings. "Mmm . . . ?" she says, still asleep. He imagines their bed, the smell of her dozing warmth rising through. He hears her swallow and lick her lips. He can see her drowsy green eyes perfectly.

"Pleasant dreams, Ellen?"

He hears the tiniest sound—a small nasal noise she sometimes makes when he touches her. She answers, "Mm hm. I'm dreaming you're here, actually. We're pushing kids on the swings. Not ours, don't worry. Somebody else's."

Martin steps by to look in on his son. Danny waits for him to leave before saying, "Ellen, why do you do that?"

"Do what."

"Dream of me."

"Why do I dream of you?" She yawns. "Why do you ask?"

"Just curious."

For a moment she doesn't say anything, and Danny hears the rustle of linen as if she's settling back into sleep. But when she speaks she sounds wide awake.

"What's going on?" she says.

He thinks of the bar, of Lois Liuski, of Ray ready to tear somebody's throat out—new evidence of what the men in his family were made of: pure red stupidity springing to life centuries ago in some young Irishman, hitching a ride across the ocean with Big John's father, picking up speed in the bloodlines of Big Frank and spilling, potent as ever, into the veins of his sons.

But all he says, finally, is "Nothing. Nothing earth-shattering."

"Really?"

"Really," he says.

"Really?"

He listens to her breathing, heavy and slow again.

"I don't dream," he tells her.

"About me?"

"About anything. Or if I do I never remember."

"That's because you live closer to daylight. To your conscious self." She yawns again. "Whereas I live closer to my subconscious self."

"Closer to dreams."

"Mm hmm."

For a while he just listens to the sound of her slipping back there — to dreams. Until, suddenly, she says his name.

"Still here," he answers.

She sighs, slipping further. "Okay," she says. "Just curious."

They hammer without talking. Every now and then they become synchronized — four fat nails sinking musically into solid wood — but it doesn't last. Fitting the next two-by-four into place they sniffle, catch whiffs of the big dinner Anna and Kate are preparing: stuffed mushrooms, turkey, pumpkin pie.

A year earlier — just after his second divorce — Big Frank and Anna moved into the woods of Lone Tree and have been living here ever since. They've built this A-Frame from the dirt up. He cross-country skis, now, their father. He listens to jazz. Last Christmas, the first time they all got together out here, Big Frank put his arm around his new wife and looked at his grown sons. He gave her a little hug as if to say, "We did all right, didn't we?"

Danny has never been too handy with a hammer and nails, but this is Thanksgiving, and if nothing else he can help lift: they are framing the outer wall of the garage and the new bedroom above it — a gigantic two-by-four crossword puzzle, so far, flat on the ground. They stand at what will be the top of the wall once they lift it into place and nail it shut. They stand in exactly the order they were born — Big Frank at the far end, Ray, Martin, then Danny. A day earlier Danny might have found this arrangement amusing — might have considered describing it to Ellen, hearing her theorize about subconscious familial constructs and so forth. Today, still tasting last night's beer at the back of his throat, he is merely annoyed.

"It's a hell of a lot bigger than we planned," Big Frank says. He hooks his thumbs in the workbelt around his wide waist.

"It's exactly how you planned," Ray says, his voice thick with hangover. "You just planned too goddam big." He pops two aspirin and makes a sour face. Despite clouds, Ray hides his eyes behind sunglasses.

Still in his sweats Martin hops from one foot to the other, rubbing bare hands briskly. He bends over to give a pull on the wall. "This is impossible! Why didn't we build it one level at a time, right onto the house?"

Big Frank studies the wall as if he hasn't heard Martin's question. Ray takes a drag on his cigarette and tells Martin, "Because, Boss, this is how Pop likes to do it."

"Well," Martin says, "I'm freezing. Why don't we just lift the sucker and get it over with?"

This cracks Ray up. "Hey," he laughs, "I'm ready when you ladies are." The wind snatches smoke from his lips.

Big Frank catches Danny's eye from his end of the frame. "What do *you* think?"

What Danny thinks is this is not what he had in mind for Thanksgiving—the four of them standing around this wall scratching their heads as if they'd already gorged themselves on food and wine before coming out here to do this absurd thing.

He thinks he might give Lois Liuski a call.

He says, "Hell, let's give it a try. Test it, at least."

Ray looks him over. "Hey, whaddaya know—college works!"

Big Frank shakes his head. "Why are you kids such jerks today?" He doesn't expect an answer, doesn't get one.

Ray flicks off his cigarette, hisses smoke through his smile. He tugs on big leather gloves.

"Okay, okay," Martin says. "What should I do? Lift here?"

"Hold on, Hercules," Ray says. He squats to get a grip.

Big Frank says, "Don't anybody hurt themselves. Lift with your legs, not with your back."

"Don't worry about our backs," Ray says.

They all find their grips.

"On three," Big Frank says. "One . . . two . . . three!"

Ray growls with effort, Martin moans demonstratively—and they stand, backs bowed in, arms stretched with the weight.

"Jesus!" Big Frank says. The top two-by-four presses against their thighs. The wind picks up, stinging Danny's eyes.

"Keep going!" Ray says. "Let's raise the sonofabitch!"

"Wait!" Martin cries. "My hands!"

"Hey, Mart," Danny grunts, "ever heard of gloves?"

Big Frank says, "Wait. Let's put it down. It's too windy."

"Jesus Christ," Ray says. "It's a windy day!"

Big Frank flushes a deep, purplish red—a color they're all familiar with from the days before he got his blood pressure under control—and says, "Down—let's get a better grip."

"Christ," Ray says. "Okay, but wait." With one long leg he hooks a cinder block and scoots it under the frame. He scoots over another and tells them to hold on. The moment he lets go the load seems to double, but he quickly stacks the two blocks and they ease the frame onto them. Ray scrambles for six more blocks and relieves Big Frank, Martin, then Danny. Freed, they flex their fingers and torque their spines. Ray lights another cigarette while Big Frank stares up into the trees, his face returning to normal hues.

Ray waits as long as he can, Danny guesses, before blurting, "Well, picking our noses doesn't seem to be working. How's about we lift the bastard?" and Big Frank turns to his oldest son exactly as if he means to slap him—at least, they all flinch as if he does—but then simply runs a hand through his own hair, shaking his head wearily.

"Damn it, Ray," he says. "What's got into you?"

No answer.

Martin grips his head, a hairy basketball, in his hands. "Whoa—drank more than I thought last night."

"Lightweight," Ray says. He pops two more aspirin.

Above them, on the second level, Anna pushes aside hanging plastic to wave with a pot-holder mitten the color and shape of a lobster. "You guys want to have Thanksgiving, or what?"

Big Frank pulls on his chin: he is a man in no hurry, Danny thinks, a man who has all day—a man who, to look at him, has never messed up a single thing his entire life.

"What do *you* think?" he calls up.

"Well, if it's too windy maybe you should put it off." She looks at Ray. "What do you think, Ray?" She's only known him a year, but already she knows enough to seek his opinion, and as soon as she does Ray is transformed.

"I think we can do it," he says eagerly. "If we can lift it to our shoulders we can just walk it into place."

"The soldiers of Iwo Jima," Danny offers dryly.

"Exactly!" Ray says. "It'll get easier as we go."

Big Frank scratches his head.

Kate appears behind Anna, smiling, nearly laughing at the four of them lined up and ready to lift. From beyond the plastic Danny hears the shrill chaotic cries of his nephews.

"Martin," Kate calls, "where are your gloves, you jerk?"

"Who needs 'em," he answers. "We're ready to lift!"

Big Frank says, "Fine. Okay."

"Jesus, are we about ready?" Ray says.

Danny says, "Everybody's goddam ready, Ray."

"Fine. Let's separate the men from the boys." He stuffs his sunglasses in a pocket. His blue eyes shine.

"Ready?" Big Frank calls.

"You guys," Anna warns. "Be careful."

"I can't watch," Kate says, and disappears.

Ray counts to three, and they heave. The wall rises to their chests, then to their shoulders; they catch the scent of fresh-cut lumber as it passes their noses. They are walking it up, going smooth, when Martin suddenly cries, "I'm too short! I'm too short!"

Sure enough, the wall has risen out of Martin's reach, and it hasn't yet occurred to him to move in for a lower grip.

Ray busts out laughing. Danny joins him; his stretched ribs ache with it. The two of them laugh so hard the whole wall trembles.

"You guys!" Anna cries.

"KEEP GOING!" Big Frank bellows, forcing down his own laughter. They all take one step back—before Martin catches on, digs in, and the wall flips up, banging the house violently. Danny and his brothers hold while their father hammers.

Danny wipes tears from his eyes. The whole scene reminds him, vaguely, of some moment from his childhood—but it won't come clear.

"Puppies," his father laughs. "I got puppies for sons."

Then he is there, in the family room before the first divorce. The room smells of cut wood from the bookshelves their father is building. He is kneeling on the carpet, measuring, when they take him by surprise. He reels, growling, with Danny riding piggy-back, Martin wrestling one hairy, immovable arm, Ray hugging a tree-trunk thigh. Ray plants his legs and heaves; his face is flushed, his eyes fierce—and the giant begins to totter. He laughs, their father, the teary laughter of a tickled child, and they step up the assault, jerking and shoving, squealing and snarling. They are the relentless extensions of one huge thing, giddy with the certainty of their fall.

"Jesus, Boss," Ray says. "I didn't think you had it in you."

Martin shoves his hands under his armpits, resumes hopping. "By the way, Ray, you're fired."

"Oh, hey — don't do me any favors!"

Anna is still up there, looking down. From her smile and the way she leans through the studs Danny thinks she's about to say something funny, precise, to sum them up. But she just hammers in a few nails, then goes to help Kate.

Big Frank pulls another nail from his pouch and holds it up. "Been looking for this," he says, and begins pounding.

Martin glances from Danny to Ray. Together, they tell him, "Last nail."

Watching his father hammer, it seems to Danny that he is not himself, standing there — that he is someone else — or that he is *some-where* else simultaneously. Then he remembers New York. Ellen. A thousand miles away they are sharing a bed, a shower, sometimes the same toothbrush. In the amazingly brief span of twelve months they have grown familiar as twins, and these men know nothing about it.

They step back to look. Danny feels the cold wind slice his ears. His nose is numb and he's starving. But he's not ready to go inside. He wants to stand awhile longer among these men before they all sit down to dinner — before they try to eat and talk and drink amidst the tireless commotion of four small boys.

After dinner, if it's not too dark, they'll nail up sheets of Celotex to keep the cold out. Tomorrow they'll lay siding. After that, he decides, dropping his hammer and following the three of them inside — after that they're on their own.

Black Ice

HIS FATHER STOLE THE PUCK. ON THE SHORE, JIMMY GRIPPED HIS STICK as his father broke clear of the pack and bore down on Johnny Ryan's father in goal. Mr. Ryan moved out from the net to meet him, trying to cut down his angle. But he was too slow, his father was on him now and Jimmy held his breath. His father's left shoulder dipped, Mr. Ryan bit. A graceful sweep right, then the backhand flip into a wide open net. Piece of cake, Jimmy imagined him saying. He relaxed his grip, let out a long, deep breath, and started to smile.

Out on the pond his father did a tight pirouette from the goal and glided over to the keg of beer. He was a beer salesman and got it at discount, wouldn't think of letting anyone else chip in. Jimmy watched him fish a plastic cup out of the sweaters strewn around the keg, saw the heads of the other men thrown back at something he'd said. His father's own laughter, faint yet jarring, broke the silence in the cove. Suddenly it all came back to Jimmy, the night before, what his father had said, and he stopped smiling. He looked away now, as if by averting his eyes he could close his ears to the sound.

The ground was cold under his father's faded green Marine Corps duffel bag, serving as a seat cushion, and Jimmy shivered slightly. He looked down at his new skates dangling over the bank, their untested silvery blades safely removed from the surrounding mix of dirt and snow. Beyond them the black ice stretched the length of the cove like a new-washed pane of glass, so clear he imagined being able to reach down to touch the dead leaves littering the pond bottom. Their clarity unnerved him, and he shivered again. He'd grown up skating on black ice, it was the best ice there was if your skates were sharp, and he knew it was thick and hard because he could see the proof in the thin white cuts his father's skates had made. Still . . . he wondered where the ice turned to water, down there. He couldn't tell really. It was so dark, that icy water; its darkness seemed to fill the cove, to darken it from below.

He let his stick fall gently onto his lap and hugged his arms tight to his stomach. Past the thick spires of pines keeping the cove in perpetual shade, the rest of the pond shimmered in the winter sun. The glare off the bluish-white surface hurt his eyes. He could see where the black ice left off and the other began, and to him it might as well have been the distant line of the horizon on some flat, arctic ocean. His father had the puck again. He could have been a million miles away.

They usually approached the pond from the main beachfront down the way, but for some reason his father had driven to this end today. Jimmy heard the cries of the kids down there, but he couldn't see them for all the trees penning the cove. Johnny Ryan would be down there, and Frankie Russo and Eddie Joyce. Briefly he considered cutting through the woods to join them. But no. He couldn't tromp through the woods in his new skates. Besides, he always played with the men on Saturday. His friends were still at the ankle-bending stage, so it was easy for him to dominate their games. Jimmy had started young. Already he could keep up with most of the men.

Saturday was their day, his and his father's. The day they forgot about tests at school, hassles with customers. On Saturdays they even skipped their daily ritual of attending mass, so they could catch the good ice. Later it got soft from the sun and the sharp blades digging at it, chewing it up. But early morning ice was hard, like glass. They were always the first ones on it, and seeing the lone cuts of their skates Jimmy sometimes imagined God's eyes watching, approving that it was them christening the virgin ice. When it was just the two of them like that, his father would make him leave his stick behind and just skate.

"Stay low! From the hips!" he'd bark, his long shadow in front of Jimmy as they whirled side by side from one end of the pond to the other. Jimmy's eyes never left his father's shadow as he matched it stride for stride, mirroring it down to the swing of its arms. Eventually the others would show up and the game began. But nothing beat their early morning skate, when they had the pond to themselves. Then, the wind in his hair, the sound of his father's hard breathing next to him seemed to lift him right off the ice, until he imagined himself skating on air.

A thin, beckoning finger of light from the slow-rising sun beamed through a crack in the pine-wall, reflecting off one of his skates. Jimmy followed the current of light back into the trees. It reminded him of the way the light left Father Martin's gold chalice when he raised it during the consecration, a single, flashing, sharp-edged light. The sun was getting up there; the regular mass would have ended and Father would be at the side altar by now. Jimmy pictured him alone at the altar and felt a flicker of guilt. Poor Father: no one there to pour out his water and wine, to answer his prayers. He stared into the trees but, mysteriously, the crack had closed, the light had disappeared. The cove was dark again.

Father Martin set the altar boy schedules and lately had been assigning more and more daily masses to Jimmy. Or "Mr. Doyle," as Father called him sometimes. He liked that, "Mr. Doyle," and since becoming an altar boy he did feel older, different somehow. He no longer worried so much about school, wasn't so easily goaded into fights by his older sister Katie. He'd even taken to padding around the house the way Father moved on the altar: softly, quietly. It drove Katie wild.

"He's doing it again, Mommy," she'd complain bitterly. "He's sneaking up on me again."

He knew he was becoming a great favorite of Father Martin. Hadn't Father complimented him just last week on the way he rang the bells during the consecration?

"Beautiful job with the bells today, Mr. Doyle," he'd said.

"Thank you, Father."

"You know, I might have you give a little clinic at my next altar boy class. The awful noises some of those guys make," Father clucked. "Why, it's a wonder old Haggerty hasn't had a heart attack, the racket Joyce makes sometimes. Imagine the poor man's shock, Jimmy. One minute he's traipsing o'er the green fields of home, the next there's a three-alarm fire going off in his head."

"My grandfather's from the same place in Ireland as Mr. Haggerty," Jimmy blurted.

"I know Jimmy, I know. And it wasn't easy for them when they came here, believe me." Father's face grew thoughtful. "No, not easy at all." He looked down at Jimmy then brightened again.

"But that was a long time ago. Nothing for my favorite little bell ringer to worry about," and he ruffled Jimmy's hair.

Blushing, Jimmy almost said "It's all in the wrist, Father," but caught himself. He didn't want to seem swell-headed. After all, at ten he was the youngest altar boy in the parish. Besides, if there was anything his father hated it was a show-off. "Stop shapin'!" he growled whenever he thought Jimmy was getting too full of himself. Like the time, a couple of weeks ago, when he'd raced his friends across the pond and started skating backwards, teasing them as they tried to catch him. He'd sensed his father's watchful eyes, turned to see his shaking head and slipped on a dead leaf frozen into the ice. His crowing friends whizzed past and he lay still, waiting for his father to lift him off the ice, the way he used to when Jimmy would fall. But his friends' shouts were dim whispers on the winter air when he realized his father had skated away. Slowly he'd picked himself up, dusting the snow from his legs.

"Kid's a born defenseman. You should see him skate backwards," he heard his father tell his mother that night, when he thought Jimmy wasn't around to overhear.

He'd found out about the side altar mass a couple of months ago. He'd just walked off the altar one day after serving mass for Father Chioffaro when he was mystified to see Father Martin setting out his vestments. Outside of a funeral there was only one mass scheduled on weekdays. He didn't say anything, but after hanging up his cassock and surplice he lingered in the back of the church, and when Father came out to the side altar with the chalice and the cruets filled with water and wine it dawned on him: a priest has to say mass every day, he remembered. Without a word he'd walked over to the side altar and taken up his post, behind Father and to his right. It was a close call to make it to school on time that day. But he ran all the way and just made it.

Now every weekday the chapel emptied after mass, and he waited alone in the pews off to the side. He loved the peace of those early mornings: the sleepy light filtering soft through the stained-glass windows, muted by the dark brown pews and confessional closets lining the wall. The candles in rows between the side and main altars, short red ones in front, behind and above them taller blue ones, casting vague shadows on the crucifix nailed into the dark wall above. Sometimes in the flickering shadows Jimmy imagined His sad eyes looking down on him and he strained in the dim light, searching them out, forgetting all about Father until the sweep of Father's cassock on the floor broke his trance. Then he moved to the small altar set into the sacristy wall and here, against the white altar cloth and whitewashed walls, the shadows deepened and took shape. Father in a simple white cowl spoke his Latin softly, so softly the words might have come from his shadow on the altar. But Jimmy didn't have to hear to know when to whisper back the right response. At mass's end Father simply nodded his thanks and Jimmy stole out the side door, then ran for school.

Of course, Sunday was the big day for everyone else. Jimmy sat benignly through the sermon, bemused at mothers and daughters in pretty dresses, fathers and sons in suitcoats and ties and fresh-shined shoes. From the altar he looked out on Miss Leary his teacher, prim in a dark dress; old Mr. Haggerty, drowsy already in the back of the church; his friends in a whispery huddle, Ryan and Russo and Eddie Joyce. They were such kids!

There'd be his family all in a row. Mom in her favorite blue dress and black felt hat with its thin-meshed veil, Katie scowly beside her, then the three little ones fidgety, buffed and polished like prized red apples on display in a supermarket. His father impassive as Father Martin spoke from the pulpit: "For all men He suffered . . . " The shifting of feet, scattered coughs. Sunday pretenders! The racket of his father honking into his handkerchief would ring out. Incredible, the volume of that honk, like a wounded goose.

He heard the honk now and looked up to see him glide into the cove. He set his teeth to stop their chattering. His father pulled up, stuffing his handkerchief back into his pocket, then leaning casually on his stick. He reminded Jimmy of a Confederate soldier leaning on his long musket, broken-nosed, gaunt, and hungry-eyed, like the one pictured in his history book.

"Hey kid, we could use some fresh legs out there."

Jimmy shrugged and looked down at the black ice. Below the surface a bright orange carp swam slowly, aimlessly back and forth, as if trying to stay warm. The sound of ice meeting ice boomed like a thunderclap somewhere out on the pond.

"Must be awful cold just sittin' there, huh? Ya cold?"

"No."

"Feel sick?"

"No."

His father looked down, idly tapping his stick against the snow caught in his skates.

"Hmm. He's not cold, he's not sick." He looked up. "What're ya, a sissy?"

Jimmy stiffened. There it was again, that same flat, hard voice from the night before. And now it all came back to him, the feeling from the night before that the voice came from someone else, from some imposter pretending to be his father. He stared at his father now and tears started in his eyes. Don't cry, he told himself, whatever you do, don't let him see you cry.

He looked down at his new skates, gleaming again from another patch of light breaking through the trees. He'd been so excited the night before when his father brought them home. New Bauers, just like the pros wore! He could smell the sharp leather, could see his father's smile when, trembling, he'd taken them out of the box. In his rush to try them on he'd cut his thumb on the edge of a blade. "Easy, kid," his father had laughed, applying a BandAid to the wound. Idly now Jimmy picked at the bandage until it came loose. He rubbed a fingernail around the frozen cut, feeling the dry, wrinkled skin.

"C'mon kid, you're missin' all the good ice," his father said, softening. "You wanta try out those new skates, don't ya?"

Jimmy started picking out patterns on the dead leaves under the ice. Softly, he said, "I should be at mass."

"What?"

"I should be at mass. Father will be alone today."

"Christ, can't you take one lousy day off from those priests? Huh?"

It was his father who'd started him going to daily mass, before he was old enough for school even. Jimmy remembered how he used to trail after him, struggling to keep pace as they left the house; two silent, shadowy figures in the pre-dawn darkness, the crunch of their boots on the dry snow echoing in the still morning air. Then arriving at the church and always that fresh feeling of rediscovery, as if he were entering an old, familiar world. Sometimes they were the only ones there. Then Jimmy couldn't help feeling it was a world made specially for them; a mysterious, dark-lit, timeless world, far removed from the slow-wakening world outside. Kneeling together in the soft light and warmth of the chapel, Jimmy would mimic his father's every move, down to the modest bow of his head, the clasp of his hands.

But now by the time his father's honking sinuses woke the house Jimmy was out the door, alone in the snowy street, arriving at the sacristy early to tend to his duties. Filling the cruets with water and wine, lighting the candles, setting out the Book. Then leading Father to the altar, to another even more private world where nothing beyond the altar rail mattered. Afterwards he had his side altar mass to serve, by which time his father would be gone.

He felt his father's gaze and raised his to see him shaking his head.

"Sit there all day, makes no difference to me." He turned, did a little hop to accelerate and headed back out to where his friends were circled around Mr. Ryan, who'd just stopped a hard shot with his head. Jimmy watched him leave the cove. The shivering he'd stifled broke with a pent-up energy, like an imploding crystal of glass. He looked out at the fresh cuts of his father's skates on the black ice and with a final, convulsed shudder closed his eyes and forced himself still.

"Hey, he didn't dent my puck, did he?" His father's shout, like clanging metal in an empty room, echoed through the still cove.

The night before, when Mr. Ryan came over to watch the hockey game with his father, Jimmy had joined them in the basement. They liked having him around to fetch their beer for them, and he felt privileged in this role, in a way. No one else in the family was allowed down there when his father had company. Although Mr. Ryan could be a pain. He drank faster than Jimmy's father and always seemed out of synch, so Jimmy would no sooner make a run than Mr. Ryan sent him up to the kitchen again.

"Kid." The game had just started and his father pointed to his empty beer can.

Jimmy automatically looked to Mr. Ryan, but there was no signal there and he ran upstairs. Returning, he caught his father in mid-sentence.

" . . . so I says to the guy, whattaya mean you only ordered ten cases? I got it written down right here, twenty cases of bar bottles. What's it, my fault you had a slow week? I gotta pay for your problems?

"So he says 'Well, I don't remember order no twenty cases.' He no speaka the Inglais too good, you know what I mean? At this point I go into my act."

His father stood up and slowly lifted his hands, palms upward, to the ceiling. Rolling his head onto his neck, he said in a loud voice "God, why me? What did I do, that you put me here in the South End with these people, me with five kids and guys half my age cleanin' up out in Brighton and Newton? Tell me, what did I do to deserve this shit? Willya tell me please?"

He shook with laughter. "I'm tellin' ya, I did everything but strike my breast three times. That poor spic didn't know what to do. Finally he says 'Okay, okay, I take the twenty.'"

"Did he really order twenty cases?" Mr. Ryan asked.

"No you dummy, that's the whole point. I padded my order, see?

Christ, I've been cheatin' those Puerto Ricans down there for years. How d'ya think I feed these kids? By charity work?" He sat down, picked up his beer and turned back to the game, still chuckling. Jimmy couldn't tell what his father thought funnier, his own performance or Mr. Ryan's dimwittedness.

"Only you, Doyle, only you," Mr. Ryan said, laughing himself now.

When the game ended and Jimmy went to bed he lay still, trying to go to sleep. From the den downstairs he heard the rustle of his mother's newspapers, the crack of a beer opening. There was a plopping sound as his father settled into his chair.

"So how was your day?"

"Not bad," he heard from his mother. There was a pause, as if she were considering something. "Jimmy's teacher called today. He was late for school again."

"That kid." Jimmy pictured his father's shaking head. "At the church?"

His mother must have simply nodded.

"Christ, don't those priests know he's got school?"

"They don't ask him to do it, he volunteers. Father Martin says he's the only kid who's ever done it, in his memory."

"Well, it's time we put an end to it."

"I suppose." There was another pause, then his mother laughed. "Father calls him his shadow. Says he's never seen such a serious little kid."

"Too serious for his own good, if you ask me. He spends too much time with those goddamn priests."

"Oh, come on Jim . . . "

His father cut her off, his voice a weary growl. "It's a hard world out there and it's about time he realized it. He's getting older now."

Suddenly alert, Jimmy rose halfway from his bed, straining for his mother's response. The house was still. He lay back, then turned onto his side, arms wrapped tight over his stomach. He closed his eyes, but soon his father's snores began to drift up from the den, deep snores that filled the quiet house. In between, his low whistling breaths were like spent waves.

Jimmy exhaled noisily, as if trying to blow the pressure in his stomach right out of him. It was no good, though, he saw it still too clearly: the dull flush of his father's broken-veined face when he'd stood, the crooked smile. The too loud voice when he'd said "God, why me?" Did his father really have to cheat, to feed him and Katie and the others? He wondered if the Puerto Ricans cheated, to get food. And if so, whom.

There was a loud snort from the den. The air whooshed out of his father's chair, there was a lurching step, a muttered "good night." His father tripped on the stairs and cursed. Through hooded eyes, Jimmy watched his shadow pass his door.

He pulled his blanket tight around him. His mother always turned down the heat after putting them to bed. Already the house seemed cold. Shivering slightly, he curled around the lump in his stomach and stared into the darkness. "For all men He suffered . . . " Father had said. Jimmy closed his eyes again, and now he could hear Father's soft voice, could see him at the altar, his face furrowed in prayer. Suddenly drowsy, he began his own whispery prayer. Our Father . . . father . . . Father . . . father . . .

Now he shook uncontrollably. The thin cuts his father's blades had made on the black ice stared up at him like an accusation. He lifted his head in time to see someone's stick catch in his father's skates, sending him crashing to the ice. The spill made him wince and he held his breath. Get up, dad, get up he urged silently, but his father lay in a heap where he'd fallen.

Jimmy stood up. Throat tight, he took a tentative step onto the ice and his legs, cramped and weak, buckled and nearly collapsed. Like a new-born foal, he righted himself and pushed off with his skates. He glided slowly out about ten yards into the cove, holding his breath, as if to make himself lighter. The ice was hard and sure. Exhaling deeply, he pivoted and glided back to the bank, where he stopped and turned. His father lay still on the ice.

Jimmy stared out at the fallen figure of his father and gripped his stick. Head down, he dug the inside edges of his blades into the black ice and began to skate. Halfway across the cove he sensed his speed pick up and churned ahead with fury, pushing hard from side to side. From the hips, just like Dad taught me, he spurred himself on. Leaving the dark cove, he felt the pressure explode out of him, mingling with the light and the wind and the cold air and seeming to lift him right off the ice, propelling him forward.

"Dad!" he cried. "Dad!"

His father turned and jumped to his feet just in time to catch Jimmy in his arms. Grinning, he lifted him and held him close.

"All right, here he is. We'll see some moves now."

"Dad, are you okay?"

His father smiled. "Sure, I'm okay, kid. I was just takin' a little rest."

"I thought you were hurt."

"Naw, who could hurt an old Marine like me?" he laughed.

Jimmy was panting. His frozen nostrils, loosened by his sprint across the ice, ran freely and he gulped in the cold air.

"You had me worried," he gasped.

"Ah, you're like your mother. You worry too much."

A flooding warmth broke inside Jimmy, melting out to his hands and feet. The cut on his finger throbbed. He stared into his father's eyes and blurted: "Dad?"

"Yeah, kid?"

"You won't cheat the Puerto Ricans anymore?"

His father met Jimmy's stare with silence. Gently, he dropped him to the ice.

"Dad?"

"Yeah, sure kid. No more cheating," he said quietly, so quietly the wind rushing over the pond seemed to steal the words right off his lips. But Jimmy was sure he'd heard them.

He swallowed freely, warm in his father's shadow, and looked around him. Out in mid-ice his father's cronies battled for a loose puck. Down by the beachfront the kids played whip-the-whip. The cove and its black ice sat off in the distance.

"Hey kid, whattaya say we show these guys where we come from."

"Yeah, let's show 'em where we come from."

The Visit

I WOULD NEVER HAVE KNOWN MY FATHER WAS DYING, IF IT WEREN'T for the letter; if Aunt Marty hadn't told me. It came during the summer I was staying with Marty and Uncle Harold, finishing a master's at Connecticut State. I didn't even know he had lived nearby in the Veterans' Home for years. I didn't know anything about him because my mother wanted it that way. Marty sensed her mistake right away and we argued and I sat in the kitchen very late that night, alone, wondering what to do.

In the morning Marty moved through the house as usual, battling the heat, pulling shades down against the sun, bitching about the humidity.

"Eight o'clock and it's already seventy-five," she said coming into the kitchen. A small air conditioner hung from the window in the breakfast nook, droning, dominating the room. The chairs and table felt like ice.

She was still in her slip, her pretty, round face made up, white summer earrings clipped in place. Her shoulders and plump breasts gleaming from a violently scented body lotion. She looked like a cocktail waitress until she stepped into her crisp blue uniform. That summer she was working for a pediatrician. The job exhausted her. She would come home at five-thirty, fall on her bed and not move for exactly one hour. One thing about Marty, you knew where you stood, which is to say when she had something on her mind, she let you know about it.

She settled at the table with her orange juice and let me know again how she felt about my father.

"Why should you go see Reilly? Now after all these years? Your mother would kill me," she said.

They always referred to my father impersonally, last name only. The family never called him John or John Reilly.

She handed me a glass of juice and rained out some Rice Krispies, then pushed the milk and sugar toward me. She kept forgetting I don't use sugar.

"What did he ever do for you? He ran off with no more thought than a tom cat. Even though he was brought up Irish Catholic, he was no good. We all told your mother that. All those Reilly boys were the same . . . a rough lot, running around. He broke your mother's heart, Katherine. Don't you forget it."

I told her I didn't see what being Catholic had to do with it. She sighed, reaching for patience, wisdom, both I suppose.

"He never gave a cent to help out. And in those days . . . well, you wouldn't remember, it wasn't easy. Divorce was hard, a scandal. What your mother went through . . . " She paused, studied me a moment. "Just forget it, Katherine."

All this was old news. At least she didn't drag the Great Depression into it again or living above the bakery where my mother worked, after he left us. The place smelled of cinnamon, rising yeast, and baking bread, donuts in hot fat. There were always cookies, and people dropping in and out. We had a kitten in that place. I don't remember what happened to it when we moved or much at all about that time. I only know things worked out for my mother. She always said I hadn't missed anything by not knowing my father.

"He's my father, " I said then. "I don't even know what he looks like."

Not moved at all, she shrugged and lit a cigarette. Smoke drifted toward the air conditioner, was sucked away.

"The man is dying. Someone owes him a visit," I said.

"Good God! The letter would have to come while you're here. I never should have told you. Harold thought I should. The VA sends everything here, you know, because *we* had to sign him in there. Harold had him working in the terminal, loading trucks just before he fell apart. His own family wouldn't give him the time of day."

She frowned, remembered something she wouldn't share, and stubbed out her cigarette.

"God rest his soul," she said suddenly and leaned forward and put her hands on mine.

It could have been my mother sitting there; the two sisters look so alike. The same plump fingers and pleading eyes. A sad touch. You can feel sadness in a touch.

"Please . . . don't get involved with him," she said.

When I didn't say anything, she relaxed a bit and rewarded me with some information.

"I'll tell you he was good looking, if that's what's on your mind," she said. "Dark Irish and always wearing some fancy brand of toilet water . . . imported from Europe somewhere. He took good care of himself, that one." She drifted off in thought a moment and went on. "You have some of his looks, his eyes. He was handsome all right. And did he know it . . . a ladies' man, you know."

She glanced at her watch and whipped the dishes to the sink. "Jesus," she said, "I'm going to be late. We've got ten camp physicals today. Hurry up, I'll drop you at school."

We didn't talk much in the car. Marty was still waiting for a promise that I wouldn't go see Reilly. How could she expect me to forget him? How can you forget a father you've never known? Reilly, always until then on the periphery of my life, was actually in it and there was no going back.

Marty double-parked and looked at me; I wasn't getting out. Everything was so confusing and unfinished.

"Didn't he ever try to see me? Not even once?"

"Jesus, you're still thinking about him. Forget about the letter. Promise you won't go see him, Katherine."

I told her what she wanted to hear and she smiled and told me it made good sense. Then she leaned across the seat and said she'd see me later, at the house. She said we'd go out, maybe see a movie because it was too hot to cook.

"I wouldn't mind going to a movie," I said and got out.

I had nothing better to do. The truth was I'd been too busy to do much and hadn't met any people my own age. To do things with, I mean. The year before I had been involved with a man who taught music at my school in Shaker Heights. It didn't work out. He wanted me to marry him and go to San Diego where he had a new job teaching band. I couldn't quit and go off like that. I wasn't ready to marry or live together either. Besides, I'd always heard that musicians were poor risks. My mother had told me they need all kinds of freedom and I would always be tagging along. Didn't she know? Reilly, when he worked, played the harp and sang in Irish taverns around town. He had a talent with ballads, some said, but I never heard him sing. I just didn't want to get involved. I still don't want to get involved with anyone.

❦

The street we lived on felt tropical, foreign in the lush, heavy night. A quarter moon was rising as we drove home, sprinklers churned over the small lawns. The neighbor's beagle, caught in our headlights, squatted at the end of his leash, looked embarrassed, and sprinted off with his owner.

Marty and Harold had been arguing over the movie, how it should have ended. It was a fight story. I didn't care how it ended. Grown men knocking each other's brains out. I closed my eyes a lot. Suddenly, Marty had an idea.

"Why don't we get out of this heat? Let's run up to the mountains this weekend," she said.

Harold was all for it but when she turned to me I made an excuse. A paper to do, reading for a quiz. They didn't try to persuade me: I supposed they would like to be alone for awhile. So did I and Marty said all right. I knew that while they were gone I would go see Reilly. Try to; I'd have to call and see if he wanted me to visit. After all those years, maybe *he* would like to forget it . . . the past . . . me . . . who could know?

I put on shorts and a halter and sat on the front steps drinking iced tea, making plans. Harold was getting his fishing gear together in the garage and then he came and stood on the driveway looking at the moon just above the trees.

"Sure you don't want to come? You can bring some work along. We'll leave you alone," he said.

"Can't really," I said. "I need the library. Research."

He came up the steps and touched the top of my head.

"Don't stay up too late," he said.

He always treated me like a daughter. Marty and Harold never had children. They are my godparents and I loved them and felt sorry about the lies, but not enough to change anything. We sat there taking in the night and sounds. You could be comfortable with Harold; he seemed so at peace with himself. He'd never said a bad thing to me about Reilly. Men can be that way, not wanting to take sides against each other. For a moment, I wanted to tell him my plan but Marty came to the door with a towel wrapped around her head and called him inside. Just as well, because it was between Reilly and me.

❦

The Veterans' Hospital sat on a high hill facing west over the gardens and pools of the municipal park. A long porch ran the front length of the brick building and was scattered with high-backed cane rockers. No one was using them. Probably too hot. The petunias along the drive lay flattened by heat, their pale blossoms sucked together.

I had called ahead, just after Marty and Harold pulled out of the driveway, to ask if John Reilly could have a visitor. They'd asked who I was. His daughter Katherine I'd said, as if I were used to saying it. It was a wait before they called back and the longer I waited the more certain I was the answer would be no.

So, I wasn't prepared to be there, walking up the wooden steps, crossing into the dark, seedy lobby. The walls shone under countless layers of glossy paint, institutional green, rippling like water on the old walls. The clerk made me wait at the reception desk while he called up to tell Reilly I was there. There was some confusion and he asked me to sit down and pointed to one of the cracked leather couches arranged in a square in the center of the lobby. A ceiling fan hummed above, moving the air slightly, but my arms and legs still stuck to the leather cushions. I sweated, afraid he wouldn't see me after all. Could he be playing a game? Bringing me there so that he could send me away? Then it would be true, all the things Marty and my mother had told me. I made up something easier to live with: he might be in bad shape, or, who knows, he may have had other children, people in his life we didn't know about. I may not have been special, after all, only an intruder. I was on my feet, heading toward the door when an orderly called me back, led me to the elevator, then down green corridors, past open doorways, sick rooms I avoided looking into. The clerk stopped before a closed door, opened it and said, "Hey, Reilly. On your best. A lady to see you."

He wasn't frail, as I'd expected, but fleshy, florid in a blue bathrobe and silky maroon pajamas. His chalky white hair needed cutting but his moustache, only beginning to gray, was trim and lightly waxed. He looked quite elegant; he could have been on a cruise, sitting under a lap robe in a deck chair rather than in the high hospital bed. He smiled and waved me in and I moved closer to the bed, waiting for him to say something, to make the first move. We were both waiting, sizing each other up. Then he started.

"Katherine . . . I'm sorry they kept you waiting down there."

"I'm a little late . . . the bus was late. I'll bet you thought I wasn't coming."

"No, I thought you'd come all right. Once you decided . . . I've been lying here wondering why."

He started to get up then, everything stiffening as he pulled the sheet aside and moved off the bed. For a moment all his style fell away as he moved toward me, leaning on the bed, then a chair, the dresser for support. His legs seemed too heavy for him but he made it and took my hand. A good cologne, woodsy, green, surrounded us.

"Just a few damn days in bed and a man can hardly stand up," he said. He was trembling, his hand shaking in mine. There was fever in his touch and I realized that his flush, the look of health, was part of his illness. I helped him into one of the chairs and he arranged himself, thanking me, smiling. I sat down facing him in the other chair and we began again.

"What do they call you? Katy? Kathy?"

"The family calls me Katherine."

"Your friends, what do they call you?"

"Kate."

"I'll call you Kate then. A good name, solid. You look like a Kate." He chuckled and told me I had my mother's freckles. Then he blurted out, "How the hell did you happen to come here?"

"Harold and Marty Phalen told me you were here. I'm staying with them, going to summer school . . . working for Harold in the afternoon . . . answering phones, filing."

"They let you come?"

"They don't know. No one knows. Marty made me promise I wouldn't."

He grinned. "She still ordering people around like a goddamned sergeant?"

"Who, Marty?"

"Yes, Marty . . . your mother wasn't like that."

"Sometimes," I said and then to be fair, "She and Harold help me out a lot."

"Well, don't tell her a thing. A little white lie never hurt anyone. Don't worry about it. I'd give plenty to see her face, if she knew. Do her good to realize some people have a mind of their own. You have to live your own life, Kate, for better or worse. But you must have learned that by now or you wouldn't be here."

He shifted around, moving his weight from one elbow to the other and flexed his hand. "Gone to sleep. My blood runs slow; bad circulation, they tell me."

"I'm sorry you're not feeling well," I said. "Please tell me when you want me to leave . . . I mean if you're uncomfortable or anything."

He dismissed my concern with a little wave of his hand, a nod. "This is nothing," he said. "But I could use a drink of water. Then we'll talk a bit. Don't worry about me."

I poured water from a carafe on the bedstand into a plastic cup and held it out. He couldn't manage it and I helped him, holding it to his lips while he drank in short gulps. A little dribbled onto his robe. Embarrassed, he brushed at the wet spot then smoothed his moustache. I tossed the cup in the wastebasket and sat down, pretending not to notice.

He asked me about myself and for a while I told him about my life, about teaching history in Shaker Heights, about working for my master's degree, and he picked up on that.

"Get all the education you can and then some. Sounds bossy. God, what right do I have to boss you?"

"I want to hear what you have to say," I told him.

"Like a father and daughter?"

"Yes, like that."

"There's a lot to say. Don't know that I can do that. Make up for all these years . . . "

He slipped into another thought. I didn't try to follow. I wasn't sure that I wanted to know everything he might want to tell me and I believe he sensed this. He didn't want to know everything either.

"I could have had an education on the army after the war. GI Bill. Didn't have enough sense to settle down to it. Stayed in the occupation army instead and ran all over Europe, what was left of it. Had some damn good times there. France, after the liberation . . . never saw anything like it."

He leaned forward, his eyes brightened and his face seemed suddenly softer.

"Have you ever been to Paris, Kate?"

"No. I've never been east of New York."

"Well, that's a shame. Never saw anything like it. What a city Paris is. The whole place seems alive, you know, like it's breathing right under your feet . . . " He paused and stared at me. "I'll bet you don't remember World War II."

"Some of it," I said but he looked skeptical. "Really, I do! We used to go to those little movie theatres and see newsreels of the battles . . . everything, at sea, Europe, too, and they made me cry. The noise, and the burials at sea, and flamethrowers and kamikazees . . . fire and death . . . my mother had to take me out into the lobby and then I started having nightmares. She didn't take me after that."

He looked away out the window. "It was a nightmare all right." Then remembering me again, he tried to be cheerful. "But it wasn't all bad; some of us survived. Fool's luck I suppose."

"I'm glad you survived," I said. "I thought a lot about you. I used to wonder if you were dead."

"Killed in the war?"

"Dead and gone."

"You really wondered about that? You're not just being . . . you know, polite or something?"

The room seemed very small with no space between us and I thought he was going to get up and touch me. I wasn't ready for that.

"I didn't come here just to be polite," I said quickly and the moment passed. Neither one of us knew where to go with it.

He wanted to show me an album then and slowly got up and pulled it from a drawer in his dresser. It was full of snapshots taken after the war in France, mostly Paris. Reilly at the Arc de Triomphe, Reilly ascending the Eiffel Tower, and in a night club with white table cloths and little lamps with fringed shades and soldiers and women sitting arms around each other. And Reilly, tanned so dark he looked foreign, exotic, sitting in an umbrella shade someplace on the Cote d'Azure . . . he couldn't remember exactly where.

This exhausted him and he handed me the album to finish on my own. A few loose prints fell into my lap and he reached to retrieve them but I saw them before he could. A younger Reilly, at the shore with a line of old gabled houses rising behind the group, posed on the beach in one of those pyramids with the men shoring up the bottom, several young women balancing on top, looking like a troop of amateur acrobats on holiday. The women had bobbed hair, wore striped bathing suits belted low on the hip. Everyone with bathing slippers, laughing, and I recognized my mother, kneeling on Reilly's broad back, mugging for the camera.

He took the picture from my lap and stared at it.

"There were some good times, you see. Don't let anyone tell you different. You came from love. Remember that Kate."

Then he closed the album and I didn't know what to say. I remember other photos, my mother's, that have parts snipped away.

One especially of my mother leaning against a tree. The body next to hers had been carefully clipped out but the contours of the missing part were still there. Someone taller than she. I always knew it had been Reilly that she had cut from her life and mine as well.

"How is she? How's your mother?"

"All right. Living in Cleveland. She has a business, real estate."

He did not seem surprised. He was pleased to hear.

"She always was a go-getter, able to take care of herself. She still pretty?"

I nodded, yes.

"Married?"

"No. She could have been though. She said she was too busy for it." Actually, there were no men she trusted but I wouldn't say that.

"You happy, Kate?"

"What a question . . . I guess so."

"You don't hold it against me? What happened?"

"I wasn't old enough to understand."

"I was a damn fool, running away . . . it was so hard to make money in those days and when you came along . . . all that responsibility. I did what I could, singing and the like."

"You don't have to tell me this."

"Oh, I do, Kate. I need to and I think you need to hear it. Marty and your mother kept after me, nothing was good enough and her family didn't like me. I just gave up on it. When I tried to send a little money now and then, your mother sent it right back. So goddamn proud, my god she wouldn't have accepted heaven from the pope. Marty kept at her then, made her bitter against me. I tried to see you once and they hauled me to jail. After that, I left for good. Then the war happened and when I came back from that I started an appliance business in Tampa but it never amounted to much. I thought of helping again, of finding you and making it right. Marty wouldn't tell me anything . . . but Harold . . . he's a good egg, he hired me . . . then I got sick and wound up in here. The end, story of my life . . . "

He stopped suddenly and pushed out of the chair, then just stood looking at me before he bent and kissed me on the forehead. His hands were on my shoulders, his palms burning with fever and I put my hands on top of his.

I remember saying, "It's all right." Over and over again while he stood there touching my shoulders.

Finally, he said, "I've wondered for a long time . . . if you were all right. My God, you don't know how I tried to love you. I do love you, in my way."

I let go then, cried and he stepped away and went back to the dresser and from the same drawer where he kept the album he pulled out a thick leather book. A Bible, I could see as he came toward me, holding it out like an offering, a proof of some kind. There was a gold cross embossed on the cover. The pages were edged in gold and it was heavy when he put it in my lap.

"This should belong to you now. Look there on the last pages, where it says births and baptisms and what not."

I was there. Katherine Elizabeth Reilly. I knew then that he knew he was dying. It was his way of telling me.

"I don't have anything to give you," I said.

"You came, that's enough. That's everything, Kate. Katherine Elizabeth Reilly. Has a ring to it. I chose Katherine, you know. Your mother chose the other."

"Is there anything I can do for you?" I asked. But he had turned away and then he excused himself. I heard his slippers scuffing down the hall, a door slammed. Later, when he came back, he seemed tired, sunken, with the look of people caught in disasters as they search through what's left of their lives.

"It's not so much what is, but what could have been. Know what I mean? That's what bothers me," he said.

It was important that we could sit together then, saying nothing, until the room grew dusky. The automatic light winked on and brought us starkly together again. Somewhere a bell rang. "Dinner," he said. "Only meatloaf but you're welcome to stay."

"I'll come again."

"You're not missing much. It's always too dry."

Somehow I got myself together and to the door and said good-bye. The elevator was full of the smell of baked hamburger and onions. I held the Bible against my chest and as I crossed the lobby the clerk called me over and asked how the visit had gone, was I one of Reilly's family?

"Yes," I said. "Yes, I'm his daughter."

With the Bible tight under my arm, I hurried out, glad for the dark and glad that no one would be home.

❦

The next day, Sunday, the clerk put my call through to the nursing station. They said my father wasn't feeling well, had been given some medication and would probably sleep all afternoon. I left a message that I would see him on Monday if it was all right with him. I would call first.

Marty and Harold came home late that night, flushed with sun, exhausted, complaining of traffic and crowded restaurants. Harold took a beer from the refrigerator and said he was going to watch the news. I sat there in the kitchen while Marty bent over the ice chest, pulling out their catch.

"Bass," she said, holding up a pale, stiff fillet. Then she began wrapping them up.

"Did you get a lot done? Finish that paper?" she asked.

"Yes . . . well almost. Most of it."

She tore off another sheet of white paper, rinsed and patted dry a fillet, deftly wrapped and taped it. I couldn't think of anything to say. I should have made something up because the silence felt dangerous. Anything could have fallen into that silence but I let it go on.

She gave me a knowing look as she opened the freezer. A cold mist surged from the drawer while she stacked the fillets in place. "Hard to study in the summer, I suppose, in this heat," she said. She slid the drawer back in and emptied the ice chest into the sink, leaving it there upside down to drain. "I couldn't do it. I know I couldn't do it." She studied me a moment.

I almost told her then about the visit. About knowing they had all lied to me, not told the whole truth about Reilly and me. I really didn't care what she thought anymore. She and my mother could carry on their own case against Reilly. Let them figure it out. But I wasn't going to give up my secret. The visit had given me a kind of strength I'd never felt before.

"You worked too hard. You look all wound up."

"I got a lot done," I said.

"It's so damn hot in here," she said suddenly. "Why isn't this air on?"

"I forgot," I said. "It was cool at the library."

Marty turned on the air conditioner. It came on with a watery starting-up sound and settled into a dull hum. She sat down and opened her blouse to the cooler air blowing across the table.

"Go get some sleep, Katherine. You don't look quite yourself," she said.

It was one of those nights when the moon came in through the window like stage light and I couldn't sleep at all. I was thinking about my father. How I had found him and what it was going to be like now. Next time, we could talk about Paris, so glowing and beautiful that he wanted me to see it.

I turned my bed light on, got out my Bible and read the family record again. There wasn't much to see. My mother's and his marriage date, my birth and baptism. Not much after all those years, but something, really something, better than nothing at all.

Alison Townsend

Persian Carpet

All fall I debate whether or not
to sell my grandmother's Persian carpet.
Kazak, late nineteenth century,
a red field woven with three large
geometrical flowers in lapis, ivory, and gold,
it would pay for a month's rent.
I tell myself there's no place for it
in this rented, wall-to-wall carpeted house.
Its pile is thin and worn, scratchy as stubble.
The selvage and fringes are stringy,
frayed-looking as a child's uncombed hair.

But it saw sixty years of sun filtered
through sandalwood, leather-bound books
and cigar smoke in my grandfather's library.
My mother told me she lay before the fire
on it as a girl, eating apples and crying
when Jo March cut her chestnut hair.
My grandfather crossed it each day,
on his way to the bay window
where he did crossword puzzles,
read race results, waited
for *The Irish Times* to arrive.
I stared into its design
whenever I got stuck on a jigsaw.
At my grandmother's wake everyone
stood upon it one last time, warming themselves
at her black marble fireplace.

So when the rug appraiser tells me
Persian carpets are valued according
to how many knots they contain per inch,
I cannot untangle myself from what has been tied
into this pattern, from family fortunes
made and lost, from the unknown relative
who traveled to the Mideast and brought it back,
from my grandmother's determination to die in the house
where she'd raised ten children and buried two,
the life my grandfather wove there with her
one more knot in what *his* father began —
the boy who sailed from Londonderry
at the time of the Famine and hired out
as a mill hand at ten, working the threads
and strands of wool at the blanket factory
until his fingers bled, and the place was his,
and he could lay down Persian carpets in every
room of the house for his children's children's children.

Grandpa

His panel truck started up like a disaster
every morning
when he was still young enough
for union work
and I swore for sure
I'd spend my life doing
"the same damn thing everyday" as he
but there were no ships for me
to go aboard a steward at age ten
my father telling me it was
time to leave the farm
no one telling me to find my own way
I could afford to dream.

Swinging a hammer for a living
working in the yard and on the site
with other men
a paperback in his tool kit,
I knew the old man was right:
"such work ain't fit for a dog"
and I knew then only for the lack myself
Grandma made it possible for him.
She was he as much as he was she
maybe more so
sitting at the table, coffee and tea
on the porch September evenings
a man who came home
needful of washing up
was all she needed from him
and come home he did
soiled and bruised
her liniment on his cuts

her hands kneading his shoulders.
Their quiet jokes in the kitchen:
—"Go on, then, Tom"—
"I'm serious, lass, that is
exactly what the man said."
They'd sit together
to watch the nightly news
for the sons of their daughter
my mother
the older sons
the sons half a world away
getting themselves made dead —
holding hands
his paper, her sewing
"Bring 'em home, ya bastards."
—"Sssh, Tom, the little ones."—

I wished I could work like he
hands as calloused as the world,
strong, to break up kindling in my hands
and still walk as he
hand in hand with "me lass"
along the bluffs north of town
near the shore
to pick wild blackberries
for a pie she'll bake.
I wanted nothing more
than to walk into the union office
where the carpenters are hired
look the man in the eye and say:
"My name is Tom Galway,
and I come for work."

Patricia Barone

Inheritance

In the middle
of my thirtieth year,

in a frame house
we didn't mean to buy
across from Kreuzer's farm,

all May I woke by dawn
wanting to grow corn.

A dream told me to plant potatoes,
in the gibbous moon's waxing shine.

I knew just what to do
preparing soil, I'd haul

black manure across the highway,
red blood meal, white bone meal

from the feed store, as if
born in the country, though I never
owned a houseplant in the city.

It was just that the landscape
looked familiar, though disguised

by lawn we ripped from one half acre,
to beard the backyard slope with peas.

By June I saw the face upon our field:
Great-grandfather Ryan, his profile —

a land-work of hoeing, ridges in the soil —
telling me to listen for the Evergreen
corn, it grew so fast I heard the silk spin.

No matter. I'd made him with my hands.

Everyone Asked about You

IT IS CHRISTMAS EVE. IN THE CRAMPED FRONT ROOM OF A MOBILE HOME in East Texas a man sits reading. On a couch across from him, just a few feet away, an elderly woman, his mother, lies resting beneath an afghan, watching him. A color television set is on in the room, tuned low to a Christmas program, but neither of them has been paying it any attention. Otherwise, there are no gifts, no wreaths or tree, no signs of the season.

After watching the man read for a moment more, the woman speaks, resuming a conversation that had been allowed to lapse.

"Are you going or not?" she says. She is extremely frail and thin. There is obviously something wrong with her. Her voice is not much more than a whisper.

The man looks up from his book. "Hm?"

"Are you going over there, or not?" she repeats. "They invited you."

There is a Christmas Eve party taking place in the house next door. It is a regular, one-story brick house, not a mobile home. Cars and pickups have been pulling in off the highway for the past half hour, parking in the driveway and up in the front yard.

"Oh, Mama," the man says, "I don't think so. They can get along fine without me."

The people next door are his mother's friends. He hardly knows them. The woman had come over with a plate of cookies that morning, had mentioned the party, and asked him if he'd like to stop by. But it was just a formality, he could tell. She hadn't really meant it. And anyhow, the book he's reading has gotten interesting. It's Barbara Tuchman's *The March of Folly*.

There is silence in the little room, except for the faint sound of "Rudolph the Red-Nosed Reindeer," coming from the TV. The man continues to look at his mother, but he feels his eyes being drawn back toward his book.

Finally the mother says, "I think you should. They're probably expecting you."

The man smiles at this. He shakes his head. "You really want me to, do you?" he says. "You think it's the proper thing to do."

The mother doesn't say anything for a moment, simply lies there on the couch. On a TV tray beside her, within reach, is a small glass half-filled with water. Beside the glass is a large red-and-white capsule.

"I think it'd be nice," she says finally.

The man is feeling the pull of the book again, but he also feels the force of his mother's will. Next door, another car or truck has just arrived, the sounds of laughter and greeting can be heard as the door is opened to the new guests.

The man closes his book.

"Okay," he says. "Maybe you're right. I guess it wouldn't hurt me to put in an appearance, would it?"

On the couch the mother smiles.

The man places the book, a paperback, on a stack of others beside his chair. He stands up. He has on a pair of shapeless corduroy trousers and an old brown cardigan sweater, the same outfit he's been wearing around the mobile home for several days.

"Can I get you anything first?" he says.

The mother is gazing up at him. He is a large man and towers over her. "I'm fine," she says. Then after a pause, "I hope you're not planning to go over there like that."

The man looks at himself: at the sweater, the corduroy trousers, the loafers on his feet. "I thought I would — why?"

The mother doesn't say anything, just continues to gaze up at him from the couch.

"What's wrong with this?" the man says. "They're not going to be dressed up over there, Mama. You know that."

The mother doesn't say anything.

"You think I ought to change clothes, do you?" he says.

"I think you'd look better," the mother says.

The man goes into the back bedroom of the mobile home, the room he has taken over since he's been there. He doesn't want to go to this party; he knows what it will be like over there. He slides open the door of the closet and unzips the plastic travel bag hanging on the clothes rod. Inside the bag, next to a dark suit, hang two white dress shirts, a gray tweed jacket with matching charcoal slacks, and three ties, all in subdued patterns and colors.

The man removes the jacket and slacks and one of the shirts from the bag and lays them out on the bed. Then he strips off what he is wearing and changes into the fresh clothes. When he's finished, he turns and regards himself in the mirror of the bedroom dresser. Tie or no tie? The hell with it, he decides, he will go the whole hog. Choosing the least subdued of the three ties — it is, after all, Christmas Eve, and he is, after all, going to a party — he steps back to the mirror and begins knotting it.

On the wall beside the mirror as he works is an assortment of photographs cropped and matted within a single large frame. The pictures, some oval, some rectangular, some round, capture the man at various stages in his life. There are shots of him as a baby, as a toddler, and as a boy of twelve. Also, as a high schooler in his football uniform, as a young Marine, and as a graduate student up in Iowa. There is a large color shot of him posed with his first wife and their three children on the steps of their Minneapolis home, and a smaller one down in the corner showing him standing with his second wife — this one taken just over a year ago now — outside a bakery shop in Paris. All told, there are a dozen pictures. He ignores them as he carefully knots his tie.

With the tie finally fixed to his satisfaction, he goes back out to the living room. His mother is as he left her, the water and the pill still on the tray beside her. He spreads his arms for her inspection.

"You look nice," she says.

He lets himself out the back, kitchen, door of the trailer and crosses the small yard to the neighbors' house.

The party inside is just as he had imagined it would be. These are plain people, his mother's neighbors, he a retired railroad worker, she a practicing beautician. The guests are mostly their children and grandchildren. The weather has been unseasonably mild, even for East Texas, and one of the sons is wearing cut-off jeans and a tank top. There is a large tree with lots of presents underneath it. The man doesn't know a soul. His initial awkwardness is never overcome. Attempts are made to include him in a few conversations, but with little success. He has been away from this part of the country too long. Questions about his mother are carefully avoided. Everyone seems to know. He nibbles at a piece of fruitcake, drinks half a cup of eggnog, and leaves as soon as he decently can.

He lets himself back in through the kitchen door of the mobile home. His mother is dozing on the couch. The red-and-white capsule is gone. The television set is still on; Christmas mass is being celebrated in a vaulted cathedral somewhere back East. He has been gone less than an hour.

His mother opens her eyes and sees him standing there, looking down at her. She smiles. While she was dozing the little green turban she wears to conceal her baldness has slipped and now sits on her head askew.

"How was the party?" she says.

"Fine," he says. "I had a good time. Everyone asked about you."

She closes her eyes again.

"Are you ready to go to bed?" he says.

She nods.

"Would you like another pill first?"

She nods again.

The man returns to the kitchen, takes one of the red-and-white capsules from a bottle on the counter, fills another small glass with water from the tap, and returns to the living room.

He elevates his mother's head and cups it with his hand as she takes her pill. Then he holds the water glass for her as she drinks.

"Ready?" he says when she's done.

She nods and places one thin arm around his shoulder. He lifts her easily — she weighs nothing — and takes her back to the small side bedroom that has become hers. When he first arrived, six weeks earlier, she could still make it back to the bedroom on her own, using just his arm for support. It has only been in the last week or so that he's had to carry her.

As he tucks her in he hears the sound of a car leaving next door and a shout of "Merry Christmas!" He arranges his mother's hands outside the covers and bends down to kiss her forehead. As he does so, she lifts a hand up off the blanket just enough to touch, then feel, then stroke, the lapel of his gray tweed jacket.

"You look nice," she says to him as she closes her eyes. "You look nice."

Susan Firer

My Mothers' Rosaries

Rosaries of night breath,
rosaries of woman smell,
rosaries of dream, spoon
rosaries blue, rosaries of yarn
knots greed rosaries, dandelion
rosaries, dough rosaries,
crystal Slovac rosaries,
baked potato rosaries, cock
hot rosaries, sunflower
yellow rosaries, phone line
rosaries, human hair
rosaries, butterfly blue
rosaries, snow rosaries,
dark cherry red burn rosaries,
say lead rosaries, flour
white first-communion rosaries,
lemon rosaries, cold-cock punch
rosaries, confessional dark
water holy rosaries, sweet apple
red rosaries, concertina sweet rosaries,
before bed rosaries, wild
asparagus rosaries, smooth
wood beaded rosaries, see
all the way to heaven rosaries.
Keep me sighted rosaries,
don't let me be pregnant rosaries,
don't let anyone die rosaries,
bring him here rosaries,
keep me sane rosaries,
keep him off me rosaries.
My mothers' rosaries fill
my mouth with dark prayer names:

My name is Susan the Baptist,
daughter of Ruth Lorraine Brophy
whose mother Katherine Boussart
came from Alsace-Lorraine
with a immigrant's trunk
full of women's lost names,
and prayers, rosaries, Maypoles, and angels.

Only the Devil

SHE ISN'T IN HER USUAL PLACE WHEN I COME OUT OF THE ELEVATOR. The two old dears who sit one on either side of her open their eyes wide.

"She's in her room," the little one says. "She hasn't come out today yet. We're saving her place."

Their heads turn in unison like spectators at a tennis match as I walk past. Whenever I talk with my mother beside the elevator, they gather around us and take part in the conversation, as though I come to visit them as well.

I walk down the wide corridor, past the open doors, marveling at the light and the brilliance of the place. There is nothing on earth like a Florida nursing home. The passage of time is suspended here; nothing suggests the end of the line. It must be like a perpetual summer camp: in Boston you go to a nursing home to die.

My mother is sitting by the window in her wheelchair, perfectly motionless. She does not move, even when I pat her hand and peck her papery cheek and settle into the armchair opposite her with a sigh.

"It's your son Dick come to see you, mother, all the way from the frozen north."

She raises an eyebrow, but otherwise gives no indication she has heard me. Her face is pallid, and the sunken cast of her eyes gives me a little chill. She's aged in the two months since I've seen her. I don't come as often in the wintertime. Being thrust into summer for a day upsets my equilibrium.

"Would you like to go out and sit with your friends, mother?"

She shrugs her wasted shoulders and continues to stare out of the window. I look out too. Her room is on the third floor, and she has a view of a little artificial lake. The developers have not entirely banished the wildlife; there's an anhinga drying its wings on the far bank and a couple of little blue herons stalking in the shallows. But apart from that — nothing but lawns of crabgrass, hibiscus hedges, and palms. It's an environment from which all sense of threat has been eliminated. Not that there's anything to fear from acres of tract housing and shopping malls. You can't even find a bar.

"Are you ever going to get married?" she says to me suddenly, turning her head, her eyes lighting up sharply.

"Never again, mother. Once bitten, twice shy."

Her eyes cloud over.

"A grown man," she says, in a blank, mystified voice.

"How did you like seeing Mark and David?"

She gives me a look of consternation.

"My kids, mother. Your beloved grandchildren. Full grown and about to fly the coop."

"Do they go to mass and the sacraments?"

"You better ask them. No good asking me."

Her consternation dissolves easily, and she smiles her puckered smile and shakes her head.

"You were always a big lad for your age," she says mildly.

She turns back to the window. We often look out the window without saying a word to each other for the entire duration of my visit, when she doesn't feel like talking. The low sun around the corner of the building casts a long shadow that divides the lake into light and dark. A bank of thunderclouds walls the treeless horizon. But day is the same as night here, almost as bright, equally benign.

"Would you like me to get you anything from the candy store downstairs, mother?"

This is something that must be carefully negotiated. If I bring candies, she's as likely to say she doesn't eat them. But she's not tuned in today.

"How's Mrs. O'Herlihy in Boston?" she says.

"I haven't seen Mrs. O'Herlihy in a long long time. Not since we lived on Ivy Street in Dorchester when I was five years old."

"You don't remember Ivy Street," she tells me shortly. "We moved to Medford when you were only two."

"Do *you* remember it?"

She opens her mouth to say something, closes it again, and purses her wrinkled lips.

"I don't remember anything any more," she says with disgust. "Except the old country."

It's true. She hardly ever asks about Boston. Perhaps it's because there's nothing to remind her of it here: no neighborhoods like up North, no neighbors who live in the houses they grew up in. No cellars. This is what makes Florida the perfect place to die: there's nothing here to distract you from your memories.

"Tell me about Ireland then, mother."

"Sure you ought to know it as well as I do by now."

"Not as well as you do, mother."

I've grown tired of telling her that I've never been to Ireland to visit her father's family in county Waterford. Sometimes she knows this and takes me to task over it, and I feel a little guilty that I haven't made time for a stopover in Ireland on my many trips to Europe. But I'm told there's not much to do there. Sometimes she thinks I've been there, and she talks to me about people I'm supposed to have met.

"Eileen O'Herlihy was a great friend of mine at home," she says eagerly. " 'Twas thinking about her namesake put me in mind of her."

"I don't think I've ever met her, mother."

"Sure how could you? Didn't she die of TB before she was twenty-five?"

She draws her brows together and bends over her old hands resting in her lap. I can see the brown mottled skin of her skull through its wispy covering of hair.

"I was a dab hand at dressmaking when I was a girl," she says. "Your father used to call me Scrap-a-nelly when he was courting me, because I could make a dress or a blouse out of any old scrap of material."

"I think I remember you used to make things for me and Eddie."

"Yerrah, those were only alterations," she says scornfully. "Taking up the legs of yeer pants, putting a tuck in yeer shirts. Though if we'd ever had a girl, I might have made things for her."

"What about your friend Eileen?" I say.

This is a little cruel of me, because I expect that she's lost the thread.

"She went for a nun, and she asked me would I make her novice's habit. Oh, Dick, what a job I had with it! There was the heavy black serge of the habit itself ('twas as much as you could do to put a hem on it), white serge for the petticoat, and these long bloomers they used to wear – they were a fright, you should have seen them! A train they tie around their waists – because it's supposed to be a wedding dress, you see – the same serge as the habit, and a leather belt. And then I had to make the band for the forehead and the piece that covers the bust out of a terrible stiff linen. And the veil too."

I stretch out my legs and watch the lake. Dusk is falling quickly. I'm glad for both our sakes that she's latched onto something. It upsets me when she rambles. Or maybe it's the place itself: you can't imagine that anybody works here, or has children here, or does anything but wait for death in a sleepy sunny daze.

"Eileen came around to the house to see it all laid out on the bed. It won't be long now, she said, until I'll be a bride of Christ. It wasn't like her at all: she was always a very outgoing sort of girl, she wasn't a holy mary, as they used to say. She told me all about the ceremony, how the novices have to lie stretched out on the floor before the altar and the solemn vows they have to take: chastity, poverty, and obedience. She was all excited about it, and sure I could hardly talk – she must have thought I was very strange – I had a lump in my throat the whole time she was telling me and I was glad when she went away and all I could think of – I suppose it was foolish – was that old song that goes, *agus d'fhág sí mise ag sileadh na ndeor.*"

"Could you run that by me one more time in the Queen's English?"

"Oh, she left me here crying after her, or something like that. It was foolish of me, I know, but I was very fond of her. Well, I went up to the convent the next evening to see her in her habit. When she came out all dressed up, I could see straightaway she wasn't herself, but she looked like a stranger beneath the veil and all and I didn't know what to say to her. She didn't say a word or look at me, but she came over to me and tried to put a letter into my hand. Such a fright as I got! But I wouldn't take it from her for anything."

"That wasn't very nice of you, mother," I say. "It was probably a letter to her boyfriend."

"It was! How did you know, Dick? But I wouldn't take it because I knew she wasn't supposed to have anything to do with the outside the night before she was to enter the order. Then the sister came in on us and she had to put the letter back inside the habit and the sister told her to go out of the room and she wouldn't look at me when she went out – and it nearly broke my heart! I was so upset I never went to see her take her vows. I used to worry about it afterwards because I heard that the nuns try to persuade young girls to join the order before they're old enough to know their own minds. There were nights I didn't sleep for thinking about it, did I do the right thing by her or not?"

A row of orange street lights blinks on at the perimeter of the lake. The roadway is deserted. I can almost feel the heat of the night. I'm not looking forward to the evening ahead. You can't find a half-way decent restaurant outside of Miami, and that's a two hour drive. I'll probably eat at the hotel, have a few drinks in the bar, and go to bed early. Maybe I'll have time to see her again in the morning before my flight back.

"Why didn't you want to be a nun yourself?"

She turns in the chair to peer at me. It is an incredulous, mocking, and at the same time searching look, as if she suspects me of trifling with her.

"Me? Is it me? Sure I was young and a little wild, and I wanted to be off with the boys!"

She settles herself in the chair again and returns her hands to her lap.

"Did I ever tell you about the day I went in the airplane?" she says. "It was me and your Auntie Evelyn went to an old carnival in Bally-truckle and they had an airplane there in the field, the first airplane that was ever seen in Waterford, I'd say, and they'd give you a spin in it for a shilling. Come on, Evelyn, says I. Well! You should have seen her face. No way will I go next or near that contraption, says she. Off I went – and left her looking after me. We flew over the whole town. I could see the Mall and the quay and Reginald's Tower and the bridge and the railway station – and our house: it was so small, it was like a doll's house. I couldn't credit it. But I wasn't in the least bit frightened: I didn't want to come down out of it. But come here till I tell you, Dick –"

She bends over and puts her face on her knees. I reach forward to take her arm, and then I see that her face is wrinkled with silent laughter. She leans back again, sighs, and wipes the tears from the corners of her eyes.

"Somebody went into Granny in John's Street where we used to live and said to her, do you know your daughter's after going off in that airplane? And she nearly had a fit there on the spot. Your Grandad told me afterwards that she ran out into the garden and looked up in the sky and said, what are we going to do at all? Sure there's nothing to do, woman, your Grandad said – you remember the quiet way he had, there was nothing could upset him – what goes up must come down. Well! When she heard that she nearly went wild and off with her down to the field. We met her on the way home. Evelyn tried to pretend that nothing had happened — she was supposed to be looking after me. But sure Mammy knew there was a bit of a *divil* in me."

There's a knock at the open door.

"Excuse me," a young nurse says. "Are you coming to dinner tonight, Mrs. Morrissey?"

A sly look comes into my mother's eyes, and they circle warily toward the window.

"She'll be there in a few minutes," I say.

The nurse bobs prettily and whirls out, leaving me with an after-image of her starched white skirt stretched taut across her hips and bottom. Her accent is not Southern, and I wonder where she comes from, what her story is. Everybody in Florida comes from somewhere else. I move forward and sit on the edge of my chair.

"I'd better be going, mother. I'll wheel you down there."

"It wasn't until a long time after that I met her again," my mother says in a sober voice.

"Met who?"

"My friend Eileen. She came up to me one day in Georges Street, and she was all talk to me. She told me she was very happy as a nun and she'd never had so much as a moment's regret. And I could see she wasn't well, though I never knew it was TB she had till afterwards. I told her I was off to the States. Isn't it well for you? she said. But when I was saying good-bye to her, she took me by the arm and says she, do you remember that letter I wanted to give you the night before I took my vows? And it all went through me again because I was still upset about not taking it from her. Don't give it another thought, girl, she says to me. It was some poor fellow I thought I was in love with — but sure it was only the devil who was tempting me."

She sits quietly looking out. The only light in the room comes from the corridor and the glow of the lights across the lake. She breathes quietly and evenly.

"Mom?"

Her eyes are closed. She's nodded off on me. I can go now. But I'm not in a hurry anymore. Boston and winter seem very far away. The peace and quiet of the atmosphere settle upon me like a shroud. I sit back in my chair and watch the last light die out of the sky, and my mind fills with images of my mother's life in a place I have never seen.

James Liddy

Epithalamium Notes

talis in vario solet
divitis domini hortulo
stare flos . . .

Lest the hoar frost grip the iridescent tent of your marriage.

I have violent dreams. By violent I mean intense and multicolored.
I see the house and on its trim lawn purple-pink flowers. Bigger
than the size of your two hands they are swollen rainbows.

Mother and father lived in a Wexford village
leaning on a stream, between the barracks and the pub.
A croppy's pike between them in the bed.

They were married in Westland Row by
Father Hubert Quinn who kept a thousand photographs of himself
in a drawer and knew the Duchess Brady, the friend of Pius XII
(O Illyrian Iris of the ancients).
Her father's brother Mick came up from Scariff her mother's
brother from Kilkee (her brother Dan was in Berlin but
Uncle James sent a thousand pounds from New York).
The breakfast was at seven A.M., Christmas Eve was a day
of abstinence so fish was served . . . not eggs, mother says
she thinks an egg never crossed the threshold of the
Shelbourne Hotel in those days . . .
They rented a car and had two punctures on the way to the
Great Southern Hotel at Galway. On to Renvyle where in
the imperturbable distance Oliver St. John Gogarty carved
the meat . . .

Perfumed or unperfumable human beings, handsome showy-flowered.

Mother, messenger of the gods to me and personification
of the rainbow, remembers she had a party before the wedding
in the Shelbourne — when she went up to change after
breakfast the booze was gone. Truly the thirties,
even for waiters.

Captain Hone came up on the Maynooth road to say the bedroom
furniture was ready. She bought a mahogany dining room
table in the Georgian House on the corner of Hume Street
and the Green. The Nolans ran it, gave as a present
a brass fender and a framed ballad The Croppy Boy.
Ten years later to Wexford . . . she carried water from the river
in an ewer to put her husband's mind asleep.

She is violet-scented orris root used in perfuming.

She gives thanks that night is spent.

The earth white with frost gives away in my dream to the
curved line of stiff erect stem, sword-shaped leaves,
purple-pink flowers. The biggest one grows and spreads to a bent
twisted Iris cloud that springs out of the head of Vinegar Hill.
The Croppy Boy Iris. I was.

I think marriage is writing feminine, treasurable, untranslatable
letters like this.

24 December 1931 to 24 December 1981

Doing These Words

On the road of eternal hallelujah
I creep along singing to myself

the curious music known to many
was what flew through the night
through all the heads
ending in the fields with

the cloud's white edges in
the dream, mine the dark color
the stone in the center.
It would take so much to change it.

Since I was born at the beginning of everything
since I was born at the beginning of day
since I awoke in the dream (hallelujah!)
and walked on the dark in
the field — now I creep along the road.

Do you address me now
because we are unable to do anything?
There is no comfort in doing these words.
The kind of poetry I want to write
is the poetry of a dead woman; it comes
from her grave in the sky.

Susan Donnelly

At the Gravesite

for Paul Leahy

He watched them tape the stencils to the stone.
This was his doing, almost his obsession,
for over a year. He'd hunted everywhere
until he retrieved the family Bible,
with its page of marriages and births.
He made his sisters rummage through their attics
for faded letters, broken at the folds,

found a family tree, spindly as a nursling,
drawn in his father's delicate script.

Stoic and private in his illness
as he'd been all his life,
he brushed off questions about the chemotherapy:
    "Oh, not too bad—" although, months later,
there were days he was too tired even to stroll
along the mall on Commonwealth Avenue.

The workmen wanted him there for one last check
of names and dates. He made sure
no widowed aunt, tubercular cousin,
loved and dishonored brother was forgotten.
Great-grandfather Daniel Driscoll's dates
set an antiquity record for the mason.
He liked that.

        Maybe it would be clear
the names were added long after the stone.
But in time, he hoped, that sense would disappear.
He watched until the air began to fill up
with a fine granite dust. Then he went home.

Jody Aliesan

Yearday

I'VE SET UP THE ALTAR: A ROSE FROM THE FAMILY SPRAY ON TOP OF your casket, pulled out when you were lying above the hole they dug, green sod cloth arranged around you. Each of us pulled one out then and I held mine upside down so it wouldn't fall apart until at the potluck in the lodge hall afterwards Sarah told me to press it right away. Now it's flat and dry, still dark purple heartblood red.

And the lump of clay is here. I picked it up from beside the hole when we finally had to help each other leave, everyone else had gone and we were still stroking the casket and talking to you, how we loved you, how we'd be back. It was hard to walk away, drive away looking back at you lying there on the hillside alone, everybody gone, finally.

I comforted myself thinking about how you were a quiet person who liked moments to yourself and probably never did get enough of them in this life, what with all of us around all the time. Certainly you didn't get any in the last year of the nursing home and very little the two years before that of hospitals and paralysis. So I thought, and it helped, that now at least you'd have some quiet, all the quiet you could want and maybe enough to begin to make up for so many people for so long.

So the bit of clay is here. And the three tie tacks I sorted out the days after the funeral. A piece of turquoise, a silver bear's foot with a bit of turquoise in the center, and an enameled dogwood flower. They don't represent most of what was in the boxes, all the signs and symbols of your life, but I liked them best and I wear them on my jacket lapels in your honor.

And here's a little gilt frame with the two pictures Mother found in your wallet, one of her holding infant me, the other of me at two years old, both with your handwriting on the back, my name and age. You carried those around with you all my life. In front of the frame, flat on this little table, a picture from the funeral: the pallbearers are sliding your casket into the hearse. We're all standing to the side. Brecken is on my left, John on my right, we have our arms around one another. You can see the top of Mother's head, she's standing in front of the three of us. John and I were saying, *Gently, gently*.

John chose the casket, and it was just right. Bronze. It was fitting you should have something heroic. When I rode behind the hearse looking ahead at you, looking behind at the long line of cars, I felt we were riding behind a chieftain. Because you were so brave and valiant at the end, because you were such a fighter when all the odds were against you and when saying let go, pass over, accept, might be philosophically correct but all wrong. Because you battled so hard to stay awake and alert and present and aware and conscious of other people and their lives right up to the last night, a year ago tonight. A year ago today, when you were in intensive care after the last surgery and in pain, so much constant pain from the gangrene, John and Brecken told you about their hike and you marveled there was snow on the trail this time of year, you'd never seen that. You said you still had so much to live for.

Laid on the picture is a spray of heather Lisa mailed from Scotland. Next to it is a stone from Tara and two Irish coins she and Kevin brought back for me. Your favorite glass with the roadrunner on it, full of water. A tomato from my garden. There's a small enameled saucer I found in a second-hand store when I was keeping up my courage. In it is a little knob of wood with holes for sticks of incense. I've been burning myrrh. The third king: *Myrrh is mine, its bitter perfume . . . sorrowing, sighing, bleeding, dying, sealed in a stone cold tomb*. So the song goes.

But I feel you're fine, now. I miss you. The human barriers that separated us I remember with sadness. I'm sorry that your time here was hard, with so much suffering, and that I ever added to it. But after you died I felt your presence great and warm and radiant around us and knew you were larger and healthier and more whole than ever in this life. That you were doing just fine.

What's left. A stack of photographs from the funeral. A vase with four cattails from the flowers people at work set waiting for me when I came back. A small glass candle holder with a stub of purple candle burning in it. That's the only light. A blue candle lying beside it, waiting. Behind all this, leaning against the wall, a photograph of a great eagle's eye carved from stone. A book opened to two pages of the Book of Kells. And Lisa's postcard of the inside of New Grange at the moment of sunrise on Winter Solstice.

Mother is on her way to Ireland. She left at nightfall and now it's dark. But you know all this already, don't you.

Father

When the clerk after last week's rent
forced the door, it was almost too late
for the undertaker's

gaudy art. He left little behind
that day his death became official:
a razor and two crumpled

dollar bills. Crossing the Textile
Avenue Bridge after his hasty
wake, I watch a sad moon drag

its empty net across the river
and remember that night a bartender
told me my father wanted to be

a tenor. I never heard him sing.
Once, behind the mills where we fished
for carp to sell to Polish women,

I hooked a fish
Leo Paradise called a trout
before it slipped the hook

and fell back to the sluggish water.
A speckled fish that made me want to sing.
Father, soon I will believe that fish was you.

Greg Delanty

Tie

Without asking, you borrowed your father's black tie,
sure that he had another black tie to wear
should some acquaintance or relation die.
But had he? He should be here somewhere.
But where? Could he be at home on this dark day,
ransacking drawer after drawer for a funeral tie?
Yes, that must be what has kept him away.
Though you are sure you saw him, tieless,
smiling over at you, before you lost him again
among the keening cortege. Leaving you clueless
to his whereabouts, till earth, splattering a coffin
(or was it the wind ululating in each prayer?),
informed you that you can never give your father
back his black tie, though you'll find him everywhere.

Leavetaking

After you board the train, you sit & wait,
    to begin your first real journey alone.
You read to avoid the window's awkwardness,
    knowing he's anxious to catch your eye,
        loitering out in never ending rain,
to wave, a bit shy, another final good-bye;
you are afraid of having to wave too soon.

And for a moment you think it's the train
    next to you has begun, but it is yours,
and your face, pressed to the window pane,
    is distorted & numbed by the icy glass,
        pinning your eyes upon your father,
as he cranes to defy your disappearing train.
Both of you waving, eternally, to each other.

Birds

crows circle
the graveyard
build nests
on the mausoleums

my father says birds
try to catch souls
of men rising
from the grave

if caught
they cannot reach
heaven, become
ghosts

he was taught
to throw stones
for his father
resting there

a crow perches
on a gravemarker
it is not family
I have no stones

Contributors' Notes

BARBARA ADAMS is the author of two collections of poems, *Hapax Legomena* (Edwin Mellen Press, 1990) and *Double Solitaire* (Geryon Press, 1982). Her stories have appeared in *Madison Review, Fiction 83, Other Voices, In-Print,* and *Home Planet News;* her poems have appeared in over thirty literary magazines, including *The Nation, Confrontation,* and *Modern Poetry Studies.* She is currently a professor of English at Pace University in New York.

JODY ALIESAN is the author of eight books and chapbooks. "Yearday" is from her most recent, *States of Grace,* published this fall in limited edition letterpress by Grey Spider Press in Seattle, Washington. Among the others are *Grief Sweat, Doing Least Harm, Desire, as if it will matter,* and *Soul Claiming.* Her work has been acknowledged by fellowships, grants, and awards from the National Endowment for the Arts, Arts Commissions of King, Pierce and Snohomish Counties, the Seattle Arts Commission, and Artists Trust. A resident of the Pacific Northwest for twenty-two years, she divides her time between Seattle and a cabin on an island near the border with Canada.

NUALA ARCHER won the Patrick Kavenaugh award for her first book, *Whale on the Line.* Her second, *Two Women/Two Shores,* was a collaboration with Ulster poet Mebhbh McGuikian; her third, *Pan/ama,* was issued in 1992 by Salmon Publishing in Galway, Ireland. She is director of the Poetry Center of Cleveland State University.

PHIL ASAPH's work has appeared in *Poetry Wales, Slant, High Plains Literary Review,* and other publications. A graduate of the creative writing program at Eckerd College, he won the Stadler Semester for Young Poets at Bucknell University, whose press also published his chapbook, *Meditation & Movement.*

JOSEPH AWAD was born in Shenandoah, Pennsylvania, of an Irish mother and a Lebanese father. He now lives in Richmond, VA. His poems have appeared in numerous journals and anthologies, most recently in *Negative Capability*, *The Chariton Review*, and *Visions*. He has published two books of poetry, *The Neon Distances* and *Shenandoah Long Ago*, the latter of which includes the poem published here.

PATRICIA BARONE's first book, *The Wind*, was published by New Rivers Press in 1987, and she has a volume of poetry forthcoming, also by New Rivers Press, in 1994. Her mother's family, composed primarily of Ryans and Nolans, settled in the Fox River Valley of Wisconsin in 1848. Her great-uncle Malachy Ryan was one of the first farmers in Outagamie County to practice crop rotation.

TRICIA BAUER's stories and poems have appeared in numerous magazines and literary periodicals, most recently in the *American Literary Review*, *Calyx*, *Indiana Review*, and the Crossing Press anthology *Eating Our Hearts Out: Women and Food*, as well as in *The New York Times*.

CATHERINE BRADY grew up in the Chicago area, where her parents settled after immigrating to the U.S. from Ireland. Her short stories have appeared in *Redbook*, *The Missouri Review*, *Greensboro Review*, and the anthology *I Know Some Things: Stories about Childhood by Contemporary Writers*, edited by Lorrie Moore. She recently completed a collection of related stories about an Irish-American family and is currently working on a novel. She lives in San Francisco.

RICHARD BRODERICK grew up in New Jersey and now lives in Saint Paul with his daughter Emma. He is a collateral descendent of Thomas Meagher, "Meagher Of The Sword." He is currently the poetry editor of *Minnesota Monthly* and he is the author of a collection of short stories, *Night Sale*, published by New Rivers Press. His fiction and poetry have appeared in numerous journals, including *Prairie Schooner*, *Clockwatch Review*, and *Minnesota Monthly*.

STEPHANY BROWN lives in Flagstaff, Arizona. Her work has appeared in *The Short Story Review*, *Other Voices*, and *If I Had My Life to Live Over*.

PIERCE BUTLER was born in Waterford City, Ireland. He holds degrees from the National University of Ireland in Cork, Harvard University, and Northeastern Unviersity, Boston. Since coming to the U.S. in 1979, he has taught at Northeastern, Harvard, the University of Massachusetts-Boston, and Babson College. He is the author of *A Malady* (Co-op Books); his stories have appeared in *Story, San Jose Studies, American Way*, and in a Joyce centenary anthology of Irish writers. He currently lives in Waltham, Massachusetts, where he is writer-in-residence at Bentley College. He is currently at work on a new novel and on a study of the short fiction of Sean O'Faolain. "Only the Devil" aired on RTE (Radio Telefís Eireann) on March 12, 1991.

ANNE CALLAN is a native Irish woman who lives now in Portland, Oregon. She teaches high school and college creative writing and literature courses. She also works as a freelance writer and editor. She earned an M.A. in poetry from John Hopkins University.

MICHAEL CAREY lives and farms 800 acres in Farragut, Iowa, with his wife Kelly and their four children. He spends winter months as a visiting artist and lectures for the Iowa Humanities Board Speakers Bureau. His books of poetry include *The Noise the Earth Makes* (Pterodactyl Press) and *Honest Effort* (Holy Cow! Press) as well as a teaching manual, *Poetry: Starting from Scratch* (Foundation Books). His work has been included in many anthologies as well as being featured in the *Wall Street Journal*.

CATHERINE CLARKE is the author of the chapbook *Red Horse*, published by Copper Beech Press of Brown University in 1981. She lives in Stillwater, New York.

DARCY CUMMINGS is three-fourths Irish and grew up in an Irish Catholic urban neighborhood. She has received fellowships from the New Jersey State Council on the Arts and Yaddo. Her work has appeared in many literary journals, including *The Spirit That Moves Us, Poetry Northwest*, and *Intro 11*.

GREG DELANTY won the Patrick Kavenaugh award in 1983; he is the author of *Cast in the Fire* (Dolmen Press, 1986) and *Southward* (Louisiana State University Press, 1992). Born in Cork, Ireland, he now lives in the U.S., where he has worked as poet-in-residence at such schools as New York University, the University of Vermont, and the Robert Frost Place. His work has appeared in many Irish anthologies, including *Bitter Harvest: Contemporary Irish Poetry* and the *Field Day Anthology of Irish Literature 500 B.C.–Present*.

KERRY DOLAN was born in Brooklyn, New York. Her stories have appeared in *Quarterly West*, *Greensboro Review*, and other magazines. Her collection of short stories, *Hit or Miss*, in which the story collected here is included, was a finalist for the Flannery O'Connor Award. A former creative writing teacher at Cornell University, she now lives in San Francisco.

SUSAN DONNELLY is the author of *Eve Names the Animals* (Northeastern University Press, 1985), winner of the 1984 Samuel French Morse Prize. She has been published in such periodicals as *Ploughshares*, *Harvard Magazine*, and the *Women's Review of Books*. She is the founder of the Every Other Thursday workshop and press in Cambridge, Massachusetts, where she lives.

FINVOLA DRURY was born in Cleveland, Ohio, in 1926, to Marie McNeil Drury and Frank Drury. In 1948 she married George F. Drury and moved to Chicago, where she taught poetry workshops at the University of Chicago. In 1959 she moved to Detroit, where for six years she chaired Wayne State University's Miles Modern Poetry Committee. During the seventies and eighties, she lived in Rochester, New York, where she served for a decade as a director of the local literary center. Her two books of poetry are *Elegy on the Death of Joric Ross* (Multifarious Press, 1983) and *Burning the Snow* (Landers and Francis, 1990). She now lives in Maine.

JOSEPH FARLEY lives and writes in Philadelphia. His poems and short stories have appeared in *Painted Bride Quarterly*, *Pearl*, *Mildred*, *Seems*, *The Cape Rock* and other magazines. "Birds" first appeared in *Painted Bride Quarterly* (1986) and then appeared in the United Kingdom in *Vigil* (1991).

JUDITH FERGUSON was born in 1959. Her mother, Teresa Ferguson, is Irish, and her father, Robert Ferguson, is Irish-American. She is a registered nurse working in the field of maternal-child health. Her poems have appeared in many magazines and journals, including

Calyx, Out/Look, and *Hanging Loose.* At present she is working on a collection of poems, *The Woman in the Street Is Still Screaming.*

SUSAN FIRER's poem "My Mothers' Rosaries" appeared in *Ms* magazine last year. She is the author of *The Underground Communion Rail* from West End Press (1992), and winner of the 1992 Cleveland State University Poetry Center Prize for *The Lives of the Saints and Everything*, 1993. Her work has been anthologized in *The Best American Poetry 1992*, and she also appeared in *The Boundaries of Twilight: A Czecho-Slovak American Writing from the New World*, from New Rivers Press.

KEVIN FITZPATRICK lives in Minneapolis, Minnesota, and works as a civil servant. He is the author of a book of poems, *Down on the Corner*, published by Midwest Villages and Voices. A founder of the *Lake Street Review*, he was editor from 1977 until its final issue in 1991. His great-grandparents on both the FitzPatrick and Hurley sides emigrated from Ireland to the United States in the mid-nineteenth century and settled in Waverly and Bird Island, respectively, in Minnesota.

JOSEPH GAHAGAN is a graduate of Saint Francis Xaivier Grade School where he first discovered the rituals of community life and where he devoutly served mass at the parish church. He has spent his time since then exploring the possibilities of where the parish boundaries begin and end. Currently, Gahagan teaches creative writing and modern literature at the University of Wisconsin-Milwaukee. His poetry and fiction have appeared in a wide variety of publications and he has won numerous awards including the 1989 *Irish Voice* Poetry Award and a 1990 New Voices award in both fiction and poetry. "Island People" is the winner of the 1992 Milwaukee Fiction Award.

TESS GALLAGHER is a poet, short story writer, and essayist, who writes and lives in Port Angeles, Washington. Her most recent books of poetry are *Moon Crossing Bridge*, (Graywolf Press, 1992) and *Portable Kisses*, (Capra Press, 1992). Her book of short stories, *The Lover of Horses*, has been reissued recently by Graywolf Press. Her essays are collected in *A Concert of Tenses* (University of Michigan Press, 1986). She has been advising on the set of the film production of *Short*

Cuts, which is based on nine stories and a poem of Raymond Carver, her late husband; the film is due for release fall 1993.

RENNY GOLDEN is a professor of criminal and social justice at Northeastern Illinois University in Chicago. Active in many political causes, she is the author of the recent *Hour of the Poor, Hour of Women*, on Central American women's political activism, which won *Crossroad Publishing's Women Studies Award* in 1991. Her poems were previously included in *Unlacing: Ten Irish-American Women Poets* (Fireweed Press, 1985).

JAMES JAY GOULD is a professor of writing and literature at Paul Smiths College in New York's Adirondack Mountains. He writes frequently on outdoor topics, and his nonfiction has appeared in the *New York Times, Washington Post, San Francisco Review of Books, Adirondack Life*, and other national and regional publications.

JOHN GRADY is working on a biography of Matthew Fontaine Maury, a Civil War scientist. He lives in Burke, Virginia with his fourteen-year-old daughter Katherine Anne.

JAMES GRIFFIN was born in New York City; his father was born in County Leitrim. He is a writer and editor in the Washington, D.C. area; his work has been published in *The Midwest Quarterly* and *The Maryland Poetry Review*.

EILEEN HENNESSY was raised in Bellmore, Long Island, and currently lives in New York City. She holds an M.A. in Creative Writing from New York University and works as an adjunct assistant professor in the Translation Studies Program there. She translates commercial and legal materials, as well as books on art history and other subjects, from French, German, Spanish, Dutch, and Italian. Her poems have appeared in *Bogg, The Quarterly, Manhattan Poetry Review*, and other journals.

TIMOTHY PATRICK JOHNSTON's work has appeared in the *New England Review, High Plains Literary Review, California Quarterly, Sycamore Review, Puerto del Sol, The Missouri Review*, and other journals. "White Sneakers," which was previously published in *Nexus*, is an excerpt from his recently-completed first novel.

WILLIAM KEOUGH is a Boston Irishman who has lived in Turkey, Ireland, and Montserrat. Holding an M.F.A. from the University of Iowa and a Ph.D. from the University of Massachusetts, he is professor of English at Fitchburg State College. He is the author of *Punchlines: The Violence of American Humor* (Paragon, 1990) and *Any Such Greenness: Poems* (Tara West, 1991). "Last Word on a Pink Dress" won the first Waterstone Short Story Prize at the 1992 Irish Cultural Festival at Stonehill College.

ROBERT LACY is a native of East Texas who has lived in Minneapolis for more than twenty years. He won a Loft-McKnight Fiction Fellowship in 1984 and the Midwest Voices fiction competition in 1985. His stories have appeared in a wide range of magazines including *The Saturday Evening Post*, *Ploughshares*, *Crazyhorse*, *Indiana Review*, and *Manoa*. His work has been anthologized in the *Best American Short Stories 1988*, *The Best of Crazyhorse*, *Stiller's Pond: New Fiction from the Upper Midwest*, and elsewhere. He writes a regular fiction-review column for the Minneapolis *Star-Tribune*.

JAMES LIDDY was born in 1934 on the Night of the Long Knives from Limerick, Clare, and New York parentage. He spent summers in the resort of Kilkee and academic years at Glenstal Abbey. His most recent books are *In the Slovak Bowling Alley*, *Art is Not for Grown-Ups*, and *Trees Warmer than Green: Notes towards a Video of Avondale House*. He is currently a professor of English at the University of Wisconsin-Milwaukee.

KATHLEEN LYNCH is a poet, fiction writer, essayist, and artist. Her work has appeared in the *Chariton Review*, *Cutbank*, *Poetry Flash*, *Reed*, *Quarry West*, and other magazines. She teaches creative writing through California Poets in the Schools. She lives in Pleasanton, California.

SHELIA MAC AVOY grew up in New York City where she attended Queens College and St. John's Law School. She currently lives in Santa Barbara and practices law. Her stories have been published in *Writer's Forum*, *Northern Review*, and *WEST/Word*.

TOM McCARTHY was raised by his Belfast grandparents in rural California. After several years of following his grandfather's trade of carpentry, he found his way into journalism. He is the former editor of *The Tenderloin Times*, a small community newspaper in San Francisco published in four languages — Khmer, Lao, Vietnamese, and English.

JOHN McFARLAND was born, raised and educated in Cambridge, Massachusetts. If he hadn't left for Bolivia as a Peace Corps Volunteer, he'd probably still be there. His first book, *The Exploding Frog and Other Fables from Aesop*, was selected as one of the best illustrated books of 1981 by *Parents' Choice Magazine*. His short fiction has appeared in *Ararat*, *Caliban*, stet, and *Wiggansnatch*, among other journals. He lives in Seattle, Washington.

ETHNA McKIERNAN is the founder and director of Irish Books and Media, one of the nation's premier sources for imported Irish literature. She is the author of *Caravan* (Midwest Villages and Voices 1989).

PATRICK McKINNON is the founder of Poetry Harbor, an arts organization centered in Duluth, Minnesota, which sponsors the literary magazine, *North Coast Review*. He also founded Suburban Wilderness Press, an international publisher of poetry, and *Poetry Motel* literary magazine. He is the author of six books of poetry, the most recent being *Cherry Ferris Wheels* (Black Hat Press, 1990) and *Walking Behind My Breath* (No Press, 1988).

WESLEY McNAIR has four volumes of poetry, including *My Brother Running*, forthcoming this year from David Godine. He has received a Guggenheim Fellowship, a Fulbright Lecturership, two NEA Fellowships, the Devins Award, and an Emmy Award for a PBS series on Robert Frost. He has also won prizes in poetry from *Poetry* and *Yankee* magazines, and is a 1993 resident at the Bellagio Center of the Rockefeller Foundation.

JACK McNAMARA is a 1973 graduate of Holy Cross College and currently works as a mail clerk in Boston. At the present time he is working on a novel of family conflict set in the 1960s and a drawerful of story ideas which he is continuing to develop. His short stories have appeared in *The Northgate Anthology of Short Stories*, *The New Press Literature Quarterly*, and *The Journal of Irish Literature*.

PATRICIA MONAGHAN is the author of two books of poetry, *Winterburning* (Fireweed Press, 1990) and *Seasons of the Witch* (Delphi Press, 1992). She has also published a nonfiction book, *The Book of Goddesses and Heroines* (E. P. Dutton, 1981, revised Llewellyn Worldwide, 1990). She is poetry reviewer for *Booklist,* the journal of the American Library Association. She holds dual Irish/American citizenship and travels regularly to Connemara.

SHEILA O'CONNOR's novel *Tokens of Grace* was published by Milkweed Editions in 1990; the town of Savage, Minnesota, and the poem of that title which appears here were the impetus for the novel. Her poems and stories have appeared in a number of magazines. In addition to her writing, she teaches poetry and fiction in a variety of settings, including the University of Minnesota and the Writers-in-the-Schools program. She lives in Minneapolis with her husband and two small children; she is currently at work on a second novel.

JOE PADDOCK's three volumes of poetry are *Handful of Thunder* (Anvil Press, 1983), *Earth Tongues* (Milkweed Editions, 1985), and *Boar's Dance* (Holy Cow! Press, 1992). He is principal author of *Soil and Survival* (Sierra Club Books, 1986). In 1988, he won the Loft-McKnight Award of Distinction for his poetry. He lives in Litchfield, Minnesota.

FRAN DOYLE PODULKA won awards from the Society of Midland Authors and the Friends of Literature for her 1974 novel, *The Wonder Jungle.* In 1989 her story "Coming Around the Horn" won an Illinois Arts Council fiction award and was included in *Chicago Works: Chicago's Best Stories* (The Morton Press, 1990). A collection of her poems, *Essentials,* was published in 1989. A native of Connecticut, she attended Michigan State and Northwestern universities; she now works on the editorial staff of *Other Voices.*

KAY MARIE PORTERFIELD is the author of several books on addiction, recovery and relationships. She edited the anthology *What's a Nice Girl Like You Doing in a Relationship Like This? Women in Abusive Relationships* (Crossing Press, 1992). Her latest book is *Blind Faith: Recognizing and Recovering from Dysfunctional Religious Groups* (CompCare, 1993).

KAREN RILE is the author of *Winter Music* (Little, Brown) and is now at work on a second novel. Her stories have appeared in *American Fic-*

tion and *The Southern Review*. One of her stories, "Defection," was listed among the 100 most distinguished stories of 1991 in *Best American Short Stories*.

A resident of Boston, MAUREEN E. ROGERS was born and raised in Worcester, Massachusetts. She received her B.A. in sociology from Emmanuel College, and has an M.S. in Management from the Massachusetts Institute of Technology. By profession, she is director of marketing for a small software firm. Her publications include the chapter on M.I.T. in *The Insider's Guide to the Top Ten Business Schools*.

GERI ROSENZWEIG was born and grew up in Ireland; she worked as a registered nurse in Ireland and London before emigrating to the U.S. Her first book of poems, *Under the Jasmine Moon*, has just been published by HMS Press in Canada. Her work has appeared in *Negative Capability*, *Christian Science Monitor*, *Visions International* and many other publications.

TOM SEXTON's latest book of poetry is *Late August on the Kenai River* (Limner Press). His poems have recently appeared in *Hayden's Ferry Review*, *The Paris Review*, and ZYZZYVA. Sexton is the poetry editor for *Alaska Quarterly Review*. Both sides of his family emigrated from Ireland during the Famine.

KNUTE SKINNER teaches at Western Washington University in Bellingham, Washington, but spends as much time as possible in Killaspuglonane, County Clare. His most recent collection is *The Bears and Other Poems*, from Salmon Publishing in Galway, Ireland.

MAURA STANTON is a poet and fiction writer who teaches at Indiana University. Her books of poems are *Tales of the Supernatural* (Godine, 1988), *Cries of Swimmers* (Carnegie Mellon, 1991) and *Snow on Snow*, for which she received the Yale Series of Younger Poets Award. She's published a novel, *Molly Companion* (Bobbs-Merrill, 1977) and a collection of stories, *The Country I Come From* (Milkweed Editions, 1988).

ALISON TOWNSEND is a poet, essayist, and reviewer whose work has appeared in *Prairie Schooner*, *Kalliope*, *Sing Heavenly Muse*, *The Georgia Review*, and *The Women's Review of Books*. She lives in Madison, Wisconsin.

MARK VINZ's great-grandmother Emma Norton provides the Irish link which is a source of "both pride and the frustration of lost connections" that he expresses in "Traces." He is the author of several collections of poems, most recently *Late Night Calls* (New Rivers Press, 1992). With photographer Wayne Gudmundson, he created *Minnesota Gothic*, winner of the 1991 Milkweed Editions "Seeing Double" competition. His short fiction has appeared in several magazines, and in newspapers via five PEN Syndicated Fiction awards. He lives in Moorhead, Minnesota, and teaches at Moorhead State University.

MAUREEN WALSH was born on the Upper West Side of Manhattan, of Irish immigrant parents who instilled in her an appreciation for heritage and a decidedly Celtic identity. She is the recipient of a National Arts Club Literary Scholarship for fiction, and an Edward F. Albee Foundation Fellowship. She teaches writing at the City College of New York and is working on a novel.

A. D. WINANS was born in San Francisco, California, and graduated from San Francisco State College. He is the author of seven books of poetry; his poetry and prose has appeared in over 300 literary magazines and anthologies. Winans is the former editor and publisher of *Second Coming* magazine and press and the organizer of the 1980 Poetry-Music festival honoring the blues great John Lee Hooker and poet Josephine Miles. Winans currently works in the civil rights field, investigating discrimination against minorities, women, and the handicapped.

Acknowledgements

"Yearday" was published in *States of Grace* (Grey Spider Press).

"For My Irish Grandmother" has also appeared in *POEM* and *Shenandoah Long Ago* (Sparrow Press).

"Holy Place" was published in *If I Had to Live My Life Over* (Paper Mache Press).

"Only the Devil" originally appeared in *American Way*.

"Where We Searched for the Fathers" was published in *Kansas Quarterly*.

"My Father, Standing At a Snowy Bus Stop" was published in *Poetry Northwest*.

"Speaking With My Father" originally appeared in *INTRO 11* – Associated Writing Programs.

"Hit or Miss" is from the collection *Hit or Miss*.

"Birds" originally was published in *Painted Bird Quarterly*. It then appeared in *Vigil*.

"My Mothers' Rosaries" was published in *Ms. Magazine*.

"Boat Ride" first appeared in *Amplitude* (Graywolf Press).

"White Sneakers" appeared in *NEXUS*.

"Walking Behind My Breath" is from the collection *Walking Behind My Breath* (No Press Chicago).

"Finding the Curves of Love" was published in *Boar's Dance* (Holy Cow! Press).

"Father" was published in *ZYZZYVA*.

"The Palace" and "John McCormack" both appeared in *The Country I Come From* (Milkweed Editions).

"Supposedly When My Father Was Young" was published in the *Summit Avenue Express*.

"Black Ice" appeared in *The Northgate Anthology of Short Stories* (Harold Shaw Publishers, Wheaton, IL)

"Absences" was published first in *Sidewalks*, Fall, '92.

"An Irish-American Air" was published in *Burning the Snow* (Landers & Francis).

"Everyone Asked About You" was published in *Great River Review*.

"Spilled Milk" has been published in *The Sun* and *Catholic Girls* (Plume).